The ATLANTIS Encyclopedia

D1628058

FRANK JOSEPH

Author of
The Destruction of Atlantis

Foreword by
BRAD STEIGER

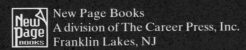
New Page Books
A division of The Career Press, Inc.
Franklin Lakes, NJ

THE ATLANTIS ENCYCLOPEDIA
EDITED AND TYPESET BY CLAYTON W. LEADBETTER
Cover design by Lu Rossman/Digi Dog Design
Printed in the U.S.A. by Book-mart Press

To order this title, please call toll-free 1-800-CAREER-1 (NJ and Canada: 201-848-0310) to order using VISA or MasterCard, or for further information on books from Career Press.

The Career Press, Inc., 3 Tice Road, PO Box 687,
Franklin Lakes, NJ 07417
www.careerpress.com
www.newpagebooks.com

Library of Congress Cataloging-in-Publication Data

Joseph, Frank.
    The Atlantis encyclopedia / by Frank Joseph ; foreword by Brad Steiger.
      p. cm.
    Includes bibliographical references.
    ISBN 1-56414-795-9
    1. Atlantis--Encyclopedias. I. Title.

GN751.J675 2005
001.94--dc22

2004059279

To William A. Donato,
the foremost explorer of Poseidia.

CONTENTS

Foreword by Brad Steiger 7

Introduction: *A Lost Civilization* 9

A: *Aalu to Aztlan* 11

B: *Bacab to Byamspa* 64

C: *Caer Feddwid to Cuchavira* 80

D: *Dardanus to Dzilke* 93

E: *Ea to Exiles of Time* 104

F: *Falias to Fu Sang Mu* 113

G: *Gadeiros to Gwyddno* 119

H: *Haiyococab to Hyne* 133

I: *Iamblichos to Izanagi and Izanami* 143

J: *Jacolliot to Jubmel* 150

K: *Ka'ahupahau to Kuskurza* 154

L: *Ladon to Lyonesse* 163

M: *Macusis to Mu-yu-Moqo* 174

N: *Naacals to Nyoe* 195

O: *Oak to Ova-herero* 208

P: *Pacata-Mu to Pur-Un-Runa* 216

Q: *Qamate to Quikinna'qu* 233

R: *Ragnarok to Ruty* 236

S: *Sacsahuaman to Szeu-Kha* 243

T: *Tahiti to Tyche* 260

U: *Ualuvu levu to Uxmal* 277

V: *Vediouis to Vue* 282

W: *Wai-ta-hanui to Wotan* 287

X: *Xelhua to Xochiquetzal* 295

Y: *Yamquisapa to Yurlunggur* 298

Z: *Zac-Mu-until to Zuni Deluge Story* 302

Afterword by Professor Nobuhiro Yoshida 305

Bibliography 307

About the Author 312

FOREWORD
BY BRAD STEIGER

I must confess that the first thing I did when I received a manuscript copy of Frank Joseph's *The Atlantis Encyclopedia* was to check for myself just how thorough the text really was. I started with Viracocha, the early Inca culture-hero, who has fascinated me since our trip to Peru, where I stood at his legendary tomb site at Machu Picchu. I thought it unlikely that many researchers would associate Viracocha's "rising" from the great depths of Lake Titicaca with his possible arrival from Atlantis after the deluge, but there he was. Score one for Joseph.

Next, I tried an even more obscure reference—Balor, the king of the giant Sea People in Irish folklore. Another hit for Joseph. And so it went with name after name, geographical location after geographical location, until I put the manuscript aside and agreed that there was no single reference work on Atlantis quite as complete as this unique work. The vast majority of the thousands of books and magazine articles published about the lost civilization of Atlantis present a particular researcher's pet theory about where the place was; whether it was really a continent, an island, or a metropolis; and where we might find bits and pieces of the vanished world to prove the validity of the author's hypothesis.

The Atlantis Encyclopedia is by no means the first book Joseph has written about this perennial subject. His *Edgar Cayce's Atlantis and Lemuria* (A.R.E. Press, 2001) showed that the Sleeping Prophet was uncanny in his correct description of these antediluvian civilizations, and Cayce reappears in this latest effort with his intriguing predictions for their future discovery. But *The Atlantis Encyclopedia* is unique because it is the largest and most comprehensive of its kind; the author was about its research for nearly a quarter of a century.

In my own *Atlantis Rising*, first published in 1973, I examined and reevaluated the evidence for what I considered the eight most prevalent theories of what the "lost continent" was or what it represented, from ancient terrestrial sea-kings, to ancient extraterrestrial colonizers. But in this extensive encyclopedia, Joseph has no particular axe to grind or theory to postulate. These are the facts, figures, fauna, flora, figments, and fantasies that surround the mystery of Atlantis. Although I have written books on many different subjects since *Atlantis Rising*, researching the true origins of humankind's sojourn on this planet remains one of my greatest passions in terms of personal research.

While I am fascinated by our plans to explore outer space—and I do support such efforts—I truly believe that it remains one of our greatest responsibilities, as a species, to discover who we truly are, before we begin our trek to the stars. I very much believe, as I titled a subsequent book on the mysteries of humankind's vast antiquity, that there have been "worlds before our own" on this planet.

Yes, once the subject of Atlantis and lost civilizations seizes your imagination and invades your dreams, you will find that you, too, must join the search for establishing the reality of what the great majority of your peers will consider nonsense. But read this impressive work by Frank Joseph, and you will discover for yourself that Atlantis is far more than a metaphor for humankind's brief glory before the dust. The subject of Atlantis can really get a hold on you. After all, Frank was kind enough to share with me that it was my *Atlantis Rising* that whetted his own appetite for the quest. Now make it your own in *The Atlantis Encyclopedia*!

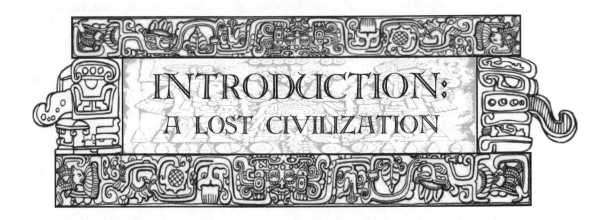

INTRODUCTION:
A LOST CIVILIZATION

The Atlantis Encyclopedia is a result of more than two decades of continuous study and international travel. It began in 1980, when I started picking up clues to the lost civilization in locations from the ruins of Troy and Egypt's desert pyramids, to Morocco's underground shrine and Britain's Stonehenge, beyond to the mountaintop city of Peru and a ceremonial center in the jungles of Guatemala. My quest took me to Polynesia's cannibal temple, the seldom seen solar monuments of Japan's remote forests, and the golden pillar of Thailand. I sought out credible proof in my own country, traveling from coast to coast, finding telltale evidence—among the world's most northerly pyramids, in Wisconsin; at Ohio's Great Serpent Mound; and in the ruins of North America's oldest city, in Louisiana. I participated in diving expeditions to the Bahamas, Yucatan, the Canary Islands, the Aegean Sea, and the Pacific Ocean. Decades of these on-site explorations was combined with research in the libraries of the world and the shared wisdom of devoted colleagues to produce this unique volume.

Of the estimated 2,500 books and magazine articles published about the lost civilization, *The Atlantis Encyclopedia* is the only one of its kind. It is an attempt to bring together all the known details of this immense, continually fascinating subject, as well as to provide succinct definitions and clear explanations. It is a handbook of Atlantean information for general readers and specialists alike. Everything one wants to know about Atlantis is here in short form. It is a source for students of archaeology, myth, and prehistory.

Unlike most other books on the subject, *The Atlantis Encyclopedia* offers fewer theories and more facts. Areas of interest include geology, astronomy, and oceanography, but with strong emphasis on the folk traditions of numerous peoples around the world who preserved memories of a great flood that destroyed an ancestral island of memorial splendor. These elements have never been presented together before in a single volume. In so doing, the common threads that weave European and Near Eastern versions to North American accounts, beyond to Polynesian and Asian renditions, accumulatively build a picture in the reader's mind of a real event encapsulated for thousands of years in the long-surviving myths and legends of mankind.

We learn that the Egyptians told of "the Isle of Flame" in the Far Western Ocean from which their forefathers arrived after a terrible natural disaster. Meanwhile, in North America, the Apache Indians still preserve memories of their ancestral origins from the sunken "Isle of Flames" in the distant seas of the East. There is the Norse Lifthraser and Lif, husband and wife refugees of the Great Flood, just as the ancient Mexicans remembered Nata and Nena, the pair who escaped a world deluge. Balor leads his people to safety in pre-Celtic Ireland, while Manibozho survives to become the founder of all North American Indian tribes. Underpinning them all is the story of Atlantis, as given to the world 24 centuries ago by the greatest thinker of classical Greece. Plato's Atlantis still lives in the folkish memories of virtually every people on Earth. Although fundamentally similar to all the rest, each version presents its own details, contributing to an overall panorama of the Atlantean experience, as dramatic as it is persuasive.

The Atlantis Encyclopedia offers equally exhaustive information about a Pacific counterpart—the lost kingdom of Mu, also known as Lemuria. Although at opposite cultural and geographical poles, the two civilizations were at least partially contemporaneous and in contact with each other, produced transoceanic seafarers who founded new societies around the globe, and succumbed in the end to natural catastrophes that may have been related. Persuasive physical evidence for the sunken realm came to light in 1985 off the coast of Yonaguni, a remote Japanese island, when divers found the ruins of a large ceremonial building that sank beneath the sea perhaps as long ago as 12,000 years. Long before that dramatic discovery, accounts of Mu or Lemuria were preserved in the oral folk traditions of numerous peoples around the Pacific Basin, from America's western coastal regions, across Polynesia and Micronesia, to Australia, and throughout Asia. As such, the story of Atlantis is incomplete without some appreciation of the complimentary role played by its Lemurian predecessor and coruler of the world.

And no comprehensive investigation of this kind can ignore the "life-readings" of Edgar Cayce, America's "Sleeping Prophet," during the first half of the 20th century. His vision of Atlantis, still controversial, is nonetheless compelling and, if true, insightful and revealing. Cayce's testimony is unique, because he spoke less of theories and history, than of individual human beings, and the high drama they lived as players on the stage of the Atlantean world.

Although it does not set out to prove the sunken capital actually existed, *The Atlantis Encyclopedia* musters so much evidence on its behalf, even skeptics may conclude that there must be at least something factual behind such an enduring, indeed global legend. For true believers, this book is a gold mine of information to help them better understand the lost civilization. Atlantologists (serious investigators of the subject) may use it as a unique and valuable reference to spring-board their own research. Students of comparative myth have here a ready source of often rarely presented themes connecting the Bronze Age to Classical World images. For most readers, however, *The Atlantis Encyclopedia* offers an easily accessible introduction to this eternally enthralling enigma.

Aalu

Ancient Egyptian for "The Isle of Flame," descriptive of a large, volcanic island in the Distant West (the Atlantic Ocean). It physically matches Plato's Atlantis virtually detail for detail: mountainous, with canals, luxuriant crops, a palatial city surrounded by great walls decorated with precious metals, etc. Aalu's earliest known reference appears in *The Destruction of Mankind*, a New Kingdom history (1299 B.C.) discovered in the tomb of Pharaoh Seti-I, at Abydos. His city was the site of the Osireion, a subterranean monument to the Great Flood that destroyed a former age of greatness.

On the other side of the world from Egypt, the Apache Indians of the American Southwest claim their ancestors arrived after the Great Flood destroyed their homeland, still remembered as the "Isle of Flames," in the Atlantic Ocean.

Ablach

In Celtic and pre-Celtic myth, an Atlantic island whose name meant "rich in apple trees." It was ruled by the Irish version of Poseidon—the sea-god, Manannan. Ablach is paralleled by the Garden of the Hesperides, a sacred grove of apple trees at the center of Atlas's island, tended by the Hesperides, who were *Atlantises*—"daughters of Atlas."

(See Garden of the Hesperides)

Abnakis

Algonquian tradition tells how the eponymous founding father, from whom this North American tribe derived its name, came "from the rising sun," the direction of the Abnakis ("our white ancestors"), after he was forewarned in a dream that the gods would sink their land beneath the sea. In haste, he built "a great reed raft" on which he sailed away with his family. Aboard were a number of animals that, in those days, could speak. The beasts grew impatient with the long voyage, ridiculed the Father of the Tribes, and were about to mutiny, when land was finally sighted. Everyone disembarked safely, but the formerly rebellious animals, as punishment for their onboard behavior, were deprived by the gods of their ability to converse with humans.

(See Noah)

Aclla Cuna

In Quechua, the language of the Incas, "The Chosen Women," or "The Little Mothers." They referred to the seven visible stars in the constellation of the Pleiades, associated with a great deluge, from which Con-Tiki-Viracocha ("White Man of the Sea Foam") arrived in South America to found Andean Civilization.

Aclla Cuna was also the name of the Incas' most sacred mystery cult composed exclusively of the most beautiful, virtuous, and intelligent women, who orally preserved the high wisdom and ancestral traditions of the red-haired Con-Tiki-Viracocha. They dressed in Atlantean colors (red, white, and black) and were provided magnificent estates at Cuzco, the capital of the Inca Empire, and the mountain citadel of Machu Picchu. The Chosen Women identified with the Pleiades, or "Atlantises," as they were known similarly in Greek myth.

Ad

A palatial island capital punished for the wickedness of its inhabitants by a terrible flood. The story of Ad is preserved in pre-Islamic traditions and mentioned in the Holy Koran, which condemned its inhabitants for building "high places for vain uses." The Adites were said to have "worshiped the sun from the tops of pyramids," a singularly un-Arabic practice more evocative of life in Atlantis. Ad was known as "the City of Pillars," or "the Land of Bronze." Plato similarly described the pillar cult of the Atlanteans, while their city was the pre-classical world's foremost clearinghouse for the bronze trade.

In Arabic tradition, the Adites are portrayed as giants (the Atlantean Titans of Greek mythology), superior architects and builders who raised great stone monuments. Even today, rural tribes of Saudi Arabia refer to any ancient ruins of prodigious size as "buildings of the Adites," and apply the expression "as old as Ad" to anything of extreme age. In the 19th century, the royal monarch of the Mussulman tribes was Shedd-Ad-Ben-Ad, or "Descendant and Son of Ad." The progenitor of the Arab peoples was Ad, grandson of the biblical Ham.

The Adites are still regarded as the earliest inhabitants of Arabia. They were referred to as "red men," for the light color of their hair. Several accounts of Atlantis (Egyptian, Irish, Winnebago, etc.) depict the Atlanteans, at least in part, as redheads. The Adites had 10 kings ruling various parts of the world simultaneously—the same number and disposition described by Plato in his Atlantis account, *Kritias*. The Adites arrived in the country after Ad was annihilated by a colossal black cloud with the ferocity of a hurricane, an obvious reference to the volcanic eruption that accompanied the destruction of Atlantis.

"Ad" is still the name of a Semitic tribe in the province of Hadramut, Saudi Arabia, whose elders claimed descent from their eponymous ancestor, the great-grandson of Noah.

(See Adapa)

Adad

The Atlantean concept of Atlas imported into Sumer (after 3000 B.C.). Adad was a fire-god symbolized by an active volcano, its summit wreathed by the constellation of the Pleiades—the "Atlantises," or daughters of Atlas. Oppenheimer writes that the Sumerian version of the flood was "catastrophic. The storm came suddenly with a loud noise and darkening the sky and a raging wind from Adad...One of the gods, Anzu, is described as tearing the sky with his talons." According to the Sumerian version of the Deluge, "No one could see anyone else. They could not be recognized in the catastrophe. The flood roared like a bull. Like a wild ass screaming, the winds howled. The darkness was total, and there was no sun."

Adapa

In Babylonian myth, Ea, the god of the seas, destroyed the great city of Ad with a catastrophic deluge, killing all its sinful inhabitants except his virtuous high priest, Adapa. This "Man from Ad" arrived in the Near East as a culture-bearer to pass on the arts and sciences, principles of government, and religion, from which all subsequent Mesopotamian civilizations traced their development. The Babylonian Ad is equivalent to the drowned capital preserved in Arabic traditions, and both are clear references to the same primeval civilization of Atlantis.

(See Ad)

Adena

Named after an Ohio mound group dating from ca. 1000 B.C., Adena represents the earliest known civilization in the American Midwest and along the eastern seaboard. Its people built colossal ridge-top or linear burial mounds of stone, often longer than 100 feet, and great conical structures; the greatest, at 66 feet high, is West Virginia's Creek Grave Mound. The Adena people also laid out sprawling enclosures oriented to various celestial phenomena. Their prodigious feats of ceremonial construction imply high levels of labor management, astronomy, and surveying. They were able metalsmiths who worked copper on a large scale, and they demonstrated carving skills in surviving stone effigy-pipes.

Their sudden, unheralded appearance after the previous and primitive Archaic Period represented a major break with the immediate past. Such a transformation can only mean that the Adena were newcomers who brought their already evolved culture with them from outside the American Midwest. Their starting date coincides within two centuries of the final destruction of Atlantis and the abrupt closure of Michigan's Upper Peninsula copper mines, which had been consistently worked for the previous 1,800 years. Given these parallel events, it appears the Adena were former Atlantean copper miners, who settled throughout the Middle West to the East Coast, following the loss of their distant homeland and the abandonment of copper mining in the Upper Great Lakes.

A majority of the Adena monuments were dismantled and their stone used by early 19th-century settlers to build wells and fences. Only a few examples still survive, because they were naturally concealed by their obscure locations, such as those at the bottom of Rock Lake, in Wisconsin, and in the wooded areas of Heritage Park, Michigan.

(See Bronze Age, Rock Lake)

Ades

Sacred mountain where the Atlantean Navel of the World mystery cult originated. Ades was later known as "Hades"—the realm of the dead in Greek myth—but associated with the death-rebirth mystery cult of Atlantis in the story of Persephone, the "Corn Maiden" daughter of the Earth Mother, Demeter.

(See Navel of the World)

An Atlantean-like engraved stone found in Illinois, provenance unknown. From the Thelma MacLaine Collection. The figure resembles the winged horses and Poseidon's trident described in Plato's account of Atlantis.

Ad-ima

In Indian myth, the first man to arrive in the subcontinent, with his wife (Heva), from an island overwhelmed by a natural catastrophe that forever cut off all communication with his homeland. In Sanskrit, the word for "first" is *Adim*, surprisingly like the biblical Adam. Later versions of the story identify the lost island with Sri Lanka, but in that the former Ceylon still exists, Atlantis was undoubtedly the location from which Ad-ima came. His name, moreover, is identifiably Atlantean, apparent in the philological relationship between "Ad-ima" and the Greek variant, "Atlas." This association is underscored by the antediluvian setting of the Ad-ima myth.

(See Heva)

Aditayas

Also known as the Daityas, offspring of Vishnu. Water-giants somewhat equivalent to the Titans of Greek myth (like Atlas and the other kings of Atlantis), the Aditayas are mentioned in *Vishnu Purana* and *Mahabharata*, two of the oldest and most revered ancient Indian literary traditions. The latter work describes them as the inhabitants of Tripura, the Triple City in the Western Ocean, doubtless the Atlantic island of Poseidon (of the trident). The Aditayas were destroyed after they engaged in a war that culminated in the sinking of Tripura, the same story retold by Plato in his account of Atlantis.

Aditi

In Indian myth, the mother of Vishnu, who conquered the Earth for the gods and became the first Aditaya, or "Upholder" of the sky (the moral order of the cosmos), and is therefore identified with Atlas. His offspring were the Aditayas (or Daityas), who supported the heavens.

(See Aditayas, Atlas)

Aegle

An Atlantis, or "Daughter of Atlas," one of the Hesperides, a trio of divine sisters who guarded the golden apples of eternal life in a sacred grove on Atlas's island.

(See Garden of the Hesperides)

Aegeon

In Greek myth, a Titan who carried civilization into the eastern Mediterranean, which he named after himself: the Aegean Sea. Aegeon is associated with Atlantean culture-bearers during the 12th century B.C. He was also known as Briareus.

(See Hecatoncheires)

Aegyptus

In Greek myth, an early king of Egypt, from whom the country derived its name. He was the grandson of Poseidon and Libya, which is to say his lineage was Atlanto-African. Aegyptus was descended from Atlantean royalty who, on their passage through the Nile Valley, married native North Africans.

Aelian

Roman biologist (third century A.D.) and author of *The Nature of Animals*, in which he reported, "The inhabitants of the shores of the Ocean tell that in former times the kings of Atlantis, descendants of Poseidon, wore on their heads, as a mark of power, the fillet of the male sea-ram [a dolphin], and that their wives, the queens, wore, as a sign of their power, fillets of the female sea-rams [perhaps narwhals]."

Queen Hatshepsut's funerary temple at Deir el-Bahri, West Thebes, was patterned after similar monumental construction in contemporary Atlantis, circa 1470 B.C.

Aethyr

The Egyptian month corresponding to our late October/early November, during which a world deluge associated with the final destruction of Atlantis was caused by the goddess Hathor.

Agadir

A city on the Atlantic coast of Morocco. Its name may have been derived from the Atlantean king mentioned in Plato's *Kritias*, Gadeiros.

Ah-Auab

Literally "white men," or "foreigners to the land," a term by which the Mayas of the Lowland Yucatan distinguished themselves from native Indian populations, because they claimed descent from fair-skinned survivors of the Great Flood.

(See Halach-Unicob, Tutulxiu)

Ahson-nutli

Among the Navajo Indians in the American Southwest, Ahson-nutli was a god who, in the days before the Great Flood, created a quartet of twin giants to support the four corners of the sky. In Plato's account of Atlantis, supreme leadership of the antediluvian civilization belonged to twin brothers, likewise Titans, or giants. Atlas, the first of these, was mythically perceived as supporting the sky on his shoulders. His name derives from the Sanskrit *atl*, "to support or uphold."

(See Atlas, Ayar-aucca)

Aiken, Conrad

Renowned 20th-century American author and master poet who wrote of Atlantis in his 1929 works, *Priapus and the Fool* and *Senlin*.

Aintzine-Koak

Literally "those who came before," the forefathers of the Basque. The ancestral Aintzine-Koak are still remembered as former inhabitants of "the Green Isle," a powerful maritime nation that sank into the Atlantic Ocean after a terrible cataclysm and from which the few survivors sailed into the Bay of Biscay, eventually bringing the holy relics of their mystery religion into the Pyrenees Mountains.

(See Atlaintika)

Ainu Deluge Myth

The Ainu are mixed descendants of a Caucasian population that inhabited Japan before Asian immigrations from Korea. They may have belonged to the same white population that inhabited the kingdom of Mu and dispersed across the Pacific Ocean after it was overwhelmed by a great flood. Remnants of this lost race also appear among 9,000-year-old skeletal remains found in Washington State (the so-called "Kennewick Man"), the untypically bearded Haida of coastal British Columbia, and in parts of Polynesia.

The Ainu recall a time when the sea suddenly rose over the land, drowning most humans. Only a few survived by climbing to mountaintops.

(See Mu)

Alalu

The Hurrians were a people who occupied Anatolia (Turkey) from the early third millennium B.C. Many of their religious and mythic concepts were absorbed by their Hittite conquerors, beginning after 2000 B.C. Among these traditions was the story of Alalu, the first king of heaven, a giant god who made his home on a mountainous island in the sea of the setting sun. His son, Kumarbi, was synonymous for the Greek Kronos, a mythic personification of the Atlantic Ocean through Roman times. In Alalu survives a Hurrian memory of the mountainous island of Atlantis.

(See Arallu, Arallu, Kronos)

Alas, That Great City

Francis Ashton's popular 1948 novel about Atlantis, influenced by Hanns Hoerbiger's Cosmic Ice Theory.

(See Hoerbiger)

Alatuir

A magic stone, the source of ultimate power, at the very center of Bouyan, the sunken island-kingdom from which the ancestors of the Slavic peoples migrated to the European Continent from the Western Ocean. Alatuir was a sacred omphalos, a large, egg-shaped stone symbol of the primeval mystery cult in Atlantis.

(See Navel of the World)

Albion

The ancient name for Britain, "The White Island," derived from the twin brother of Atlas. Albion was said to have introduced the arts of shipbuilding and astrology, the leading material features of Atlantis. "The White Island" concept associated with Atlantis is also found in Aztec Mexico, North Africa, and India. The spiritual arts Albion brought to Britain were believed to have formed the basis for Druidism.

(See Atala, Aztlan, Blake)

Algonquian Flood Myth

Native tribes of the American Northeast preserved a tribal memory of their ancestral origins on a large island in the Atlantic Ocean. After many generations, signs and portents warned the inhabitants of impending disaster. Some magnitude of the evacuation that took place is suggested in the 138 boats said to have been prepared for the emergency. According to Algonquian elder Sam D. Gill, it began when "the Earth rocked to and fro, as a ship at sea." The quakes became so powerful the island "was cut loose from its fastenings, and fires of the Earth came forth in flames and clouds and loud roarings." As the flotilla of refugees made good their escape, "the land sank down beneath the waters to rise no more." The survivors eventually landed along the eastern seaboard of North America, and married among the indigenous peoples to become the forefathers of the Algonquian tribes. There is no more succinct and credible version of the Atlantis catastrophe and its aftermath.

Alkynous

The king of Phaeacia (Atlantis) in Homer's *Odyssey*. The monarch's name is a derivative of the leading Pleiade most directly associated with Atlantis, Alkyone.

Alkyone

An "Atlantis," a daughter of Atlas and the sea-goddess Pleione; leader of her divine sisters, the Pleiades. Alkyone may be a mythic rendering of Kleito, the woman in Plato's account of Atlantis, who likewise bore culture-bearers to the sea-god Poseidon. Her title was "The Queen who wards off Storms." To the Druids at Boscawen-Uen, Mea-Penzance, Scotland's Callanish, and other megalithic sites throughout Britain, the Pleiades represented fearful powers of destruction through the agency of water.

The same dreadful association was made by the Egyptians. The so-called "Scored Lines" of the Great Pyramid at Giza were in alignment with the star

Alkyone of the Pleiades, in the constellation of Taurus the Bull, at noon of the spring equinox (March 21) in 2141 B.C. Suggestion that the Alkyone alignment was deliberately intended by the pyramid's designer is supported by the fact that the feature corresponding to the Scored Lines in the so-called "Trial Passages" is a flat surface that could have been used as a pelorus for stargazing (Lemesurier, 193).

In view of the Great Pyramid's function, at least partially, as a monument to Atlantis, the third-millennium B.C. date may commemorate some related anniversary, either of the Atlantis catastrophe itself or an Atlantean arrival in the Nile Valley. Lemesurier suggests as much: "The Pleiades were firmly linked in the Egyptian tradition with the goddess Hathor, the 'goddess of the Foundation', and instigator of the primeval 'deluge'." Hathor, or Aether, was, after all, the Egyptian version of Alkyone, herself the personification of Atlantis (151).

"The Egyptians observed three solemn days that ended when these stars [the Pleiades] culminated at midnight. These days were associated with a tradition of a deluge or other race-destroying disaster. The rites began on the seventeenth day of Aethyr, which agrees with the Mosaic deluge account, namely, the seventeenth day of the second month of the Jewish year" (154). Both the Egyptian Aethyr and the second month of the Jewish year correspond to our late October/early November. With the year provided by a proper lunar calculation of the date given by Plato in *Kritias* and Egyptian records of the XX Dynasty, we arrive at a date for the final destruction of Atlantis: November 3, 1198 B.C.

Ama

A Japanese tribe, of numerical insignificance, with genetic links to populations directly descended from the Jomon Culture of the ninth millennium B.C. Today, the Ama live around the Saheki Gulf (Ohita prefecture). Their oldest known settlements were at Minami Amabe-gun (Ohita prefecture), Amabe-cho (Tokushima prefecture), Kaishi-cho in Sado (Niigata prefecture) and Itoman-cho (Okinawa prefecture). These areas coincide with some of the country's oldest habitation sites. The Ama believe they are direct descendants of foreigners from a high civilization across the sea in the deeply ancient past. The visitors, remembered as the Sobata, preached a solar religion, and its symbol, a rising sun, became the national emblem of Japan. It also signified the direction from which the Sobata came; namely, the eastern Pacific Ocean. Their island kingdom, Nirai-Kanai, was eventually overwhelmed by a great flood and now lays at the bottom of the sea.

To commemorate these events, the Ama still conduct an annual ceremony at the eastern shores of Japan, held in early April or October. At dawn, the celebrants gather on the beach to face the dawn and pray for the souls of their ancestors, the Sobata. Following purification with seawater, a designated leader walks into the ocean, up to his neck, bearing a small tree branch in his hand. After a pause, he turns to face the shore. Emerging from the water, he is greeted with the wild beating of drums and joyful chanting, as though he had survived some catastrophe.

In *The Lost Continent of Mu*, James Churchward stated that the sunken civilization of the Pacific was symbolized by the Tree of Life. The word for "timber" in

Chinese is *mu*. In Japanese and Korean, *mu* signifies that which does not exist, referring perhaps to the vanished Nirai-Kanai signified by the tree branch carried through the water by the Ama celebrant.

(See Mu, Nirai-Kanai, Sobata)

Amadís

This opera by the French composer Jules Massenet premiered in Monte Carlo, in 1927, and was based on the Breton folk legend of King Perion who, with his family, barely escaped before his island kingdom was swallowed up by the sea with its wicked inhabitants. The story of Amadis belongs to "the Green Isle" oral traditions of a sunken island city still preserved among various western coastal populations in Belgium, the Netherlands, Brittany, Biscay (among the Basque), Spain, and Portugal.

Amaicaca

Remembered by the Carib Indians of Venezuela as a deluge hero who escaped some natural catastrophe in "a big canoe" that settled at the top of Mount Tamancu after the flood waters receded. *Amaicaca* resembles Edgar Cayce's *Amaki* and the Colombian *Amuraca*.

Amaiur

The legendary first king of the Basque is equated with biblical parallels of Tubalcain, a grandson of the flood hero in Genesis, Noah. *Amaiur* means, "Monarch of Maya," a kingdom referred to as the Green Isle, swallowed by the Atlantic Ocean. In Greek myth, Maya was one of the seven Pleiades, daughters of the goddess Pleione and the Titan Atlas, and hence, an "Atlantis."

(See Maia, Pleiades)

Ambrosia

As a daughter of Atlas, she was an Atlantis, one of the five Hyades. Her name means "immortality."

(See Hyades)

Ami

A tribal people of Taiwan, whose flood story shares details in common with deluge accounts in other parts of the world. As explained by John Canon MacCullow: "They say at that time [in the remote past] the mountains crumbled down, the Earth gaped, and from the fissure a hot spring gushed forth, which flooded the whole face of the Earth. Few living things survived the inundation." The Tsuwo version describes birds dropping many thousands of stones into the cataclysm, suggesting a meteor bombardment. The only persons to survive were a brother and sister, whose responsibility it was to repopulate the planet.

Their first offspring were living abortions, which became fish and crabs, because the pair committed the sin of incest without asking dispensation from the sun-god. Having angered him, they applied to the moon-goddess. She forgave them, and the woman gave birth to a stone, from which sprang new generations of mankind. In this final detail of the Ami deluge myth is the rebirth of humanity from a stone, the same theme encountered in Greek myth and numerous other flood accounts around the world.

(See Asteroid Theory, Deucalion)

Amimitl

"The Harpoon" or "Harpooner," a title applied to the Aztec god of the sea, Atlahua. His name is an apparent derivative of Atlas. He was also known as "He Who Divides the Waters" and "Inventor of the Trident," both of which clearly define Atlantean associations. Plato told how the sea-god Poseidon "divided the waters from the land" to create Atlantis. Moreover, the trident was Poseidon's emblem of maritime power. Brundage reports that Atlahua was "venerated in a temple on the legendary island of Aztlan," Atlantis, obviously enough (93). Remarkably, the ancient Egyptians remembered the Mesentiu, "The Harpooners," a culture-bearing people who arrived by sea from the Distant West to establish dynastic civilization at the Nile Delta.

Amma

In Yoruba and Benin traditions, she was among the few royal survivors of a great flood when the Atlantic Ocean overflowed very long ago. Amma arrived safely on the shores of West Africa, where she became the first ruler.

Ammianus Marcellinus

A fourth-century Roman historian who classified the destruction of Atlantis as a *chasmatiae*, a natural disaster in which seismic violence breaks open great fissures in the Earth to swallow large tracts of territory during a single event.

Ampheres

One of the 10 original Atlantean kings listed by Plato (in *Kritias*). His name means "he who encompasses," or "fitted or joined on both sides," suggestive of a power center located midway between Western Europe and the Outer Continent of the Americas, such as the Azore Islands, where possible Atlantean remains have been found. Ampheres might be linked to the amphora, or drinking vessel of King Gradlon, king of Ys, in Brittany's pre-Christian tradition of a sunken island.

(See Azores, Outer Continent)

Amphictyonies

Term for political confederations of sometimes large kingdoms in classical Greece, derived from "Amphictyon," son of Deucalion and Pyrrha, the couple who survived the Great Flood. Deucalion was a nephew of Atlas and, therefore, an Atlantean. Amphictyon helped reestablish civilization by reading omens, particularly in dreams. He was also the first post-deluge survivor to mix water and wine, which means he preserved the antediluvian Dionysiac mystery religion in Greece. The amphictyonies reflect not only his name, but the political organization of Atlantean civilization, which was a confederation of kingdoms, as described by Plato in *Timaeus* and *Kritias*.

A-Mu-Ra-Ca

In the early 16th century, when they first walked ashore at what is now Colombia, the Spaniards were informed by their Indian hosts that they had appeared in "the Land of A-Mu-Ra-Ca." Bearing the royal title, "Serpent," A-Mu-Ra-Ca, they said, was a bearded white man not unlike the Conquistadors themselves. He had long ago arrived after a terrible flood out at sea forced him and his followers to seek refuge. He afterward taught the natives the benefits of agriculture, medicine, and religion, then built the first of several stone cities. A-Mu-Ra-Ca's resemblance to the "Plumed Serpent," known by the identical name to the northerly Mayas and Aztecs, means that the same set of Old World culture-bearers arrived throughout the Americas.

It suggests, too, that the name given to the New World did not derive from a contemporary Italian mapmaker, but rather the Atlantean flood hero. The Europeans did not use native names for lands they conquered, because they sought to lend greater legitimacy to their New World holdings by rechristening them with Old World names. Thus, the Atlanto-Colombian "A-Mu-Ra-Ca" was changed to the "America" of Amerigo Vespucci for political reasons. It does indeed seem strange that the New World would have been christened after the first name of the cartographer. Supporting the indigenous provenance of "America," Columbus himself, on his third voyage to the New World, met Indian natives who introduced themselves as "Americos" (Jimenez and Graeber, 67). The same tribe was identified by Alonso de Ojeda on his second voyage to Hispaniola. Moreover, the "land of perpetual wind," reference to a mountain range in the province of Chantoles, between Juigalpa and Liberdad, in Nicaragua, was known to the Mayas as "Amerisque," and so recorded in the sailing logs of Columbus, as well as the writings of Vespucci.

Intriguingly, *A-Mu-Ra-Ca* appears to mean "Ra's Serpent from Mu." *Ca* ("Serpent") describes a powerful wise man, most likely a priest-king. The appearance of Ra, the Egyptian sun-god, is hardly less amazing than that of Mu, the Pacific Ocean land said to have perished in a natural catastrophe before the destruction of Atlantis.

(See Mu)

A-Mu-ru

In Colombian native traditions, the great oceanic kingdom destroyed by a natural catastrophe from which the culture hero, A-Mu-Ra-Ca, led his followers to South America. In Akkadian, the language of Sumer's Semitic conquerors at the close of the third millennium B.C., *A-Mu-ru* means "Western Lands." The name, in both Colombian Muysica and Akkadian, refers to the lost Pacific Ocean civilization of Mu.

(See Mu)

An

In Sumerian tradition (circa 3500 to 2500 B.C.), a capital city on the island of Atu, which was overwhelmed by a cataclysmic deluge.

Andros Platform

Andros is the largest of the Bahama Islands, south of Bimini, where an underwater feature discovered in 1969 has been associated with Atlantean civilization ever since. Floridians Dr. Gregory Little and his wife, Lora, found a sunken site in Nicolls Town Bay, near the extreme northeast end of Andros 34 years later. They learned of its general position from a former dive operator, Dino Keller, who claimed to have navigated his boat inside a coral reef usually approached on the outside. There, in 1992, Keller observed a large structure similar to the so-called "Bimini Wall," under some 10 feet of water.

Following Keller's directions, in March, 2003, Dr. Little snorkeled about 600 yards from shore to find a 1,375-foot long, 150-foot wide arrangement of cyclopean blocks in three well-ordered sloping tiers interspersed by two bands of smaller stones. Although standing 15 feet beneath the surface, its top section is 10 feet deep, as described by Keller. The large stones comprising the tiers average 25 × 30 feet, and 2 feet thick. Each of the three tiers is 50 feet wide. Some suggestion of a ramp was discerned leading from the floor of the harbor lagoon to the top of the platform.

The feature's regular appearance and almost uniformly square-cut blocks, given its location at a natural harbor in the North Atlantic Current, suggest it may have been a quay, breakwater, or port facility of some kind. Underscoring this characterization, together with the ramp, are a number of 5-inch wide and deep rectangles resembling post-holes cut into some of the cyclopean stones just below the uppermost tier. These holes may have held mooring pylons used to tie up docked ships. Most if not all of the blocks themselves appear to have been quarried from local beach rock and deliberately set in place, a marine construction practice common in the ancient Old World.

Dr. Little believes the formation could only have been built 10,000 years ago, when sea levels were low enough for its creation. But archaeologists are certain that nothing of the kind existed in the post glacial epoch. Sea levels would have dropped sufficiently, however, between 1600 and 1500 B.C., during the middle to late Bronze Age—a far more likely period for construction, if only because similar harbor works were already in use throughout the eastern Mediterranean by that time. Moreover, Lake Superior copper mining was simultaneously nearing the zenith of its output. A port located off the North American coast, situated in the heart of the North Atlantic Current, would have been a valuable asset for freighters carrying cargos of mined copper back to their headquarters in Atlantis.

An Atlantean connection is, after all, suggested in the Andros platform's six alternating bands of stone: 6 was the sacred numeral of Atlantis, whose city-planners incorporated the holy number in the capital's alternating stone walls, according to Plato's description of the sunken civilization.

(See Bimini Road, *Kritias*)

Annals of Cuauhtitlan

An Aztec chronicle of earliest Mesoamerican beginnings, from when the first civilizers arrived on the eastern shores of Mexico after a destructive flood. "For fifty two years the waters lasted," it reports. "Thus, they [an ancestral people] perished. They were swallowed by the waters, and their souls became fish. The heavens collapsed upon them, and in a single day they perished. All the mountains perished [under the sea]."

These "Annals" compare with the Babylonian deluge story of Ishtar (the Sumerian Inanna), wherein the goddess laments how her people were "changed into fish" by a great flood that overwhelmed a former kingdom. So too, the Aztecs chose virtually the same words Plato used to describe the destruction of Atlantis "in a single day and night." That "the heavens collapsed upon them" also suggests a celestial event as part of the Deluge.

(See Asteroid Theory, Berosus, Inanna)

Annwn

From the Brythonic *an* ("abyss") and *dwfn* ("world"), known throughout Celtic myth as "Land Under Wave," or the "Revolving Castle" (Caer Sidi); formerly a fortified island of great natural beauty with freshwater streams and a circular-shaped city, at the center of which was a magic cauldron of immortality. These details clearly point to Atlantis, while Annwn's cauldron is a pre-Christian reference to the Holy Grail—another legendary link with the sunken civilization.

Antaeus

Possibly a pre-Platonic mythological rendering of Greek victory over the forces of Atlantis. Like Atlas, Antaeus was a Titan, the son of Poseidon and Gaia (Kleito, described as the mother of Atlas in *Kritias*, was likewise an Earth Mother goddess). Similar to the imperialist Atlanteans, he was everywhere invincible, until Heracles overcame him on the Atlantic shores of North Africa, fronting the position of Atlantis, "beyond the Pillars of Heracles," according to Plato. Archaeological finds throughout Atlantic coastal Morocco reveal consistent themes related to Heracles. Also, a similarity appears to exist between the names *Antaeus* and *Atlas*.

(See Atlas, Kleito)

Anubis

Greek for a funeral-god known to the Egyptians as Anpu. Although most Egyptologists describe him as jackal-headed, his title, "The Great Dog," demonstrates he was canine cephalic. And, like the seeing-eye dog, Anubis loyally guided the recently deceased through the darkness of death. He was a spirit-guide, who comforted the *ba*, or soul, leading it to the Otherworld. Prayed to as "The Westerner," Anubis was said to have "written annals from before the flood" which destroyed his island-home in the Distant West, from whence he arrived to reestablish his worship in Egypt. He was also known as the "Great Five," the sacred numeral of Atlantis, according to Plato. Hence, the funeral rites associated with his divinity became Egyptian mortuary practices after their importation from the sunken civilization.

(See Plato)

Apaturia

"The Gathering of the Clans," an ancient Greek religious festival lasting three days and staged every year, during which the *phratriai*, or various clans of Attica, met to discuss national affairs, celebrate their common culture, and publicly present children born since the previous Apaturia. The name means "shared relationship," underscoring the Greek heritage shared with all the tribal groups of Ionia. In his account of Atlantis (*Timaeus*), Plato wrote, "Now, the day was that day, the third of the festival of Apaturia, which is called the Registration of Youth (the Koureotis), at which, according to custom, our parents gave prizes for recitations, and the poems of several poets were recited by us boys." One youth, Amynander, makes a speech in praise of Solon, which begins the story of Atlantis, as it was brought to Greece from Egypt by the great Athenian law-giver.

Whether the tale was, in fact, recounted at each Koureotis ("Shearing Day," a ceremonial haircut; the last day of the festival and its climax) or Plato merely used the occasion as a related backdrop for his narrative, the Apaturia made an altogether appropriate setting for celebrating victory over the invading Atlanteans. It was an annual affair of national patriotism, in which the common greatness of the Greeks was honored. Interestingly, the previous day was known as Anarrhysis, or "the Day of Rescue." Nothing beyond its provocative name survives, but it may have been a commemoration of survivors from the Atlantean disaster. Moreover, the Apaturia was held in honor of Dionysus, whose myth portrays the god of rebirth as a culture-bearer following some catastrophic flood. Each Apaturia took place during the harvest time of Pyanopsion (the "Bean Month"), in late October/early November; according to the Egyptians, Atlantis was defeated by the Greeks and destroyed by a cataclysm of nature in their corresponding month of Aethyr (late October/early November).

(See Plato, Solon, *Timaeus*)

Arallu

In Babylonian tradition (circa 2100 B.C.), a great, mountainous island in the Distant West, where freshwater springs and a year-round temperate climate were enjoyed by the spiritually enlightened inhabitants. Arallu was the Babylonian version of Atlantis.

Arianrhod

Or Caer Arianrhod, the Celtic "Fortress of the Silver Wheel," referring to the concentric walls of Atlantis decorated, according to Plato, with precious metals. In some versions of her myth, Arianrhod was a woman who was responsible for the sinking of Caer Arianrhod, a Brythonic legend common along the Carnarvon coast, where a reef out at sea is associated with the remains of her sunken castle. According to Book I of *Taliesin*, a medieval collection of Welsh traditions with deeply prehistoric roots, "There is a *caer* of defense (a fortified city) under the ocean's wave." Artists and magicians went to Caer Arianrhod for the most advanced instruction, a Welsh recollection of the sophisticated civilization universally associated with Atlantis.

Arnobious Afer

A Christian rhetorician and early Church founder famous for dramatizing the fate of Atlantis in his sermons as a warning against the moral corruption of society. His use of the sunken civilization as an historic object lesson illuminates late third-century Roman thought, because it demonstrates the general acceptance of Atlantis as a real place.

Asteroid Theory

G.R. Corli, a French astronomer in 1785, was the first researcher to conclude that the fragment of a passing comet collided with the Earth to destroy Atlantis. The earliest thorough investigation of the Atlantis Problem was begun nearly 100 years later by the father of Atlantology, Ignatius Donnelly. His second book on the subject, *Ragnarok: Age of Fire and Gravel* (1884), proposed that the island civilization had been annihilated by a comet's collision with the Earth. At a time when established scientists did not even recognize the existence of meteorites, his speculation was roundly dismissed as untenable fantasy. He was supported by only a few contemporary thinkers, such as the Russian physicist Sergi Basinsky, who argued that a meteor impact with the Earth had been great enough for the simultaneous destruction of Atlantis and rise of Australia.

But in the 1920s and 30s, Donnelly's theory was revived and supported by the German physicist, Hanns Hoerbiger, whose controversial "Cosmic Ice" paradigm included the Atlantean catastrophe as the result of Earth's impact with a cometary fragment of frozen debris. His British contemporary, the influential publisher, Comyns Beaumont, had already come to the same conclusion independently. During the post-World War II era, Hoerbiger was championed by another well-known Austrian researcher, H.S. Bellamy. Meanwhile, Beaumont's work was taken over entirely by Immanuel Velikovsky in his famous *Worlds in Collision* (1950), which elaborated on the possibility of a celestial impact as responsible for the sudden extinction of a pre-Flood civilization.

As intriguingly or even as plausibly as these catastrophists argued, their proofs were largely inferential. But the extraterrestrial theory began to find persuasive material evidence in 1964, when a German rocket-engineer, Otto Muck, announced his findings of twin, deep-sea holes in the ocean floor. They were caused by a small asteroid that split in half and set off a chain reaction of geologic violence along the length of the Mid-Atlantic Ridge, a series of subsurface volcanoes, to which the island of Atlantis was connected.

Athanasius Kircher's 17th-century map of Atlantis. Photograph by Wayne May.

In the late 1980s and early 90s, astronomers Victor Clube and Bill Napier affirmed an asteroidal or meteoric explanation for the destruction of Atlantis. They demonstrated, however, the greater likelihood of a virtual Earth-bombardment, or "fire from heaven," as our planet passed through or near a cloud of large debris that showered down dozens or even hundreds of meteoritic materials, as opposed to Muck's single collision.

Particularly since the publication of Muck's convincing evidence, leading scholars—such as the world's foremost authority on Halley' Comet, Dr. M.M. Kamiensky (member of the Polish Academy of Sciences); Professor N. Bonev (Bulgarian astronomer at the University of Sofia); and Edgerton Sykes (the most important Atlantologist of the post-World War II era)—believed the final destruction of Atlantis was caused by an extraterrestrial impact or series of impacts. Preceding these scientific investigations by thousands of years are the numerous traditions of a great deluge caused by some celestial event, recounted in societies on both sides of the Atlantic Ocean.

Many, if not most, of these worldwide folk memories invariably link a heaven-sent cataclysm with the Flood. Beginning with the first complete account of Atlantis, Plato's *Timaeus*, the fall of an extraterrestrial object foreshadows the island's destruction when Psonchis, the Egyptian narrator of the story, tells Solon, the visiting Greek statesman, about "a declination of the bodies moving around the Earth and in the heavens, and a great conflagration of things upon the Earth recurring at long intervals of time."

Inscriptions on the walls of Medinet Habu (Upper Nile Valley), the "Victory Temple" of Pharaoh Ramses III, tell how the Atlantean invaders of Egypt were destroyed: "The shooting-star was terrible in pursuit of them," before their island went under the sea. Ibrahim ben Ebn Wauff Shah, Abu Zeyd el Balkhy, and other Arab historians used the story of Surid, the ruler of an antediluvian kingdom, to explain that the Great Flood was caused when a "planet" collided with the Earth.

In North America, the Cherokee Indians remembered Unadatsug, a "group" of stars—the Pleiades—one of whom, "creating a fiery tail, fell to Earth. Where it landed, a palm tree grew up, and the fallen star itself transformed into an old man, who warned of coming floods." As the modern commentator, Jobes, has written of Unadatsug, "The fall of one star may be connected with a Deluge story; possibly the fall of a Taurid meteor is echoed here."

A complimentary version occurs in the Jewish Talmud: "When the Holy One, blessed be He, wished to bring the Deluge upon the world, He took two stars out of the Pleiades." Similar accounts may be found among the Quiche Maya of the Lowland Yucatan, the Muysica of Colombia, the Arawak Indians of Venezuela, the Aztecs at Cholula, the classical Greeks, and so on.

Asterope

One of the Pleiades, an Atlantis, daughter of Atlas by Pleione.

Astrology

Literally, the "language of the stars," from the Greek *logos astra*, a scientific analysis of the mathematical relationships linking human character and the prediction of future events to positions and movements of the heavenly bodies. In the ancient world, astrology and astronomy (the observation of celestial events) comprised a single discipline. They finally split apart only in the early 19th century, when astrology was banished by rationalists to the realms of metaphysics or superstition.

Astrology undoubtedly emerged after and from astronomy, when correspon-dences between cosmic activity and human behavior were first noticed. This inter-relationship was embodied in the mythic personality of Atlas, the founder of both sciences. In Greek myth, he was the first astronomer-astrologer. Indeed, his capital city, Atlantis, was the child ("Daughter of Atlas") of his astronomical character, in that its layout of concentric rings was a reflection of the cosmic order.

The city and the Titan were architectural and mythic expressions, respectively, of the Atlanteans' own founding of and excellence in astronomy-astrology, as evidenced by the numerous stone structures that still survive in what was once the Atlantean sphere of influence. Many of these monuments (Britain's Stonehenge, Ireland's New Grange, America's Poverty Point, etc.) not only conform to the era and construction styles of the Atlanteans, but were skillfully aligned with significant cosmic orientations and built to compute often sophisticated celestial data.

At

Found in cultures around the world where traditions of Atlantis-like experiences have been preserved in folk memory, and usually denoting a sacred mountain (from the Mount Atlas of Atlantis), often volcanic and sometimes symbolized by a holy altar, such as the Samoan Atua. Throughout the prehistoric New World of the Americas, *At* invariably defines an eastern location (Aztlan, etc.), while, in Old World traditions, it is associated with western places (Atum, etc.)—appropriately enough, because mid-ocean culture-bearers sailed from Atlantis to both east and west. As such, in numerous cultures around the world, *At* is a prefix, a word, or a name in itself, defining a sacred mountain associated with ancestral origins, commonly after a world-class deluge.

Ata

An extinct volcanic mountain of the Tongatapu group in the southwest Pacific, and revered by the Tonga islanders as a natural memorial to red-haired, fair-skinned gods who arrived long ago to somehow "bless" the natives.

At-ach-u-chu

The premiere founding father of Andean civilization, revered from deeply prehistoric times to the Spanish Conquest of the 16th century. He was consistently described as the tall, red-haired, bearded, fair-skinned culture-bearer from a distant land in the East who arrived on the shores of Lake Titicaca after surviving some terrible deluge. The Peruvian natives called him "The Teacher of all Things," and knew him as the man who established the arts of civilization in South America, including agriculture, religion, astronomy, weights and measures, social organization, and government.

He was the elder of five brothers, known collectively as Viracochas, or "white men." At-ach-u-chu is better remembered by his title, Kontiki-Viracocha, or "White Man of the Sea Foam"; in other words, he was a foreigner who arrived by ship, "sea foam" being a poetic description of its bow wave. All features of this supremely important figure in Andean tradition, beginning with the At in the head of his name, clearly define him as the leader of survivors from the final destruction of Atlantis, who reestablished themselves by creating a hybrid civilization, a mix of local cultures with Atlantean technology, in Peru and Bolivia.

At-ach-u-chu was said to have moved on after a few years, traveling to the west. A curious variation of this folk memory from Nazca, site of the great lines and effigies seen properly only from altitude, has him rising into the air and flying toward the setting sun. Other than this last suggestion of prehistoric aviation, At-ach-u-chu's resemblance to similarly fair-faced culture-bearers appearing after a great natural disaster in the Atlantic Ocean are common throughout the Americas, from the Menomonie Indians of Michigan's Upper Peninsula, to the Aztecs' Quetzalcoatl and the Mayas' Kukulcan. These related founding heroes from over the sea apparently represent the impact native peoples experienced from the large-scale arrival of Atlantis refugees.

The South American At-ach-u-chu bears a striking resemblance to Atcha, remembered by the ancient Egyptians as a far-off, splendid, but vanished city echoing lost Atlantis. Here *At-ach-u-chu* could mean "The Man from Atcha (Atlantis)."

Ataentsik

The ancestor-hero of the Algonquian Passamaquoddy Indians, Ataentsik arrived on the eastern shores of Turtle Island (North America) from "the first island in the sea." His name, function as a founding father, and origin define him as an Atlantean visitor. Among the Hurons, however, Ataensik is the name of "Sky Woman," who, perishing, gave life to all creatures.

Atagi

Members of a tiny group of highly select and enigmatic Shinto priests, said to preserve the most deeply ancient wisdom from Japanese prehistory, as embodied in their ceremonial robes, which are primitively cut to deliberately suggest profound age. Their arcane rituals open with the members of the priesthood blowing conch-shell trumpets, the only such example in all Japan. The Atagi philological resemblance to "Atlantis," their emphasis on the great antiquity of their cult, and its unique sea-oriented symbolism bespeak the continuing survival of early Atlantean religious influences in Japan.

Atago

A hill lying at the center of Tokyo is described in myth as the place where the gods brought civilization to Japan.

(See Atagi, Atami)

Ataka

Described in the Harris Papyrus, a 133-foot long document dated April 14 (Epiphi 6), circa 1180 B.C., summarizing in detail the political, cultural, religious, and military accomplishments of Ramses III, Pharaoh of the XX Dynasty, who defended his kingdom from invading "Sea Peoples" identified with Plato's Atlanteans. After their defeat, he declares in the Harris Papyrus, "I sent out an expedition to the land of Ataka for the great foundries of copper which are in that place. Our transport ships were loaded. Having located the foundries loaded with metal, loaded as myriads upon our ships, they sailed back to Egypt, arriving safely. The cargo was piled in stores as hundreds of thousands of the color of gold. I let the people see them like marvels."

Ataka appears to be an Egyptian linguistic inflection of the Atlanteans' original name (the prefix "At" often designated Atlantean holdings) for Michigan's Upper Peninsula, in North America, where they engaged in extensive copper mining. Plato describes them as preeminent miners of the world's highest-grade copper (orichalcum). Ramses mentions "foundries," implying the large-scale mining operations that went on in Ataka, and which certainly existed throughout the Upper Great Lakes area up until his time, when they were abruptly and coincidentally shut down. The great quantities of copper his expedition took from Ataka required transport ships sailing a great, hazardous distance (they returned "safely"), while their "color of gold" suggests Plato's gold-like orichalcum and Michigan's high-grade copper. Only from the Upper Peninsula could Ramses have obtained such large amounts of exceptional copper. The Egyptians were well-accustomed to seeing riches of all kinds, but the prodigious stores of the world's best copper made even them "marvel."

It would appear that, after the Atlanteans' defeat and capture by Ramses, they divulged the location of their copper sources in North America. His transports ventured a transatlantic crossing, "located the foundries loaded with metal, loaded as myriads upon our ships, they sailed back to Egypt." He does not indicate any trade negotiations or military operations in Ataka, but simple seizure of the vast amounts of copper, as though there was no one there with whom to barter or fight. Historians know that at this time, the early 12th century B.C., the Michigan mines were likewise abandoned. With the sudden, simultaneous collapse of Atlantean Civilization, their copper treasure was easy pickings for the victorious Egyptians.

In the name *Ataka* may survive the closest reference to the Atlanteans' copper-mining region in the Upper Great Lakes.

Atala

"The White Island" described in the great Indian epic *Mahabharata* and in the epic poems, the *Puranas*, as the mountainous homeland of a powerful and highly civilized race located in "the Western Sea" on the other side of the world from India. *Vishnu Purana* located Atala "on the seventh zone" of heat, which corresponds to 24 to 28 degrees latitude, on a line with the Canary Islands. *Mahabharata* likewise locates Atala, "an island of great splendor," in the North Atlantic, where its inhabitants worshiped Narayana. This was the "Son of the Waters" and "the blessed supporter" (Atlas, "the supporter"), who was later responsible for a world-flood. Atala itself sank in a violent storm. All this unquestionably bespeaks Atlantis and its destruction. In Hindu myth, Atala was the center of seven realms. "They are embellished with the magnificent palaces in which dwell great snake-gods [compare with Valum, "Kingdom of Serpents," from which Votan, the Quiche Mayas' founding father, arrived in Middle America]—and where the sons of Danu are happy. There are beautiful groves and streams and lakes." This description mirrors Plato's description of Atlantis in *Kritias*.

The six regions surrounding Atala correspond to another Atlantean allegory, the Tower of Babel, which "was built after the model city in the sphere of Saturn." Saturn, or Kronos, was synonymous for the Atlantic Ocean in Greek and Roman myth. Moreover, the fifth-century Greek poet Nonnus described "Atlas, in the enclosure of the Seven Zones." Among the sacred numerals of Atlantis, Seven signified the completion of cycles, while Six stood for the perfection of human forms. "The sons of Danu" recur in other parts of the world directly affected by the Atlantis experience, such as the Irish Tuatha da Danann ("the Followers of Danu") and the Dananns (the sons of Danaus, himself a son of Poseidon, brother of Atlas, and the founder of civilized Greece). Berber traditions likewise describe Atala as an island of miners, wealthy in gold, silver, copper, and tin. Not content with these riches, they launched a military invasion that swept eastward across North Africa, a conquest cut short by a flood that drowned their homeland, the same Atlantean War and inundation described by Plato. The Berbers predicted that Atala will one day rise to the surface of the sea that long ago overwhelmed it. Berber tribesmen of the Shott el Hameina, in Tunisia, still refer to themselves as the "Sons of the Source, Atala." A Norse version of Atala was Landvidi, similarly known as the "White Land."

On the other side of the Atlantic Ocean, in the American South, Atala is the word for "mountain" among the Cherokee Indians, who may have used it to describe a 40-foot high pyramid found in Georgia. Etowah Mounds is today an archaeological park including a prehistoric ceremonial center of large earthen temple-mounds built around 900 A.D., and abandoned in the early part of the 14th century, but whose earliest origins are still undetermined. The Cherokee also preserve a deluge legend that tells of survivors arriving on the shores of Turtle Island (North America) from "a great lodge" drowned in the Eastern Sea. The survival of this term, *Atala*, and its undeniably Atlantean details among peoples as widely separated as India, Morocco, and Georgia comprise persuasive evidence on behalf of a historic Atlantis.

Atalanta

Modern Talanto, a rocky islet west of the entrance to the Greek port city of Piraeus. Also the name of another Greek island in the fjord of Euboea, whose name was changed to Talandonisi.

In Greek myth, Atalanta was a virgin huntress, who vowed to marry the man able to beat her in a foot race. There were many suitors, but she outran them all, save Hippomenes, who cunningly dropped three golden apples, one by one, which, in her desire for the fruit, she stopped to pick up, thereby forfeiting her victory and virginity. Almost immediately after this contest, however, she and Hippomenes incurred the wrath of Zeus by copulating in the god's sacred precinct. He turned the couple into a lioness and a lion. Their son, Pathenopaeus, grew up to become a leader of the Argives (one of the Seven Against Thebes).

While outwardly the story of Atalanta appears to have nothing to do with Atlantis, Rene Guenon wrote that the three golden apples dropped by Hippomenes were from the Hesperides, the three daughters of Atlas (that is, Atlantids or "Atlantises"). Guenon also concludes that Atalanta's role as heroine of the Caledonian bear hunt signified change from a solstitial to an equinoctial method of measuring time; from reckoning the starting point of the annual cycle with the appearance of the Pleiades (Hesperides), instead of the Great Bear, thus implying the ascendancy of Atlantean civilization over a former culture.

The Atlantean character of Atalanta's name and her punishment at the hands of Zeus (who likewise condemned the Atlanteans in Plato's version for their immorality) parallel Atlantis in a garbled mythic tradition. Her husband, Hippomenes, is likely Atlantean as well, because at least some names in Plato's account are similarly equine: Elasippos ("Knightly Horse-Rider," one of the original 10 Atlantean kings), Leukippe ("White Mare," the first lady of Atlantis), and so on. Like all the other daughters of Atlas, Atalanta gave birth to a foremost culture-bearer, signifying the Atlanteans who voyaged to other lands, where they became the progenitors of new societies.

Atalanta: A Story of Atlantis

A 1940s musical by British composer Sir Gerald Hargreaves, who also wrote the libretto and designed its lavish sets. The story is set in the Atlantean court, where two factions of aristocrats argue for and against war. At the height of their debate, the Greek hero, Achilles, fresh from his triumph over the Trojans, arrives to plea for peace. But a warlike faction carries the day, and he flees with his lover, the princess Atalanta, as Atlantis sinks beneath the sea, as punishment by the gods.

Atali

In Cherokee tradition, the place from which their ancestors disbursed throughout the world immediately after the Great Flood that brought a former age to a close.

Atalya

An important proof for Atlantis found in various parts of the world, specifically and appropriately, within the Atlantean sphere of influence. "Italy" is a derivation of its more ancient name, used even in late Roman times, "Italia"—a corruption of "Atalya," or "Land of Atlas," the eponymous king of Atlantis, who likewise brought civilization to the Italian peninsula. An alternative but closely related Roman myth describes the origin of "Italy" from the country's earliest ruler, Italus, a brother of Atlas. In *Kritias*, Plato mentions that the Atlanteans occupied Etruria, the homeland of the Etruscans in western Italy.

Atalya is also the name of an ancient, ceremonial mound in Biarritz. The Basque still revere this mound as symbolic of the Great Ancestral Mountain in the sea, from which their seafaring forebears traveled into the Bay of Biscay after the sinking of "the Green Isle."

Atalya appears on the "Opposite Continent" among the Aztecs, who similarly venerated a holy mountain in the Valley of Mexico by the same name. Atalaia is the name of a small Quechua Indian town in the High Andes about one day's journey from Cuzco, formerly the capital of the Inca Empire. A pre-Inca civilization was the Chavin de Huantar, and in the ruins of Atalya, one of its early cities, archaeologists found important collections of ancient ceramics. Chavin de Huantar began suddenly after 1200 B.C., coinciding with the final destruction of Atlantis. Some survivors apparently migrated to Peru, where they established this ceremonial center of Atalya.

Near Lake Atitlan, in Guatemala, stands a round, Atlantean-style tower in a ruined fortress known as Atalaya. Similarly, the nuraghe stone towers of the Balearic Isles in the western Mediterranean are talayots, "a diminutive of Atalaya, meaning 'Giant's Burrow'" (Tyndale, quoted in Blackett). Southern Portugal was the Atlantean kingdom of Elasippos, featuring Bronze Age tumuli, or domed tombs, dating to the height of Atlantean civilization (1500 to 1200 B.C.). Atalya is a *Kritias*-like mountainous valley found at Gran Canaria, one of the Canary Islands, anciently the Atlantean kingdom of Diaprepes.

Bolivia's Silustani, with its enigmatic stone circle and tower. Photograph by William Donato.

Atami-san

Mt. Atami, on the northeastern coast of Japan's Izu-hanto, the Izu Peninsula (Shizuoka prefecture ken, Honshu), facing Sagami-nada (the Gulf of Sagami), an enormous but extinct volcano, the ancient source from which the city of Atami, built within the crater, derives its name. Almost half sunk into the sea, Atami-san presents an Atlantean appearance.

Atami was an important resort as early as the fifth century A.D., although Neolithic finds in the crater prove the site has been occupied from much earlier times, when the name originated. "Atami," an Atlantean linguistic survivor, has no meaning in the Japanese language.

Atana

Meaning a "cultic center" or "sacred site" in Linear B, *Atana* is a linguistic term archaeologists use to describe a Greek language spoken on the island of Crete after 1500 to about 1200 B.C. "Atana" is comparable to sacred places around the world identified with variants of "Atlantis."

Atanua

The Marquesans' memory of Atlantis, described in their oral epic "Te Vanana na Tanaoa": "Atanua was beautiful and good, adorned with riches very great. Atanua was fair, very rich and soft. Atanua produced abundantly of living things. Atea [and his brothers] dwelt as kings in the most beautiful palaces supported on thrones. They ruled the space of heaven and the large, entire sky and all the powers thereof [astrology]. The first lords dwelling on high. Oh, throne placed in the middle of the upper heavens! The great lord Atea established in love to love the fair Atanua. A woman of great wealth is Atanua. From within Atea came forth Ono [a terrible sound, the explosion of Mt. Atlas erupting]. Atea produces the very hot fire."

These lines from "Te Vanana na Tanaoa" vividly compare with Plato's description of Atlantis and its destruction. Atea's, like that of Atlas's association with a volcanic mountain, was recognized by the early 20th-century anthropologist Abraham Fornander: "In this sense, it would appropriately convey the idea of the lurid light which accompanies an eruption of the volcano."

Atanum

The Indian name for a river in Washington State. It means "water by the long mountain." Here, as elsewhere throughout the world, a name appears among a native people, combining the "At" prefix to describe a mountain bounded by water. In this instance, "Atanum" suggests the ancient Egyptian Atum (god of the Primal Mound) and/or Nun (the sea-god who sank it), both intimately connected with the Egyptian version of the Atlantis story.

Atao

According to archaeo-linguists, a masculine name in Linear A, the language spoken by the Minoans, who raised a great civilization on Crete from 3000 to 1500 B.C. "Atao" may be the Minoan version of the Greek "Atlas," the eponymous Titan of Atlantis.

Atapaska

The Ascohimi Indians' flood-hero, who arrived on the shores of North America after some oceanic catastrophe. They relate that the world was deluged as the result of a powerful earthquake, during which the air became extremely hot, followed by a prolonged period of intense cold. Their tribal memory accurately describes a celestial collision of a comet or associated meteoric debris with the Earth, preceding the aftereffect of a so-called "dust veil event," wherein thousands of cubic kilometers of ash are extruded into the atmosphere, blocking sunlight and drastically lowering world temperatures. Just such a catastrophe connected with the final destruction of Atlantis and simultaneous close of the Bronze Age did indeed take place around the start of the 13th century B.C.

The Athabascan Indians of Alaska derived their tribal name from their Atlantean ancestor, Atapaska.

Atara

Among the Guanche, the original inhabitants of the Canary Islands, the word for "mountain," apparently derived from and related to the Atlantean mythic concept of the sacred mountain of Atlas.

Atarantes

"Of Atlantis." A people residing on the Atlantic shores of Morocco and described by various classical writers (Herodotus, Diodorus Siculus, etc.).

Atas

Natives inhabiting the mountainous central region of Mindanao, a large southern island in the Philippines. They tell how the Great Flood "covered the whole Earth, and all the Atas were drowned except for two men and a woman. The waters carried them far away." An eagle offered to save them, but one of the men refused, so the bird took up the other man and woman, carrying them to safety on the island of Mapula. Here the Atas were reborn and eventually multiplied sufficiently to conquer the entire Philippines. The Atas still claim descent from these light-skinned invaders who, over time, intermarried with the Negritos and aboriginal peoples.

Atauro

A small island near East Timor, memorializing in native tradition a larger landmass, long ago swallowed by the sea.

Atcha

In ancient Egyptian, a distant, splendid, vanished city, suggestive of Atlantis. The prefix "At" recurs among ancient Egyptian mythic figures associated with overtly Atlantean themes (Atum, Atfih, At-hothes, etc.).

Atchafalaya

Known as the "Long River" to the Choctaw Indians of Louisiana. Its resemblance to the shorter Egyptian name Atcha is suggestive, especially in view of the Choctaws' own deluge myth. Here, too, "At" is used to identify water, one of the three Atlantean themes (city, mountain, and/or water) associated with this prefix by numerous cultures around the world.

Atea

The Marquesans regarded Atea as their ancestral progenitor who, like the Atlanto-Egyptian Atum, claimed for himself the creation of the world. Fornander wrote, "In the Marquesan legends the people claim their descent from Atea and Tani, the two eldest of Toho's twelve sons, whose descendants, after long periods of alternant migrations and rest in the far western lands, finally arrived at the Marquesas Islands."

Like Atlas, Atea was his father's first son and a twin. With his story begins the long migration of some Atlanteans, the descendants of Atea, throughout the Pacific. Fornander saw Atea as "the god which corresponds to Kane in the Hawaiian group" and goes on to explain that "the ideas of solar worship embodied in the Polynesian Kane as the sun, the sun-god, the shining one, are thus synonymous with the Marquesan Atea, the bright one, the light." Atum, too, was a solar deity.

Atemet

The dwelling place and/or name of the goddess Hat-menit, who was depicted in Egyptian temple art as a woman wearing headgear fashioned in the likeness of a fish. Worshiped at Mendes, where her title was "Mother," she was somehow connected to the Lands of Punt often associated with the islands of Atlantis. Budge believed Atemet was a form of Hathor, the goddess responsible for the world flood. Atemet's Atlantean name, fish-crown (queen of the sea), and connections to both Punt and Hathor identify her with some of the leading features of the Atlantis story.

Atemoztli

Literally "the Descent of Waters," or the Great Flood, as it was known to the Aztecs. A worldwide cataclysm accompanied by volcanic eruptions, its few survivors arrived from over the Sunrise Sea (the Atlantic Ocean) to establish the first Mesoamerican civilization. "Atemoztli" was also the name of a festival day commemorating the Deluge, held each November 16—the same period associated with the final destruction of Atlantis (late October to mid-November). Atemoztli's philological resemblance to Atemet, the Egyptian deluge figure, is clear.

Atennu

Egyptian sun-god, as he appears over the sea in the west. Another example of the "At" recurring throughout various cultures to define a sacred place or personage with the Atlantic Ocean.

Atep

The name of the calumet or "peace pipe" in the Siouan language. The Atep was and is the single most sacred object among all Native American tribes, and smoked only ritually. It was given to them by the Great Spirit (Manitou) immediately after a catastrophic conflagration and flood destroyed a former world or age, which was ruled over from a "big lodge" on an island in the Atlantic Ocean.

The survivors, who came from the east, were commanded by the Great Spirit to fashion the ceremonial pipes from a mineral (Catlinite) found only in the southwest corner of present-day Minnesota (Pipestone National Monument) and Barron County (Pipestone Mountain), in northwestern Wisconsin. In these two places alone the bodies of the drowned sinners had come to rest, their red flesh transformed into easily worked stone. The bowl represented the female principle, while the stem stood for the male; both signified the men and women who perished in the flood. Uniting these two symbols and smoking tobacco in the pipe was understood as a commemoration of the cataclysm and admonition to subsequent generations against defying the will of God.

The Atep was a covenant between the Indians and the Great Spirit, who received their prayers on the smoke that drifted toward heaven. It meant a reconciliation between God and man, a sacred peace that had to be honored by all tribes. The deluge story behind the pipe, the apparent philological relationship of its name to "Atlas" or things Atlantean—even the description of the Indians' drowned ancestors as red-skinned (various accounts portray the Atlanteans as ruddy complected)—confirm the Atep as a living relic of lost Atlantis.

Ater

The Guanche Atlas, also worshiped in the pre-Conquest Canary Islands as Ataman ("the upholder," precisely the same meaning for the Greek Titan), and Atara ("mountain," Mount Atlas).

Ateste

The Bronze Age capital, in northern Italy, of the Veneti, direct descendants of Atlantis.

Atfih

More of an Egyptian symbol than an actual deity, he supported the serpent, Mehen, that protectively surrounded the palace in which Ra, the sun-god, resided. Here, Atlantis is suggested in the serpent, symbolizing the Great Water Circle (the ocean) and in Ra's palace, center of a solar cult, while Atfih, whose name means "bearer," was Atlas, who bore the great circle of the heavens.

At-hothes

The earliest known name of Thaut, (Thoth to the Greeks, who equated him with Hermes), the patron god of wisdom, medicine, literature, and hieroglyphic writing, who arrived in Egypt after a deluge destroyed his home in the Distant West. These western origins, together with the "At" beginning his name, define him as an Atlantean deity. Arab tradition identifies him as the architect of Egypt's Great Pyramid on the Giza Plateau. Edgar Cayce, who certainly knew nothing of these Arab accounts, likewise mentioned Thoth as the Atlantean authority responsible for raising the Great Pyramid.

(See Cayce)

At-ia-Mu-ri

Site of impressive megalithic ruins in New Zealand, believed by John Macmillan Brown, a leading academic authority of Pacific archaeology in the 1920s, to be evidence of builders from a sunken civilization. The name of the site is particularly interesting for its combining of At[lantis] and Mu, at this midpoint between the two sunken kingdoms.

(See Mu)

Atinach

The name by which the natives of Tenerife referred to themselves, it means "People of the Sky-God." Antinach derived from Atuaman, the Canary Island Atlas.

Atitlan

A lake in the Solola Department in the central highlands of southwestern Guatemala, where Quiche-Maya Civilization reached its florescence. Atitlan was named after its volcano surrounded by lofty mountains, a setting that could pass for a scene from Plato's description of the island of Atlantis in *Kritias*. Blackett describes Atitlan as "the large and rich capital, court of the native kings of Quiche and the most sumptuous found by the Spaniards." The lake's name was apparently chosen to match its appropriately Atlantean environment; this, together with its obvious derivation from "Atlantis," and the extraordinary splendor of its culture, identify Atitlan's foundation by Atlantean colonizers.

Atiu

An extinct volcano forming an atoll among the southern Cook Islands in the southwest Pacific. "At," associated with volcanic islands, occurs throughout the Pacific Ocean.

Atius

Among the Pawnee Indians of North America, the sky-god, who controlled and understood the movements of the sun, moon, and stars. The similarity of his name and function to Atlas are affirmed by the Pawnee flood story.

Atjeh

A mountainous area of Indonesian Sumatra bordering a sloping plain reminiscent of Plato's description of Atlantis. Even in this remote corner of the world, "At" was anciently applied to sacred mountains.

Atl

"Water" in Nahuatl, the Aztecs' spoken language. The ancient Mexican *Atl* is likewise found in Atlantis, a water-born civilization. *Atl* also occurs on the other side of the Atlantic Ocean among Morocco's Taureg peoples, for whom it also represents "water." Atlantis' former location between Mexico and Morocco suggests a kindred implication between the Nahuatl and Taureg words.

In the Aztec calendar, "4-Atl" signifies the global deluge that destroyed a former "Sun" or age, immediately after which the Feathered Serpent arrived with his followers to found Mesoamerican civilization. The date 4-Atl is depicted on the Aztec Calendar Stone as a celestial bucket of water inundating a half-sunken stone pyramid, a self-evident reference to the final destruction of Atlantis.

(See Quetzalcoatl)

Atla

As described in the *Hyndluljod Saga*, she was a giantess, the mother of Heimdall, an important Norse god. Atlantean elements evident in the mythic relationship between Heimdall and Atla begin in the obvious derivation of her name. She was also a "daughter of the ocean," who gave birth to her divine son "at the edge of the world, where land and sea meet." So too, in Greek tradition, the Pleiades were daughters of Atlas—"Atlantises"—whose sons founded new civilizations. According to MacCullow (111), Atla personified at once the waves of the deep and the "Heavenly Mountain," Himinbjorg, from which Heimdall derived his name, just as Atlantis was known after the sacred Mount Atlas. Even in modern Norwegian, *himinbjorg* refers to a mountain sloping down to the sea. Like the Mayas' fair-skinned Itzamna, who brought civilization to Yucatan after a great flood in the Atlantic Ocean, Heimdall was "the White God," the father of mankind.

Another Atla is a town in Mexico's central plateau region, inhabited by the Otomi Indians who preserve the mythic heritage of their Aztec ancestors beneath a Christian gloss. Some Otomi tribes are among the most culturally conservative peoples in Middle America, refusing to wear modern dress and still preserving ritual kinship institutions handed down from pre-Spanish times. Because of this maintenance of prehistoric traditions, anthropologists regard the Otomi as reliable guides to Mesoamerica's past.

Pertinent to our study is the Otomi *acatlaxqui*, the Dance of the Reed-Throwers. Every November 25, 10 dancers assemble in Atla's main square, dressed in red and white cotton costumes, and wear conical headgear. From the points of these paper hats stream red ribbons. Each dancer carries a 3-foot long reed staff decorated with feathers and additional reeds attached. The performers form a circle, at the center of which one of their number, dressed as a girl, rattles a gourd containing the wooden image of a snake. The acatlaxqui climaxes when the surrounding dancers use their reeds to create a dome over the central character, taken as a sign to begin a fireworks display.

The dance is not only deeply ancient, but a dramatic recreation of Otomi origins. The 10 dancers symbolize the 10 kings of Atlantis, portrayed in their conical hats streaming red ribbons, suggesting erupting volcanos. The reed was synonymous for learning, because it was a writing instrument. The Aztecs claimed their ancestors came to America from Aztlan, "the Isle of Reeds." The boy "girl" dancer at the center may signify the Sacred Androgyne, a god-concept featured in an Atlantean mystery-cult. More likely, the female impersonator is meant to represent Atlantis itself, which was feminine: "Daughter of Atlas." His gourd with the wooden snake inside for a rattle is a remnant of the same Atlantean mystery-cult, in which serpent symbolism described the powers of regeneration and the serpentine energy of the soul.

Forming a dome over the central performer may signify the central position of Atlantis, to which all the allied kingdoms paid tribute, or it could represent the sinking of Atlantis-Aztlan beneath the sea, an interpretation underscored by the fireworks timed to go off as the dome is created. The Otomi's acatlaxqui-Atlantean identity is lent special emphasis by the name of the town in which it is annually danced, Atla. Moreover, November is generally accepted as the month in which Atlantis was destroyed. The name, *Otomi*, likewise implies Atlantean origins: *Atomi*, or *Atoni*, from the monotheistic solar god, Aton.

Atlahua

Aztec sea-god with apparent Atlantean provenance.

Atlaintika

In Euskara, the sunken island, sometimes referred to as "the Green Isle," from which Basque ancestors arrived in the Bay of Biscay. Atlaintika's resemblance to Plato's Atlantis is unmistakable.

(See Belesb-At)

Atlakvith

A 13th-century Scandinavian saga preserving and perpetuating oral traditions going back 1,500 years before, to the late Bronze Age. *Atlakvith* (literally, "The Punishment of Atla[ntis]") poetically describes the Atlantean cataclysm in terms of Norse myth, with special emphasis on the celestial role played by "warring comets" in the catastrophe.

Atlamal

Like *Atlakvith*, this most appropriately titled Norse saga tells of the "Twilight of the Gods," or Ragnarok, the final destruction of the world order through celestial conflagrations, war, and flood. *Atlamal* means, literally, "The Story of Atla[ntis]."

Atlan

Today's Alca, on the Gulf of Uraba, it was known as Atlan before the Spanish Conquest. Another Venezuelan "Atlan" is a village in the virgin forests between Orinoco and Apure. Its nearly extinct residents, the Paria Indians, preserve traditions of a catastrophe that overwhelmed their home country, a prosperous island in the Atlantic Ocean inhabited by a race of wealthy seafarers. Survivors arrived on the shores of Venezuela, where they lived apart from the indigenous natives. In Nahuatl, the language of the Aztecs, "Atlan" meant, literally, "In the Midst of the Sea." Atlan's philological derivation from Atlantis, kindred meaning, and common account of the lost island comprise valid evidence for Atlanteans in Middle and South America, just where investigators would expect to find important cultural clues.

Atland

The Northern European memory of Atlantis, as preserved in the medieval account of a Frisian manuscript, the *Oera Linda Bok*, or "The Book of How Things Were in the Old Days."

(See *Oera Linda Bok*)

Atlanersa

King of Nubia in the fifth century B.C. The name means "Prince or Royal Descendant (ersa) of Atlan," presumably the Atlantis coincidentally described by Plato in Athens at the same time this monarch ruled Egypt's southern neighbor. Unfortunately, nothing else is known about Atlanersa beyond his provocative name, nor have any Atlantean traditions been associated with the little that is known about Nubian beliefs.

Atlantean

As a pronoun, an inhabitant of the island of Atlas or its capital, Atlantis. As an adjective, it defines anything belonging to the culture and society of the civilization of Atlantis. In art and architecture, Atlantean describes an anthropomorphic figure, usually a male statue, supporting a lintel often representing the sky. Until the early 20th century, "Atlantean" was used to characterize the outstanding monumentality of a particular structure, an echo of the splendid public building projects associated with Atlantis.

Atlantean War

The Egyptian priest quoted in Plato's Dialogue, *Timaeus*, reported that the Atlanteans, at the zenith of their imperial power, inaugurated far-reaching military campaigns throughout the Mediterranean World. They invaded western Italy and North Africa to threaten Egypt, but were turned back by the Greeks, who stood alone after the defeat of their allies. Successful counteroffensives liberated all occupied territories up to the Strait of Gibraltar, when a major seismic event simultaneously destroyed the island of Atlantis and the pursuing Greek armies. The reasons or causes for the war are not described.

The Egyptian priest implies that the Greeks perished in an earthquake on the shores of North Africa (northern Morocco) fronting the enemy's island capital. He spoke of "the city which *now* is Athens" (author's italics), meaning that the Greeks he described belonged to another city that preceded Athens at the same location during pre-classical times. This represents an internal dating of the war to the late Bronze Age (15th to 12th centuries B.C.) and the heyday of Mycenaean Greece.

There is abundant archaeological evidence for the Atlanteans' far-ranging aggression described by the Egyptian priest. Beginning in the mid-13th century B.C., the Balearic Isles, Sardinia, Corsica, and western Italy were suddenly overrun by helmeted warriors proficient in the use of superior bronze weapons technology. At the same time, Libya was hit by legions of the same invaders described by the Greek historian Herodotus (circa 500 B.C.) as the "Garamantes." Meanwhile, Pharaoh Merenptah was defending the Nile Delta against the Hanebu, or "Sea Peoples." His campaigns coincided with the Trojan War, in which the Achaeans (Mycenaean Greeks) defeated the Anatolian kingdom of Ilios and all its allies. Among them were 10,000 troops from Atlantis, led by General Memnon. These widespread military events from the western Mediterranean to Egypt and Asia Minor comprised the Atlantean War described in *Timaeus*.

It is possible, however, that Atlantean aggression was not entirely military but more commercial in origin. Troy, while not a colony of Atlantis, was a blood-related kingdom, and the Trojans dominated the economically strategic Dardanelles, gateway to the Bosphorous and rich trading centers of the Black Sea. It was their monopoly of this vital position that won them fabulous wealth. In fact, it appears that the Atlanteans founded an important harbor city in western coastal Anatolia just prior to the Trojan War (see Attaleia). But the change of fortunes in Asia Minor also won them the animosity of the Greeks, who were effectively cut off from the Dardanelles. This was the tense economic situation that many scholars believe actually led to the Achaean invasion of Troy.

The abduction of Helen by Paris, if such an event were not merely a poetic metaphor for the "piracy" of which the Trojans were accused, was the dramatic incident that escalated international tensions into war—the last straw, as it were, after years of growing animosity. Thus, the victorious Greeks portrayed the defeated Atlanteans as having embarked upon an unprovoked military conquest, when, in reality, both opposing sides were engaged in economic rivalry, through Troy, for control of the Bosphorous and its rich markets. These commercial causes appear more credible than the otherwise unexplained military adventure supposedly launched by the Atlanteans in a selfish conquest of the Mediterranean World, as depicted in *Timaeus*. On the other hand, our pro-Atlantean example of historical revision is at least partially undermined by the Atlanteans' unquestionable aggression against Egypt immediately after their defeat at Troy and again, 42 years later.

(See Memnon)

Atlanteotl

An Aztec (Zapotec) water-god who "was condemned to stand forever on the edge of the world, bearing upon his shoulders the vault of the heavens" (Miller and Rivera, 4). This deity is practically a mirror image in both name and function of Atlas-Atlantis, powerful evidence supporting a profound Atlantean influence in Mesoamerica.

Atlantes

Described by many classical writers (Herodotus, Diodorus Siculus, etc.), a people who resided on the northwestern shores of present-day Morocco. They preserved a tradition of their ancestral origins in Atlantis, and appear to have been absorbed by the eighth-century invasion of their land by the forces of Islam. Notwithstanding their disappearance, their Atlantean legacy has been preserved by the Tuaregs and Berbers, who pride themselves on their partial descent from the Atlantes.

Atlanthropis mauritanicus

A genus name assigned by the French anthropologist, Camille Arambourg, to *Homo erectus* finds at Ternifine, Algeria. It represented a slight development, considered "superfluous" by some scholars, of a type along the Atlantic shores of North Africa and may indicate that early man followed migrating animal herds across former land bridges onto the island of Atlantis. There the abundance of game and temperate climate fostered further evolutionary steps toward becoming Cro-Magnon. The Atlanthropis mauritanicus hypothesis is bolstered by Cro-Magnon finds made in some of the Canaries, the nearest islands to the suspected location of Atlantis. *Atlanthropis mauritanicus* is also referred to as *Homo erectus mauritanicus*.

Atlantiades

Atlantises, Daughters of Atlas.

Atlantic Ocean

The sea that took its name from the land that once dominated it, Atlantis, just as the Indian Ocean derived its name from India, the Irish Sea from Ireland, the South China Sea from China, and so on.

Atlantica

A four-volume magnum opus by Swedish polymath Olaus Rudbeck. Published in the year of his death, 1702, *Atlantica* was eagerly sought out by Sir Isaac Newton and other leading 18th-century scientists. It describes "Fennoscandia," roughly equivalent to modern Sweden, as the post-deluge home of Atlantean survivors in the mid-third millennium B.C.

(See Rudbeck)

La Atlantída

Literally "Atlantis"; an opera (sometimes performed in concert form) by Spain's foremost composer, Manuel de Falla (1876 to 1946). When a youth, de Falla heard local folktales of Atlantis, and learned that some Andalusian nobility traced their line of descent to Atlantean forebears. De Falla's birthplace was Cadiz, site of the Spanish realm of Gadeiros, the twin brother of Atlas and king mentioned in Plato's account (*Kritias*) of Atlantis.

La Atlantida describes the destruction of Atlantis from which Alcides (Hercules) arrives in Iberia to found a new lineage through subsequent generations of Spanish aristocracy. One of the opera's most effective moments occurs immediately after the sinking of Atlantis, when de Falla's music eerily portrays a dark sea floating with debris moving back and forth upon the waves, as a ghostly chorus intones, "El Mort! El Mort! El Mort!" ("Death! Death! Death!").

Atlantida is also the title of a Basque epic poem describing ancestral origins at "the Green Isle" which sank into the sea.

Atlantika

In their thorough examination of the so-called "Aztec Calendar Stone," Jimenez and Graeber state that *Atlantika* means "we live by the sea," in Nahuatl, the Aztec language (67).

Atlantikos

Ancient Greek for "Atlantis," the title of Solon's unfinished epic, begun circa 470 B.C.

Atlantioi

"Of Atlantis." The name appears in the writings of various classical writers (Herodotus, Diodorus Siculus, etc.) to describe the contemporary inhabitants of Atlantic coastal northwestern Africa.

Atlantis

Literally "Daughter of Atlas," the chief city of the island of Atlas, and capital of the Atlantean Empire. From the welter of accumulating evidence, a reasonable picture of the lost civilization is beginning to emerge: As Pangea, the original supercontinent, was breaking apart about 200 million years ago, a continental mass trailing dry-land territories to what is now Portugal and Morocco was left mid-ocean, between the American and Eur-African continents pulled in opposite directions. This action was caused by seafloor spreading, a process that moves the continents apart by the operation of convection currents in the mantle of our planet. The resultant tear in the ocean bottom is the Mid-Atlantic Ridge, a seismic zone of volcanic and magmatic activity extending like a narrow scar from the Arctic Circle to the Antarctic. The geologic violence of the Ridge combined with rising sea levels to eventually reduce the Atlantic island's dry-land area.

About 1.5 million years ago, early man (*Homo erectus mauritanicus*, or *Atlanthropis mauritanicus*) pursued animal herds across slim land bridges leading from the western shores of North Africa onto the Atlantic island. These earliest inhabitants found a natural environment of abundant game, extraordinarily fertile volcanic soil with numerous freshwater springs, rich fishing, and a year-round temperate climate. Such uniquely superior conditions combined to stimulate human evolutionary growth toward the appearance of modern or Cro-Magnon man. With increases in population fostered by the nurturing Atlantean environment, social cooperation gradually developed to produce the earliest communities— small alliances of families for mutual assistance. These communities continued to expand, and in their growth, they became complex. The greater the number of individuals involved, the greater the number and variety of needs became, as well as technological innovations created by those needs, until a populous society of arts, letters, sciences, and religious and political hierarchies eventually emerged. The island of Atlas was, therefore, the birthplace of modern man and home of his first civilization.

Time frames are very controversial among Atlantologists, and this issue is addressed in the text that follows. Conservative investigators tend to regard Atlantean civilization as having come into its own sometime after 4000 B.C. By the end of that millennium, the Atlanteans were mining copper in the Upper Peninsula of North America; establishing a sacred calendar in Middle America; building megalithic structures such as New Grange in Ireland, Stonehenge in Britain, and Hal Tarxian at Malta; as well as founding the first dynasties in Egypt and Mesopotamia's earliest city-states.

The island of Atlas was named after its chief mountain, a dormant volcano. The chief city and imperial capital was Atlantis, arranged in alternating rings of land and water interconnected by canals. High walls decorated with gleaming sheets of polished copper alloys and precious stones, featuring regularly spaced watchtowers, encircled the outer perimeter, which was separated from Mt. Atlas on the north by a broad, fair plain. The inner rings were occupied by a spacious racetrack, for popular events of all kinds; military headquarters and training fields; a bureaucracy; the aristocracy; and the royal family, who resided in a palace near the Temple of Poseidon, at the very center of the city. This temple was the most sacred site in Atlantis—the place where holy tradition claimed that the sea-god Poseidon mated with a mortal woman, Kleito, one of the native inhabitants, to produce five sets of male twins. These sons became the first Atlantean kings, from whom the various colonies of the Empire derived their names. The first of these was Atlas, earliest ruler of the island in the new order established by Poseidon.

By the 13th century B.C., the Atlantean Empire stretched from the Americas to the western shores of North Africa, the British Isles, Iberia, and Italy, with royal family and commercial ties as far as the Aegean coasts of Asia Minor. The Atlanteans were responsible for and dominated the Bronze Age, during which they rose to the zenith of their material and imperial success to become the leading power of late pre-classical times. However, their expanding trade network eventually clashed with powerful Greek interests in the Aegean, resulting in a long war that began at Troy and spread to Syria, the Nile Delta, and Libya, climaxing at the western shores of North Africa.

Initially successful, the Atlantean invaders suffered defeats at the hands of the Greeks, who had just pushed them out of the Mediterranean World when a natural catastrophe destroyed the island of Atlantis, along with most of its population, after a day and night of geologic upheaval. The same event simultaneously set off a major earthquake in present-day Morocco, where the pursuing Greek armies had gathered, and engulfed them, as well. Atlantean survivors of the destruction arrived as culture-bearers in different parts of the world, founding new civilizations in the Americas, and left related flood legends as part of the folk traditions of peoples around the globe.

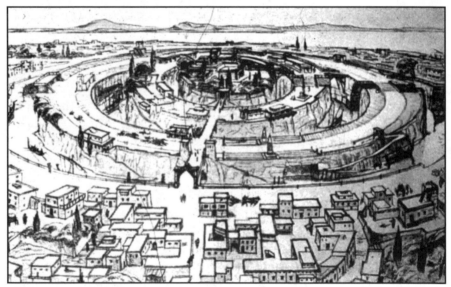

Illustration of Atlantis based on the description in Plato's Kritias. *From Unser Ahnen und die Atlanten, Nordliche Seeherrschaft von Skandinavien bis nach Nordafrika, by Albert Herrmann.*

Atlantis: The Antediluvian World

The first modern, scientific examination of Atlantis begun in 1880 by Ignatius Donnelly and published two years later by Harper Brothers (New York). Certainly the most influential book on the subject, it triggered a popular and controversial revival of interest in Atlantis that continues to the present day.

Donnelly's use of comparative mythologies to argue on behalf of Atlantis-as-fact is encyclopedic, persuasive, and still represents a veritable gold mine of information for researchers. His geology and oceanography were far ahead of his time, while his conclusions were largely borne out by advances made during the second half of the 20th century in the general acceptance of seafloor spreading and plate tectonics. *Atlantis: The Antediluvian World* has been unfairly condemned for its relatively few failings, mostly by Establishment dogmatists and cultural isolationists to whom any serious suggestion of Atlantis is the worst heresy. But no scholarly position has been able to remain unscathed after 100 years of scientific progress, and, for the most part, Donnelly's work has stood the test of time. In the first 10 years after its publication, the book went through 24 editions, making it an extraordinary best-seller, even by modern standards. It has since been translated into dozens of languages, has sold millions of copies around the world, and is still in print—all of which qualifies the book as a classic, just as vigorously condemned and championed today as it was more than a century ago.

Atlantis: The Antediluvian World poses 13 fundamental positions, which formed the basis of Atlantology. These predicate that:

1) Atlantis was a large island that lay just outside the Strait of Gibraltar in the Atlantic Ocean.

2) Plato's account of Atlantis is factual.

3) Atlantis was the site where mankind arose from barbarism to civilization. Donnelly was the first to state this view, which, although not mentioned in Plato's Dialogues, is suggested by the weight of supportive evidence found in the traditions of peoples residing within the former Atlantean sphere of influence.

4) The power of Atlantis stretched from Pacific coastal Peru and Yucatan in the west to Africa, Europe, and Asia Minor in the east.

5) Atlantis represented "a universal memory of a great land, where early mankind dwelt for ages in peace and happiness"—the original Garden of Eden.

6) The Greek, Phoenician, Hindu, and Scandinavian deities represented a confused recollection in myth of the kings, queens, and heroes of Atlantis.

Although important Atlantean themes interpenetrate both Western and Eastern mythologies, as he successfully demonstrated, Donnelly overstated that relationship by reducing all the ancient divinities to merely mythic shadows of mundane mortals.

7) The solar cults of ancient Egypt and Peru derived from the original religion of Atlantis.

8) Egypt, whose civilization was a reproduction of Atlantis, was also the oldest Atlantean colony.

Early Dynastic Egypt was a synthesis of indigenous Nilotic cultures and Atlantean culture-bearers who arrived at the Nile Delta during the close of the fourth millennium B.C. The hybrid civilization that emerged was never a "colony" of Atlantis, although Donnelly was right in detecting numerous aspects of Atlantean culture among the Egyptians.

9) The Atlanteans, responsible for the European Bronze Age, were the first manufacturers of iron, as well.

While persuasive evidence for this last argument is scant, Donnelly's identification of the Atlanteans with the bronze-barons of the Ancient World is among his most valid and important positions.

10) The Phoenician and Mayan written languages derived from Atlantis.

Phoenician letters evolved from trade contacts with the Egyptians, whose demotic script was simplified by merchants in Lebanon. If Egyptian and Mayan hieroglyphs are both Atlantean, they should be at least partially intertranslatable, which they are not. Even so, they may have evolved into separate systems over the millennia from a shared parent source in Atlantis, because at least a few genuine comparisons, known as *cognates*, between the two have been made.

11) Atlantis was the original homeland of both the Aryan and the Semitic peoples.

What later became known as the so-called "Indo-Europeans" may have first arisen on the Atlantic island, and the Atlanteans were unquestionably Caucasoid. But such origins are deeply prehistoric, and any real proof is very difficult to ascertain. More likely, the Atlanteans were direct descendants of Cro-Magnon types, whose genetic legacy has been traced to the original inhabitants of the Canary Islands, the native Guanches, direct descendants of Atlantis. Donnelly mistakenly accepted the Genesis story of the Great Flood and related references in Old Testament and Talmudic literature as evidence for Aryan (Japhethic), as well as Semitic origins in Atlantis. In truth, the Hebrews incorporated some ancient Gentile traditions, such as the Deluge, into their own mosaic culture. Even so, the Phoenicians were in part descended from the invading "Sea Peoples" of lost Atlantis in the early 12th century B.C.

It was the depredations of these Atlantean survivors-turned-privateers that ravaged the shores of Canaan, thereby making possible a takeover of the Promised Land by the Hebrews. They intermarried with the piratical Gentiles to produce the mercantile Phoenicians. Their concentric capital at Carthage and prodigious seafaring achievements were evidence of an Atlantean inheritance. These influences, however, are after the fact (the destruction of Atlantis). Even so, Edgar Cayce spoke of a "principle island at the time of the final destruction" he called "Aryan." Later, he described "the Aryan land" as Yucatan, where a yet-to-be discovered Hall of Records contains original documents pertaining to Atlantis.

12) Atlantis perished in a natural catastrophe that sank the entire island and killed most of its inhabitants.

13) The relatively few survivors arrived in various parts of the world, where their reports of the cataclysm grew to become the flood traditions of many nations.

The late 19th-century publication of *Atlantis: The Antediluvian World* marked the beginning of renewed interest in Atlantis, and is still among the best of its kind on the subject.

(See Cayce)

Atlantis, the Lost Continent

A 1961 feature film by George Pal based less on Plato than the wildest statements of Edgar Cayce. Its bromidic screenplay, vapid dialogue, wooden acting, and bargain-basement "special effects" have made *Atlantis, the Lost Continent* into something of a cult classic for Atlantologists with a sense of humor.

Atlantis, the Lost Empire

Presented in a flat, dimensionless animation characteristic of the Disney Studio since the death of its founder, this 2001 production has far less in common with Plato than even George Pal's unintentionally comic version. A sequel to *Atlantis, the Lost Empire*, released two years later, was even more miserable, but demonstrated that popular interest in the subject is still strong 24 centuries after Plato's account appeared for the first time.

Atlantology

The study of all aspects related to the civilization of Atlantis; also refers to a large body of literature (an estimated 2,500 books and published papers) describing Atlantis. It calls upon many related disciplines, including archaeology, archaeo-astronomy, comparative mythology, genetics, anthropology, geology, volcanology, oceanography, linguistics, nautical construction, navigation, and more.

Atlas

The central figure in the story of Atlantis, he was the chief monarch of the Atlantean Empire, ruling from its island capital. Atlas was the founder of astrology-astronomy (there being made no original distinction between the two disciplines), depicted as a bearded Titan or giant supporting the sphere of the heavens on his shoulders, as he crouches on one knee. He thus became a symbol and national emblem for the Atlanteans and their devotion to the celestial sciences. In Sanskrit, *atl* means "to support or uphold."

Parallel mythic descriptions of Atlas are revealing. His father, in the non-Platonic version, was Iapatus, also a Titan, who was regarded as the father of mankind. After his defeat by the Olympians, Iapatus was buried under a mountainous island to prevent his escape, suggesting the sunken island and punishment meted out to Atlantis by the gods, as described in Plato's account. Clymene was the mother of Atlas. She was a sea-nymph who personified Asia Minor. Interestingly, "Atlas" is the name of a mountain in Asia Minor (modern Turkey) near Catal-Huyuk, which, at 9,000 years old, is among the most ancient cities on earth. Thus, in Atlas's parentage are represented the Far West of the Atlantic islands (Iapatus) and the eastern extent of Atlantean influence (Anatolia) in Clymene. Her parents were Tythys, "the Lovely Queen of the Sea," and Oceanus, the oldest Titan, known as the "Outer Sea," or the Atlantic Ocean itself—all of which underscore Atlas's oceanic identity, contrary to some scholars who confine him to Morocco and the Atlas Mountains.

Plato's version of Atlas's descent makes Poseidon, the sea-god, his father, and Kleito, the native girl of the ocean isle, his mother. These discrepancies are unimportant, because the significance of myth does not lie in its consistency, but in its power to describe. The Titan's transformation into a mountain took place after he fetched the Golden Apples for Heracles, who temporarily took Atlas's place in supporting the sky. He had been condemned to this singular position as punishment for his leading role in the Titanomachy, an antediluvian struggle between gods and giants for mastery of the world. But Perseus, Heracles' companion, took pity on Atlas and turned him into a mountain of stone by showing him the Gorgon Medusa's severed head.

This largely Hellenistic myth from early classic or late pre-classic times added peculiarly Greek elements, which clouded a far older tradition. Even so, certain details of the original survive in the Titanomachy, the Atlanteans' bid for world conquest, of which the depredations of the so-called "Sea Peoples" against Pharaoh Ramses III's Egypt, Homer's *Iliad*, and Plato's Atlanto-Athenian War were but various campaigns of the same conflict.

According to Sumerian scholar Neil Zimmerer, Atlas was indigenously known in West Africa, where he was remembered as "the king of Atlantis, and fled when the island sank into the sea. He established a new kingdom in Mauretania."

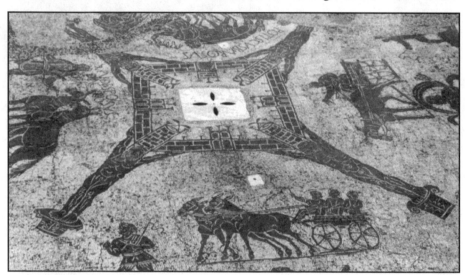

A first-century A.D. mosaic at Ostia, the port city of ancient Rome, depicts four Atlases, representing the cardinal directions, as they support Atlantis, signifying its central importance in maritime history.

Atlatonan

The "Daughter of Tlaloc," a blue-robed virgin ritually drowned as a sacrifice to the Aztec rain-god. Her fate and philological resemblance to Atlantis, literally, "Daughter of Atlas," are too remarkable for coincidence.

(See Tlaloc)

Atlcaulcaco

"The Waste of Waters," a month in the Aztec calendar commemorating the Great Flood, the first month calculated by the Aztec Calendar Stone, during which a blue-robed virgin was ritually drowned to honor the rain-god. Plato described the royalty of Atlantis as favoring blue robes during ceremonial events.

Atlixco

An Aztec outpost in south-central Mexico near a sacred volcano, Itztac-cihu-atl, associated with the earlier Mayas' version of Atlas, Itzamna, "the Lord of Heaven," and "the White Man." Itztac-cihu-atl means "Great in the Water," a clear reference to Mt. Atlas, the great peak on the island of Atlantis.

Aton

Among the oldest deities worshiped in Egypt, he was the sun-god who alone ruled the universe, suggesting an archaic form of monotheism, which may have been the "Law of One" Edgar Cayce said functioned as a mystery cult in Atlantis up until the final destruction. His "life-readings" described the Atlantean Followers of the Law of One arriving in Egypt to reestablish themselves. Egyptian tradition itself spoke of the Smsu-Hr, the Followers of Horus (the sun-god), highly civilized seafarers, who landed at the Nile Delta to found the first dynasties. Shortly thereafter, Aton dwindled to insignificance, as polytheism rapidly spread throughout the Nile Valley.

It was not until 1379 B.C., with the ascent of Amenhotep IV, who changed his name to Akhenaton, that the old solar divinity was given primacy. All other deities were banned, allowing Aton to have no other gods before him. The religious experiment was a disastrous failure and did not survive the heretical Pharaoh's death in 1362 B.C., when all the old gods were restored, except Aton. His possible worship by Cayce's Followers of the Law of One, along with the "At" perfix, suggest the god was imported by late fourth-millennium B.C. Atlanteans arriving in Egypt. Aton's name appears to have meant "Mountain Sun City" ("On" being the Egyptian name for the Greek Heliopolis, or City of the Sun-God), and may have originally referred to a religious location (that is, Atlantis) rather than a god. Indeed, he was often addressed as "The Aton," the sun disc—a thing, more than a divine personality.

(See Cayce)

Aton-at-i-uh

The supreme sun-god of the Aztecs depicted at the center of their famous "Calendar Stone," actually an astrological device. His supremacy, astrological function, and philological resemblance to the Egyptian Aton imply a credible connection through Atlantis. Additionally, young Egyptian initiates of the Aton cult were required to have their skulls artificially deformed after the example of their high-priest, Pharaoh Akhenaton, a practice that would identify them for the rest of their lives as important worshippers of the Sun Disk. Surviving temple art from his city, Akhetaton (current-day Tell el-Amarna), show the King's own children with deformed heads. On the other side of the world, the sun-worshipping elite among the Mayas in Middle America and the pre-Inca peoples of South America all practiced skull elongation. At both Akhetaton and Yucatan, the newborn infant of a royal family had its head placed between cloth-covered boards, which were gently drawn together by knotted cords. For about two years, the malleable skull was forced to develop into an oblong shape that was considered the height of aristocratic fashion.

According to chronologer Neil Zimmerer, Aton-at-i-uh was originally a cruel Atlantcan despot who crushed a rebellion of miners by feeding them to wild beasts. He was supposedly responsible for the destruction of Atlantis when he blew up its mineshafts during his frustrated bid to assume absolute power. Aton-at-i-uh's reputation lived on long after his life, eventually transforming into the Aztec God of Time, which destroys everything. As the sun was associated with the passage of time, so Aton-at-i-uh personified both the supreme solar and temporal deity.

At-o-sis

A monstrous serpent that long ago encircled a water-girt palace of the gods located across the Sunrise Sea, according to the Algonquian Passamaquoddy Indians. Their concept is identical to the Egyptian Mehen, with its mythic portrayal of Atlantis. Many tales of At-o-sis describe him as lying at the bottom of "the Great Lake" (the Atlantic Ocean), with the remains of the gods' sunken "lodge." Interestingly, the Passamaquoddies' "Sunrise Sea" is in keeping with the Egyptian sun-god, Ra, encircled by the Mehen serpent.

(See Atfih, Ataentsik)

At-otarho

Among the North American Iroquois, a mythic figure with a head of snakes for hair, similar to the Greek Medusa, who was herself associated with Atlantis.

Atrakhasis

"Unsurpassed in Wisdom," the title of Utnapishtim, survivor of the Great Flood portrayed in the Sumerian *Epic of Gilgamesh*. Scholars believe the story predates by 1,000 years its earliest written version, recorded around 2000 B.C. in cuneiform script on 12 clay tablets. The prefix "At" combines with the epic's early third-millennium B.C. origins to indicate that Utnapishtim belonged to the First Atlantean Deluge, in 3100 B.C.

Atri

In Hindu myth, one of 10 Prajapatis, beings intermediate between gods and mortals, known as the progenitors of mankind, and assigned by Manu to create civilization throughout the world. Atri may be an Indus Valley version of Atlas, who likewise had nine brothers, Titans, who similarly occupied a position between the Olympians and men. The Prajapatis were sometimes associated with the Aditayas, the "upholders" of the heavens (sustainers of the cosmic order), just like Atlas, who supported the sky. Atri's prominent position as a world-civilizer echoes the far-flung Atlantis Empire.

Atsilagigai

Literally, the "Red Fire Men" in Cherokee tradition. The name more broadly interpreted means the "Men from the Place of Red Fire," Cherokee ancestors. Some of them escaped the judgement of heaven, when the Great Flood drowned almost all living things. Atsilagigai refers to culture-bearers from a volcanic island, and is a Native American rendering of the word "Atlantean."

Atso, or Gyatso

Tibetan for "ocean," associated with the most important spiritual position in Boen-Buddhism, the Dalai Lama. The Mongolian word for ocean is *dalai*, a derivative of the Sanskrit *atl* for "upholder," and is found throughout every Indo-European language for "sea" or "valley in the water," as though created by high waves: the Sumerian Thallath, the Greek thallasa, the German Tal, the English dale, and so on. Dalai, according to Tenzin Gyatso, the 14th Dalai Lama of Tibet, stems from the Tibetan word for "ocean" that forms his name. Although *Dalai Lama* has sometimes been translated as "Ocean of Wisdom," it really means "Wise Man (Guru) of (or from) the Ocean," a title that appears to have originated with the pre-Buddhist Boen religion somewhat absorbed by the creed introduced from India in the eighth century.

Atlantologists have speculated since the late 1800s that the history and religious tenets of Atlantis are still preserved in some of Tibet's secret libraries or even encoded in the very ritual fabric of Tibetan religion itself. Some investigators discern traces of the Atlantean mystery cults in Boen-Buddhism, particularly the central importance placed on the doctrine of reincarnation and the sand mandalas designed to portray the celestial city, with its concentric layout of alternating rings of land and water powerfully reminiscent of Plato's sunken capital, even to the sacred numerals and elephants of Atlantis recurring through the sand-paintings. These considerations seem stressed by Atlantean influences in the high-holy terminology of Tibetan just discussed: Gyatso, Dalai, and so forth.

Edgar Cayce spoke of an unnamed person from the land now known as Tibet, who visited Atlantis at a time when Atlantean teachings were being disseminated. Perhaps this refers to the early spread of spiritual concepts to Tibet from Atlantis

and accounts for the Tibetan "Wise Man from the Ocean." In other "life-readings," Cayce mentions a "correlating" of Atlantean thought with Mongolian theology.
(Cayce, 957-1 M.53 3/12/30; 938-1 F.29 6/21/35; 1159-1 F.80 5/5/36)

Att

A word in the language of the ancient Egyptians signifying a large pool or lake, a body of water. As elsewhere in Egyptian and the tongues of other peoples impacted by the Atlantis experience, "Att" has an aquatic reference.

Attaleia

Modern Antalya, in western coastal Turkey, chief port of ancient Anatolian Lycia, founded (actually refounded in classical times) by Attalos II of Pergamon, circa 150 B.C. Recent excavations unearthed material evidence demonstrating civilized habitation at Attaleia in the form of stone bulwarks and harbor facilities dated to the late or early post-Bronze Age (circa 1300 to 900 B.C.) Attalus II rebuilt the site, following closely the original walls, which were laid out in concentric circles interspaced with watchtowers. Its architectural resemblance to Atlantis; early date, during which Atlantis was at the zenith of its military influence, which stretched as far as the eastern Mediterranean; identity as an Atlantis-like harbor capital; and the Atlantean character of its name all suggest that Attaleia was originally founded by Atlanteans in Asia Minor, perhaps to assist their Dardanian allies in the Trojan War (1250 to 1240 B.C.)

Attawaugen

Known to native Algonquian speakers in Connecticut as a sacred hill associated with the arrival of their forefathers on the eastern shores of North America following a catastrophic flood that engulfed an ancestral homeland.
(See Atum)

Attewandeton

An extinct aboriginal tribe cited in the oral traditions of Upper Michigan's Menomonie Indians as responsible for having committed genocide against the "Marine Men," identified with Plato's miners from Atlantis.
(See Bronze Age)

At-tit

In pre-Columbian Guatemala, an ancestral goddess who preached "worship of the true God," suggesting she was a practitioner (probably high priestess) of the Followers of the Law of One, which Edgar Cayce claimed was the second most influential cult in Atlantis at the time of its final destruction. At-tit's name and character identify her as an important Atlantean visitor to Middle America.

(See Cayce)

Atu

In Sumerian myth, a sacred mountain in the Western Sea, from whence the sky-goddess, Inanna, carried the Tablets of Civilization to Mesopotamia after Atu was engulfed by the sea.

Atua

In Maori, "Altar of the God," found among various Polynesian islanders. They regard its memory as a sacred heirloom from their ancestors and a symbol of the holy mountain, the original homeland of their ancestors who largely perished when it sank beneath the surface of the ocean. Atua is also the name of a district in Western Samoa, whose inhabitants speak the oldest language in Polynesia. The cult of Atua, the chief god worshiped by the Easter Islanders, arrived after he caused a great people to perish in some oceanic cataclysm.

Atuaman

Similar to the Polynesian Atua and the Egyptian Atum, Atuaman was the most important deity worshiped by the Guanches, the original inhabitants of the Canary Islands. His name means, literally, "Supporter of the Sky," precisely the same description accorded to Atlas. Atuaman is represented in pictographs, especially at Gran Canaria, as a man supporting the heavens on his shoulders, the identical characterization of Atlas in Western art. Among archaeological evidence in the Canaries, the appearance of this unquestionably Atlantean figure—the leading mythic personality of Atlantis—affirms the former existence of Atlantis in its next-nearest neighboring islands.

Atuf

According to the Tanimbar Austronesian people of southeast Maluku, he separated the Lesser Sundras from Borneo by wielding his spear, while traveling eastward with his royal family from a huge natural cataclysm that annihilated their distant homeland. It supposedly took place at a time when the whole Earth was unstable. The chief cultural focus of the Tanimbar is concentrated on the story of Atuf and his heroism in saving their ancestors from disaster. "Thereafter they had to migrate ever eastward from island refuge to island refuge," writes Oppenheimer, and "as if to emphasize this, visitors will find huge symbolic stone boats as ritual centres of the villages" (278). North of Maluku, a similar account is known to the islanders of Ceram and Banda. In their version, their ancestors are led to safety by Boi Ratan, a princess from the sunken kingdom.

Atum

Among the most ancient of Egyptian deities associated with a Sacred Mountain, the origin of the first gods, Atum was the first divinity of creation. He created the Celestial Waters from which arose the Primal Mound. Shu, the Egyptian Atlas, declares in the Coffin Texts, "I am the son of Atum. Let him place me on his neck." In Hittite mythology, Kumarbi, a giant arising from the Western Ocean, placed Upelluri on his mountainous neck, where he supported the sky, and is today regarded by mythologists as the Anatolian version of Atlas.

Atum says elsewhere in the same Texts, "Let my son, Shu, be put beneath my daughter, Nut [the starry night sky], to keep guard for me over the Heavenly Supports, which exist in the twilight [the far west]." His position beneath Nut indicates Shu's identification with Atlas as the patron of astronomy. "The Heavenly Supports" were known to Plato and his fellow Greeks as "the Pillars of Heracles," beyond which lay Atlantis-Atum.

The 60th Utterance of the Pyramid Texts reads, "Oh, Atum! When you came into being you rose up as a high hill. You rose up in this your name of High Hill." As Clark explains:

> When the deceased, impersonated by his statue, was crowned during the final ceremony inside the pyramid, he was invested with the Red Crown of Lower Egypt. A heap of sand was put on the floor and the statue placed upon it while a long prayer was recited, beginning, 'Rise upon it, this land which came forth at Atum. Rise high upon it, that your father may see you, that Ra may see you.' The sand represents the Primal Mound. The instruction to the king is to ascend the mound and be greeted by the sun. This implies that the mound can become the world mountain whereon the king ascends to meet in his present form, the sun.

This, then, is the concept of kingship descended from the supreme sun-god, Ra, on his holy mountain of Atum, the gods' birthplace. It was this sacred ancestral location, reported Egyptian tradition, that sank beneath the sea of the Distant West, causing the migration of divinities and royalty to the Nile Delta. Atum's philological and mythic resemblance to Mount Atlas, wherein the Egyptian deity is likewise synonymous for the sacred mountain and the god, defines him as a religious representation of the original Atlantean homeland.

Atur

A unit of nautical measurement used by the ancient Egyptians that meant, literally, "river" (more probably, an archaic term for "water") and corresponded to one hour of navigation covering 7,862.2 meters, equal to a constant speed of about 4.5 miles per hour. The term was a legacy from the Egyptians' seafaring Atlantean forefathers, as is apparent in the prefix "at" and its definition as a nautical term.

Atziluth

The Cabala, literally "the received tradition," is a mystical interpretation of Hebrew scriptures relying on their most ancient and original meanings. The cabalistic term *Atziluth* refers to the first of four "worlds" or spiritual powers that dominated the Earth. It signified the "World of Emanations" or "Will of God," the beginning of human spiritual consciousness. Philological and mythological comparisons with Atlantis, where modern man and his first formalized religion came into existence, appears preserved in the earliest traditions of the Cabala.

Autlan

Located in the foothills of the Sierra Madre Occidental Mountains, Autlan was the home of the highly civilized Tarascans of Michoacan. The only Mesoamericans known to have established regular trade with the civilizations of coastal Peru, because of their seafaring abilities, the Tarascans' superior bronze weapons enabled them to fight off the Aztecs. Their chief ceremonial center was at Tzintzuntzan, renowned for its outstanding Atlantean architectural features, including circular pyramidal platforms profuse with the sacred numerals of Atlantis, 5 and 6, mentioned by Plato (in *Kritias*). Autlan's philological resemblance to "Atlantis" and the Atlantean features of the Bronze Age-like Tarascans define both the site and its people as inheritors from the drowned island civilization.

Autochthon

Literally, "Sprung from the Land," he was the sixth king of Atlantis listed in Plato's *Kritias*. Autochthon was also mentioned in Phoenician (Canaanite) myth—the Sanchoniathon—as one of the Rephaim, or Titans, just as Plato described him. The first-century B.C. Greek geographer Diodorus Siculus wrote of a native people dwelling in coastal Mauretania (modern Morocco), facing the direction of Atlantis, who called themselves the Autochthones. They were descendants of Atlantean colonizers who established an allied kingdom on the Atlantic shores of North Africa. According to the thorough Atlantologist Jalandris, "Autochthon" was a term by which the Greeks knew the Pelasgians, or "Sea Peoples" associated with Atlantis.

Avalon

From the Old Welsh Ynys Avallach, or Avallenau, "The Isle of Apple Trees." The lost *Druidic Books of Pheryllt* and *Writings of Pridian*, both described as "more ancient than the Flood," celebrated the return of King Arthur from Ynys Avallach, "where all the rest of mankind had been overwhelmed." Avalon is clearly the British version of Atlantis, with its grove of sacred apple trees tended by the Hesperides, Daughters of Atlas (that is, Atlantises). Avallenau was also the name of a Celtic goddess of orchards, reaffirming the Hesperides' connection with

Atlantis. Avalon was additionally referred to as Ynys-vitrius, the "Island of Glass Towers," an isle of the dead, formerly the site of a great kingdom in the Atlantic Ocean. Avalon has since been associated with Glastonbury Tor—roughly, "Hill of the Glass Tower"—a high hill in Somerset, England. During the Bronze Age, the site was an island intersected by watercourses, resembling the concentric layout of the island of Atlantis. Underscoring this allusion is the spiral pathway that spreads outward from the Tor, because Plato described Atlantis as having been originally laid out in the pattern of a sacred spiral.

In Geoffrey of Monmouth's *Vita Merlini*, Avalon is called "the Fortunate Isle," the same title Classical Greek and Roman writers assigned to Atlantic islands generally and to Atlantis specifically. The Welsh Ynys Avallach and English Ynys-vitrius were known along the Normandy coast as the Isle of Ys, which disappeared beneath the waves. Avalon is also a town in Burgundy named after the sunken island city, because some of its survivors reached Brittany.

(See Ablach, Ys)

Awun

One of the divine twins in the Chinese version of Atlantis.
(See Infoniwa)

Ayar-aucca

The third and last wave of foreign immigration into prehistoric South America comprised refugees from a natural catastrophe—the sudden obliteration of their once mighty kingdom in fire and flood. Appropriately remembered as the "War-like People," they were undoubtedly veterans of failed Atlantean wars in the eastern Mediterranean and survivors from the final destruction of Atlantis, in 1198 B.C. Their Atlantean identity is confirmed by the Incas themselves. They described the Ayar-aucca as four twin giants who held up the sky. But they eventually grew tired of their exertions on behalf of an ungrateful humanity, and let it fall into the sea, creating a worldwide deluge that destroyed most of mankind.

One of the Ayar-aucca arrived in Cuzco, where he transformed himself into a *huaca,* or sacred stone, but not before mating with a local woman to sire the first Inca. Henceforward, Cuzco, known as "the Navel of the World," was the capital of the Inca Empire. The Ayar-aucca is the self-evident Peruvian rendering of the Bronze Age Atlantis catastrophe, incorporated into the Incas' imperial foundation myth.

(See Ahson-nutl, Navel of the World)

Ayar-chaki

This second wave of foreigners in South America suddenly appeared as "Wanderers" or immigrants from earthquakes and floods that made continued residency at their distant homeland impossible. Their leader was Manco Capac and his wife, Mama Ocllo. They established the "Flowering Age," when the "Master Craftsmen" built Tiahuanaco about 3,500 years ago. Indeed, radiocarbon testing at the ceremonial center yielded an early construction date of +/-1600 B.C. (Childress, 139). Their sinful homeland was destroyed in a flood sent as punishment from the gods, who spared Manco Capac and his large, virtuous family. The Ayar-chaki were refugees from geologic violence that beset much of the world with the return of a killer comet between 1600 and 1500 B.C., the same celestial phenomenon that forced the earlier Ayar-manco-topa and the later Ayar-aucca to flee their seismically unstable oceanic homelands for higher ground.

Ayar-manco-topa

Bands of men and women who arrived along the northern coasts of Peru, where they built the earliest cities, raised the first pyramids and other monumental structures, understood applied mathematics, cured illnesses with medicines and surgery, and instituted all the cultural features for which Andean civilization came to be known. In the Chimu version, they were led by King Naymlap, who landed with his followers in "a fleet of big canoes." The Ayar-manco-topa correspond to the Salavarry Period in Andean archaeology, when the first South American pyramidal platforms with rectangular courts appeared in Peru. The Ayar-manco-topa were probably Lemurian culture-bearers fleeing the worldwide geologic upheavals that particularly afflicted, but did not yet destroy, their Pacific Ocean homeland at the close of the fourth millennium B.C.

(See Lemuria)

Azaes

The ninth king of Atlantis listed in Plato's *Kritias*. On the Atlantic shores of Middle America, he was known as Itzamna, leader of the ancestral Mesoamericans' "Greater Arrival," that first wave of Atlantean culture-bearers from across the Sunrise Sea, recorded by the Mayas. Portrayed as a fair-skinned, bearded figure among the beardless natives, his title was "The First One." He holds up the sky in the temple art of Yucatan's foremost Maya ceremonial center, Chichen Itza, which was named after him and his descendants, the Itzas. Chichen Itza is particularly noted for its Atlantean statuary and sculpted relief.

Azaes-Itzamna was probably a real colonizer from Atlantis, who established his allied kingdom, which eventually took his name. In Yucatan, *Azaes* means "the Parched or Thirsty One," appropriate to the arid conditions of Middle America, where sufficient drinking water was always a question of paramount importance and the Atlantean Tlaloc was a rain-god of highest significance. Another title for Itzamna was "Lizard," the Mayas' symbol for a bringer or harbinger of rain and, hence, abundance.

Azores

Ten major islands in the North Atlantic comprising 902 square miles, lying 740 miles west of Portugal's Cape Roca from the island of San Miguel. The Azores are volcanic; their tallest mountain, Pico, at 7,713 feet, is dormant. Captain Diego de Sevilha discovered the islands in 1427. Portugal's possession ever since, they are still collectively and officially recognized by Portuguese authorities as "os vestigios dos Atlantida," or "the remains of Atlantis." The name "Azores" supposedly derives from Portuguese for "hawks," or Acores. The Hungarian specialist in comparative linguistics, Dr. Vamos-Toth Bator, believes instead that "Azores" is a corruption of "Azaes," the monarch of an Atlantean kingdom, as described in Plato's account (*Kritias*).

None of the islands were inhabited at the time of their discovery, but a few important artifacts were found on Santa Maria, where a cave concealed a stone altar decorated with serpentine designs, and at Corvo, famous for a small cask of Phoenician coins dated to the fifth century B.C.

The most dramatic find was an equestrian statue atop a mountain at San Miguel. The 15-foot tall bronze masterpiece comprised a block pedestal bearing a badly weathered inscription and surmounted by a magnificent horse, its rider stretching forth a right arm and pointing out across the sea, toward the west. King John V ordered the statue removed to Portugal, but his governor's men botched the job, when they accidentally dropped the colossus down the mountainside. Only the rider's head and one arm, together with the horse's head and flank and an impression of the pedestal's inscription, were salvaged and sent on to the King.

These items were preserved in his royal palace, but scholars were unable to effect a translation of the "archaic Latin," as they thought the inscription might have read. They were reasonably sure of deciphering a single word—"cates"— although they could not determine its significance. If correctly transcribed, it might be related to *cati*, which means, appropriately enough, "go that way," in the language spoken by the Incas, Quechua. Cattigara is the name of a Peruvian city, as indicated on a second-century A.D. Roman map, so a South American connection with the mysterious San Miguel statue seems likely (Thompson 167–169). Cattigara was probably Peru's Cajamarca, a deeply ancient, pre-Inca site. Indeed, the two city names are not even that dissimilar.

In 1755, however, all the artifacts taken from San Miguel were lost during a great earthquake that destroyed 85 percent of Lisbon. While neither Santa Maria's altar in the cave nor San Miguel's equestrian statue were certifiably Atlantean, they unquestionably evidenced an ancient world occupation of the Azores, and the bronze rider's pointed gesture toward the west suggests more distant voyages to the Americas. Roman accounts of islands nine days' sail from Lusitania (Portugal) describe contemporary sailing time to the Azores. The first-century B.C. Greek geographer Diodorus Siculus reported that the Phoenicians and Etruscans contested each other for control of Atlantic islands, which were almost certainly the Azores. We recall Corvo's Phoenician coins, while the Etruscans were extraordinary bronze sculptors, who favored equestrian themes, such as the example at San Miguel. Both the Phoenicians and Etruscans were outstanding seafarers.

Atlantologists speculate the Etruscans did not discover the islands, but learned of them from their Atlantean fathers and grandfathers. The Azores' lack of human habitation at the time of their Portuguese discovery and their paucity of civilized remains may be explained in terms of the Atlantis catastrophe itself, which forced their evacuation and, over the subsequent course of centuries of geologic activity, buried most of what survived under lava flows, which are common in the islands. The oldest known reference to the Azores appears in Homer's *Odyssey*, where he refers (probably) to San Miguel as *umbilicus maris*, or "the Navel of the Ocean," the name of an Atlantean mystery cult.

(See Ampheres)

Aztecs

A Nahuatl-speaking people who established their capital, Tenochtitlan, at the present location of Mexico City, in 1325 A.D. Over the next two centuries, they rose through military aggression to become the dominant power in pre-Conquest Middle America. Although their civilization was an inheritance from other Mesoamerican cultures that preceded them, the Aztecs preserved abundant and obvious references to Atlantis in their mythic traditions. Despite the millennia that separated them from that mother civilization, their royal ancestry, though not entirely unmixed with native blood, could still trace itself back to the arrival of Quetzalcoatl, the "Feathered Serpent," an Atlantean culture-bearer.

Aztecatl

The Aztecs themselves drew their national identity from this term, which means, "Man of Watery (that is, *sunken*) Aztlan," the Aztec name for Atlantis.

Aztlan

An island civilization in the Atlantic Ocean from which the ancestors of the Aztecs arrived in America following a destructive flood. A clear reference to Atlantis, Aztlan was remembered by the Aztecs as "the Field of Reeds," "Land of Cranes" (denoting its island character), and "the White Island." On the other side of the world, the ancient Egyptians referred to an island in the Atlantic Ocean from which the first gods and men arrived at the Nile Delta as Sekhet-aaru, or "the Field of Reeds." To both the Aztecs and the Egyptians, reeds were symbolic for wisdom, because they were used as writing utensils. Atlantis was likewise known as "the White Island" to North African Berbers, ancient Britons, and Hindus of the Indian subcontinent.

(See Albion, Atala)

Bacab

A Mayan name given to anthropomorphic figures usually carved in relief on sacred buildings. They simultaneously represent a single god and his own manifestation as twin pairs signifying the four cardinal directions. The Bacabs are portrayed as men with long beards, distinctly un-Indian facial features, and wearing conch shells, while supporting the sky with upraised hands. Their most famous appearance occurs at a shrine atop Chichen Itza's Pyramid of the Kukulcan, the Feathered Serpent, in Yucatan. Placement in the holy-of-holies at this structure is most appropriate, because the Mayas venerated Kukulcan as their founding father—a white-skinned, yellow-bearded man who arrived from over the Atlantic Ocean on the shores of prehistoric Mexico with all the arts of civilization. Bacab is synonymous with Kukulcan and undoubtedly a representation of Atlas in Yucatan. Indeed, the conch shell worn by the Chichen Itza Bacabs was the Feathered Serpent's personal emblem, symbolic of his oceanic origins.

Plato tells us that sets of royal twins ruled the Atlantean Empire, which was at the center of the world. So too, the Bacabs are twins personifying the sacred center. Among the many gifts they brought to the natives of Middle America was the science of honey production, and even today they are revered as the divine patrons of beekeeping. In ancient Hindu tradition, the first apiarists in India were sacred twins called the Acvins, redoubtable sailors from across the sea. Each brother Bacab presided over one year in a four-year cycle, because Bacab was the deity of astrological time. In Greek myth, Atlas, too, was the inventor and deity of astrology-astronomy.

Mexican archaeologists have associated the post-Deluge arrival of the Bacabs in Guatemala with the foundation date of the Mayas and the start of their calendar: August 10, 3113 B.C. This date finds remarkable correspondence in Egypt, where the First Dynasty suddenly began around 3100 B.C. after gods and men were said to have sailed to the Nile Delta when their sacred mound in the Distant West began to sink beneath the sea. The Babylonian version of the Great Flood that produced Oannes, the culture-bearer of Mesopotamian civilization, was believed to have taken place in 3116 B.C. Clearly, these common dates commemorated by disparate peoples define a shared, seminal experience that can only belong to Atlantis.

Bahr Atala

Literally, the "Sea of Atlas," a south Tunisian archaeological site known as Shott el Jerid. With concentric walls enclosing what appears to be a centralized palace, it resembles the citadel of Atlantis, as described by Plato. Nearby hills are locally referred to as the Mountains of Talae, or "the Great Atlantean Water." Bahr Atala was probably an Atlantean outpost in Tunis during the Late Bronze Age, from the 16th to 13th centuries B.C.

Balam-Qitze

According to the cosmological *Popol Vuh*, the Mayan "Book of Counsel," he was unanimously elected chief by the U Mamae to lead the "Old Men" across the Atlantic Ocean from Patulan-Pa-Civan, their realm drowning beyond the eastern horizon. Balam-Qitze appears to have been the authentically Atlantean name of a leader who conveyed survivors from Atlantis to Yucatan.

(See Giron-Gagal, U Mamae)

Bailey, Jean

An 18th-century French Atlantologist who traced Atlantean influences into Scandinavia.

(See Rudbeck)

Balearic Islands

An archipelago in the western Mediterranean Sea, ranging from 50 to 190 miles off the east coast of Spain, forming two distinct island groups, which are actually a continuation of the Andalusian Mountain chain. An Early Bronze Age people settled in the Balearics who were notable for their military aggressiveness, as evidenced in surviving representations on stone stelae of helmeted warriors bearing long swords. They were invaders of the Mediterranean from Atlantis, during that empire's later, imperialistic phase, as described by Plato. Their Atlantean identity is underscored by a number of great, stone watchtowers, found mostly on Majorca, still remembered as *talaia* or *talayot*, derivatives of *Atlas*.

Balor

In Old Irish folklore, he was the king of the Formorach, a giant "Sea People." Balor led them to Ireland, where they arrived as its first inhabitants after a great flood destroyed their former kingdom. Later renditions of his myth put his original homeland in Spain or North Africa. Although corruptions of the earliest version, they nonetheless properly indicate the general direction from which the Formorach came, because the island of Atlantis lay about 200 miles west of Gibraltar.

Basilea

In Greek folk tradition, the sister of Atlas, who was elected the Queen of Atlantis after the death of her husband, Uranus, an early king. Her name, in fact, means, "queen." She remarried with Hyperion, and bore him a son and daughter, Helios and Selene, deities of the sun and moon, respectively. A variant of her myth had the other Atlantean kings, afraid Hyperion would seize the throne of Atlantis and establish his family as a usurping dynasty, conspire to assassinate him and his son. Their deaths occasioned the suicide of Selene and the madness of Basilea. According to Lewis Spence, "When her subjects endeavored to restrain her, a terrible tempest of rain, thunder, and lightning broke forth, and she was seen no more." He believed her story signified the triumph of the powers of darkness over light (Helios), a reference to the Atlantis catastrophe itself, when neither sun nor moon were visible because of ash clouds which encircled the globe.

The "Arcane Tradition," he writes, reported that, after her disappearance, Basilea took the place of her dead daughter to become the moon-goddess, and assisted Atlas in his creation of astrology-astronomy.

Basque

The English and French word used to describe a people who refer to themselves as the Euskotarak. They inhabit the Bay of Biscay in both France and Spain, including the western foothills of the Pyrenees Mountains. There are only about 1.25 million Basque people, living mostly in Europe but also in communities in South and North America, particularly the state of Nevada. Stocky, with auburn hair and gray eyes, they are genetically distinct from both French and Spanish and speak a unique tongue totally unrelated to any European language. Euskara is spoken by approximately half a million persons worldwide. It shares some affinity with Finno-Urgic Patumnili, the tongue of ancient Troy; Etruscan, as spoken by the pre-Roman civilizers in west-central Italy; Guanche, belonging to the native inhabitants in the Canary Islands; and, most surprisingly, Nahuatl, the language of the Aztecs, in ancient Mexico. Each one of these disparate peoples played important roles in the story of Atlantis.

A revealing cognate is "Atalya," the name of a prehistoric ceremonial mound in Biarritz, in Basque country. "Atalaia" is also a site in southern Portugal featuring Bronze Age tumuli, or domed tombs, dating to the high imperial phase of Atlantis, in the 13th century B.C. Another "Atalya" is a Guanche region high in the central mountains of Gran Canaria that could pass for a scene taken directly from Plato's account of Atlantis. "Atalya" is the name of a holy mountain in the Valley of Mexico, venerated by the Aztecs at the time of their discovery by the Spaniards in the 16th century.

Clearly, "Atalya" carries the same meaning in Euskara, Iberian, Guanche, and Nahuatl, the Aztec language; namely, the description of a sacred mountain, mound, or mound-like structure, and apparently derivative of "Atlas," the holy peak at the center of the island of Atlantis. The "Atalya" of the Basque, Iberians, Guanches, and Aztecs were probably meant to commemorate, in both word and configuration, that original Mount Atlas, from which their ancestors fled the destruction. Indeed, they all preserved stories of a great flood that preceded the establishment of their own civilizations.

Parallels between Euskara and pre-Columbian speech are underscored by a traditional ball game known alike to Europe's Euskotarak and the ancient Maya of Middle America. Rules of the Basque Pelota are identical in numerous details to the otherwise unique Maya version. "These similarities," observed the noted German Atlantologist, Otto Muck, "form a bond between peoples on two sides of the Atlantic, pointing to a common cause, a common center: Atlantis, heartland of this long-vanished maritime power."

There is an additional link between the Basques and the ancient Canary Islanders: the Guanches practiced a singular goat cult with rituals likewise observed in traditional Basque witchcraft. Basque folktales still recount the Aintzine-koak, their seafaring forefathers who arrived in the Bay of Biscay after "the Green Isle," Atlaintika, went under the waves. *Atlantida* is a national Basque poem describing their ancient greatness in Atlaintika, its fiery collapse into the sea with most of its inhabitants, and the voyage of survivors to southwestern Europe. Although composed in the 19th century, "like many other epics committed to paper long after their first telling," according to a *Reader's Digest* investigation, "it is based on age-old folk belief and oral tradition."

In 1930, the famous German writer Ernst von Salomon reported a claim made by a native of the Pyrenees: "The Basque are the last of a more beautiful, freer, prouder world, long ago sunk beneath the sea."

Historian Robert Gallop writes, "These fireside tales of the Basques are a strange hotch-potch of legends which must have reached them from east and south and north, and—who knows?—perhaps even from the west, if there is anything to the Atlantis theory!" (165).

Racially, the Basque have been associated by some anthropologists with the pre-Indo-European people who occupied the western Mediterranean until the eighth century B.C. If so, the Euskotarak may be the last direct descendants of Atlantis, and their strange language is perhaps the same heard in that lost world, more than 3,000 years ago.

(See Atlaintika, Belesb-At, Muck)

Bath

See Orichalcum, Findrine.

Battle of Mag Tured

Also known as Moytura, a military campaign in which the Formorach were defeated by the Tuatha da Danann, as described in *The Book of Invasions*. Stripped of its mythic colors, Mag Tured tells how the Atlanteans lost control of Ireland to Celtic invaders.

The Begetting of Nanna

A late third-millennium B.C. Sumerian epic in which Atlantis is described, according to Noah Kramer: "Behold, the Bond-of-Heaven-and-Earth, the kindly wall, its pure river, its quay where the boats stand, its well of good water, its pure canal!" Here, at the birthplace of the gods, they "built the lofty stage-tower on the nether-sea, and chapels for themselves," devised the first laws, and founded the science of astronomy-astrology.

The Babylonian version of the Sumerian Ea was Marduk, who "made supreme the glorious city, the seat dear to their [the gods'] hearts, constructed an enclosure around the waters." In a liturgical text, Ea is described as "the lord who dwells in a fane in the midst of the ocean" (Gaster, 135).

These mythic accounts of Enki's "sea-house," Ninhursag's "cosmic mountain" and Ea's "glorious city in the midst of the ocean" are self-evident portrayals of the same homeland of civilization Plato depicts in his Atlantis dialogue. Ninhursag's "Bond-of-Heaven-and-Earth" is Atlas, "the Upholder" of the heavens, inventer of astrology-astronomy, etc.

(See Atlas)

Belesb-At

The Basques' sunken "Green Isle" from which their ancestors arrived in the Bay of Biscay. "Belesb" is a prefix or title referring to the sun-god Bel, whose symbol, the oriphile swastika, adorns many of the oldest houses in the Pyrenees, and is still revered as a Basque national emblem. Belesb-At is a clear reference to Atlantis.

(See Basque, Atlaintika)

Belial

The last generations of Atlantis in the 14th and 13th centuries B.C. over-indulged themselves in luxury and military aggression. Their monopoly of the copper trade made them the wealthiest, most influential people in the civilized world, enabling them to build an empire unrivaled in size and splendor until the Roman Imperium. National affluence became the new religion, personified in Belial, less a god than the deification of materialism. His followers grew increasingly obsessed with technology to maintain and generate luxuries, while earlier nature cults fell into decline through popular obsession with shallow distractions, until his became the dominant state-monotheism.

Belial was an accurate projection of the decadent Atlanteans, when transient wealth, power, and pleasure alone interested them. In his name, they despoiled not only other peoples, but the Earth itself, until their homeland was obliterated by a natural catastrophe. The worship of Belial escaped with his surviving followers, who transplanted his cult in the British Isles and the Near East. Over time, his narrow materialism was interpreted by the ancient Irish to signify deserved abundance. They re-enshrined him in their Beltane festival, celebrating the munificence of the sun and the goodness it implied. Staying closer to his original conception, the plutocratic Babylonians appropriately made him their chief god: Bel, "Lord of Heaven and Earth."

His Atlantean identification is certain, because he brought about the catastrophe in the Babylonian version of the Great Flood. His rehabilitation from the wicked god responsible for the destruction of Atlantis is described in the Sumerian *Epic of Gilgamesh*, where Bel is ordered by his superior, Ea, another flood-god: "You did not listen to my counsel and caused the deluge. Yes, punish the sinner for his crimes and the evil-doer for his wickedness, but be merciful and do not destroy all mankind" (Mackenzie). Henceforward, Bel was worshiped as a protector of the virtuous and the maker of kings. But he was seen for what he really represented by the writers of the Old Testament, where his name became the epithet for an evil or subversive person. In later Jewish apocryphal literature, Belial was synonymous for Satan himself.

Benoit, Pierre

Author of the popular *L'Atlantide* (1920), among the most successful novels about the lost civilization, translated in England as *Atlantida* and in the United States as *The Queen of Atlantis*. An atmospheric silent movie version in 1929, produced by the renowned German director G.W. Papst and starring Brigitte Helm, has since become a "classic" film. It was remade 20 years later in Hollywood with Maria Montez and Jean Pierre Aumont.

(See Dionysus of Mitylene)

Benten, or Benzaiten

Goddess of civilization (music, eloquence, fine arts, seamanship, etc.), which she brought to ancient Japan from her lost kingdom across the sea on a great ship.

Her shrines at Biwa-ko, or Lake Biwa, and in Tokyo, at Shinobazu, are adorned with discernably Atlanto-Lemurian symbolism. In keeping with her identity as the country's earliest culture-bearer, the oldest indications of human occupation are found around the shores of Lake Biwa.

(See Chikubujima, Shinobazu)

Bergelmir

A Norse giant, who, with his wife, escaped the catastrophic flood that destroyed a former age. They sired a new race, the Jotnar, after establishing his realm, Jotunheim. Bergelmir's myth is similar to other ancient traditions around the world describing a cataclysmic deluge from which only a few survivors emerge to found new dynasties, races, or kingdoms.

Berlitz, Charles

American author (1913 to 2003) of *The Mystery of Atlantis* (1974) and *Atlantis, the Eighth Continent* (1984), which revived popular interest in the subject after more than 40 years of general neglect. As the innovative president of an internationally famous language training school in France that he inherited from his grandfather, Maximilian (1878), his expertise in various tongues, ancient and modern, led him to conclude that many derived from a single, prehistoric source. Beginning in the Bahamas, Berlitz followed his line of research back to the lost civilization of Atlantis. His renowned credentials as a professional linguist with 26 years as an intelligence officer in the U.S. Army helped restore credibility to Atlantean studies, which continue to this day.

Berosus

A Chaldean high priest who lived around the turn of the third century B.C. Although the Greeks knew him as "Berosus," his real name was Bel-Usur, a priest of Bel in Babylon. The worship of Belial, the icon of a controlling cult in Atlantis during its last years, was carried to Mesopotamia after the destruction, and reestablished as "Bel" in a new temple, as described by Berosus, who, serving there, read the story of the Atlantean flood. His three-volume history of Babylon, written in Greek, was regarded by scholars throughout classical times as authoritative. During 1928, his reputation for accuracy was reaffirmed by German archaeologists, who found corroborating evidence described in a late-Babylonian tablet discovered at the ruins of Uruk, the former capital, predating Berosus by 1,000 years.

He opened his first volume by describing the origins of Babylonian civilization, which began with the arrival of culture-bearers after a great flood. Their leader was the half-man, half-fish Oannes, who came from the sea with all the arts and technology from a preceding high culture. His characterization is not to be taken literally, but was more a poetic metaphor signifying Oannes's prodigious seafaring skills, in much the same way an outstanding swimmer is described as "half fish." Oannes came ashore daily to instruct the natives of Eridu in the secrets of canal-building, irrigation, agriculture, literature, mathematics, civil engineering, metallurgy, pottery, music, art, astrology-astronomy, city-planning, temple-building—all the arts of civilization. He also exercised power over the souls of the ocean, perhaps a reference to an Atlantean priest who conjured the spirits of the dead in the submerged Atlantis.

In the Akkadian language, he was known as Nun-Amelu, a comparison Bailey makes with the Egyptian Nun, a god of the primal sea, who carried men and gods to the Nile Valley after a flood in the Distant West. A contemporary of Berosus, the Greek writer, Orpheus, reported that "Egypt and Chaldea are twin sisters, daughters of Poseidon," the sea-god creator of Atlantis. Bailey also reproduces the impression of a Sumerian cylinder seal portraying Oannes, known to the Sumerians as Ea, paying homage to a bearded figure bent on one knee while supporting the sky—the classic image of Atlas reproduced throughout the ancient world—thereby associating the Mesopotamian culture-bearer with Atlantis.

In his second volume, Berosus described in some detail the Deluge itself, characterizing it as a worldwide natural catastrophe that wiped out most of humanity and obliterated a former kingdom of enormous power and wisdom. He wrote that there were "ten kings before the flood," some of whose surviving descendants sailed to Mesopotamia, where they reestablished civilization between the Tigris and Euphrates Rivers. Since then, every Babylonian monarch had to prove direct descent from these antediluvian regents before legitimately assuming the throne. In *Timaeus*, Plato also said that there were 10 kings of the Atlantis Empire previous to its destruction.

Berosus was almost certainly privy to the same kind of original Atlantean documents Plato and/or Solon saw at the Temple of the Goddess Neith, in the Egyptian city of Sais, in the Nile Delta.

(See Oannes)

Bimini Road

Bimini is an island in the Bahamas, 55 miles east of Miami, Florida, approximately 7 miles long and 1/3 mile across at its widest point. Its modern inhabitants are descendants of West African slaves imported by Spain and Britain beginning in the mid-16th century. They replaced the resident Caribs, who arrived only a few generations before and after whom the Caribbean Sea was named. Bellicose cannibals from Middle America's mainland, the Caribs feasted on the island's earliest known inhabitants, the Lucayans, a linguistic branch of Arawak Indians. Before their extermination (consumption?), the Lucayans were described by Spanish explorers as able craftsmen (surviving Lucayan celts and hammer-stones attest to their refined skills), with noticeably lighter complexions and auburn hair, even occasional blue eyes. These untypical traits may have been genetic traces of contacts with pre-Columbian visitors from Europe, or even racial evidence for an Atlantis pedigree, in view of the following information.

The origin and meaning of "Bimini" are unknown. However, the name appears in the Ancient Egyptian language as Baminini, which means, "Homage (*ini*) to the Soul (*ba*) of Min." Min was the Egyptians' divine protector of travelers on far-off journeys, a particularly appropriate god to be worshiped at distant Bimini, if indeed the island had been visited by voyagers from the Nile Valley. Material evidence for an Egyptian or, at any rate, an Egyptian-like presence in the western Atlantic appeared during the late 1930s, when James Lockwood, Jr., an American archaeologist in Haiti, saw a stone statue of the ancient Egyptian god of the dead, Anubis, that had been discovered on an off-shore island.

The Lucayans knew Bimini as "Guanahani," another curious connection with the Ancient World, because the name translates as "the Island (*hani*) of Men (*guana*)" in the language of the Guanches. These were native inhabitants of the Canary Islands, off the northwest coast of North Africa, until their utter demise at the hands of the Spanish in the 15th and 16th centuries. Although no monumental buildings were found on Bimini, in Arawak, *Guanahani* meant "the Place of the Encircling Walls"; in Arawak, *hani* was also synonymous for "crown" or "wreath." This oldest known name for the island may have referred to a large stone formation lying in 19 feet of water less than 2 miles off Bimini's northernmost point.

It is composed of so far unnumbered but certainly no less than 5,000, mostly square-cut blocks running in a straight line for about 1,900 feet, before swinging back on itself to create a J-formation. To early observers, it resembled a paved road running across the bottom of the sea. But the general consensus of investigators since then tentatively identifies the structure as a cyclopean wall, not unlike Andean examples found in Peru, specifically, at Cuzco and Sacsahuaman. Unfortunately, it continues to be known by its first and misleading appellation.

In 1933, Edgar Cayce, during one of his trance states, said that records from Atlantis still existed "where a portion of the temples may yet be discovered, under the slime of ages of sea water—near what is known as Bimini." The little island was not Atlantis itself, he explained, but its outpost, known many thousands of years ago as Alta, extending (politically) to east-coastal Florida, and part of a wider Atlantean administration known as Poseidia, comprising the Lesser Antilles. In 1940, the

If removed from its underwater location, the Bimini Road would resemble the Peruvian walls of Sacsahuaman.

"Sleeping Prophet" predicted, "Poseidia will be among the first portion of Atlantis to rise again. Expect it in '68 and '69; not so far away!" The so-called "Bimini Road" was, in fact, "discovered" in 1968 by maverick archaeologist Mason Valentine, while looking for Atlantean remains around the island in hopes of confirming Cayce's prophesy.

Since then, the underwater site has been subjected to continuous investigation by researchers convinced it is an Atlantean ruin and critics sure it is nothing more than a natural formation of beach rock. The latter, despite their standard array of academic credentials, have for more than 30 years failed to show an analogous arrangement of beach rock, not only at Bimini, but anywhere else in the world. Allegedly similar examples from Loggerhead Key, Dry Tortugas, or near Sri Lanka, cited as evidence for its entirely natural provenance, are so unlike the linear, organized blocks found at Bimini that such comparisons are worthless. Moreover, core-drillings at the Bimini Road, beginning in the mid-1980s, extracted micrite, which does not occur in beach rock. Some of its stones contain conglomerations of aragonite and calcite, patterns likewise missing from beach rock.

Florida geologist, Eugene A. Shinn, a harsh critic of theories on behalf of the Bimini structure's artificiality, radio-carbon dated the stones, which range in age from 2,000 to 4,000 years before present. The oldest end of this time parameter coincides with the Middle Bronze Age, just when port facilities resembling the Bimini site were being constructed in the Near East, and Atlantis was nearing the apogee of its material greatness, according to researchers who argue that Plato's sunken city flourished from 3000 to 1200 B.C.

Serious investigation of the Bahama site began in the late 1960s under the direction of Valentine and his scientific colleague, Dimitri Rebikoff, continuing into the 1970s and early 80s through the work of Dr. David Zink, whose *Stones of Atlantis* was the first full-length book published on the subject. During the 1990s and early years of the 21st century, numerous underwater expeditions to Bimini conducted by William Donato, president of The Atlantis Organization (Buena Park, California), have contributed significantly toward a general appreciation of the structure's real identity.

The underwater ruin appears to be the foundation of a continuous rampart which originally formed an elongated oval (the Lucayans' "Encircling Wall"?) to shelter seagoing vessels. A harbor at the north end of Bimini makes abundant maritime sense, because its location serves two fundamentally important prerequisites for transoceanic travel: First, the island stands directly in the path of an Atlantic current that travels like an underwater conveyor belt—northward, parallel to New England shores, then due east toward the Azores, the British Isles, and Western Europe. Second, Bimini is the last landfall for fresh water before a transatlantic voyage from North America.

The discovery at Bimini of additional, prehistoric evidence underscores the site's ancient, man-made identity. These include colossal effigy mounds shaped like fish and other zoomorphic and geometric figures, together with additional blocks also found at 19-foot depths, about 3 miles northeast of the road, resembling Tiahuanaco's squared columns in the high Andes of Bolivia. But what divers see at Bimini today are the ruins of a ruin. As recently as the early years of the 20th century, the surface

A lone, square pillar lies half buried in the sand, under 19 feet of water, at Bimini's Moselle Shoals. Photograph by William Donato.

This block at the Bimini Road is similar to other "fingerprint masonry" found in the Andean walls at Cuzco, Machu Picchu, and Sacsahuaman. Photograph by William Donato.

of the Road was visible at low tide, when its location was even designated "a navigational hazard." Older natives still living in the 1990s personally testified they saw waves washing over the tops of the stones on numerous occasions when they were young, although most inhabitants of the island avoided the site with superstitious dread. In the early 1920s, a Florida salvage company dismantled the structure down to its bottom course. The blocks were removed to Miami, where they were used as fill for the city's new quayside.

Cayce may in fact have described the Bimini Road as early as 1932. He said in a reading for May 5:

> This we find (at Poseidia) not an altogether walled city, but a portion of same built so that the waters of these rivers became as the pools about which both sacrifice and sport, and those necessities for the cleansing of the body, home and all, were obtained, and these—kept constantly in motion so that it purified itself in its course;—water in motion over stone—purifies itself in twenty feet of space.

The base of the Bimini Road is 1 foot short of 20 feet underwater. Rivers do not exist on the island today, but they did in its geologic past. Cayce seems to have portrayed the Road, not as part of a harbor, but a ritual and recreational feature.

Ongoing investigations at Bimini with increasingly sophisticated search technology may prove that "the Place of the Encircling Walls" was indeed Cayce's Alta, where ships 3,000 years ago, heavy-laden with copper ore mined in North America, replenished their provisions of fresh water on the last leg of their return voyages to Atlantis.

(Cayce 364-12 5/6/32)

Blake, William

Famed English poet and artist (1757 to 1827) whose visionary style—radically advanced for his own time—is still highly valued by modern audiences. In his free verse epic, *America*, Blake wrote of "those vast, shady hills between America and Albion's shore now barred out by the Atlantic Ocean, called Atlantean hills."

He paraphrased British myth in characterizing Albion as a flood hero who led a contingent of survivors from Atlantis to England, which derived its early name from him. Blake held that both ancient Britain and pre-Columbian America were indebted to Atlantean culture-bearers. It says something for the credibility of an historic Atlantis that men of William Blake's genius believed the drowned civilization was something more than fable, as its less-renowned skeptics continue to insist.

(See Albion)

Bochica

He is still known to various Indian tribes in coastal Colombia, Venezuela, and Brazil, such as the Chibchas, near Bogotá, Colombia, as a white-skinned giant with a long beard who supported the sky on his shoulders, until he dropped it, causing the whole world to burst into flame and flood at the same time. The disaster destroyed his home across the sea, forcing his children to migrate for their lives to South America, where they became the ancestors of today's native peoples. After this catastrophe, Bochica reassumed his burden of the heavens, which he still supports, but causes earthquakes when he shifts the weight on his shoulders. In variants of his myth, he condemned a demon responsible for the natural disaster, Chibchacum, to hold up the sky, while Bochica took up residence on the world's first rainbow. Ever since, rainbows are not only associated with the god, but venerated as commemorative phenomena of the ancestral flood.

This tribal memory of what can only be the destruction of Atlantis is ignored by skeptics of the lost civilization. But why else would a dark-skinned people unable to grow beards concoct a pre-Columbian story about a bearded, white giant causing a great flood? Moreover, the South American deluge myth contains many elements found around the world, such as the annihilation of a distant, splendid kingdom; some celestial disturbance; the arrival of racially alien survivors, who become the ancestors of future leaders; and so on. Like Plato's *Kritias*, in which Zeus destroys Atlantis for the iniquity of its inhabitants, Bochica brings about the catastrophe to punish a sinful mankind.

(See Cuchavira, Zuhe)

Bon

An important Feast of the Dead held in the middle of the seventh lunar month, around August 14 or 16, when spirits return to visit their earthly homes in Japan. Bon Odori are hypnotic outdoor dances held at this time. They are shamanic exercises used to induce altered states of consciousness for commiserating with the spirits. Bon concludes after sundown with burning lanterns floating across the sea to guide the departed back to the Otherworld. The festival is not unlike Thailand's Lak Krathong or the Roman Lemuria, all of which aim at propitiating ghosts from Mu, the Pacific Ocean civilization lost beneath the seas in ancient times.

(See Lak Krathong, Lemuria, Mu)

Bralbral

According to Sumerian scholar Neil Zimmerer, Bralbral was an Atlantean who founded the Kingdom of Baralku (mentioned in Polynesian folk traditions), in Lemuria, sharing the leadership with his two sisters, Djanggau and Djunkgau.

(See Lemuria)

The Bronze Age

Bronze was the Ancient World equivalent of plutonium in the Atomic Age. Before its appearance, tools and weapons were made of either stone (usually granite and flint) or copper. Bronze was entirely superior to both, and whoever possessed it wielded a quantum advantage in military and industrial affairs. But it was difficult to manufacture, because it depended on the quality of the copper used and was combined with zinc and tin. None of the three minerals occurred in abundance throughout Europe and the Near East, where demands from every kingdom for the new metal erupted after its discovery at the turn of the fourth millennium B.C.

The only real sources for tin were found in southern Spain and parts of England. As some indication of the copper's importance, the modern island of Cypress derives its name from "Kippur," the Assyrian word for copper, because it was one of the few locations where it was mined in some abundance. But even there, its quality was not consistently first-rate. Despite insufficient supplies of copper, zinc, and tin, by 1500 B.C., the great powers, and even most of the lesser ones, had outfitted their often massive armed forces with vast arsenals of superb bronze weapons. The superpowers—Egypt, the Hittite Empire, Troy, Minoan Crete, Mycenaean Greece, and Assyria—ranged against themselves literally millions of bronze swords, spears, and battering rams, their soldiers outfitted with bronze helmets and shields. In ostentatious displays of wealth, kings would sometimes bedeck the walls of their cities with great sheets of gleaming bronze, or fill their squares and temples with the bronze statues of gods and heroes.

An enormous industry arose, specializing in the manufacture of bronze tools absolutely essential to craftsmen, artisans, and armorers from Ireland to Mesopotamia. Clearly, native mineral deposits, especially of copper, were insufficient, both in quantity and quality, to have even begun to keep pace with such a grand-scale supply and demand. For more than a century, historians have asked themselves, "Where did the ancients obtain the copper necessary to make so many bronze items?" The Old World Bronze Age began around 3000 B.C., reached peak production from the 16th to 13th centuries B.C., then came to an abrupt end about 1200 B.C. It was not logically superceded by the advent of the Iron Age, but followed instead by the precise opposite of all human progress: a 4-century long Dark Age, during which the lamp of civilization was extinguished in Europe, Asia Minor, and the Near East, excepting only Pharaonic Egypt, which had nevertheless entered a decline from which she would never recover. Moreover, iron had been known to Egyptian workers since early dynastic times, while Hittite arms were already bolstered by iron lance-heads and axes.

Curiously, the Bronze Age exactly parallels another, although intimately related mystery: the excavation of prodigious amounts of the world's highest-grade copper ore from the Upper Great Lakes Region of North America. Beginning circa 3000 B.C., a people, described in Menomonie Indian oral tradition as fair-complected "Marine Men," applied sophisticated mining techniques that would not be seen again until the Industrial Age. They extracted a minimum of 500 million pounds of copper, all of which vanished with the white-skinned miners by 1200 B.C., when the pits were suddenly abandoned. That is the same date for the final destruction of Atlantis, whose inhabitants Plato described as the world's wealthiest minerologists.

Bear Butte, South Dakota, where Native Americans from across the continent gather to commemorate the Atlantean Deluge.

Clearly, it was the seafaring "Marine Men" of Atlantis who discovered the Upper Peninsula's rich mineral deposits, mined them, and sold high-grade copper to the tool and weapons manufacturers of Europe, Asia Minor, and the Near East. Together with copper, tin was mined along Michigan shores, evidence for the manufacture of bronze, with which the Native American Indian residents were unfamiliar. The North American source was jealously preserved as a state secret upon which the Atlantean monopoly depended. When Atlantis was destroyed around 1200 B.C., the secret went with her and the Bronze Age ended for lack of quality copper supplies. The three most influential and interrelated aspects of ancient times—the Bronze Age, Atlantis, and the Upper Great Lakes copper mining—share the same time parameters.

Bull Worship

In *Kritias*, Plato describes an important ceremony undertaken by the kings of Atlantis in the Temple of Poseidon. This monumental structure was situated at the very center of the island, its own perfect center defined by a free-standing column of great antiquity. It was made of solid orichalcum, an alloy of high-grade copper and fine gold manufactured only in Atlantis. The pillar contained the original laws of the land, as inscribed by the first monarchs themselves. Around its base, subsequent Atlantean leaders consulted every fifth and sixth year on matters of state.

Before ruling on any final judgements, they prayed to Poseidon for guidance, then removed clubs and nooses from a sacred vessel. Without assistance, the 10 men captured one of several bulls allowed to roam freely in the vicinity of the temple, where they had been maintained by priests. The kings brought their captured bull into the sanctuary, then cut its throat over the top of the orichalcum column, allowing blood to course over the inscription, which ended with a curse against anyone who knowingly violated the laws of Atlantis. The bull's remains were gathered into separate containers. Its flesh was roasted, later divided into several portions for the kings' ritual meal and as a gratuity to the temple priesthood. The rest, together with all the bones and most of the blood, were tossed into a sacrificial fire.

Afterwards, the kings cleaned the pillar, utensils, and sacred precinct, then mixed a bowl of wine, into which was dropped one clot of bull's blood for each of them. They received their drink in golden cups, swore an oath on behalf of themselves and their descendants to uphold the law of their forefathers, emptied their wine into the sacred flames, and drank a fresh cup of bull's blood wine in a pledge of atonement for any sins they may have committed. Only after completing this libation did they sit down to their sacramental meal.

Bulls were associated with divine regents in Sumer, Egypt, Assyria, Minoan Crete, Greece, Rome, Iberia, and Ireland. All of these cultures featured traditions of a great deluge from which their ancestors came with all the accoutrements of a high civilization, including, most importantly, matters of kingship. In each people, their king was ritually identified with a sacred bull, because it was important for a leader to identify with the tremendous strength and aggressiveness epitomized by such an animal. In pre-Celtic Ireland, the new monarch had to undergo a ceremonial bath of bull's broth, which he then drank from an Atlantean-like golden cup.

The Egyptian Hape, better remembered by his Greek name, Apis, was the sacred bull of Memphis. Like the bulls at the Temple of Poseidon, he was allowed to roam free in a courtyard of the temple. After reaching his 25th year, "he was killed with great ceremony," according to Mercatante, just as the Atlantean bull was ritually slaughtered every fifth year (the divider of 25). The manner of his death was unique: he was drowned in a cistern. Was his religious execution meant to symbolize his cultic origins in drowned Atlantis? The dead animal was believed to be reincarnated in a new bull, "the Golden Calf,"—the same idol adored by the Israelites under Aron in Exodus 32:4—which began again the process of identification with Hape.

Romans participating in the mysteries of Mithra drank the blood of a slaughtered bull "as a sacramental act," in which they were purified of their sins and "born again for eternity"—all reminiscent of the atonement sought by the Atlantean kings when they drank wine with bull's blood. Their sacrificial meal even finds echoes in the Last Supper, where Jesus tells his apostles that the wine they drink is his own blood. The Messiah, too, was identified with the bull—a white one—in the apocryphal Book of Enoch.

What might very well be an authentic artifact from Atlantis was discovered during the 1889 excavation of a Bronze Age tomb at the Greek town of Vapheio, in Laconia, 5 miles south of Sparta. The item was an embossed gold cup depicting a bull roundup, wherein the hunter is portrayed using only lassos—a scene straight out of Plato's *Kritias*. The item's Atlantean identity is reinforced when we recall that he said the kings who met in the Temple of Poseidon after their bull hunt toasted in cups of gold.

Archaeologists believe the Vapheio cup is not Greek, but from Crete, dating to the first Late Minoan Period, about 1500 B.C. This date marks the florescence of the Atlantis Empire and its widening influence throughout the Mediterranean. Minoans may have made the cup to commemorate some kingly alliance forged in the bull ceremony between their country and the Atlanteans. Or the object may in fact be an import originally manufactured in Atlantis and brought somehow to Crete, from where it was looted by invading Mycenaean Greeks. In any case, an Atlantean provenance for the Vapheio cup seems inescapable.

This scene from the Cretan Vapheio cup duplicates a ritual recounted by Plato in his description of Atlantis.

Burotu

Revered by the Fiji Islanders of the western Pacific as their ancestral paradise before it sank beneath the sea. The island is known as Buloto in distant Tonga and Samoa. To the aborigines of Australia, it is remembered as Baralku, thereby demonstrating a very broadly known tradition among disparate peoples all apparently effected by a common event. According to native oral accounts, Tonga's ancient Ha'amonga ("The Burden of Maui"), a monumental arch almost 20 feet high, had its 105 tons of coral limestone ferried by survivors from Burotu. These were the Hiti, or giants of that lost realm. Their ancestral island was destroyed when the "heavens fell down," and fire married water to produce the Samoan islands. Like the Roman Lemuria, the souls of the dead return to Bolutu in annual ceremonies. The Fiji Burotu may be philologically related to Rutas, another name by which Mu was known in Asia.

(See Mu, Rutas)

Bussumarus

In Gallic folk traditions, a leader of 60 "Sea People" marines during their aggression against Europe immediately before and after the final destruction of Atlantis.

Byamspa

"When he found out that the Kingdom of Lemuria would sink under a gigantic tidal wave," according to chronologer, Neil Zimmerer, Byamspa led a group of fellow seers into the Himalayas of Tibet.

Caer Feddwid

The "Court of Carousal," also known as Caer Siddi and Caer Arianrhod, an opulent island kingdom featuring fountains and curative fresh water springs, but long ago lost beneath the waves of the Atlantic Ocean. Caer Feddwid is one of several Welsh versions of Atlantis.

(See Arianrhod, Gwyddno, Llyn Syfaddon)

Calypso

An Atlantis, daughter of Atlas by Thetis, a sea-goddess. Calypso's residence was a sacred cave on the island of Ogygia, where she had the power to grant eternal life to mortal human beings. She personifies the Atlantean Navel of the World mystery cult, with its cave rituals and promises of immortality. "Ogygia" derives from Ogyges, a flood hero in Greek mythology, implying that Calypso's island and Atlantis were one and the same.

(See Ogyges)

Ca-Mu

Literally "He from Mu," a flood hero of the Arovac Indians described as a tall, white-skinned, fair-haired and bearded "magician" who arrived on the shores of Panama after having been driven from his kingdom far across the sea by a terrible cataclysm. Ca-Mu is regarded as the man from whom all Arovac have since descended.

(See Mu)

Cayce, Edgar

Born in 1877, in Kentucky, he was known as "the Sleeping Prophet," because he uttered predictions and medical cures while in a deep trance. Until his death in Virginia, 68 years later, Cayce dictated thousands of "life-readings" he allegedly obtained from a kind of spiritual record he claimed to be able to read while experiencing an altered state of consciousness. Until his 47th year, he never uttered a word about Atlantis. But in 1922, he suddenly began recalling life in a place with which he was otherwise allegedly unfamiliar. Cayce's descriptions of the doomed civilization are sometimes remarkable for their uncanny credibility. For example, his portrayal of the migration of Atlanteans into the Nile Valley following the destruction of their Empire is entirely convincing. Many otherwise obscure names of persons and places he associates with the Atlantis experience likewise seem to reflect real events.

His son, Hugh Lynn Cayce, knew his father "did not read material on Atlantis, and that he, so far as we know, had absolutely no knowledge of the subject." The evocative, often verifiable detail of his readings in which Atlantis was described is all the more astounding when we realize he knew little about the vanished culture in his waking hours. As his son wrote:

> They are the most fantastic, the most bizarre, the most impossible information in the Edgar Cayce files. If his unconscious fabricated this material or wove it together from existing legends and writings, we believe that it is the most amazing example of a telepathic-clairvoyant scanning of existing legends and stories in print or of the minds of persons dealing with the Atlantis theory.

Edgar Cayce's conscious ignorance of the sunken civilization is not surprising. His formal education was meager, and his points of reference were more spiritual than historical or academic. His grasp of the past was often biblical, rather than scholastic. It seems clear then, that the subject was outside the purview of both his background and essentially Christian view of the world. But his readings are self-evidently plausible, because they often contain information that made little or no sense at the time they were uttered, but have been since confirmed by subsequent verification.

Perhaps most impressive of all is that obscure, even fleeting, references he made to Atlantis during the early 1920s were occasionally repeated only once, but within an exact same frame of reference, after more than two decades. Persuasive elements of Cayce's "life-readings" such as these give even skeptics pause, and encourage many investigators, regardless of their spiritual beliefs, to reconsider everything he had to say about Atlantis. His prediction of finding its first physical remains not far from the United States was a case in point described in the "Bimini" entry. Until Cayce spoke of Bimini, and even long after some of his "life-readings" were published, no researchers bothered to consider that small island as a possible remnant of Atlantean Civilization.

But how did the massive stone structure come to lie at the bottom of the sea? According to Cayce's "life-readings," the Atlantean lands underwent three major periods of inundation. They did not disappear altogether in a single cataclysm. The natural disaster described by Plato represented only the final destruction of

Edgar Cayce, America's most renowned psychic of the 20th century, often envisioned life in Atlantis.

Atlantis. A typical reading exemplifying these various epochs of upheaval took place in 1933, when Cayce told a client that he once dwelt "in the Atlantean land before the third destruction." The first seismic unrest dropped much of its territory beneath sea-level, followed several millennia later by renewed geologic violence which sank the remaining dry land, save for the tops of its tallest mountains. These volcanic peaks became known in historic times as Madeira, the Azore and Canary Islands, together with Atlas, on which the city of Atlantis arose. The ultimate destruction took place when Mount Atlas detonated, scoured and hollowed itself out with ferocious eruptions, then collapsed into the sea. Present interpretation of this evidence confirms the accuracy of Cayce's clairvoyant view of the Atlantean catastrophe. As he said, "the destruction of this continent and the peoples was far beyond any of that as has been kept as an absolute record, that record in the rocks still remains."

For someone of no formal education, Cayce's grasp of archaeology and geology was extraordinary, even prophetic. When he said in the 1930s that the Nile River flowed across the Sahara Desert to the ocean in early Atlantean times, no scientist in the world would have considered such an apparently outlandish possibility. Yet, in 1994, nearly half a century after his death, a satellite survey of North Africa discovered traces of a former tributary of the Nile that connected Egypt with the Atlantic Ocean at Morocco in prehistory. Persuasive elements of Cayce's "life-readings" encourage many investigators to reconsider his documented statements about Atlantis. But they are troubled by his characterization of the

Atlanteans as the builders of a technology superior to 20th-century accomplishments. Because Cayce has been verified in at least some important details, other researchers believe he was telling the whole truth, however difficult it may be for some to grasp, about the sunken civilization.

Regardless of the response he elicits, an important part of Edgar Cayce's legacy is the Association for Research and Enlightenment (A.R.E.) he founded and which continues to prosper in his home at Virginia Beach. It contains the largest library of its kind in the world, featuring not only all of his "life-readings," but many hundreds of books, papers, feature articles, and reference materials about Atlantis. The A.R.E. is also deeply involved in scientific investigation and study on behalf of the lost realm, including lectures and expeditions to various parts of the world, particularly at Andros and Bimini.

(See Andros Platform, Bimini Road)

Recreation of a Bronze Age stevedore carrying a typical "oxhide" ingot of copper, the basis of Atlantean wealth.

Ce-calli

Described in the Aztec *Anales de Quahititlan* as "the Great Water," the world-class deluge that destroyed a former age of greatness and wickedness.

Celaeno

In Greek myth, daughter of the sea-goddess Pleione hence, one of the Pleiades, or "Atlantises." Celaeno taught occult science to mortals. From her name derive all words pertaining to things "celestial," not only because she herself became a star in the night sky, but through her knowledge of astrology invented by her father, Atlas. Celaeno's myth tells of arcane spirituality and practices invented in Atlantis, as carried by survivors of its destruction to the reestablishment of civilization in new lands. She married Lycus, a king of the Blessed Isles, whose name was a term in circulation throughout classical times referring to any unspecified group of Atlantis islands, such as the Canaries or Madeira.

Chatwin, C.P.

A leading 20th-century naturalist, who stated in 1940 that the migratory behavior of certain butterflies and birds in the North and South Atlantic strongly suggested the former existence of the island civilization described by Plato.

(See Heer)

Cellarius, Christophe

A prominent late 18th-century French geographer who made a public statement supporting the historical credibility of Plato's Atlantis based on evidence he found in the fragments of ancient maps.

(See de Gisancourt)

Cerne

A name by which Atlantis was once known, according to the 1st-century B.C. geographer Diodorus Siculus. "Cerne" is also the name of a prehistoric hill-figure in Dorset, England. The 180-foot image of a naked man wielding a club in his right hand probably was made to represent Gogmagog, a giant said to have been armed with an immense war club. If so, then the bioglyph's Atlantean identity comes into focus. In Celtic myth, Gogmagog was a leader of Britain's first inhabitants, descendants from the Titan Albion, brother of Atlas, like the giant Fomors, the earliest residents of Ireland. Culture-bearers from Atlantis arriving in several other parts of the world, as far away as the shores of Peru, were often described in local folk memory as "gigantic."

Chac

A rain-god, or more appropriately, the sky-god worshiped by the Mayas. They portrayed him in temple art as a bearded man with a long nose and supporting the heavens on his shoulders, like the eponymous and sacred mountain from which the island of Atlantis derived its name: Atlas. Chac sometimes appears Christ-like in wall paintings, as he bears a cross on his back. But it was actually a symbol for the four cardinal directions, defining Chac's origin at the center of the world, just as Atlantis was located between of the Old and New Worlds. Chac is perhaps identical to Bacab, because he also was four divine persons in one, each "chac" representing a particular point of the compass. They appeared in symbolic red for east, black for west, white for north, and yellow for south. These colors corresponded to the directions personified by the chacs. White seems associated with the snow and ice far above the Rio Grande River. Yellow perhaps signified the intense heat of the sun toward the Equator. If these interpretations are correct, then the Mayas possessed far wider knowledge of the world beyond their home in the Lowland Yucatan than credited by conventional archaeologists.

The West is universally regarded as a place of death (the dying sun, etc.), hence its black characterization. Red is a color often associated with Atlantis, where Plato wrote that its public and even some of its private buildings were made of red stone, or volcanic tufa. The Atlanteans themselves were said to have been red-haired. But the color more probably refers to sunrise.

Chac-Mool

A representation of the Maya rain- and sky-god in a reclining position, while holding a bowl over his navel, usually in the medium of sacred statuary. As visitors ascend the grand staircase to the Temple of the Warriors, at Chichen Itza, in Yucatan, they come face to face with the life-size statue of a chac-mool resting at the top. Nearby, inside the Pyramid of the Feathered Serpent, they climb a rising passageway that terminates at the center of the structure in a chamber containing another life-size chac-mool, extraordinary for its blue eyes. This racial anomaly, together with the bearded, Atlas-like figures carved in the walls of the shrine just above, identify the chac-mool as an Atlantean concept—and a particularly important one it is, too. The manner in which the chac-mool at the Pyramid of the Feathered Serpent is holding a bowl over its stomach and its position at the center of the building define an early mystery cult in Atlantis.

(See Navel of the World)

Chalchiuhtlicue

The Aztec goddess who changed victims of the Great Flood into fish. The same transformation appears in the deluge myths of the Babylonians and American Lakota Sioux. Chalchiuhtlicue was honored during an annual ceremony in which priests collected reeds, dried them out, then placed them inside her shrine. The reeds symbolized wisdom, as writing utensils, but also "the Place of Reeds," Aztlan, her overseas' homeland. Temple art represented Chalchiuhtlicue seated on a throne, around which men and women were shown drowning in huge whirlpools. Her name, "Our Lady of the Turquoise Skirt," refers to the feminine Atlantis, the "Daughter of Atlas," in the midst of the sea. Chalchiuhtlicue's myth is a self-evident evocation of the natural catastrophe.

(See Aztlan, Sekhet-aaru)

Chief Mountain

Located in northern Montana, Chief Mountain is especially revered by North America's Blackfoot tribes, who believe its summit alone stood above the waters of the Great Flood, which rose to drown the rest of the world in the deeply ancient past. Shamans ascend its slopes to annually commemorate the escape of a single survivor, who later became the first ancestral chief of the Blackfoot, after marrying a Star Maiden sent from the Great Spirit.

(See Nowah'wus)

Chien-Mu

Described in the *Chou-li*, an ancient Chinese book of rites, as a place where Earth and sky met at the cosmic axis. Here, time and space became irrelevant, the four seasons merged into each other, pairs of opposites were resolved, and the alternating principles of yin and yang no longer strove against each other, but grew peaceful in balanced harmony. Chien-Mu signifies the sacred center, the still-point reached in deep meditation. Its name implies that these concepts are to be associated with the Pacific Motherland of Mu, the original Navel of the World, where they were first developed and employed in reaching high levels of spiritual attainment.

(See Navel of the World)

Chikubujima

Shrine to Benten, or Benzaiten, the goddess who brought civilization to Japan in a great ship from across the sea. Chikubujima's location on the shores of Lake Biwa, or Biwa-ko, is not entirely legendary, because along its shores are found the earliest evidence for human habitation in the islands. It was here that culture-bearers from Lemuria probably first landed in Japan.

(See Benten, Lemuria, Shinobazu)

Chimu

A pre-Inca people who raised a powerful civilization, Chimor, that dominated the Peruvian coast from circa 900 A.D., until their defeat by the Incas during the late 15th century. The capital, Chan-Chan, lies just north of Trujillo, and was founded, according to Chimu historians, by Taycana-mu. He had been sent on a culture-founding mission by his superior, who ruled a kingdom in the Pacific Ocean. Another important Chimor city was Pacatna-mu, christened after an early Chimu general who became the regional governor. The so-called "Palace of the Governor" at Chan-Chan features a wall decorated with a frieze depicting a sunken city— fish swimming over the tops of contiguous pyramids. The scene memorializes the drowned civilization of Mu, from which the ancestors of the Chimu—literally, the "Children of Mu"—arrived on Peruvian shores after the catastrophe. Their Lemurian heritage likewise appears in other significant names, such as Taycana-mu, Pacatna-mu, and so on.

(See Mu)

Chintamani

Also *Cintimani*, Sanskrit for "magical stone from another world." Now at the Moscow Museum, the Chintamani is an exceptionally clear quartz crystal, once in the possession of Nicholas Roerich, a German-American Russian, prominent artist, mystic, and world-traveler of the early and mid-20th century. His paintings are still valued for their stark, though pure numinosity. Most of them are on public display at New York's Roerich Museum. Childress writes, "ancient Asian chronicles claim that a divine messenger from the heavens gave a fragment of the stone to

Emperor Tazlavoo of Atlantis. According to legend, the stone was sent from Tibet to King Solomon in Jerusalem, who split the stone and made a ring out of one piece" (*A Hitchhiker's Guide to Armageddon*, 216–217).

The Chintamani is also known in China and Japan as the "Jewel-That-Grants-All-Desires," and was believed to have originally belonged to the Makara, a dragon- or dolphin-god, living in a palace at the bottom of the sea, underscoring its Atlantean provenance.

(See Tuoai)

Chronology

There are three primary chronologies for the history of Atlantis. Plato writes that its destruction took place 11,400 years ago, although he provides no date for its foundation. The origins of Atlantean Civilization should have preceded its end by at least five centuries, in order for it to have attained the cultural heights he wrote that it enjoyed, thereby placing its beginning sometime after the turn of the 13th millennium B.C. Edgar Cayce said that Atlantis was far older, emerging about 100,000 years ago. In another 50,000 years, the Atlanteans had developed a technologically advanced civilization. The first of three major cataclysms occurred at this time, followed by another about 30,000 years ago. The final destruction took place around 10,000 B.C., roughly the same period Plato reported.

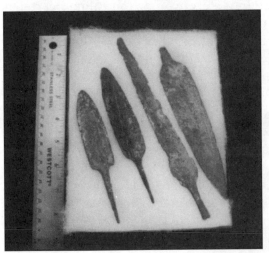

These 4,000-year-old weapons were found at Michigan's Upper Peninsula, where the Atlanteans undertook colossal mining enterprises. Photograph by Wayne May.

Most serious Atlantologists today find these time parameters unrealistic. While at least some investigators believe Cayce's "life-readings" may shed light on the story of Atlantis, they point out that persons in trance states, while capable of recalling vivid, even accurate images, enter into a timeless consciousness, just as a sleeper, when awake, may remember the clear details of a dream, but his sense of time while dreaming is totally unlike anything when he is awake. Modern man (*Homo sapiens-sapiens*) had only just evolved 100,000 years ago and was in no condition to found civilization. Plato's 11,4000-year-old date for the destruction of Atlantis is also troubling.

Anthropologists have learned much about the level of human accomplishment during the mid-12th millennium B.C., but they found not the merest hint that anything resembling a civilization existed then. As even that prominent Atlantologist, Lewis Spence, remarked as long ago as 1924, "I would suggest that no city or civilized state of Atlantis existed at the period alluded to by Plato—9600 B.C." Moreover, geologists know that the mid-ocean tropical island Plato describes would not have been possible when he wrote it existed, because the North Atlantic was, at that time, plunged into the final phase of the last Ice Age. They realize, however, that the Alleroed Interstadal was a warm phase during the Devensian glaciation in Europe's Pleistocene Ice Age, when massive, catastrophic flooding did indeed occur about the time of a literal reading of Plato's date for the destruction of Atlantis. Even so, enough of at least the general outlines of human culture and the level of material achievement during the Pleistocene reveal that the sophisticated civilization described by Plato, let alone Cayce, bore nothing in common with post-glacial society.

Researchers need to ask, "What kind of years was Plato writing about? We assume they were solar years, identical to our own calendar. But what if he was using a different calendrical system? What would that make of his date for Atlantis?" This, in fact, is the root of the problem that was solved as long ago as the early 1950s, when a German Atlantologist, Juergen Spanuth, pointed out that the Egyptian priests who relayed the Atlantis story to Solon (and almost certainly Plato himself) used a lunar, not a solar calendar. When they spoke of time it was always in terms of the cycles of the moon. Indeed, their temple in which they preserved Atlantean records was dedicated to a moon-goddess, Neith.

Recalibrating Plato's solar date into its original lunar years, a more realistic period for the destruction of Atlantis is revealed circa 1200 B.C. As soon as Atlantologists learned of the corrected time scale, they were themselves deluged by a wealth of confirming evidence that placed Atlantis squarely in the Bronze Age. Pre-Columbian traditions, Egyptology, climatology, geology, even astronomy, all combined to underscore the revised date, and thereby provided more quality arguments for the credibility of Atlantis than ever before. Moreover, Plato's own description of Atlantis belongs to an arch-typical Late Bronze Age capital. Indeed, the Classical Greek writer Apollodorus maintained the tradition that Zeus, depicted by Plato as the destroyer of Atlantis, endeavored to annihilate mankind at the end of the Bronze Age.

But the unusual ringed design of Atlantis suggests much older Neolithic origins from and upon which the city grew over thousands of years. These deeply prehistoric beginnings are far more difficult to define than the Atlantean cataclysm. Based on the known dates of megalithic sites in the British Isles and Spain, Atlantis perhaps began its rise as a Neolithic settlement more than 6,000 years ago. By the mid- to late fourth millennium B.C., it may have reached a high level of civilization.

Both Plato and Cayce mentioned more than one Atlantean deluge preceding the final disaster, and there does appear to have been at least one major upheaval before obliteration took place. Berosus, the Chaldean historian who wrote of the Great Flood from which his Babylonian ancestors came, stated it occurred on the 15th day in the month of Daisios—around June 15, 3116 B.C. This date compares almost exactly with the origin of the Maya calendar, said to have been brought to Yucatan by a white-skinned, yellow-bearded flood survivor—Kukulcan, the

Feathered Serpent—on August 10, 3110 B.C. The First Egyptian Dynasty, set up by gods and men fleeing their sacred mound sinking in the Distant West, began around 3100 B.C. So too, the earliest manifestations of arts and cities in the Cyclades Islands and Troy date to sudden arrivals from the west around 3000 B.C. Ireland's greatest megalithic site, New Grange, was built before 3100 B.C. Even work on Britain's Stonehenge began around the same time.

Such abrupt, simultaneous developments in various parts of the world, where traditions tell of founding fathers fleeing some terrible cataclysm, bespeak an Atlantean upheaval serious enough to generate mass evacuations, without utterly destroying the island. This 5,000-year-old event appears to have been associated with flood heroes among various societies—the Egyptian Thaut, the Sumerian Utnapishtim, the Babylonian Xiuthtros, the Hebrew Noah, the Greek Deucalion, the Maya Itzamna, and so on. Severe as the late fourth-millennium B.C. upheaval may have been, Atlantis survived, was rebuilt, and eventually prospered for another 1,900 years.

Being closer to us in time, the final catastrophe is provided with more precise dating information. Scribes at Medinet Habu, in Thebes, Upper Egypt, recorded the invasion of Atlantean "Sea Peoples" at the Nile Delta in 1190 B.C., eight years after the loss of their western homeland to the sea. "Day of the Dead" festivals around the world correlate with archaeo-astronomy to place the cataclysm in early November. An abundance of supporting evidence tends to confirm that Atlantis was finally destroyed on or about November 3, 1198 B.C.

Chumael-Ah-Canule

Described as "the First after the Flood," in *The History of Zodzil*—a 16th-century collection of Maya oral traditions heard firsthand by Juan Darreygosa—he escaped the deluge that engulfed his island kingdom in the Atlantic Ocean, arriving first at the island of Cozumel, off the Yucatan coast. Proceeding to the Mexican mainland, Chumael-Ah-Canule and his immigrating fellow country-men built Chichen Itza, or "Mouth of of the Well of Itza," and 149 other cities, including Mayapan, Izamel, Uxmal, and Ake. His account suggests that not only these ceremonial centers, but Mesoamerican civilization itself was founded by Atlantean culture-bearers.

Cichol Gricenchos

King of the Fomorach, the earliest Atlantean inhabitants of Ireland. He opposed the arrival of a later Atlantean settlers, the "Family of Partholon," survivors of the 2100 B.C. cataclysm that wracked Atlantis.

(See Fomorach)

The Codex Chimal-Popoca

An Aztec version of the Great Flood from which their ancestors arrived on the eastern shores of Mexico. It reports, in part, "There suddenly arose mountains the color of fire. The sky drew near to the Earth, and in the space of a day, all was downed." *The Codex Chimal-Popoca* reads almost identically to Plato's *Timaeus* and *Kritias* dialogues, where he states that Atlantis was destroyed "in a single day and night."

Collins, Andrew

British author of *Gateway to Atlantis*, in which he identifies the lost civilization with Cuba. Five years after its release in 1997, mineral prospectors probing the waters off the island's northwest coast claimed to have picked up sonar images of what appeared to be a sunken city more than 2,000 feet beneath the surface.

Coronis

An Atlantis, one of seven daughters born to Atlas and the ocean-nymph Aethra. Coronis was the mother of Aesculapius by the god of healing, Apollo, after whom the modern word "scalpel" is derived. The Greeks revered Aesculapius as the founder of modern medicine. He in turn fathered two sons, Machaon and Podaliris, who were the earliest physicians after their father, and spread his scientific principles throughout the world. His only daughter, Hygeia, was the goddess of health.

This lineage demonstrates an important theme common to all the daughters of Atlas; namely, that their offspring were the first in their fields of high endeavor and the progenitors of civilization. Through poetic metaphor, these founding-father myths preserve national memories of culture-bearers who escaped the destruction of Atlantis to reestablish civilization in new lands. As such, the story of Coronis reminded the Greeks that they received the tenets of their medical science from an Atlantean immigrant.

Cosmas

A sixth-century Alexandrian monk who endeavored to prevent his fellow Christian theologians from anathematizing Plato's account of Atlantis by drawing parallels between the Atlantean catastrophe and the biblical flood. Cosmas failed, and anything about the sunken city was condemned as "demonically inspired," along with the rest of classical civilization.

Coxcoxtic

He and his wife, Xochiquetzal, were sole survivors in one of several Aztec versions of the Great Flood. During the previous era in which they lived, humanity spoke the same language. But their offspring in post-diluvial times received the gift of speech from a variety of birds. The children of Coxcoxtic and Xochiquetzal grew up speaking many different tongues. Later, they left their parents to wander over the face of the Earth, spreading new languages around the world. Their myth refers to the cultural unity of Atlantean times destroyed by a natural catastrophe, and scattered around the globe.

(See Xochiquetzal)

Coyolxauqui

Aztec version of the earlier Maya Ixchel, the White Lady, who brought civilization to Middle America from a lost kingdom in the Atlantic Ocean after a great flood.

(See Ixchel)

Crannog

Also known as "the ruined city of Kenfig," Crannog is familiar in both Irish and Scottish traditions as a sunken city. "Og" is a derivative of the Atlantean catastrophe in the British Isles, Greece, and South America.

(See Ogma, Ogriae)

Crow Deluge Story

The Crow Indians tell that the Great Spirit, angry with the sins of the world, destroyed all mankind with a great flood. After the cataclysm, he created another humanity by scooping up a handful of dust. Blowing upon it, the first black birds and a new race of people sprang into existence together. When he asked them what they wished to be called, they chose the name "Crow" after the birds that had appeared with them. The Crow, like virtually all Native Americans, trace their origins back to a catastrophic deluge. Similar to Plato's account of Atlantis, the Crow flood story relates that a people were destroyed by the supreme being for their moral decay.

Crystal Skull

The life-size representation of a female human skull carved from a single piece of quartz crystal. Its earliest documented history began in 1936, when the Crystal Skull was obtained in Mexico from an unknown source by a British buyer, and put up for public auction in London eight years later, when it was purchased by a travel author, F.A. Mitchell-Hedges. After his death in the following decade, it passed to his adopted daughter, Anna, in Kitchener, Ontario, Canada, where it remains at this writing.

Both she and her father claimed the Crystal Skull was made in Atlantis, although without foundation. Even so, as a Mesoamerican symbol, it is associated with Ixchel, a transparently Atlantean figure worshiped by the Maya as the goddess of healing and psychic power who arrived on the shores of Yucatan as a flood-survivor. Her later Aztec version as Coyolxauqui was accompanied by a crystal skull, emblematic of the moon and her identification as a lunar deity.

The Mitchell-Hedges Crystal Skull demonstrates an extraordinarily high level of craftsmanship, perhaps even a technology superior not only to that of the ancient Mexicans, but to our own, as well. Whether or not it is an authentic Atlantean artifact, it was probably used originally in an oracular function on behalf of Ixchel to predict the future or offer intuitive medical advice for her Maya or Aztec clients.

(See Ixchel)

Plaster cast of the Crystal Skull, created during a forensic reconstruction of the actual cranial remains after which the jeweled masterpiece was modeled.

Cuchavira

A goddess who led survivors from the watery destruction of their former realm in the Atlantic Ocean to the shores of Colombia, where they intermarried with native peoples to engender the Muysca Indians.

(See Bochica)

Dardanus

The offspring of Electra, in other words, a son of Atlantis; his mother was an "Atlantis," a daughter of Atlas, his grandfather. As Virgil wrote in *The Aeneid* (Book VIII, 135–138), "Dardanus, who was first father to our city, Ilium, and made her strong, was, as the Greeks relate, sprung from Electra, the daughter of Atlas." She warned Dardanus of a coming deluge, and he fled to the northwest coast of Asia Minor. There he became the monarch of a new kingdom, Troy. The straits controlled by the Trojans were named after him, and are still known as the Dardanelles. The Trojans sometimes referred to themselves as "Dardanians" to emphasize descent from their Atlantean forefather. He gave them the Palladium, a sacred stone from Atlantis, as the centerpiece of their religion they revered until it was seized by victorious Greeks in the Trojan War.

The historical myth of Dardanus signifies the arrival in Troy of culture-bearers from Atlantis following a major, but not final natural catastrophe 5,000 years ago, which coincides with the earliest date or event-horizon archaeologists find at Ilios, the Trojan capital.

Day of the Dead

A relationship between early November and a day of the dead is not only worldwide but very ancient. The "Days of Death" celebrated in early November were among the most important Aztec festivals, and appear to have dated to Maya or even Olmec times, in the 13th century B.C. The Aztecs began their ceremonies with the heliacal rising of the Pleiades. They began at dawn over several days until the constellation was completely obscured by the sun. Their Atemoztli, or "Falling Waters," occurred every November 16, when the end of the Fourth Sun or Age, brought about by a world flood, was commemorated.

The Atlantean identity of this calendar festival is affirmed by the god who presided over it, Tlaloc, the Maya Chac, portrayed in temple art as a bearded man bearing the cross of the sky on his shoulders, the Mesoamerican Atlas. More than a philological correspondence existed between the Aztec Atemoztli and Atemet. The Egyptian goddess, Hathor, in her guise as Queen of the Sea, was depicted in sacred art wearing a crown in the image of a fish. Her role in the Great Deluge is described in her own entry.

The Mayas throughout Yucatan and Peten hung small packets of cake on the branches of the holy Ceibra, especially where the tree was found standing among clearings in the forest or at crossroads. These little sacrifices were made of the finest corn available, and intended for the spirits of the dead, as indicated by their name, *hanal pixan*, or "the food of the souls." For the Mayas, the Ceibra Tree was a living memorial of the Great Flood from which their ancestors survived by sailing to Yucatan. The hanal pixan decorated this most sacred tree for the first three days of each November. Meanwhile, in the High Andes of Peru and Bolivia, the Incas performed the Ayamarca, or "carrying the corpse" ceremony every November 2.

The appearance of the Pleiades at that time simultaneously signaled the beginning of Hawaii's most important celebration, the annual Makahiki festival. In the Kona district on the Big Island, it honored the arrival of Lono at Kealakekua. He was a white-skinned, fair-haired "god" who recently escaped a catastrophic deluge. Lono was associated with all manner of cataclysmic celestial events, together with devastating earthquakes and floods. At the western end of the Pacific, celebrants still participate in the Loi Krathong the night of the full moon by launching candle-illuminated model boats into the Gulf of Thailand. Designed to honor the sea-goddess, the lotus-shaped little vessels made of banana leaves bear flowers, incense and a coin to the spirits of their ancestors who perished in the Great Flood. The Loi Krathong, depending on the appearance of the full moon, may occur from November 2–12.

The Japanese have traditionally celebrated Bon, the Feast of the Dead, since prehistoric times in a manner virtually identical to the Loi Krathong. They set adrift fleets of burning lanterns to guide ancestral spirits across the sea. Ceremonies last for several consecutive nights, and include Bon-Odori—hypnotic outdoor dancing, often in cemeteries. Bon was partially appropriated by Buddhism in its early struggle with native Shinto traditionalists, when the annual date of its celebration was probably shifted to the middle of the seventh lunar month, around August 14. A similar "day of the dead" festival is still conducted on the island of Taiwan, and, until the Communist revolution, in China, where it was known as the Feast of Lanterns. Another Japanese ceremony of the dead does indeed take place from the last week of October to the first days of November. This is the Tsunokiri, or ritual "Antler-Cutting" at the Kasuga Taisha shrine, near Nara. The sacred bucks are lassoed by a priest, who carefully saws off their antlers; they signify life, due to their regenerating velvet. Deer also symbolize the sun, so cutting their antlers implies the sun's loss of power—darkness.

The Assyrians conducted elaborate rituals on behalf of the dead during Arahsamna, their month that included the end of October and the beginning of November. It was then, they believed, that the sun-god and the god of the Pleiades entered the land of the dead to rule.

The ancient Persian New Year began after November 1, and was known as Mordad, a month sacred to the Angel of Death. Mordad derived from the earlier Marduk of the Babylonians. They revered him as "the Lord of the Deep," who caused the Great Flood, and November belonged to him. It is reported in the Old Testament (Genesis, Chapters 7 and 8) that the World Deluge began on the 17th day of the second month, concluding on the 27th day of the second month the following year. In the ancient Hebrew calendar, the Second Month was known as Cheshvan, and equivalent to the end of our October and the start of November. Both the 17th and 27th days occur in early November. Non-biblical Jewish tradition relates that Noah regarded the appearance of the Pleiades at dawn—identically to the Aztec Atemoztli cited previously—of the 17th of Cheshvan, as an omen signifying the onset of the flood.

The Roman Catholic "All Souls' Day" is set aside for special prayers on behalf of the dead, and takes place every November 2. It was officially adopted in 998 by Odilo, the Abbot of Cluny. He supposedly decided to institute All Souls' Day after having learned about an island where the lamentations of the dead could still be heard. The inclusion of this island is a discernable mythic reference to Atlantis. The Egyptian version of the Deluge happened during Aethyr, a name associated with the Greek Alkyone, one of the Pleiades, because the month was regarded in the Nile Valley as "the shining season of the Pleiades." Aethyr, like the Assyrian Arashamna, corresponded to late October/early November. The name has several revealing connotations in Egyptian myth, proving its significance over a long period of time. The story of Osiris tells of the man-god who, through the mysteries of Isis, his wife, achieved new life. He was locked inside a coffin that was thrown into the sea on the 17th day of Aethyr, our November 2.

It was henceforth known as a day of death and rebirth. Aethyr is a variant of Hathor. The sun-god, angry with mankind, commanded Hathor to punish Earth's inhabitants. Her obedient onslaught was catastrophic, so much so, the other gods, fearing all humanity would perish, unloosed a worldwide deluge of beer. Drinking it up, she became too intoxicated to complete her genocidal task. Her great festival in the name of this event was among the most popular public occasions throughout the Nile Valley, and held for several days around November 1. She was herself sometimes depicted in sacred art as a cow walking away from a funeral mountain. The earliest name by which she was known appears to have been At-Hor, or At-Hr, "Mountain of Horus," an apparent philological relation with things Atlantean. Her funeral mountain is similarly suggestive of death-dealing Mount Atlas and November associations with days of the dead. The lioness-headed goddess, Sekhmet, was used by the Egyptians to describe the fiery comet that brought about the destruction of Atlantis. She was actually Hathor in her vengeful guise. Both deities were aspects of the same goddess.

The Pleiades are associated with Hathor, too. Writing about the worldwide day of the dead festivals in the 19th century, R.G. Haliburton, wondered:

> It is now, as was formerly, observed at or near the beginning of November by the Peruvians, the Hindoos, the Pacific Islanders, the people of the Tonga Islands, the Australians, the ancient Persians, the ancient Egyptians, and the northern nations of Europe, and continued for three days among the Japanese and the ancient Romans. This startling fact at once drew my attention to the question, How was this uniformity in the time of observance preserved, not only in far distant quarters of the globe, but also through that vast lapse of time since the Peruvian and the Indo-European first inherited this primeval festival from a common source?

Haliburton's question is answered by internal evidence of the festivals themselves. Together they describe in common a natural cataclysm that killed huge numbers of their ancestors. Some of them survived to replant civilization in other lands. The only event that measures up to this universal Festival of the Dead is the destruction of Atlantis. Indeed, astronomy combines with historical myth to provide the precise day of the catastrophe. Comet Encke's autumnal meteor shower very closely, if not exactly corresponds to such festivals. Most of them were and are concentrated in the first days of November, just when the Taurid meteor stream in the wake of Comet Encke, associated with the early 12th-century destruction of Atlantis, reaches its intensity.

de Acosta, José

A 16th-century Spanish missionary. After learning numerous oral traditions firsthand from native Mexicans, he was convinced that their rich body of Mesoamerican myth preserved the unmistakable folk memory of culture-bearers from Atlantis.

The mountain city of Peru's Machu Picchu, where the Chosen Women preserved the history of Atlantis.

Restoration of the Aztec Calendar Stone featuring the central figure of Aton-at-i-uh surrounded by squared scenes of four global catastrophes.

One of two 10-foot tall statues at Tiahuanaco, in the Bolivian Andes, bears a marked resemblance to Easter Island's moai, suggesting both cultures were influenced by intermediaries from Mu.

Tiahuanaco's Gateway of the Sun. Ancient ceremonial gates found from Bolivia, across the Pacific, to Japan trace back to the lost civilization of Mu.

Cuzco's modern mural to the glory of Andean Civilization, with its Atlantean founder, Viracocha, at the center. *Cuzco* means "navel" in Quechua, the Inca language, and refers to the Atlantean mystery cult, "Navel of the World."

Monolith on the shore of Lanzarote, in the Canary Islands, incised with rings suggesting the concentric design of nearby Atlantis.

Ornately sculpted monoliths depicting heroes of the Greater and Lesser Arrivals from Atlantis dominate the main plaza of Copan, the Mayas' ceremonial city in Honduras.

A kiva at Bandalier, New Mexico, where tribal peoples used this ritual meditation chamber to commemorate the survival of their ancestors from the Great Flood.

Tiahuanaco, in the Bolivian Andes, "built after the Flood."

Copan's Rosalila Pyramid is decorated with stylistic representations of Kukulcan, the Mayas' "Feathered Serpent," with a blond mustache.

Chac, the Maya version of Atlas, holds a bowl from which a pair of bird heads pointing in opposite directions define his position at the center of the world.

At-otarho, a mythic figure among the North American Iroquois, is similar to Medusa, one of the Greek Gorgons associated with Atlantis.

Notice the precisely placed and cut, 100-ton blocks of Peru's Sacsahuaman.

A Chac-Mool atop the Mayas' Temple of the Warriors, Chichen Itza, Yucatan.

A 17th-century statue of Mu Kung, the mythic ruler of a Pacific Ocean paradise from which he derived his name before the island was over-whelmed by rising seas.

Spain's Lady of Elche, the terra-cotta representation of a royal woman from the Atlantean kingdom of Gadeiros (Seville Archaeological Museum).

Ceremonial pyramid at Guatemala's Tikal, built by the Mayas in commemoration of the Atlantean "Feathered Serpent" culture-bearer.

Facade of Yucatan's "Palace of the Governor," Uxmal, dedicated to Chac, the Maya version of Atlas.

The Incas' Coricancha, or "Enclosure of Gold," was dedicated to the spiritual concepts brought to Peru by Viracocha, a red-haired flood survivor from the destruction of his oceanic homeland.

The massive stairway fronting Uxmal's Pyramid of the Magician.

de Carli, G.R.

Prominent, late 18th-century French scholar who went public with his belief in a historical Atlantis.

(See de Gisancourt)

de Gisancourt, L.C. Cadet

A pioneering chemist, who joined fellow scholar G.R. de Carli and geographer Christophe Cellarius during 1787 in declaring that the Atlantis described by Plato was located on an Atlantic island.

Delphi

The foremost oracle of the ancient Old World, perched on Mount Parnassus above the Gulf of Corinth, in Greece. It was governed by a *hoisioi*, or "college" of priests required to trace their family lineage to Deucalion before taking office, because he was believed to have brought the principles of divination to Delphi from a former Golden Age overwhelmed by the Deluge. Mount Parnassus itself was consecrated to Poseidon, the sea-god of Atlantis. Delphi's Omphalos stone characterized it as "the Navel of the World," after the Atlantean mystery cult of the same name. Practioners from Atlantis appear to have arrived on the shores of the Gulf of Corinth, where they reestablished the antediluvian spiritual center no later than the late third millennium B.C.

(See The Deluge, Deucalion, Navel of the World)

The Delphic oracle in Greece was presided over by priests directly descended from survivors of the Atlantean flood.

The Deluge

Known around the world, this virtually universal human tradition is mankind's outstanding myth. Modern researchers are still astounded by the general uniformity of its story, even of many details held in common by peoples separated by often great geographical barriers and many centuries. These traditions describe two or three Atlantean catastrophes, while sometimes confusing elements of them all. For example, the Greeks knew of the Ogygian flood and a later disaster associated with Deucalion. Plato's account of Atlantis appears separate from both, but may be identical with Deucalion's deluge. Edgar Cayce, too, spoke of three Atlantean floods.

The Egyptians recorded four separate events, the earliest being the sinking of a great ceremonial "mound" from which gods and men sailed to the Nile Delta, where they founded dynastic civilization. The second cataclysm took place when Ra, the sun-god, ordered Hathor to exterminate mankind, but was ultimately prevented by a flood of beer. A third appears in the *Story of the Shipwrecked Sailor*, a piece of mythic fiction investigators believe was based on real circumstances. The final Egyptian version was recorded by XX Dynasty scribes, who wrote that the island kingdom of their enemies, the "Sea Peoples," perished at sea. All four trade details among themselves, blurring any sharp distinctions there may have been at one time.

Conservative Atlantologists admit to four different geologic upheavals. The first may have comprised a series of major earthquakes and floodings that took place at the end of the 4th millennium B.C., followed around 2100 B.C. by another natural disaster. A penultimate cataclysm struck in the late 17th century B.C., when Atlantis was damaged but swiftly rebuilt, despite the partial emigration of its population. The final catastrophe was far more abrupt, lasting, in Plato's words, only "a day and a night." It occurred in early November, 1198 B.C., according to contemporary temple records at the "Victory Temple" of Medinet Habu, in West Thebes, Upper Egypt.

Desana Flood Story

A remote Amazonian people, they still recall the ancient tribal memory of a time when the sun-god punished their sinful ancestors. "Everything caught fire" in a world-conflagration that was soon after extinguished by a universal flood.

Deucalion

In Greek myth, he and his wife, Pyrrha, were the only survivors of a great deluge which otherwise exterminated all mankind. The human race is descended from this pair, a way of expressing in myth the Atlantean heritage of every Greek born thereafter, because Deucalion's uncle was none other than Atlas himself.

The Deucalion Flood belongs to a major, but not final geologic upheaval in Atlantis circa 3,700 years before present, during which some survivors arrived as culture-bearers in the Eastern Mediterranean. The Sumerian scholar Neil Zimmerer, likewise associated the coming of Deucalion with a natural catastrophe around 1700 B.C. not unrelated to Thera, a volcanic island in the Aegean Sea whose eruption was part of a third Atlantean destruction.

Deucalion's "ark" was said to have come to rest on Mount Parnassus, at the Gulf of Corinth, where the most important religious center of the Classical World, Delphi, was instituted. In other words, the Delphic Mysteries were imported from Atlantis.

(See Delphi)

Diaprepes

Listed by Plato in *Kritias* as an Atlantean king. Diaprepes means "The Brightly Shining One," and for that reason is associated with a great volcanic mountain in the Canary Islands, Tenerife's Mt. Teide.

Dilmun

Described in the Sumerian *Epic of Gilgamesh* as the antediluvian homeland of civilization lost after the Great Flood. Dilmun is possibly a Sumerian version of "Mu."

(See Mu, Ziusudra)

Dimlahamid

The Canadian Atlantis.
(See Dzilke)

Di-Mu

The Chinese Earth Mother who gave life to all things at the beginning of time. The Pacific civilization where mankind supposedly originated was likewise known as "Mu, the Motherland," according to James Churchward.

(See Mu)

Diodorus Siculus

Greek geographer born in Agryrium, Sicily, around 50 B.C., who wrote a world history of 40 books divided into three parts. Although widely read for centuries, only the first five volumes survived the collapse of classical civilization.

Book I features a report he learned while traveling through Mauretania, modern Morocco-Algeria, when that kingdom was being renovated by the scholarly king, Juba II. A Romanized Numidian prince, Juba preserved a Carthaginian account of Atlantis Diodorus included in his history.

It told of an army of women warriors from the Caucasus Mountains of Central Asia led by Queen Merine. Her 30,000 infantry and 20,000 cavalry marched across Libya to the Atlantic shores of Mauretania, from which they launched an invasion of Atlantis. After razing its walls, the city fell, and was renamed after its Amazonian ruler, which means, "Sea Queen." She concluded a friendship treaty with the vanquished Atlanteans, even going so far as to repair damages caused during the war. In the midst of this constructive peace, Atlantis was attacked by another sea people, the Gorgons. Although Atlanto-Amazonian resistance was at first successful, the enemy returned in greater numbers, effected a landing, and soundly defeated the combined forces of Queen Merine. She and her followers were not only driven into the sea, but pursued back to Mauretania. There, a ferocious battle took place in which both sides suffered heavy losses. The Gorgons returned to Atlantis, while the Queen buried her dead in three, colossal mounds, then led her bloodied troops across Libya toward Egypt, where her friend, Pharaoh Horus, rebuilt the Amazon army.

Diodorus's account appears to describe Atlantis after early geologic upheavals forced the evacuation of many of its inhabitants, leaving the city under-defended. Queen Merine tried to take advantage of Atlantean weakness, but was soon routed by other Atlanteans (Gorgons) from neighboring islands. These events appear to have taken place during the late fourth or early third millennium B.C., as implied by Pharaoh "Horus," perhaps King Hor-aha, the first monarch of Dynastic Egypt, who reigned before 3000 B.C.

Dionysus of Mitylene

Also known as Dionysus of Miletus, or Skytobrachion, for his prosthetic leather arm, he wrote "A Voyage to Atlantis" around 550 B.C., predating not only Plato, but even Solon's account of the sunken kingdom. Relying on pre-classical sources, he reported that, "From its deep-rooted base, the Phlegyan isle stern Poseidon shook and plunged beneath the waves its impious inhabitants." The volcanic island of Atlantis is suggested in the "fiery," or "Phlegyan," isle destroyed by the sea-god. This is all that survives from a lengthy discussion of Atlantis in the lost *Argonautica*, mentioned 400 years later by the Greek geographer Diodorus Siculus as one of his major sources for information about the ancient history of North Africa.

As reported in the December 15, 1968 *Paris Jour*, a complete or, at any rate, more extensive copy of his manuscript was found among the personal papers of historical writer, Pierre Benoit. Tragically, it was lost between the borrowers and restorers who made use of this valuable piece of source material after Benoit's death.

(See Benoit)

Donnelly, Ignatius

Born in Moyamensing, a suburb of Philadelphia, Pennsylvania, in 1831, Ignatius Donnelly became a young lawyer before moving with his new wife to the wilds of Minnesota, near Saint Paul. There he helped found Nininger City, named after its chief benefactor, William Nininger, but the project collapsed with the onset of national economic troubles. A born orator, Donnelly turned his writing and organizational skills to politics in a steady rise from state senator, congressman, lieutenant governor, and acting governor. A futuristic reformer, he owed no political allegiances, but regarded politics only as a means to promote his ideals, which were often far in advance of his time, including female suffrage. He was the first statesman to design and implement programs for reforestation and protection of the natural environment.

Despite his busy life as a politician, Donnelly was a voracious reader, mostly of history, particularly ancient history. Sometime before the Civil War, his sources of information opened into a veritable cornucopia of materials when he was sent to Washington, D.C., on state business. There he had access to the National Archives, which then housed the largest library in the United States, if not the world. Donnelly immersed himself in its shelves for several months, delegating political authority to others, while he virtually lived among stacks of books. His study concentrated on a question that had fascinated him since youth: Where and how had civilization arisen? Although his understanding of the ancient world broadened and deepened at the National Archives, the answer seemed just as elusive as ever.

Not long before he was scheduled to return to Minnesota, he stumbled on Plato's account of Atlantis in two dialogues, *Timaeus* and *Kritias*. The story struck Donnelly with all the impact of a major revelation. It seemed to him the missing piece of a colossal puzzle that instantly transformed the enigma into a vast, clear panorama of the deep past. The weight of evidence convinced him that Atlantis was not only a real place, but the original fountainhead of civilization.

Bronze bust of Ignatius Donnelly, the founder of Atlantology, at the state capitol of Minnesota, St. Paul..

For the next 20 years, Donnelly labored to learn everything he could about the drowned kingdom, even at the expense of his political career. Only in the early 1880s did he feel sufficiently confident of his research to organize it into a book, his first. With no contacts in the publishing industry and in threadbare financial straits, he entrained alone for New York City, and headed for the largest book producer he could find, Harper. It was his first roll of the dice, but it immediately paid off. His manuscript, *Atlantis: The Antediluvian World*, was immediately accepted and released in 1882.

Before the turn of the 20th century, it went through more than 23 printings, selling in excess of 20,000 copies, a best seller even by today's standards. The book has been in publication ever since and translated into at least a dozen languages. It won international renown for Donnelly, even a personal letter from the British Prime Minister, William Gladstone, who was so enthusiastic about prospects for discovering Atlantis, he proposed a government-sponsored expedition in search of the lost civilization.

Ragnarok: The Age of Fire and Gravel, was the author's sequel, but by the time of its release in 1883, his critics in the scientific community began marshalling bitter criticism against Donnelly, a non-degreed intruder into their academic feifdoms. They intimidated him with their high-handed skepticism, and he published no more books about Atlantis. He wrote social novels, and returned to politics as a populist leader. Ignatius Donnelly died at the home of a friend, just as the bells of New Years Day, 1901, the first moment of a new century, were chiming in Saint Paul.

(see *Atlantis: The Antediluvian World*)

Dooy

The light-skinned, red-haired forefather of the Nages, a New Guinean tribe residing in the highlands of Flores. He was the only man to survive the Great Flood that drowned his distant kingdom. Arriving in a large boat, he had many wives among the native women. They presented him with a large number of children, who became the Nages. When he died peacefully in extreme old age, Dooy's body was laid to rest under a stone platform at the center of a public square in the tribal capital of Boa Wai. His grave is the focal point of an annual harvest festival still celebrated by the Nages. During the ceremonies, a tribal chief wears headgear fashioned to resemble a golden, seven-masted ship, a model of the same vessel in which Dooy escaped the inundation of his Pacific island kingdom.

(See Mu)

Doyle, Sir Arthur Conan

Famed British author of the Sherlock Holmes mysteries wrote about Atlantis in *The Maracot Deep* for a 1928 serialization by *The Saturday Evening Post*, subsequently published in book form.

Dwarka

A magnificent city built and governed by Krishna, a human manifestation of the god Vishnu. Although sometimes thought to have been located on a large island off India's northwest coast, Dwarka's actual position was uncertain.

Like Plato's Atlantis, it was encircled by high, powerfully built walls similarly sheeted with gold, silver, and brass set in precious stones guarding monumental buildings and organized into spacious gardens during a golden age. This period came to an abrupt end with the dawning of the Age of Kali, the cosmic destroyer, in 3102 B.C., according to the *Vishnu Purana*. It tells tells how "the ocean rose and submerged the whole of Dwarka."

The late fourth-millennium B.C. date coincides with the first Atlantean cataclysm, which inaugurated cultural beginnings in South America (the Salavarry Period), Mexico (with the simultaneous institution of the Maya calendar), the start of dynastic civilization in Egypt, the foundation of Troy, and so on. Krishna's semi-divine origins parallel those of Atlas, the first king of Atlantis, the son of Poseidon the sea-god, by Kleito, a mortal woman.

Dzilke

Also known as Dimlahamid, the story of Dzilke is familiar to every native tribe across Canada. Among the most detailed versions are preserved by the We'suwet'en and Gitksan in northern British Columbia. They and other Indian peoples claim descent from a lost race of civilizers, who built a great city from which they ruled over much of the world in the very distant past. For many generations, the inhabitants of Dzilke prospered and spread their high spirituality to the far corners of the Earth. In time, however, they yielded to selfish corruption and engaged in unjust wars. Offended by the degeneracy of this once-valiant people, the gods punished Dzilke with killer earthquakes. The splendid "Street of the Chiefs" tumbled into ruin, as the ocean rose in a mighty swell to overwhelm the city and most of its residents. A few survivors arrived first at Vancouver Island, where they sired the various Canadian tribes. Researcher Terry Glavin, relying on native sources, estimated that Dzilke perished around 3,500 years ago, the same Bronze Age setting for the destruction of Mu around 1500 B.C. and Atlantis, 300 years later.

Ea

In Sumerian mythology, he was the Lord of the Waters, the sea-god who presented the secrets of a high civilization to the early inhabitants of Mesopotamia following a great flood. The Babylonians knew him as Oannes. Ea's Atlantean identity is confirmed by his portrayal on a cylinder seal in which he bids farewell to a central, Atlas-like figure, probably Enlil.

In the Babylonian version of the Great Deluge, Ea warns Utnapishtim, the flood hero, by telling him, "Oh, reed hut, reed hut! Oh, wall, wall! Oh, reed hut, listen!"

In the North American Pima deluge story, the flood hero survived by enclosing himself in a reed tube. The Navajo version recounts that the survivors made their escape through a giant reed. Implications of these folk memories on behalf of the Atlantean catastrophe are unmistakable.

Ehecatl

In the Aztec calendar, the second "Sun," or World Age, was terminated by a global disaster, 4-Ehecatl, or "Windstorm," possibly a characterization of air blasts caused by meteors exploding before they could impact the Earth. Ehecatl is the most overtly Atlantean version of the Feathered Serpent, because he was portrayed in sacred art as a man supporting the sky on his shoulders, like Atlas. Temples dedicated to Ehecatl, such as his structure at the very center of Tenochtitlan, the Aztec capital, were invariably composed of circular walls, often in red, white, and black stones or

A shrine to Ehecatl, the Aztec Atlas, features five tiers, incorpoorating the Sacred Numeral of Atlantis (Mexico City subway).

paint—the same configuration and colors Plato said typified Atlantean building styles.

Ekadzati

The brilliant Queen of Shambhala, in ancient, pre-Buddhist Tibet, where she and her people were descendants of immigrants from Lemuria. According to chronologer Neil Zimmerer, they wanted to return after the first of several natural disasters failed to destroy their Pacific homeland, but she eventually convinced them that Lemuria was doomed.

(See Lemuria)

Elasippos

The Atlantean king of what is now Portugal. Lisbon's Castel de San Jorge was built atop a fortified city the Romans took from its Celtic defenders. Before

View of Lisbon from the hill-top Castle of Saint George, a late medieval fortification built over the former Atlantean city of Elasippos, from which the Portuguese capitol derived its name.

its Lusitanian occupation, it served as a protected trading center with the Phoenicians. They called it *Alis Ubo*, or "Calm Roadstead," a reference to its felicitous harbor. Lisbon's Roman designation, Felicita Julia, carried a similar implication. But its original name was Olisipo ("Walled Town"), which bears a striking resemblance to the Atlantean *Elasippos* (in *Geographical Sketches*, by Strabo the Greek historian, circa 20 B.C.). The descent from Elasippos to Olisipo to Lisboa (Lisbon) is apparent.

Electra

An Atlantis, the mother of Dardanus, founder of Trojan civilization. The myth is in common with those of her sisters, the Pleiades, in that they were mothers of culture-creators, who restarted civilization after the Great Flood. Interestingly, "Electra" means "amber," a medium for ornamentation much prized in the ancient world, but available from only two major sources: the shores of the Baltic Sea, largely from what is now Lithuania, and the Atlantic islands of the Azores, Madeiras, and Canaries. Because Atlas has never been associated with the north, Electra's amber name and the Atlantic source for the mineral combine to reaffirm her Atlantean provenance.

(see Dardanus)

Ele'na

"Land of the Star (or Gift)," one of three versions of J.R.R. Tolkien's Atlantis. (See Numinor)

Elephants

According to the *Kritias*, there were "numerous elephants" on the island of Atlantis. Later, when describing the palace of the king, Plato writes that the entire ceiling of the structure's meeting hall was made of sculpted ivory. His brief but important mention of the creature simultaneously establishes the veracity of his narrative and confirms the near-Atlantic location of the sunken kingdom. A 1967 issue of *Science* magazine reported the discovery of elephant teeth from the Atlantic Continental Shelf running 200 to 300 miles off the Portuguese coast.

Multiple specimens were recovered from at least 40 different underwater sites along the Azore-Gibraltar Ridge, sometimes at depths of only 360 feet. The tusks were taken from submerged shorelines, peat deposits, sandbanks caused by surface waves crashing against ancient, long submerged beach-lines and depressions which formerly contained freshwater lagoons. These features defined the area as formerly dry land standing above sea level. The *Science* writer concluded, "Evidently, elephants and other large mammals ranged this region during the glacial stage of low sea level at least 25,000 years ago."

Moreover, African elephants are known to have inhabited the northwestern coastal areas of present-day Morocco, fronting the position of Atlantis, and at the junction of a vanished land bridge leading out into the ocean, as late as the 12th century B.C., if not more recently. Homer, too, wrote that the Atlanteans worked in great quantities of ivory, fashioning ornately carved ceilings from this precious medium. The presence of a native population of elephants on the island of Atlantis would have been a ready source for the material.

These two points in the *Kritias*—the existence of elephants in Atlantis and the Atlanteans' generous use of ivory—form internal evidence for herds of such animals which have been additionally confirmed by deep-sea finds. Unless he read it in an authentic document describing Atlantis, Plato could never have guessed that elephants once inhabited an area of the world presently covered by the ocean, hundreds of miles from the nearest landfall.

Elianus

A second-century Greek naturalist, who recounted in Book XV of his *Historia Naturalis* that the rulers of Atlantis dressed to show their origins from the sea-god Poseidon. Like all other works by Elianus lost with the fall of classical civilization, *Historia Naturalis* survives only in quoted fragments.

El-Khadir

In Muslim legends, a pre-Islamic figure referred to as the "Old Man of the Sea," a survivor of the Great Flood. Edgerton Sykes wrote that El-Khadir was previously known as Hasisatra, a derivation of the Sumerian deluge hero.

(See Xiuthros)

Elmeur

According to Edgar Cayce, an Atlantean prince who lived at a time when the Law of One cult was being formed. "Elmeur" suggests a phonetic variant of *Evenor*, an early Atlantean mentioned in Plato's account, *Kritias*.

Elohi-Mona

Cherokee oral tradition tells of a group of five Atlantic islands known collectively as Elohi-Mona, from which their sinful ancestors arrived on the shores of North America following a world-class conflagration eventually extinguished by the Great Flood.

In Edgar Cayce's version of Atlantis, he likewise spoke of five islands lost during the second Atlantean catastrophe. The number of islands may have served at least partially as the basis for Plato's statement in the *Kritias* that 5 was a sacred numeral revered in Atlantis.

Elohi-Mona is remarkably similar to *Elohim*, or "gods," from the singular *eloh*, found in the Old Testament. The Cherokee *Elohi-Mona* and Hebrew *Elohim* appear to have derived from a common source in Atlantis.

(See Atali, Cayce)

Endora

An Atlantis, one of seven Hyades by the sea-goddess Aethra. These daughters of Atlas are best understood as names for cities or territories directly controlled by Atlantis. Endora is the name of a particular place in the Atlantean sphere of influence, although it can no longer be associated with any known location. When their myth tells us that the Hyades and Pleiades were transformed into stars and constellations, we are being informed by way of poetic metaphor that they died, but their spirits live in heaven. As such, they enshrine the memory of the Atlantis Empire and its various cities and provinces, from which survivors arrived in new lands, just as the Hyades' and Pleiades' offspring escape a Great Flood to found new kingdoms.

Enigorio and Enigohatgea

Divine twins in the Iroquois creation story, brothers of a virgin birth, they were survivors in North America after all other life had been wiped out by a world-wide deluge. The flood was swallowed by a Great Frog, which Enigorio killed to release its waters, creating peaceful lakes and rivers. In the Huron version, the brothers are known as Tsentsa and Tawiscara. According to Plato, the first rulers of Atlantis were likewise divine twins.

Enki

In Sumerian myth, a sea-god who traveled on a worldwide mission to civilize mankind in his great ship, *The Ibex of the Abzu*. Like the Egyptian Ausar, the Greek Osiris, Enki was a pre-flood culture-bearer from Atlantis. The Abzu was the primeval waste of waters out of which arose his "Mountain of Life."

Enlil

The Sumerian Atlas, known as the Great Mountain, who held up the sky. Enlil was famous as the conqueror of Tiamat, the ocean, just as Atlantis dominated the seas. In the *Epic of Gilgamesh*, where he is known as Bel, Enlil is responsible for the Deluge.

Enuma Elish

A poem dramatizing the Deluge from which the Oannes "fish-men" crossed the sea to establish civilization throughout Mesopotamia. The *Enuma Elish* was recited during each New Year's festival at the Sumerians' Easgila ziggurat, itself dedicated to the sunken realm of their ancestors.

Eochaid

King of the Atlantean Fomorach, who defeated later invaders from Atlantis, but was murdered under treacherous circumstances.

(See Fomorach, Nuadu)

Esaugetuh Emissee

The Creek Indians' "Lord of the Wind," like the Aztec *Ehecatl*, the Sumerian *Enlil*, the Egyptian *Shu*—all ethnic variations of Atlas. In his creation legend, Esaugetuh Emissee escaped a universal flood by climbing to the summit of a mountain at the center of the world, Nunne Chaha. As the waters receded, he fashioned the first human beings from moist clay.

Nun was the Egyptian god of the Primeval Sea, out of which arose the first dry land, sometimes described as a "sacred mound" or mountain, where the earliest humans were created. It also gave birth to the gods during the Tep Zepi, or the "First Time." Nun was represented in temple art as a man plunged to his waist in the ocean, his arms upraised to carry the solar-boat with its divine and royal passengers. He held them above the Flood engulfing their mountainous homeland in the Far West, and brought them to the Nile Delta, where they reestablished themselves in Dynastic civilization. Nun saved both gods and mankind from the same disaster he caused at the behest of Atum, who had commanded a great deluge to wash away the iniquities of the world.

The Sumerian Ninhursag, "Nin of the Mountain," arose out of the Abzu, the Primordial Sea, to create an island blessed with all kinds of herbs, wine, honey, fruit trees, gold, silver, bronze, cattle, and sheep. But when Enlil, like the Egyptian Atum, ordered a Great Flood, Ninhursag sank under the waves of the Abzu. The god who actually caused the Deluge was Ningirsu, "Lord of Floods." Enlil's wife was Ninlil, the sea, mother of all. Ninazu, the "Water Knower," dwelt in Arallu (the Egyptian Aalu, the Greek Atlantis). In Phoenician, the word for "fish" was *nun*.

The Norse *Ginunngigap* was the sea that swallowed the world and doomed to repeat the catastrophe at cosmic intervals for all eternity. The Ginunngigap, too, was said to have brought forth the first land on which humans appeared.

The Native American *Nunne-Chaha* could not be clearer in its reflection of the "Nun" theme threading its Atlantean story from Egyptian and Sumerian through Phoenician and Norse myth. Nunne Chaha was the "Great Stone House" on an island in the primeval Waste of Waters. The island was said to have been surrounded by a lofty wall, and watercourses were directed into "boat-canals."

The Egyptian Nun was also known as *Nu*, and *Nu'u* was responsible for the Hawaiian *Po-au-Hulihia*, the "Era of the Over-Turning," the great flood of *Kai-a-ka-hina-li'i*, "the Sea that made the Chiefs fall down."

Escape from Atlantis

A 1997 feature film, in which the protagonists sail through the Burmuda Triangle, and are suddenly transported back to Atlantis. *Escape from Atlantis* is one of several Hollywood movies (including *Cocoon*, for example) based on the premise that Atlantis lies in the Bahamas.

Etelenty

Ancient Egyptian for "Atlantis," as it appears in *The Book of the Coming Forth by Day*, better known today as *The Book of the Dead*—a series of religious texts buried with the deceased to help the soul along its underworld journey through death to its spiritual destiny. According to Dr. Ramses Seleem's 2001 translation, "Etelenty" means "the land that has been divided and submerged by water." Its Greek derivation is apparent, and was probably the same term Solon heard spoken at Sais, which he transliterated into "Atlantis."

(See Solon)

Etruscans

The pre-Roman people who raised a unique civilization in west-central Italy, circa 800 B.C. to 200 B.C. Although racially Indo-European, their largely untranslated language was apparently related to Finno-Urgic, making them distantly related, at least linguistically, to Hungarians, Estonians, and Finns. They referred to themselves as the Rasna; "Etruscan" was the collective name by which the Romans knew them because of their residence in Tuscany. Their provenance is uncertain, although they appear to have been a synthesis of native Italians, the Villanovans, circa 1200 B.C., with foreign arrivals, most notably from northwest coastal Asia Minor.

Trojan origins after the sack of Ilios, formerly regarded by scholars as entirely fanciful, seem at least partially born out by terra-cotta artifacts featuring Trojan motifs. Etruscan writing compares with examples of Trojan script, and Aeneas' flight from Troy appears in Etruscan art.

Recreation of an Etruscan temple, Via Guilia Museum, Rome, that resembled Atlantean counterparts.

In Plato's *Kritias*, we read that Atlantean expansion extended to Italy, and specifically, that Etruria came under the influence of Atlantis. Some significant Atlantean themes survive in Etruscan art, such as the large terra-cotta winged horses of Poseidon at Tarquinia. Some scholars suspect that the name "Italy" is Etruscan. If so, it is another link to Atlantis, because *Italy* is a derivation of *Italus*, or "Atlas."

Euaemon

A king of Atlantis mentioned in Plato's account, *Kritias*. In non-Platonic Greek myth, Euaemon married Rhea—after her husband, Kronos, was banished by the victorious Olympians—and fathered Eurylyptus, the king of Thessaly. Several elements of the Atlantis story appear even in this brief legend. Kronos was synonymous for the Atlantic Ocean, "Chronos maris" to the Romans. Rhea was the Earth Mother goddess, referred to as Basilea by the 1st-century B.C. Greek historian Diodorus Siculus, who reported that she had been venerated by the Atlanteans. They probably knew her by names mentioned in *Kritias*: either Leukippe, Poseidon's mother-in-law, or Kleito, the mother of Atlantean kings.

Euaemon's role as a progenitor of Thessaly's royal lineage is likewise in keeping with the tradition of Atlantean monarchs as far-flung founding fathers. Euaemon has an intriguing connection with the Canary Islands, where the Guanche word for "water" was *aemon*. On the other side of the Atlantic Ocean, the Arawak Indians of coastal Venezuela and Colombia believed a god called Aimon Kondi drowned the world to punish the wickedness of men.

But Euaemon appears to be most closely identified with Eremon, the founder of a united, pre-Celtic Ireland. His similarity with the fourth monarch of Atlantis is more than philological. Long lists of regents' names were kept in ancient Ireland by successive generations of *files*, or poet-historians. They traced each ruler's line of descent from Eremon as a means of establishing royal legitimacy. In the *Book of Invasions*, a medieval compilation of oral traditions rooted in early Celtic and pre-Celtic times, Eremon is described as the leader of a "Sea People" who landed on Irish shores in 1002 B.C. The date is interesting, because it is precisely 200 years after the final destruction of Atlantis in the Bronze Age. These relatively close time parameters and Eremon's appearance in two unrelated ancient sources on either side of Western Europe, together with his Irish characterization as the king of a "Sea People" arriving as refugees in a pre-Celtic epoch, clearly define him as an Atlantean monarch.

Eremon was said to have sailed to Ireland with fellow storm-tossed survivors after an oceanic catastrophe that drowned most of his people, known as the Milesians. Though originally founded by an earlier race, the seat of Irish kings, Tara, was named after Eremon's wife. She herself was a daughter from the royal house of the Blessed Isles lost beneath the sea. All these native elements remarkably combine to identify themselves with Plato's account. His Euaemon was doubtless the Eremon of Irish tradition.

(See Basilea, Kleito, Kronos, Leukippe)

Eumelos

According to Plato in *Kritias*, the Greek name for Gadeiros, an Atlantean monarch in Spain.

Eupolemus

A first-century B.C. Greek author of a lost history of the Jews in Assyria. Surviving fragments tell how Babylon was founded by Titans after the Great Flood. They built the so-called "Tower of Babel," destroyed by a heavenly cataclysm which dispersed them throughout the world. In Greek myth, Atlas was leader of the Titans. The cometary destruction of Atlantis, his island kingdom, and flight of his people across the globe are represented in the fate of the Tower of Babel.

Evenor

"One of the original Earth-born inhabitants" on the island of Atlas, according to *Kritias*. "Evenor" means "the good or brave man," who lived and died before Atlantis was built. Evenor's myth implies that his homeland had a human population previous to the development of the megalithic pattern upon which the city was raised. This means that the island was at least inhabited in Paleolithic times, during the Old Stone Age, 6,000 or more years ago. We may likewise gather that the original creation of Atlantis was a product of Neolithic megalith-builders, thereby dating its foundation to circa 4000 B.C. However, it almost certainly began as a ceremonial center, like Britain's Stonehenge. As it grew over time, the sacred site expanded to become, in its final form, a Late Bronze Age citadel and city.

There is something singularly provocative in Evenor's story, because it relates that civilization was not native to his island, but an import. His daughter, Kleito, married Poseidon, an outsider, who came from across the sea to lay the concentric foundations of the city. In other words, an external influence initiated its construction, perhaps by culture-bearers from some community older even than Atlantis itself. Civilization, at least as it came to be known after 3000 B.C., may have first arisen on the island of Atlas, but seafaring megalith-builders from another unknown homeland may have arrived to spark its Neolithic beginnings.

Modern Berber tribes of North Africa still preserve traditions of Uneur and his "Sons of the Source," from whom they trace their lineage. Evenor and Uneur appear to be variations on an original Atlantean name.

Exiles of Time

A 1949 novel about Mu by Nelson Bond. In his destruction of the Pacific realm through the agency of a comet he anticipated late 20th-century scientific discoveries concerning impact on early civilization by catastrophic celestial events.

Falias

One of four pre-Celtic ceremonial centers renowned for their splendor and power, sunk to the bottom of the Atlantic Ocean during separate catastrophes. These lost cities correspond to Ireland's four alien immigrations cited by *The Book of Invasions* and the quartet of cataclysms that afflicted Atlantis around 3100, 2100, 1620, and 1200 B.C. Gaelic tradition states that Falias was the original homeland of Ireland's first inhabitants, the Fomorach, from whence they carried the Stone of Death, "crowned with pale fire." It recalls the Tuoai, or "Fire Stone," of Atlantis, as described by Edgar Cayce.

(See Finias, Fomorach, Gorias, Murias, Tir-nan-Og, Tuoai Stone, Tuatha da Danann)

Fand

The Irish "Pearl of Beauty," wife of a sea-god, the Celtic Poseidon, Manannan. They dwelt in a kingdom known as "Land-under-Wave," on an island in the West, the concentric walls of their city lavishly decorated with gleaming sheets of precious metal virtually the same as Plato's description of Atlantis. In the Old Irish legend of the Celtic hero, Cuchulain, Fand appears as a prophetess living alone in a cave on an island in the mid-Atlantic. Here she is identical to Calypso, the sibyl of Ogygia, a daughter of Atlas and, consequently, an "Atlantis."

Fathach

The poet-king of Atlantean immigrants in Ireland, the Fir Bolg. From his name derived the Irish term for "Druid," *Fathi. Fathach* may be one of the few words we know with any degree of certainty is at least close to the spoken language heard in Atlantis.

(See Fir Bolg)

Fatua-Moana

"Lord Ocean," who caused a worldwide deluge, but preserved some animals and a virtuous family from the calamity. When the waters abated, all other life had been drowned, and the survivors disembarked on the first dry land they saw, Hawaii. This pre-Christian version of the Flood is remarkably similar to the Genesis account of Noah, suggesting the Marquesas' and biblical versions both stem from an actual natural catastrophe experienced in common.

Fenrir

A cosmic wolf that swallowed the sun at the time of the Great Flood, spreading darkness over the whole world. His Norse myth is a dramatic metaphor for the phenomenal clouds of ash and dust raised by the Atlantean cataclysm, which obscured daylight and plunged the Earth into temporary, but universal darkness.

Fensalir

"The Halls of the Sea," the divine palace of the Norse Frigg, the Teutonic Fricka, or Frija, as Odin's wife, the most powerful goddess in the Nordic pantheon. Fensalir may have been the Norse Atlantis.

Findrine

In a Celtic epic, *The Voyage of Maeldune*, the Irish explorer lands at a holy island with a city laid out in concentric rings of alternating land and water interconnected by a series of bisecting canals. Each artificially created island is surrounded by its own wall ornamented with sheets of priceless metals. The penultimate ring of land has a wall sheathed in a brightly gleaming, gold-like metal unknown to Maeldune, called "findrine." The place he describes can only be Plato's Atlantis, where the next-to-innermost wall was coated in orichalcum, a metal the

Greek philosopher is no less at a loss to identify, stating only that pure gold alone was more esteemed. Findrine and orichalcum are one and the same, most likely an alloy of high-grade copper and gold the Atlantean metallurgists specialized in producing because of their country's monopoly on Earth's richest copper mines, in the Upper Great Lakes Peninsula.

(See Formigas, Orichalcum)

Finias

The sunken city from which Partholon and his followers arrived in Ireland from the second Atlantean flood, circa 2100 B.C. The sacred object of Finias was a mysterious spear.

(See Falias, Gorias, Murias, Partholon, Tir-nan-Og, Tuatha da Danann)

Fintan

The leader of the Fomorach, a sea people who sailed from the drowning of their island home to the shores of Ireland. Fintan's, along with that of his wife, Queen Kesara, may be among the few authentic Atlantean names to have survived. In Celtic tradition, Fintan drowned in the Great Flood, and was transformed into a salmon. Following the catastrophe, he swam ashore, changed himself back into human shape, and built the first post-diluvian kingdom at Ulster, where he reigned into ripe old age. His myth clearly preserves the folk memory of Atlantean culture-bearers, some of whom perished in the cataclysm, arriving in Ireland. Remarkably, the Haida and Tlingit Indians of North America's Pacific Northwest likewise tell of the Steel-Headed Man, who perished in the Deluge, but likewise transformed himself into a salmon.

(See Fomorach)

Fir-Bolg

Refugees in Ireland from the early third-millennium B.C. geologic upheavals in Atlantis. Their name means literally "Men in Bags," and was doubtless used by the resident Fomorach, themselves earlier immigrants from Atlantis, to excoriate the new arrivals for the hasty and inglorious vessels in which they arrived: leather skin pulled over a simple frame to form a kind of coracle, but the only means available to a people fleeing for their lives. The Fir-Bolg nonetheless reorganized all of Ireland in accordance with their sacred numerical principles into five provinces. According to Plato, the Atlanteans used social units of five and six.

The Fir-Bolg got along uneasily with their Fomorach cousins, but eventually formed close alliances, especially when an outside threat concerned the future existence of both tribes. The last Fir-Bolg king, Breas, married a Fomorian princess.

The Fir-Bolg joined forces with the Fomorach in the disastrous Battle of Mag Tured against later Atlantean immigrants, the Tuatha da Danann. Fir-Bolg survivors escaped to the off-shore islands of Aran, Islay, Rathlin, and Man, named after Manannan, the Irish Poseidon. The stone ruins found today on these islands belong to structures built by post-diluvian Atlanteans, the Fir-Bolg.

The Flood

See The Deluge.

Foam Woman

Still revered among the Haida Indians of coastal British Columbia and Vancouver Island as a sea-goddess and the patron deity of tribes and families. Foam Woman appeared on the northwestern shores of North America immediately after the Great Flood. She revealed 20 breasts, 10 on either side of her body, and from these the ancestors of each of the future Raven Clans was nurtured. In South America, the Incas of Peru and Bolivia told of "Sea Foam," Kon-Tiki-Viracocha, who arrived at Lake Titicaca as a flood hero bearing the technology of a previous, obliterated civilization. Foam Woman's twenty breasts for the founders of the Raven Clans recall the 10 Atlantean kings Plato describes as the forefathers of subsequent civilizations.

Fomorach

Also known as the Fomorians, Fomhoraicc, F'omoraig Afaic, Fomoraice, or Fomoragh. Described in Irish folklore as a "sea people," they were the earliest inhabitants of Ireland, although they established their chief headquarters in the Hebrides. Like the Atlanteans depicted by Plato, the Fomorach were Titans who arrived from over the ocean. Indeed, their name derives from *fomor*, synonymous for "giant" and "pirate." According to O'Brien, Fomoraice means "mariners of Fo." An Egyptian-like variant, Fomhoisre, writes Anna Franklin, means "Under Spirits." In the Old Irish *Annals of Clonmacnois*, the Fomorach are mentioned as direct descendants of Noah.

Their settlement in Ireland, according to the *Annals*, took place before the Great Flood. They "lived by pyracie and spoile of other nations, and were in those days very troublesome to the whole world"—a characterization coinciding with the aggressive Atlanteans portrayed by Plato's *Kritias*. The *Annals'* description of the Fomorach's sea-power, with their "fleet of sixty ships and a strong army," is likewise reminiscent of Atlantean imperialism. They represented an early migration to Ireland from geologically troubled Atlantis in the late fourth millennium B.C, about the time the megalithic center at New Grange, 30 miles north of Dublin, was built, circa 3200 B.C.

Some 28 centuries later, the Fomorach were virtually exterminated by the last immigrant wave from Atlantis, the Tuatha da Danann, "Followers of the Goddess Danu," at the Battle of Mag Tured. The few survivors were permitted to continue their functions as high priests and priestesses of Ireland's megalithic sites, which their forefathers erected. This Fomorach remnant lived on through many generations to eventually become assimilated into the Celtic population, after 600 B.C. The most common Irish name is Atlantean. "Murphy" derives from O'Morchoe, or Fomoroche. The Murphy crest features the Tree of Life surmounted by a griffin or protective monster and bearing sacred apples, the chief elements in the Garden of the Hesperides.

(See Garden of the Hesperides)

Formigas

An Irish rendition of Atlantis found in the ninth-century *Travels of O'Corra* and *Voyage of Bran*. Formigas "had a wall of copper all around it. In the center stood a palace from which came a beautiful maiden wearing sandals of findrine on her feet, a gold-colored jacket covered with bright, tinted metal, fastened at the neck with a broach of pure gold. In one hand she held a pitcher of copper, and in the other a silver goblet." Plato portrayed the Atlanteans as wealthy miners excelling in the excavation of copper and gold. The findrine mentioned here appears to be his orichalcum, the copper-gold alloy he stated was an exclusive product of Atlantis.

(See Findrine, Orichalcum)

Fortunate Isles

Also known as the Isles of the Blest in Greek and Roman myth. They are sometimes used to describe Atlantis, such as during Hercules' theft (his 11th labor) of the golden apples from the garden of the Hesperides that were protected by daughters of Atlas. In other contexts, the Fortunate Isles were believed to still exist, and seem to have been identified with the Canary Islands. Phoenician, Greek, and Roman amphorae have been found in the waters surrounding Lanzarote and other islands in the Canaries. The Fortunate Isles and Isles of the Blest were synonymous for the distant west and used as a metaphor for the afterlife.

Fountains of the Deep

German author Karl zu Eulenburg's 1926 novel in which a passenger liner runs aground on Atlantis after a part of the sunken civilization rises to the surface. *Die Brunnen der grossen Tiefe* is an original, imaginative tale.

Frobenius, Leo

Early 20th-century German explorer and founder of modern African studies. His pioneering collection of Yoruba oral traditions describing a catastrophic flood in the ancient past and subsequent migration of survivors, together with anomalous bronze manufacture among the Benin, convinced Frobenius that native West Africans preserved folk memories of Plato's Atlantis.

Fu Sang Mu

In Chinese myth, a colossal mulberry tree growing above a hot "pool" (sea) in a paradise far over the ocean, toward the east. The land itself is hot. No less than nine suns perch in Fu Sang Mu's lower branches. White women renowned for their beautiful, long hair tend the *li chih*, or "herb of immortality," in a garden at the center of the island. The lost Pacific civilization of Mu was chiefly characterized by a sacred Tree of Life, and its climate was said to have been very hot.

(See Chomegusa, Horaizan, Mu)

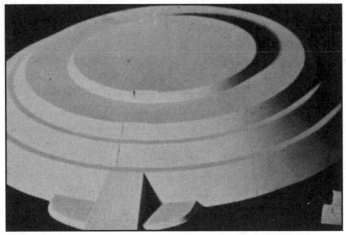

Restoration of the Cuicuilco Pyramid in this Mexico City Museum model reveals its concentric design, a hallmark of Atlantean monumental construction.

Gadeiros

The second king named in Plato's account of Atlantis, *Kritias*. Gadeiros was assigned to a region of south-Atlantic Spain, and the modern city of Cadiz is indeed the ancient Gades known to the Romans. But the name is found elsewhere throughout the Atlantean sphere of influence. Agadir is in Tunisia, while another Agadir, a southern port in Morocco, was utterly destroyed during a series of earthquakes and tsunamis that killed more than 20,000 persons between February 29 and March 1, 1960. Fronting as it does the suspected location of Atlantis, Agadir's fate reaffirms the geologic feasibility of an Atlantis-like catastrophe occurring in that area of the world.

But Plato is not the only source for information about Gadeiros. The Gauls themselves spoke of their first chiefs arriving at the mouth of the River Tagus, in or very near present-day Lisbon. There they settled for a time, naming their first town Porto Galli ("Port of the Gauls"), from which derives modern Portugal. Eventually they moved into the Continent to become the earliest leaders of the Gallic tribes. Their king who led them from the sunken Turris Vitrea, or "Island of Glass Towers," was the "Chieftain of the Peoples," Hu-Gadarn, likewise claimed by the Druids. They told their Roman conquerors that the Celts were partly descended from refugees of a drowned land in the Far West. Legend begins to merge with history at this point when we consider Celtic origins in the early 12th century B.C. Tumulus culture—the same period that witnessed the dispersal of Atlanteans from their engulfed homeland.

Hu-Gadarn is mentioned in the Welsh *Hanes Taliesan*, the "Tale of Taliesan," where he is known as Little Gwion. If this affectionate diminutive seems derivative of the Trojan capital, Ilios, (*Wilion* in Hittite and perhaps the Trojan language, as well), the impression is deepened when Hu-Gadarn says, "I am now come here to the remnant of Troia." Troy was allied with Atlantis through common blood-ties (See Electra). Although Hu-Gadarn is regarded as the first ancestor of the Cymry, the Welsh people, his Atlantean identity is no less apparent: "I have been fostered in the Ark," he confesses. *Hanes Taliesan* reports, "He had been fostered between the knees of Dylan and the Deluge," arriving in Wales after a worldwide flood whipped up by a monstrous serpent.

"Hu" was not part of his name, but rather a title referring to his royal lineage. So, the Welsh Gadarn and Plato's Gadeiros, both kings, appear to be one and the same monarch.

Gamu

An island among the Maldives, directly south of the Indian subcontinent at the equator, featuring stone structures similar to Yucatan's Pyramid of Kukulcan, at Chichen Itza. Both sites have local traditions of racially alien culture-bearers responsible for initiating civilization. "Gamu" apparently derives from "Mu," the Pacific kingdom contemporary with Atlantis.

(See Kukulcan, Mu, Redin)

Garamantes

A "Chariot-People" described by the Greek historian Herodotus (circa 500 B.C.) as invaders of the Mediterranean World at the time of the Trojan War (1250 B.C.). The Garamantes' red and yellow rock paintings may still be seen at Tin-Abou Teka, in Tunisia. They wore the same armored vests and crested, horned helmets as the Atlantean "Sea Peoples" depicted on the walls of Medinet Habu, Pharaoh Ramses III's "Victory Temple" in West Thebes. The Garamantes were part of a massive invasion force from Atlantis, which tried to conquer Egypt after the Atlantean catastrophe, in 1198 B.C.

Garden of the Hesperides

The Hesperides were *Atlantises*, daughters of Atlas by Themis, goddess of justice, knowledge, and nature. In *Kritias*, Plato mentions that 5 was the sacred numeral of Atlantis, and there were five Hesperides: Aigle, mistress of magic;

Arethusa, who bore another set of daughters, the Hyades; Erythea, mistress of Earth-powers; Hespera, personification of the planet Venus, whose cycles determined their ceremonial schedules; and Hestia, virginal keeper of the perpetual flame at the heart of the universe. Their chief duty was to tend and protect the Tree of Life at the center of Atlas' garden, which he left in their care. The Tree produced unique golden apples which none but the most holy and purified beings could touch, because they granted immortality to anyone who ate them. To assist the Hesperides in its protection, a serpent called Ladon entwined about the bough.

Despite these precautions, Heracles managed to steal a golden apple, as one of the duties he was forced to perform during his 12 labors. It would end up in the possession of Eris, the goddess of dissension, who had been snubbed by her fellow deities at the big wedding celebration of Helen and Paris. Aware of Olympian jealousies, she inscribed only three words on the apple—"For the fairest"—and surreptitiously rolled it among the immortal guests. From the petty bickering it generated, the Trojan War, with all its attendant horrors and tragedy, developed. This myth was cited to demonstrate the calamitous consequences of abusing spiritual power.

The Hesperides were originally known as *Hesperu Caras* (Leonard, 178). To the Guarani Indians, the Caras were light-skinned goddesses who arrived on the eastern shores of South America after escaping a terrible cataclysm. The same name and account are known to the Brazilian Goiaz. All white people are still referred to as *Cara-ibas* by the Chevantes of Matto Grosso, in Brazil. The mid-16th-century historian, Gonzalo de Orviedo, learned from the natives of the West Indies that their islands were synonymous with the Hesperides. From this and abundant, similar oral evidence he collected throughout Middle America, de Orviedo was the first researcher to conclude that the indigenous inhabitants were descended from survivors of the Atlantis catastrophe. Their remote and isolated native traditions clearly preserved a folk memory of Atlantean visitors.

The Hesperides were Atlantean priestesses of the primeval and most holy mysteries of Atlantis. Their mystery cult promised immortality for successful initiates, as signified by the Tree of Life with its snake, a symbol of regeneration because of the animal's ability to slough off its old, dead skin and emerge with a new one. Comparisons with the Garden of Eden in Genesis are unavoidable, and doubtless represent an Old Testament corruption of the Atlantean original.

The Hesperides are sometimes given as seven in number. As such, they may correspond to the seven major *chakras*, or metaphysical energy centers that, collectively, comprise the human personality. So too, the Tree of Life symbolizes the spinal column, along which the chakras are arranged. This interpretation suggests that kundalini yoga originated in Atlantis, from which it spread around the world. Indeed, the Tree of Life is a theme frequently encountered in many European and Asian traditions of Atlantis and Lemuria, respectively.

"Ides" of Hesperides means "in the midst of," or "the all-powerful mid-point," implying the ceremonial revolution of the planet Venus, the Greek Hespera, around the ritual core of the cult. But Hestia may have been the most centrally important as a fifth, central point of the Hesperides. She was entrusted with the perpetual flame, that initial spark that created the universe and is located at its very center. Hestia presided over the sacred fire at the hearths of private homes, as well as in public temples. Hers was the torch with began the Olympic Games. The Hesperides were venerated in Rome as the most holy concept, with particular emphasis on Hestia as Vesta. Her temple enshrined a perpetual flame attended by virgins known as Vestals.

Edgar Cayce said that sacred flames were tended in the Atlantis Temple of Fire, always by women, like the Hesperides. He mentions Ameei, Asmes, Assha, Ilax, and Jouel (like the five Hesperides, who they possibly impersonated) in separate readings as priestesses "to the fire worship."

The Gate-Keepers

In the Nile Valley, the Gate Keepers were deified guardians of the pillars of Sekhet-Aaru, the "Field of Reeds." Like much in Egyptian myth, Sekhet-Aaru was regarded simultaneously as a real place and a religious metaphor. Elements of both the historical and the spiritual combined and interacted. Sekhet-Aaru's description in the Egyptian *Book of the Dead* as an island for the souls of the departed located in the far western ocean and featuring concentric walls clearly identifies it as a poetic rendering of Atlantis, itself characterized by Plato as a "sacred isle."

The "pillars" of the Gate Keepers are the Pillars of Hercules, an ancient reference to the Straits of Gibraltar, dividing Europe and Africa from the Atlantic realm, including the pillar-cult that was practiced in Atlantis at the Temple of Poseidon, according to Plato in *Kritias*. The names of some of these mythical Gate-Keepers echo the Atlantean experience: Mistress of the World, Mistress of Destruction, Lady of the Flames, Covering Deluge, and so on.

Gateway to Remembrance

A 1948 theosophical novel about Atlantis by Phyllis Cradock. Even the Atlantis debunker, L. Sprague De Camp, admitted that he found *Gateway to Remembrance* "a skillfully wrought and absorbing narrative."

Gaueteaki

A Melanesian creation-goddess revered at Bellona Island and throughout the Solomon Islands, where secret rituals inform her followers how they may overcome death and attain eternal life. Gaueteaki is worshiped in the unusual form of a smooth, black stone. This is the Omphalos, or "Navel Stone," centerpiece of the chief mystery-religion in Atlantis, carried by surviving initiates around the globe following the destruction of their homeland. She is also known as *Gauteaki*.

(See Navel of the World)

Geiger, Wilhelm

Leading Iraniologist and doyen of Middle Eastern archaeology, whose stellar academic credentials lent Atlantology important credibility in the early 20th century. Referring to the ancient Athenian military commander and statesman, Alcibiades I, as cited by Plato, Geiger remarked:

> Quite unique stands the statement, "He was a Greek, or one of those who came forth from the continent on the other side of the Great Sea." This last expression is very obscure. It sounds too mysterious to designate the Greeks of Asia Minor. Is it, perhaps, some reminiscence of the passage of primitive man to the six Keshvars (mythic realms in Iranian tradition)? Or of Atlantis?

Gigantomachy

In Greek myth, a conflict between the Titans and the Olympians that could be a metaphor for the Atlanto-Athenian War described by Plato. Atlas was a Titan, and the Gods might have been fashioned into glorified images of the victorious Greeks. For his participation in the Gigantomachy, which he led after the resignation of Kronos, Atlas was condemned to bear the sky on his shoulders. His punishment was probably a mythic device to reaffirm the conquest of Atlantis, because in other traditions he supports the sphere of the Zodiac, not in an image of defeat, but as the inventor of astrology-astronomy.

Ginunngigap

In Norse myth, a great deluge that once drowned the whole world. After the waters receded, the first dry land was exposed. In various sagas, Ginunngigap was survived by various flood heroes who founded human society.

(See Esaugetuh Emissee)

Giron-Gagal

According to the Quiche cosmological book, the *Popol Vuh*, the Giron-Gagal was a power-crystal presented to Balaam-Qitze by Nacxit, the "Great Father" of Patulan-Pa-Civan, the Mayas' version of Atlantis. He was about to lead a company of "Old Men," the U Mamae, across the ocean to Yucatan. The Giron-Gagal was a "symbol of power and majesty to make the peoples fear and respect the Quiches."

(See Balaam-Qitze, Chintamani, Nacxit, Patulan-Pa-Civan, The Tuaoi Stone, U Mamae)

Glooskap

The Micmac Indians' flood hero, who arrived on the eastern shores of Nova Scotia from "beyond the sea."

Gloyw Wallt Lydan Gaelic Liathan

Literally "The days when the high seas parted the old kingdom," a lost, medieval epic describing an Atlantis-like flood and the arrival of survivors in ancient Wales, where they became its first kings.

Die Goetterdaemmerung

In Germanic myth, the "Twilight of the Gods"—a worldwide cataclysm, brought about by "fire from heaven" and a universal deluge. Also known as *Ragnarok*.

Gogmagog

British flood hero whose 150-foot-long image was cut into Dorset's chalk hills, near the town of Cerne-Abbas in the south of England, during the late Stone Age. Gogmagog features the "og" appellation identifying Atlantean figures in Old Irish and biblical traditions.

Golden Age

In Greek myth, the first age of mankind, when happiness, truth, and right prevailed on Earth. It was known as a "golden" age, not for any abundance of gold wealth, but because the sun was universally worshiped as a beneficent god. As such, some researchers point to the numerous solar orientations of ancient structures throughout the world, such as Ireland's 5,200-year-old tomb at New Grange, with its "roof-box" aligned to the winter solstice. Identical alignments occur throughout the world among North America's prehistoric mounds; on the Pacific island of Tonga; formerly at Heliopolis, the Egyptian Onur, in the Upper Nile Valley; and at many other locations. This epoch was also known as "the Age of Chronos," a Titan associated with the Atlantic Ocean ("Chronos maris" to the Romans). Indeed, Plutarch wrote that Kronos, after his defeat in the Gigantomachy, was imprisoned "under a mountain" on Ogygia; this is an apt description of volcanic Mount Atlas, because Ogygia was the island of Calypso, which is as much to say the island of Atlantis.

Thus the Golden Age may refer to an early, pre-imperial period of Atlantis in the fourth millennium B.C., when seafaring culture-bearers were establishing the spiritual-scientific principles of a solar cult around the world.

(See Fand)

Gorgons

In Greek myth, a trio of sisters: Euryale, the "Far-Flung," or "Far Away"; Stheino, "Strength"; and, most famous of all, Medusa, "Queen," or possibly "Sea Queen." Their names imply that they were not always the monsters of classical times, but originally titles of the triadic lunar goddess. Orphic mystics in fact referred to the moon as "Gorgon Head." The Gorgons' unfortunate transformation came about with the destruction of their Atlantean homeland.

To save Andromeda from being sacrificed for Poseidon, Perseus decapitates Medusa's head—writhing with snakes instead of hairs—for use as a weapon that will turn his opponents to stone. Barbara Walker writes that this aspect of Medusa's power was perverted from its original function "to enforce taboos on secret Mysteries of the Goddess, guarded by stone pillars formerly erected in honor of her deceased lovers." Its lethal potential may have been changed to reflect the traumatic effects of the Atlantean cataclysm. Medusa's parentage was Atlantean; she was the offspring of Phorcys, "the Old Man of the Sea," and Ceto, daughter of Oceanus.

Gorgons were characteristically portrayed in Greek art as monstrous women with exposed teeth, fangs, and tongue. Precisely the same figures appear at two widely separated pre-Columbian American sites connected by common themes to Atlantis: (1) at Colombia's San Agustin, where the Atlantean kingdom of Musaeus was located and the Muysica Indians preserved the story of a great flood, and (2) at Peru's Chavin de Huantar, a pre-Inca city built just when Atlantis was destroyed, in 1198 B.C.

Even in Late Classical Times, the Canary Islands were known collectively as "Gorgonia" by Greek and Roman geographers. The Gorgons were identified with these Islands by the Iberian geographer, Pomponius Mela, who lived at Tingentera, near the Pillars of Heracles, today's Strait of Gibraltar, in 40 A.D. The Canary Islands' association with Gorgons finds additional historical foundation in the names its original inhabitants, the Guanches, gave to different areas of their main island, Tenerife—Gorgo and Gorgano. In the *Posthomerica* (Book X, 197), the Atlantic provence of the Gorgons is explicit: "Gilded Perseus was killing fierce Medusa, where the bathing place of the stars are, the ends of the Earth, and the sources of deep flowing Oceanus, in the West, where night meets the timeless, setting sun."

Aethiopia, where Atlas was transformed into a mountain, was identified in early classical times, not with Abyssinia, but North Africa's Atlantic coast. The Gorgons, "Daughters of Night," were said to live in the western extremes of Oceanus, a theme underscored first by Medusa's marriage to Poseidon, and again through her son, the monarch of Erytheia, the Atlantean kingdom of Gadeiros (Cadiz) in Atlantic Spain. The Gorgons' location in the Far West was reaffirmed by Ovid, and placed specifically in the Atlantean realm by Hesiod, who wrote that they "dwell beyond the glorious ocean, where are the clear-voiced Hesperides." Palaephastus recorded that Athena herself was worshiped as "Gorgo" in the

Fortune Isles (that is, the Canary Islands). Even in Greece, her surname was Gorgophora. In Libya, Athena was actually referred to as "Medusa." Given her cult's arrival in Greece from the west, via Libya, Athena may have been originally an Atlantean goddess. This interpretation is underscored by the Gorgons themselves, who were described in their earliest myths as residents of the near-Atlantic, but relocated in later accounts to Libya. Her Egyptian incarnation as Neith is particularly cogent, because it was at her temple in Sais that the story of Atlantis was enshrined, according to Plato.

The Gorgons' legendary power to turn men and objects into stone suggests the numerous islets in the vicinity of the Canary Islands, many of them fashioned into fantastic simulacrum by the actions of wind and wave over time. Mela's association of the Canary Islands with the abode of the Gorgons may have derived from numerous rocks he saw fashioned into bizarre forms by constant wave action. The rocks were deadly for sailors, hence the Gorgons' lethal reputation.

Gorgon means "grim-faced" and implies "the works and agencies of Earth," referring to geologic upheaval. Lewis Spence writes (in *The Occult Sciences in Atlantis*):

> Thus we find the Gorgon women connected with those seismic powers which wrought the downfall of Atlantis...It was indeed the severed head of Medusa, the "witch," which, in the hands of Perseus, transformed Atlas into a mountain of stone. The proof, therefore, is complete that the myth of the Gorgon sisters is assuredly a tale allegorical of the destruction of Atlantis and of those evil forces, seismic and demonic, which precipitated the catastrophe.

Gorias

A sunken city from which the Nemedians arrived in Ireland after the Third Atlantean Flood during the early 17th century B.C. The sacred object of Gorias was a mysterious "dividing sword."

(See Falias, Finias, Murias, Nemedians, Tir-nan-Og, Tuatha da Danann)

Great Pyramid

According to Edgar Cayce, the Great Pyramid on the Giza Plateau was built as a cooperative effort between Egyptian residents, who formed the labor force, and Atlantean architects, in a successful effort to politically combine immigrants from the west with native population through a shared public works project. He is at least fundamentally seconded by researcher, Kurt Mendelssohn, who concluded that the monument was raised as a state-forming act that called upon the participation of the entire population in the cause of national unification. Placing its construction at the very beginning of Dynastic civilization, Mendelssohn believed its completion coincided with and actually brought about the creation of ancient Egypt.

Arab accounts told of a pre-flood king, Surid (pronounced *shu-reed*), who was forewarned of the coming cataclysm, and commanded to establish the Great Pyramid as "a place of refuge." Shu, the Egyptian Atlas, was likewise portrayed as a man supporting the sphere of the heavens on his shoulders. Perhaps the Arab Surid was actually the Egyptian Shu, the most Atlantean of all the gods. The same Arab writers reported that the Great Pyramid's grand architect was Thoth, the Egyptian god of literature and science, the divine patron of learning, keeper of the ancient wisdom. He was equated by the Greeks and Romans with Hermes and Mercury, respectively, and these names are used interchangeably with Thoth in various traditions, Arabic and Western, describing the Great Pyramid's chief engineer.

Khafre's Pyramid, at the Giza Plateau, where refugee Atlanteans and Nile residents cooperated to create Pharaonic civilization.

Edgar Cayce certainly neither heard nor read anything of these obscure traditions in the 1930s or 40s. Yet, during one of his trance-states, he too spoke the name of the genius most responsible for raising the Pyramid: Thoth. Of all the deities associated with the structure, either astronomically or spiritually, the Egyptian Hermes is the most Atlantean. His surviving myth recounts simply that he arrived at the Nile Delta before the beginning of Egyptian civilization carrying with him a body of knowledge preserved on "emerald tablets" from a flood that overwhelmed his homeland in the primeval sea.

According to the Classical geographer Diodorus Siculus, "The Egyptians themselves were strangers who in very remote times settled on the banks of the Nile, bringing with themselves the civilization of their mother country, the art of writing and a polished language. They had come from the direction of the setting sun, and were the most ancient of men." Other contemporary writers described Egypt as the "daughter of Poseidon," the sea-god creator of Atlantis.

(See Cayce)

Great Sphinx

The most famous anthropomorphic monument on Earth, its earliest known name was Hu, or "guardian." The Greek word, *sphinx*, describes various elements "bound together," referring to the human head atop its lion's body. Rain erosion appears to fix the creation of the Great Sphinx to circa 7000 B.C., a conclusion both conventional scholars and Atlantologists find troubling; the former refuse to believe that it dates before 2600 B.C., while many of the latter are unable to envision an eighth-millennium B.C. Atlantis. Regardless of who built the Great Sphinx, it was modified on several occasions over time. The head, for example, is clearly dynastic, and may indeed have been sculpted around the period assigned to it by most Egyptologists. Its face could have belonged to Pharaoh Chephren (or Khafre), as they insist, although evidence suggests he did not build the Great Sphinx, but only restored it in the VI Dynasty, when it was already centuries old. Who the original head or face depicted could not be determined after the pharaoh reworked it into a self-portrait.

At its inception, the monument more likely resembled a crouching lion. Although it may or may not have been constructed by Atlanteans, they were probably responsible for at least one of its modifications, if not its conception. As a lion, the Great Sphinx signified the constellation Leo, traditionally associated with heavy rainfall, even floods. As such, it suggests the immigration of Atlanteans after their homeland experienced extensive geologic disturbances in 3100 B.C., when they brought civilization to the Nile Delta. Interestingly, the famous Dendera zodiac painted on the ceiling of a New Kingdom temple begins in Leo on the vernal equinox of 9880 B.C. While this year was millennia before the suspected beginning of civilization in Egypt, it coincides with the literal date for Atlantis reported by Plato.

Greater Arrival

The Mayas of Middle America recounted two worldwide floods separated by many centuries. The first of these was the Greater Arrival of Itzamna and Ixchel. They survived the loss of their kingdom in the Atlantic Ocean, but arrived to present the Mayas' ancestors with the gifts of civilization. These included hieroglyphs, mathematics, temple-building and astronomy-astrology from Itzamna, "the Lord of Heaven." Weaving, medicine, and religion were gifts from his wife, Ixchel. Her name means "the White Lady," while Itzamna was portrayed in sacred art with the distinctly un-Indian features of a bearded man with a long nose. The Itzas were his followers, who named their most famous ceremonial site in Yucatan, Chichen Itza, after him. The Itzas were also known as the *Ahaab*, or "Foreigners to the Land," a title that literally meant "White Men." They are portrayed on the 27th stele at Yaxchilan, the 11th stele at Piedras Negras, and on the Temple of the Warriors at Chichen Itza as bearded, long-nosed figures with Europoid features.

They and their leader were said to have come from Tutulxiu, the "Land of Abundance," or "the Bountiful," far across the sea, "where the sun rises." The worship of Ixchel survived the disappearance of the Mayas around the turn of the 10th century among the Aztecs as Coyolxauqui. Maya temple art depicts her struggling in the waters of the Great Flood, as her possessions lie strewn across the water. Itzamna was the Atlantean king mentioned in Plato's *Kritias* as "Azaes."

The Greater Arrival is probably a seminal event that marked the opening of the Maya calendar on August 11, 3110 B.C. This date is remarkable, because it is virtually identical to Babylonian records of the Great Flood, and coincides with the founding of Egypt's First Dynasty; the sudden construction of Ireland's oldest prehistoric site at New Grange; the start of work at Stonehenge in England; Troy's earliest archaeological date; the sudden flowering of megalithic construction at Malta; the beginning of Minoan civilization; the first Indus Valley cities; and on and on. Of the traditions that survive from these early cultures, all of them recall an oceanic catastrophe from which their civilizing ancestors escaped to restart civilization in new territories.

(See Lesser Arrival)

Tiahuanaco, in the Bolivian Andes, "built after the Flood."

Green Isle

Known among various ethnic communities along the coasts of the European Continent from Brittany and the Bay of Biscay to Basque Spain, the Green Isle is still sung in folksong and told in oral tradition. It is described as a beautiful, fertile island which very long ago disappeared during a storm in the Atlantic Ocean. Sailing from the cataclysm, ship-loads of survivors landed to make new lives for themselves, often becoming the founders of royal families in Western Europe.

gSum-pam-Khan-po

Still widely respected 18th-century Tibetan scholar who described the arrival of Tibet's first king in Yarling, then the nation's capital, from "the Land of Mu." The new monarch supposedly had webbed fingers, an indigo brow and the images of wheels tattooed on the palms of both hands. His webbed fingers signified the overseas character of his Lemurian homeland, while his indigo forehead corresponded to the dark-blue color associated in kundalini yoga with the "Third Eye" of psychic power located in the fifth chakra. Indeed, his tattooed hands imply that he introduced knowledge of the chakras, or spiritual "wheels," to Tibet. Chakras are energy centers rising from the base of the spine to the crown of the head, and operate as vortices connecting the mind and body through the soul.

According to British researcher Chris Ogilvie-Herald, "Even in the mountains of Tibet there survives a tradition of a cataclysm that flooded the highlands, and comets that caused great upheavals."

(See Mu)

Guanches

Native inhabitants of the Canary Islands. "Guanche" is a contraction of *Guanchinerfe* ("Child of Tenerife") the name of the largest of the islands. They were discovered by Portuguese explorers in the mid-15th century, but subsequently exterminated by the Spaniards through wars and disease. A few, far from pure-blooded Guanches may still survive, but their lineage is doubtful. Although their estimated population of 200,000 resided in most of the Canary Islands, they were concentrated on Tenerife, Gran Canaria, Fuerteventura, Las Palmas, and Lanzarote. Tall, fair-haired, and light-eyed, the Guanches were a white race some modern investigators believe were the last examples of Cro-Magnon man.

The Guanches raised massive, finely crafted step pyramids not unlike those in Egypt and Mesoamerica. Many of these structures were built of the native volcanic tufa, pumice, and lava stone—the same materials Plato described as the construction components of buildings in Atlantis. The Guanches' chief deity was Atlas, known to them as "Ater." Variants of the name reflect his attributes by which he was known in Greece: Ataman, "Upholder of the Sky"; Atara, "Holy Mountain," etc. Approximately 25 percent of Guanche personal names began with "At." The Guanches told the Portuguese their islands were anciently part of a larger homeland engulfed by the sea, a cataclysm their forefathers survived by climbing to the top of Mount Teide, Tenerife's great volcano, the highest peak in Europe. Guanche oral tradition of this catastrophe concluded with the words, *Janega qyayoch, archimenceu no haya dir hando sahec chungra petut*—"The powerful Father of the Fatherland died and left the natives orphans."

The Atlantis story was preserved at the Canary Islands perhaps in far greater detail than even Plato's account before the imposition of Christianity, which affected Guanche culture like a blight. Perhaps the most revealing of all surviving material connecting the Canary Islanders to Atlantis is found in the *Tois Aethiopikes* by Marcellus. In 45 A.D., he recorded that "the inhabitants of the Atlantic island of Poseidon preserve a tradition handed down to them by their ancestors of the existence of an Atlantic island of immense size of not less than a thousand stadia [about 115 miles], which had really existed in those seas, and which, during a long period of time, governed all the islands of the Atlantic Ocean." Pliny the Elder seconded Marcellus, writing that the Guanches were in fact the direct descendants of the disaster that sank Atlantis. Proclus reported that they still told the story of Atlantis in his day, circa 410 A.D.

Atlantis in the Canary Islands does not end with these ancient sources. Like the Atlanteans in Plato's account, the Guanches met for prayer by forming a circle around a sacred pillar with arms raised and palms open in the Egyptian manner.

The Christians threw down all the pillars they could find, but at least one perfectly preserved specimen survived in the Barranco de Valeron on Tenerife.

The Canaries received their name probably sometime in the mid-first century from Roman visitors, who observed the inhabitants' worship of dogs (*canarii*) in association with mummification, two more ritual ties to the Nile Valley, where dog-headed Anubis was a mortuary god. But the Islands appear to have been so characterized five centuries earlier, when the Greek historian Herodotus wrote of the Kynesii, who dwelt the farthest away of men, in the west, on an island beyond the Mediterranean Sea. *Kyneseii* means "dog-worshippers." Centuries previous to the discovery of the Canary Islands there were medieval accounts of the *Cynocephalii*, a dog-headed people living somewhere in the vicinity of Northwest Africa. In the Old Testament story of Japheth's son, after the flood he:

> ...abandoned the society of his fellow men and became the progenitor of the *Cynocephalii*, a body of men who by this name denoted that their intelligence was centered on their admiration for dogs. Following this line of thought we note that when men are represented as dog-headed one interpretation is that they are to be regarded as pioneers of human progress through hitherto untrodden ways" (Howey, 166).

Dogs always played significant roles in Egyptian society. Herodotus describes how Egyptian males shaved their heads in mourning after the death of a family dog, just as they did for their fellow humans. In Book II of his *History*, he writes that the consumption of wine or bread or any other food that happened to be in the house at the time of the animal's death was not permitted. The wealthy had lavish tombs built specifically for their dogs. An entire sacred city, Cynopolis, was the center of a canine cult reminiscent of the Canary Islanders, and the location of an immense cemetery for dogs, which were mummified and buried with their masters.

But there is no indication that the Pharaonic Egyptians themselves knew the Guanches ever existed. Numerous comparisons between them indicate diffusion from west to east, as Atlantean influences spread from the vicinity of the Canary Islands, across the Mediterranean, and to the Nile Delta in pre-dynastic times. Persistence of mummification, dog-worship, pyramid-building, and so on among the Guanches, centuries after these practices vanished from Egypt, was a remnant from Atlantean epochs. The Canary Islands' "Egyptian" cultural characteristics can only be explained by their origin in the Atlantic, not in the Nile Valley, where they arrived later, circa 3100 B.C. In other words, civilization spread to both the Canary Islands and the Nile Delta from Atlantis.

Guatavita ceremony

In pre-Spanish Colombia, prior to becoming king, a prince of the Muyscas Indians boarded his royal barge at the edge of Lake Guatavita. While thousands of his well-wishing subjects gathered on theshore, the young man was rowed out to a designated location, where he was stripped naked and his body smeared with a glutinous resin, then entirely sprinkled with gold dust. Thus transformed, the aspirant to the throne assumed the title of Noa, "the Gilded One." After sufficiently displaying himself, he dove into the lake, leaving a glittering trail of gold flakes through the crystal-clear water. When most of them were washed away, he swam back to the barge, and was helped aboard, his shoulders draped for the first time with the blue robe of kingship. The initiation ritual dramatized his direct descent from the Musscas' founding father, Noa, a rich king from across the sea who had been thrown adrift by a terrific flood that destroyed his island home. The gold dust streaming from the swimming prince signified the ancient loss of ancestral wealth.

A similar deluge story repeated by the neighboring Orinoco Indians told of the *Catena-ma-noa*, the "Water of Noa." Resemblance to the biblical Noah in ether version is striking, but suggestions of lost Atlantis are not missing. The Muyscas' newly installed king clearly identified with the survivor of a sunken realm, while the royal initiate's blue robe recalls the azure raiment worn by the kings of Atlantis, as described by Plato.

These overtly Atlantean details associated with Guatavita are remarkably underscored by the origins of the site itself. The lake is an astrobleme, a crater caused by a meteor and later filled with water. And while the geologic date of its formation is uncertain, its impact as concurrent with cometary events involved in the Atlantis destruction is at least suggested by the oral and ceremonial evidence. In other words, Lake Guatavita was recognized as a result of the same celestial catastrophe, perhaps a large fragment of meteoritic debris accompanying the killer-comet; hence, the ritual activity, fraught with Atlantean overtones, surrounding its location since prehistoric times.

Gucumatz

The Quiche Maya flood-hero who traveled over the Sunrise Sea following the loss of his island home beneath the waves, arriving on the shores of Yucatan with a troupe of followers who instituted Mesoamerican Civilization. Gucumatz, described in the *Popol Vuh*, the sacred book of the Quiches, would seem to be the same founding-father figure as Kukulcan, the "Feathered Serpent."

Gwyddno

In Welsh tradition, the Prince of Cantref y Gwaelod, a splendid city sunk beneath the sea—some say in Cardigan Bay, although this may be a later, localized version of the Atlantis story. Also known in Celtic myth as "Longshanks," Gwyddno possessed a magic cauldron which was among the original, ancient treasures of Britain. This sacred object comprises a theme belonging to the Atlantean mystery cult, a motif often found in other parts of the world in conjunction with Atlantis imagery.

(See Navel of the World)

Haiyococab

Recounted in the Dresden Codex as the Aztec "Water Over Earth," from which "the Earth-upholding gods escaped when the world was destroyed by a deluge. Language used to describe the Haiyococab clearly refers to Atlantean culture-bearers from the cataclysm that struck their homeland.

Halach-Unicob

Meaning "Lords," "True Men," "the Lineage of the Land," "Great Men," or "Priest-Rulers," the Halach-Unicob are ancestors of the Maya who are identified and portrayed on the 27th stele of Yaxchilan, the 11th stele at Piedras Negras, and at Chichen Itza's Temple of the Warriors as bearded figures with long, thin noses and a European cast of facial features. Inscriptions at these sites repeat that the Halach-Unicob arrived in Yucatan from Tutulxiu, a radiant kingdom far across the Atlantic Ocean, long since swallowed by the sea.

(See Ah Auab, Tutulxiu)

Harimagadas

A select group of Guanche women at the Canary Island of Tenerife who sacrificed themselves by jumping from a towering cliff into the sea. This act was meant to propitiate the sea-god and prevent him from sinking their island, as long ago happened to an ancestral kingdom. The ritual deaths of these virgins was an apparent recollection of and response to the destruction of Atlantis, which occurred approximately 600 miles north of Tenerife.

Harimagadas translates from Old High German for "Holy Maidens," at least one indication of the linguistic impact Atlantis made on two widely disparate peoples and the common Atlantean heritage so many cultures share.

Har-Sag-Mu

"Mu of the Mountain Range," where Zu, the Sumerian sky-god, settled after causing a terrible cataclysm. Thereafter, "stillness spread abroad, silence prevailed." In the later Babylonian version, as preserved in the Assyrian library of Ashurbanipal, Zu stole the Tablets of Destiny from his fellow gods, and brought them to Har-Sag-Mu. His self-transformation into a bird of prey, in order to fight off a serpent guarding the Tablets, recurs throughout worldwide imagery of an eagle battling a snake, from the Greek Delphi and Norse Yggdrasil to Aztec Mexico and pre-Columbian Colombia.

It is also associated with the chakra system of spiritual conflict between the kundalini serpent wound around the base of the human spine and Garuda, the eagle of an enlightened crown chakra. Zu's myth implies that this metaphysical concept was brought directly from heaven to Har-Sag-Mu, a sacred mountain on the Pacific island of Mu. Zu's theft of the Tablets of Destiny, which first described kundalini yoga, parallel the Western myth in which the brother of Atlas, Prometheus, stole fire from the gods and gave it to mankind. That "Promethean heat" appears to have been no less analogous to kundalini energy, because the Greek Titan suffered the daily digestion of his liver by an eagle.

During his "life-reading" of April 17, 1936, Edgar Cayce told of immigrants from the Atlantean catastrophe arriving in the Near Eastern "lands of Zu."

(See Cayce, Mu)

Hathor

The Egyptian goddess of fiery destruction. She was identified in the wall texts of Medinet Habu, West Thebes, with a flaming "planet," in other words, a comet, that destroyed the island home of the "Sea People" who invaded the Nile Delta in the early 12th century B.C. These were the Atlanteans described by Plato in their attempted conquest of the eastern Mediterranean. To extinguish the blazing island, she sank it beneath the sea. In what may be a variation of this same destruction, Hathor provoked the gods to inundate the world with a flood aimed at preventing her from burning up all humanity. In this version of her myth appears a dangerous comet threatening all human life, but ending with a world deluge.

Hau-neb

A name appearing throughout the wall texts of Medinet Habu, the "Victory Temple," erected by Pharaoh Ramses III in West Thebes to commemorate his triumph over invading Atlanteans. They were known by early 12th-century B.C. Egyptians as the *Hau-neb*.

Hawichyepam Maapuch

Sea-goddess of California's Chemehuevi and Mohave Indians, who believe she was responsible for keeping the Great Deluge from totally obliterating all life on Earth. She spared the last two creatures, Coyote and Puma, who sought refuge at the summit of Charleston Peak. As the flood receded, they descended the mountain to repopulate the world and pay homage to Hawichyepam Maapuch. She is part of the Native American rendition of the Flood, which destroyed a former age of greatness when human arrogance made the Indians' ancestors turn from their gods.

He Alge tid Kem

"How the Bad Days Came," a section from the Frisian version the destruction of Atlantis.

(See Oera Linda Bok)

Hecatoncheires

In Greek myth, "Titans of Ocean," inventors of the first warships, each one with 50 heads and 100 arms. After their defeat by the Olympian gods, they were buried under volcanic islands far out at sea. Their fate and description suggests the Hecatoncheires were metaphors for Atlantean battle cruisers. Their 100 "hands" were actually oars, while their 50 "heads" corresponded to as many marines on deck. Cottus, Gyges, and Aegeon, also known as *Briareus*, formed the trio of "Hundred-Handed Ones," corresponding to the three harbors of Atlantis described in *Kritias*, and may have been the names of flagships in the Atlantean navy, its 1,200 vessels divided into three battle divisions of 400 ships each. As long ago as 1882, Ignatius Donnelly believed the Hecatoncheires "were civilized races, and that the peculiarities ascribed to the last two refer to the vessels in which they visited the shores of the barbarians. The empire of the Titans was clearly the empire of Atlantis."

Gyges appears to have been *Ogyges*, who gave his name to the second great flood associated with the late third-millennium B.C. cataclysms that struck Atlantis.

(See Aegeon, Ignatius Donnelly)

Heer, Oswald

A German paleobiologist who was the first scientist to suggest, in 1835, that the migratory patterns of certain birds and fish in the North Atlantic might be residual behavior genetically imprinted over successive generations by the former existence of Plato's Atlantis.

(See C.P. Chatwin)

Heitsi-Eibib

The Namaqua Hottentots' flood hero who "came from the east," landing in the west of Cape South Africa, a very long time ago, with fellow survivors from a sunken kingdom. He was the captain of a "swimming house" filled with people and animals. Despite its resemblance to the biblical Noah, the story of Heitsi-Eibib predates any contacts with missionary Christianity. Both the Namaqua version and Genesis shared the same origin in describing culture-bearers from the Atlantean catastrophe.

Helig Voel ap Glannog

A Welsh version of Atlantis.

(See Gwyddno, Llyn Syfaddon)

Hemet Maze Stone

A gray boulder emblazoned with the intricate design of a labyrinthine maze enclosed in a 3 1/2-foot square. The petroglyph is located on a mountainside just west of Hemet, California, some 90 miles southeast of Los Angeles. Accumulation on its surface of a light patina known locally as "desert varnish" suggests the incised carving was executed between 3,000 and 4,000 years ago, despite the insistence of mainstream archaeologists, who insist, on tenuous physical evidence, that it could be no more than a few centuries old.

About 50 maze-stones have been identified throughout California, in Orange, Riverside, Imperial, and San Diego counties, and at least 14 examples of labyrinthine rock art are known in the remote area of Palm Springs. All of them have been found within 150 miles of each other, and virtually every one is rectangular, although varying in size from 4 inches to several feet in diameter. They are invariably located on boulder-strewn mountainsides, and are perhaps the remnants of a pilgrimage route dedicated to commemorating a seminal event in the deep past.

The maze itself is in the form of a swastika, a sacred symbol for numerous Native American tribes across the continent. Among the Hopi Indians, the hooked cross signifies the migration of their tribe from the east following a great flood that overwhelmed early mankind. Although it is not known if Hopi forefathers carved the Hemet Maze Stone, the Atlantean significance of their ancestral myth is suggested by its westward oriented design. These implications are complimented by a late 15th-century example of Mexican featherwork in a similar, swastika-like design (with reversed orientation, however) belonging to a transparently Atlantean figure in Mesoamerican myth, Chalchiuhtlicue; "Our Lady of the Turquoise Skirt" was the Aztec goddess of death at sea. Hopi sand paintings, spiritual devices for the removal of illness, are often formed into swastikas, with the patient made to sit at its center.

In the bottom-left corner of the square outline of the Hemet Maze Stone is a simple, much smaller, reversed, or right-oriented hooked cross, known in Buddhism as the *sauvastika*. Both swastikas and sauvastikas are common images throughout Asia, where they denote Buddha's right and left foot, respectively, and refer to his missionary

William Donato at California's Hemet Maze Stone.

travels throughout the world. As such, the Buddhist swastika-sauvastika and California petroglyph appear to share a parallel symbolism which both Asians and ancient Americans may have received independently from a common source. James Churchward, a 20th-century authority on Mu, stated that the swastika was the Pacific civilization's foremost emblem. He referred to it as "the key of universal movement," a characterization complimenting both Hopi and Buddhist symbolism.

(See Chalchiuhtlicue, Churchward)

Hennig, Richard

A notable historian who, in 1925, persuasively argued for a historical Atlantean presence in the region of Spanish Cadiz, scene of the ancient Iberian city of Tartessos. Although he erred in identifying Tartessos with Atlantis itself, Hennig demonstrated that the Atlantean kingdom of Gadeiros held sway over Atlantic Spain during pre-Classical times. Unfortunately, his work has never been fully translated into other languages; hence, his important contribution to Atlantology is little-known outside Germany.

(See Gadeiros, Ellen Whishaw)

Heroic Age

In his *Works and Days*, Hesiod describes five ages of mankind prior to his time (circa 700 B.C.) at the beginning of classical times. These were the ages of Gold,

Silver, Bronze, Heroism, and Iron. They coincide remarkably well with modern archaeology in some respects, and roughly correspond to the fourth-millennium Neolithic Period, when golden sunlight, not gold coin, was most prized by the megalith-builders. Long after incorporating solar alignments into their standing stones, a shift to lunar orientations was followed by the Bronze Age, characterized by Hesiod as extremely bellicose.

The Heroic Age comprised the last century or so of the Bronze Age to include the Trojan War, and ended with the destruction of Atlantis. Hesiod wrote of the Iron Age as a period of general ignorance, savagery, and decline—all of which typify the Dark Age that overspread Europe, Asia Minor, and most of the Near East for nearly five centuries after the Atlantean holocaust.

Hesiod's *Works and Days* traces some discernably Atlantean themes. The Silver Age, which climaxed when Atlantis suffered massive geologic upheavals circa 2100 B.C., came to its conclusion as it was "engulfed by Zeus," who likewise ordered the final destruction of the Atlantean capital in Plato's account. Hesiod characterized Bronze Age men as extraordinarily large of stature (the Atlanteans were descendants of "Titans"), and outstanding metalsmiths, who crafted great walls of bronze; in *Kritias*, the Atlanteans are described as wealthy metallurgists who ringed their city with bronze-sheeted walls.

Heva

The legendary "first woman" who, together with Ad-ima, arrived at the Indian subcontinent after the Great Flood destroyed a former age of civilized greatness. Throughout Polynesia, numerous island traditions recall a similar catastrophe in which the ancestral kingdom of Hiva was lost. Both appear to be reflections of the same deluge account, a suspicion underscored by Heva herself, referring to the drowned land she and her husband escaped.

(See Ad-ima)

Hiintcabiit

The Arapaho Indian version of a horned giant who arose from the bottom of the sea to save victims of the Great Flood by carrying them to the eastern shores of Turtle Island, or North America. On the walls of Ramses III's "Victory Temple," in West Thebes, some of the Atlantean invaders he fought wore horned helmets. In Greek myth, the Atlanteans, like Hiintcabiit, are depicted as Titans.

(See Wolf Clan)

Hina-lau-limu-kala

"Hina-of-the-Leaves-of-the-Limu-kala," or seaweed, a patroness of Hawaiian sacred practices known as *kahuna*, inherited from the drowned Motherland of Lemuria.

(See Lemuria, Limu-kala)

Hiti

In Samoan myth, antediluvian giants who ruled the world before "the heavens fell down" to set their island aflame. As it sank into the sea, new lands emerged from the depths to become the Samoan Islands.

Hmu

The original name of the Miao or Hmong, whose earliest historical period began with their migration from China into the Laotian Peninsula, just 5 centuries ago. But they are unique among all Southeast Asian peoples for their strong Caucasoid racial heritage predating any contacts with modern Europeans. A persistent creation myth described their origins as a Caucasian people in the Indo-Aryan homeland, a folk tradition confirmed by recent DNA testing, which establishes genetic traces back hundreds of generations to the Steppes of Central Russia. Hmong oral traditions also tell of a great deluge, after which their ancestors, the Hmu arrived in South East Asia. The Hmong still refer to themselves as "Hmu."

(See Mu)

Hoerbiger, Hanns

Austrian engineer who first published his *Welteislehre* (*WEL*), or *Cosmic Ice Theory*, in 1913. Interest in Hoerbiger's *Glazial-Kosmogonie* was eclipsed soon after by World War I, so his book could not achieve recognition until the 1920s, when it became an international best-seller in the millions of copies, and almost dominated the cosmological sciences for nearly 25 years. *WEL* was based on the supposition that large fragments of ice from passing comets have often altered the natural, geologic and human history of our planet, most notably, the destruction of Atlantis.

After Hoerbiger died in 1931, his ideas were popularized by a fellow Austrian, Hans Bellamy, in England. But any serious consideration of *Welteislehre* was dismissed from all academic thought following World War II, for political if not always scientific reasons. However, the ongoing discovery of icy moons and planets in our own solar system and beyond, as revealed by space probes from the 1970s onward, has done much to validate at least some of his fundamental conclusions.

During the last decade of the 20th century, Hoerbiger's belief that Atlantis was destroyed through the agency of cometary debris was given powerful impetus by archaeo-astronomers who identified Comet Encke as the celestial culprit most likely responsible for the Atlantean catastrophe.

(See Asteroid Theory)

Ho-ho-demi-no-Mikoto

Cited in the *Nihongi*, a Japanese collection of pre-Buddhist myths, histories and traditions, as a divine hero who descended to the ocean floor in an overturned basket. On his arrival, he visited a sunken palace belonging to the sea-god. Its described towers and walls are reminiscent of the stone structure found by scuba divers in 1985 off the coast of the Japanese island of Yonaguni.

(See Mu, Yonaguni)

Honomu

One of several place names in Hawaii commemorating the lost civilization of the Pacific, it means literally "Sacred Mu."

(See Lono, Mu)

Horaizan

Known throughout the Ryukyu Islands of southern Japan as a sunken kingdom of great antiquity and former splendor. It derived its name from the island's highest mountain, Horai, on the summit of which grew the Tree of Life.

(See Hesperides, Mu, Yonaguni)

Hotu-matua

The legendary founding father of Easter Island arrived from over the sea with a fleet of his family and followers after surviving a great catastrophe. The god of earthquakes, Poku, had upended Hotu-matua's homeland with a crowbar, sinking Hiva into the ocean depths.

(See Lemuria, Mu)

Hrim Thursar

In Scandinavian myth, a new race begat by the only man and woman to survive the Great Flood. All Norse traced their descent to the Hrim Thursar, or "Hoar Frost."

Huitzilopochtli

In Aztec myth, he was the divine leader who rescued an ancestral people from his devastated island kingdom in the Atlantic Ocean, Aztlan. Arriving in the Valley of Mexico, they built a new capital to commemorate their lost city, when Tenochtitlan was constructed on a rocky island at the center of a man-made lake. That Aztlan was the Nahuatl word for the Greek Atlantis is no less obvious than Huitzilopochtli's identification with Atlas: The 14th-century *Codex Borgia*, at the Biblioteca Apostolica Vaticana, depicts Huitzilopochtli supporting the sky on his shoulders. In other words, he was remembered as a leader who guided a large contingent of survivors from the destruction of Atlantis to Mexico, where they founded Mesoamerican civilization.

(See Atlas, Aztlan)

The Hulluk Miyumko

The California Miwok name for the Pleiades. The Hulluk Miyumko were female deities who gave birth to "beautiful star chiefs," just as the Atlantean Daughters of Atlas bore sons who were the first leaders of men.

(See Pleiades)

Hun yecil

"The Drowning of the Trees," identically known to the later Aztecs as Hun-Esil; an episode from the Mayas' cosmological book, the *Popol Vuh*. It tells how survivors of an Atlantic cataclysm built a temple near the banks of the Huehuhuetan River to thank the gods for their escape. The Hun yecil is associated with the final destruction of Atlantis.

Huruing Wuhti

In the Hopi Indian creation story, they were a pair of women who survived the Great Flood. The Huruing Wuhti were later venerated as mother goddesses, because they gave birth to the Hopi people, suggesting Atlantean culture-bearers and tribal progenitors in the American southwest. Chronologist, Neil Zimmerer, writes that the Huruing Wuhti derived their name from a single survivor of the Atlantis catastrophe, who "fled north with many others to start a new kingdom."

Hyades

"Rainy" or "Deluge," these Atlantean Daughters of Atlas became a formation of stars in the night sky. When they appear, another constellation of Atlantises, the Pleiades, is in conjunction with the sun at the time of the rainy season, suggesting the deluge that destroyed Atlantis.

Hy-Breasail

Another name for Atlantis in Celtic myth. Some of the Atlantean Tuatha da Danann, after severe military reverses in Ireland, were said to have returned to Hy-Breasail. As late as the 17th century, the island was still pictured and so named on Irish maps of the mid-Atlantic. As encyclopedist, Anna Franklin, observes, "maps have even existed which usually depict it as round, divided in the centre by a river, leading to comparisons with Atlantis." She goes on to relate that "a red-hot arrow was fired" into Hy-Breasail before it was dragged to the bottom of the ocean by the sea-god, Manannan. This variation of the legend suggests the comet or meteor fall that brought about the final Atlantean destruction, an implication reemphasized by Manannan, the Celtic counterpart of Poseidon. Hy-Breasail may be related to the Norse Yggdrasil that grew at the center of the world, itself reminiscent of the Tree of Life at the center of the Garden of the Hesperides, a Greek variation on the Atlantis theme.

Brazil was named by Portuguese sailors familiar with the story of Hy-Breasail. Their suspicions concerning some connection between the lost island and South America were abundantly confirmed by numerous native folk traditions of a sunken realm from which other white-skinned visitors preceded the modern Europeans in antiquity.

(See Garden of the Hesperides, Maia, Tuatha da Danann)

The Hydrophoria

An annual festival held in Athens to commemorate the near extinction of mankind during the Great Flood, from which only Deucalion (a nephew of Atlas) and his wife, Pyrrha, survived. The Hydrophoria was intended to propitiate the spirits of the dead who perished in the cataclysm by pouring libations of water, signifying the Deluge, into a hole in the ground. A virtually identical commemoration was conducted in Syria, at Hierapolis, by the Phoenicians, but the name of their flood hero is no longer known.

The Hydrophoria did not memorialize the final destruction of Atlantis, but a previous period of serious geologic upheaval that caused the migration of many Atlanteans throughout the world, as personified in Deucalion and Pyrrha. While some Atlantologists believe this previous "deluge" was an early or mid-third millennium B.C. partial evacuation of the island nation, others assign it to a period immediately anterior to the sudden flourishing of civilization in many parts of the world, including the Nile Valley, Mesopotamia, the Troad, Crete, the Indus Valley, Yucatan, and so on, around 3100 B.C.

(See Haucaypata)

Hyne, Cutcliffe J.

Author of *The Lost Continent* (1900), one of the better fictional portrayals of Atlantis that continues to stand the test of time. Even the professional debunker, L. Sprague De Camp, believed Hyne's "novel is a competent piece of storytelling: fast, well-constructed, colorful, with the leading characters well-drawn and occasional flashes of grim humor." *The Lost Continent* imaginatively describes Atlantis though the adventures of Deucalion, the Greek flood hero.

(See Deucalion)

Iamblichos

An important fourth-century neo-Platonist philosopher who insisted upon the historical validity of Plato's Atlantis account, but stressed, as did Plato, its allegorical significance.

(See Krantor of Soluntum, Plato)

Iberus

A Titan associated by Roman scholars with the Spanish peninsula; hence, Iberia. His identification in non-Platonic myth as the twin brother of Atlas signifies the close relationship between Atlantis and its affiliated kingdom in Spain.

(See Gadeiros)

Igh and Imox

Among the Chiapenese, a husband and wife who arrived in Central America across the Atlantic Ocean from their splendid kingdom before it was destroyed by a catastrophic flood.

Ik

Literally "breath," in Mayan, for a glyph comprising a "T" in the center of a square, at the top of which a pair of snakes extend left and right. James Churchward identified "T" as the chief emblem of Mu, symbolizing the Tree of Life venerated at the Pacific civilization. The opposing serpents of the Ik-glyph appear to signify Lemurian spiritual energies and/or cultural influences spreading east and west from the central kingdom, which is itself represented by a square embodying the four cardinal directions. The Mayan "breath" and Mu's Tree of Life refer to the same concept.

(See Churchward, Mu)

Inanna

The Sumerian mother-goddess, who lamented that the souls of the drowned had become fish in the sea during a cataclysmic flood. After the catastrophe, Inanna carried the Tablets of Civilization to the Fertile Crescent between the Tigris and Euphrates Rivers, where society was reborn. The Hittites worshiped her as *Inaras*, who annually renewed her virginity in a ritual festival, the *Purulli*, from which the Jewish "Purim" derived. Inanna was known as *Ishtar* to the Babylonians.

Infoniwa

In Chinese myth, a young king invented civilization on a distant island through the guidance of twin gods, Infoniwa (sometimes *Infoniwoo*) and Awun. They promised to protect his people by warning them in advance of any impending danger. At the precise center of the kingdom, in a holy shrine, were statues of the divine brothers; if the faces of these statues turned red, they warned, the island would be destroyed.

For many years, the king and his subjects were virtuous and prosperous. With opulence, however, came greed. The people grew cynical of any spiritual values and laughed at their king's belief in the gods' warning as ridiculous superstition. One night, a blasphemous prankster stole into the shrine and, as a joke, daubed the faces of Infoniwa and Awun with red paint. The king, an old man now and the progenitor of many fine offspring, still honored the gods. When he saw their painted statues, he summoned his royal household and ordered an immediate evacuation. Loaded down with all their possessions as they hurriedly made for the royal yacht, the king and his family members were derided in the streets by mobs of insolent people. But as the ship disappeared over the horizon, the island was convulsed by earthquakes and sank with all its inhabitants into the depths of the sea. Meanwhile, the king with his wife and children landed safely on the shore near Shanghai, where they established China's first imperial dynasty.

Although Atlantis was on the other side of the world from China, the resemblance of this legend in so many particulars with Plato's fourth-century B.C. account argues for a common source. In both the Chinese and Greek versions, the divine founders are twins, while a prosperous, formerly upstanding people degenerate into selfishness and are punished with the inundation of their island kingdom. In most flood myths around the world, only a patriarch with his family and followers survive, because he believed a warning of some kind that was scorned by others. So too, the deluge hero becomes the founding father of a civilization, people, or dynasty, whose descendants assert their legitimacy by tracing their unbroken lineage to him.

Iopus

In Virgil's *Aeneid*, "long-haired Iopus, pupil of mighty Atlas," was a Carthaginian leader who learned from the Titan about astronomy; comets ("the fires of heaven"); human origins; meteorology; and the Hyades, daughters of Atlas and, therefore, "Atlantises." These studies are preeminently Atlantean, even suggestive of the final destruction. Iopus represented the scientific and cultural legacy of lost Atlantis subsequently inherited by the Phoenicians, who used such knowledge to become the foremost mariners of classical times.

(See Hyades)

The Ipurina Flood Story

Indians of the Upper Amazon's Rio Purus describe a deluge of fiery water which long ago burned up the entire rain forest: "On Earth, all was dark as night, and the sun and moon were hidden."

(See Asteroid Theory)

Iraghdadakh

Literally "the Old man," a deluge hero of the Aleut Indians of the Aleutian Archipelago, who repopulated the world after it was devastated by a great flood, by casting stones on the Earth. This was the same method used by the Greek Deucalion and dozens of other flood heroes around the globe, and it points to a common, pre-Christian missionary experience.

(See Deucalion)

Irin Mage

In the Tupi-Guarani story of the creation, early humanity was virtually wiped out by a terrible fire from heaven. It was sent from the supreme god, Monan, in punishment for the sins of the world. But a powerful magician, Irin Mage, appeared at the last moment and summoned a worldwide deluge to extinguish the flames.

In this South American myth is preserved a folk memory of the cometary havoc wrought worldwide immediately prior to the destruction of Atlantis. Chronologer, Neil Zimmerer, writes that Irin Mage "fled Atlantis when the island sank into the sea, and founded the Nation of Tupinamba," in prehistoric Brazil.

Isla Mujeres

The "Isle of Women" is a narrow, small island 7 miles long, about 3 miles offshore at the northeast point of Yucatan. It was named by the Spaniards, who first landed in the 1520s, for the numerous stone statues they found of what they assumed were representations of different women. Actually, the statues—apparently several hundred of them—portrayed various manifestations of a single deity, the lunar-goddess Ixchel, to whom the island was consecrated as a sacred center; hence, its absence of native population. Isla Mujeres was used by the Mayas only as a place of spiritual pilgrimage.

At the far southern point of the island stands a small, ruined shrine housing the remains of an altar. The site was ransacked and the island's statues demolished, their fragments tossed into the sea on orders of Catholic friars who condemned such artwork as satanic. In addition to her attributes as the divine patroness of childbirth and prophesy, Ixchel, "the White Lady," was the mother of the Maya people. They venerated her as the survivor of a great deluge that destroyed her former kingdom in the Atlantic Ocean. As such, her chief places of worship on islands like Isla Mujeres and Cozumel were chosen to reflect her Atlantean origins.

(See Ixchel)

Island of Jewels

In Hindu myth, a paradisiacal realm in the eastern Pacific Ocean, from which the founders of the Brahman caste arrived in India during the distant past. The island was hidden by a misty ether known as the *akasha*, a poetic metaphor for "ancient memory" or "forgetfulness." Its beaches were formed of powdered gems, and the forests were perpetually in bloom. At the center of the island was located a magnificent palace, where all wishes were granted.

(See Mu)

Isle of the Sun

A magnificent island kingdom in the middle of the Atlantic Ocean, from which Manco Capac, his wife, and followers fled during a time of wide-spread degeneracy. Their sinful homeland was destroyed in a flood sent as punishment from the gods. Later, the story was transferred to Lake Titicaca and its small island, which was named Isla del Sol after Maco Capac's oceanic homeland.

(See Manco Capac, Pu-Un-Runa)

Isle Royale

A Lake Superior island near Michigan's Upper Peninsula, where many millions of pounds of copper ore were mined by Atlantean entrepreneurs from 3000 B.C. to 1200 B.C.

(See Bronze Age)

Itaba Tahuana

The divine ancestor of Haiti's Taino natives. He married the four winds, who bore him two sets of twins, from whom early humanity descended. Most of them were sinful, so Itaba Tahuana destroyed them with a cataclysmic flood.

This figure is doubtless a folk recollection of the Atlantean catastrophe, complete with his twin offspring and marriage to the four "winds," that is to say, the four cardinal directions, placing him at the center of the world. Even Itaba's name is an obvious derivation of "Atlas."

Italus

According to Plutarch, "some say again that Roma, from whom the city was so-called, was daughter of Italus and Leucaria." Italus was the Latin version of Atlas, while Leucaria was a sea-goddess, one of the Sirens, an inflection of Leukippe, the first woman of Atlantis. Plato outlined the limits of Atlantean influence in Europe by extending them to western Italy.

(See Atlas)

Itzamna

The Mayas' earliest culture-bearer, the "White Man," who preceded the arrival of the more famous Kukulcan, or "Feathered Serpent." The latter appears to have represented survivors from the final destruction of Atlantis, in 1198 B.C. Itzamna was the original founder of Mesoamerican civilization. He and his wife, Ixchel, the "White Lady," were among immigrants fleeing westward during the late fourth millennium B.C., when their Atlantean homeland was beset with the first in a series of four geologic upheavals. In the Maya cosmology, the *Chilam Balam*, and Juan Darreygosa's 16th-century *Historia de Zodzil*, Itzamna bears the title "Serpent from the East" and is described as "the first after the flood." He arrived on the eastern shores of the island of Cozumel, where the ruins of several temples to him and Ixchel still stand, just off the Yucatan peninsula.

Moving to the mainland, he built the first version of Chichen Itza and 140 other ceremonial centers and cities. The Mayas believed Itzamna brought all the arts of civilization to Yucatan after the Great Flood. These included city-planning, astronomy-astrology, agriculture, writing, organized labor, sculpture, mathematics, book-illumination, government, and music. He is portrayed in temple art, such as friezes at the Maya ceremonial center of Tikal, in Guatemala, as a long-nosed, bearded man rowing his boat across the sea from which he came.

(See Ixchel)

Temple to Itzamna, on the island of Cozumel, where he was said to have first landed in Yucatan, following the watery destruction of his distant homeland.

Marxist rebels climb to the top of Tikal's highest pyramid. Although completed long after the destruction of Atlantis, it preserved several references to the sunken civilization.

Ix Chebel Yax

The Maya goddess of household affairs and wisdom, she was daughter of Itzamna and Ixchel. As such, Ix Chebel Yax was among the first generation of Yucatan-born Atlantean refugees from the final destruction of their homeland. She taught spinning, weaving, dyeing, and basketry, as learned from her mother, the White Lady—qualities which describe the introduction of civilization to Middle America.

Ixchel

The Mayas' "White Lady," who brought the civilized arts of weaving, medicine, and prophesy from her lost kingdom over the Atlantic Ocean after a great flood. Both she and her Aztec incarnation, Coyolxauqui, were symbolized by a crystal skull, signifying their special relationship to the moon (the heavenly crystal skull) and, hence, psychic powers. In temple art and surviving codexes, Ixchel is depicted angrily wielding a sky-serpent, or comet, with which she threatens to bring about a deluge for the destruction of a sinful mankind. Other portrayals show her over-turning a vase to drench the world with water, likewise suggesting the flood. In the Codex Mendoza, Ixchel appears with her husband, Itzamna, the "White Man," riding the flood toward Yucatan, her baggage spilling out on the waves. Her myth unmistakably describes Ixchel as a culture-bearer from Atlantis.

(See Crystal Skull, Itzamna)

Ix Pucyola

An obscure sea-deity, perhaps the Mayan name for Atlantis. Ix Pucyola means "She, the Destroyer in the Heart of Water."

Izanagi and Izanami

The Japanese creators of all life on Earth. From the Celestial Bridge, or Milky Way, Izanagi stirred the ocean with his jeweled spear. Out of the agitated waters arose the island of Onogoro, where he built an octagonal tower located at the center of the world. Afterwards, while giving birth to fire, Izanami died and went to the Underworld. In mourning for his wife, Izanagi undertook a quest to find her, but she could not return with him because she had tasted a single fruit grown in the dark kingdom. Henceforward, she became the Queen of the Land of the Dead.

This is almost precisely the Western legend of Persephone, an allegorical myth for the fundamental tenet of eternal rebirth belonging to the Atlantean Navel of the World mystery cult. It appears again in the octagonal tower, its eight sides representing the cardinal and sub-cardinal directions defining the sacred center.

The resemblance of this Japanese couple to another pair of founders in ancient Mexico is an additional theme connecting Atlantis. Izanagi and Izanami compare with Itzamna and Ixchel, the husband-and-wife creators of Maya civili-zation, who arrived at the shores of Yucatan following a terrible deluge.

Jacolliot, Louis

French scholar (1837 to 1890) who collected local and regional myths during a long sojourn through India, where his fluency in Sanskrit enabled him to read about Rutas, a great and highly cultured kingdom that sank beneath the Pacific Ocean in the deeply ancient past. Returning to France, Jacolliot published his findings in *Historie des Vierges*, to popular acclaim.

(See Rutas)

Jambu

A Tantric version of mankind's birthplace in the "Island of the Blest," perhaps the most common epithet for Atlantis. Also regarded as the "Land of the Rose-Apple Tree," the Hesperides' Atlantean Tree of Life, Jambu was similarly circular in configuration, with the god Shiva's "Diamond Seat" at the island's sacred center. Shiva is the Hindu Poseidon, whose "seat," a chariot, was set up in the center of Atlantis.

The S.S. *Jesmond*

A ship associated with the controversial discovery of Atlantis in 1882. On March 1, the 1,465-ton steam schooner was on a routine transatlantic voyage bound from France to New Orleans with a cargo of dried fruit, when Captain David Amory Robson observed "the singular appearance of the sea" some 200 miles southwest of Madeira. Great billows of mud clouded the water, together with a vast carpet of dead fish numbering an estimated .5 million tons spread over 7,500 square miles. At the same moment, a slight submarine volcanic eruption was reported by monitoring stations in the Azores and Canaries.

The following morning, the *Jesmond*, still on course, was confronted by an unknown island that gave every indication of having just risen from the sea. It was large, about 30 miles across from north to south, and mountainous, with a smoldering volcano. Captain Robson led a small landing party to investigate the new island. Black basalt predominated, and a fine ooze, with millions of dead fish, seemed to cover everything. The place was utterly barren and cut by numerous fissures, from which steam rose constantly. By accident, one of the sailors found a flint arrowhead. Excited by this discovery, the men began randomly digging. Almost at once, they shoveled up many more arrowheads, together with a few small knives.

Robson returned on March 3 with ship's tools and 15 volunteers. Before nightfall, they unearthed the stone statue of a woman; it was a bas-relief sculpted into one side of an oblong rock and slightly larger than life-size, heavily encrusted with marine growth. Further inland, the men came upon two walls of unmortared stone. Nearby, they excavated a sword made of some unfamiliar yellow metal, followed by a number of spear-heads, ax-heads, and metal rings. Finally came pottery figures of birds and other animals, plus two large flat-bottom jars containing bone fragments and a virtually intact human skull. With weather deteriorating, Captain Robson brought the finds aboard his vessel, marked the island's position (latitude 250 North, longitude 230 40' West), then hoisted anchor. He arrived in New Orleans at noon, March 31.

The *Jesmond*'s encounter was described first in a front page story of a local periodical, then quickly syndicated to more than a dozen newspapers across the country. A reporter for the New Orleans' *Times-Picayune* wrote that the artifacts, which he personally handled, did not impress him as fakes, and he wrote that the Captain offered to "show the collection to any gentleman who is interested." On May 19, Robson returned to London—without his finds, the whereabouts of which have not been known since. Lawrence D. Hill, whose investigation of the *Jesmond* incident is the most thorough, concluded that the sword and other metal objects were *tumbaga*, an alloy 80 percent gold and 20 percent copper. Robson, writes Hill, had the artifacts melted down and split the resultant gold with his crew. The ship's log was discarded by the British Board of Trade in keeping with its policy of destroying such documents after seven years.

The episode was not a hoax, because the mysterious island was sighted at the same location by James Newdick, captain of another steamer, the *Westbourne*, sailing for Marseilles out of New York. Moreover, as mentioned previously, an undersea seismic event was simultaneously recorded in the Azore and Canary Islands. The location of the arisen island, although within the immediate sphere of Atlantean influence, implies it was not actually Atlantis itself, but probably the scene of a colony or closely allied kingdom.

Some internal evidence in the *Jesmond* story supports an Atlantean interpretation: Hill believed the metal sword Captain Robson found was tumbaga, which is as much as saying it was *orichalcum*; this is a term Plato uses to define an alloy technique metalsmiths used in Atlantis, when they combined rich copper with gold.

A modern undersea research expedition to the position recorded by Captain Robson seems justified.

Job

Regarded as the oldest book in the Hebrew bible, 26:5–6 recounts, "The primeval giants tremble imprisoned beneath the waters with their inhabitants. The unseen world [the bottom of the sea] lies open before them, and the place of destruction is uncovered." These enigmatic references appear to describe the Atlanteans, described by Plato as Titans, and sunken Atlantis in "the unseen world."

Jormungandr

The name of the Midgaard Serpent in Norse myth and a metaphor for geologic violence particularly associated with the mid-Atlantic Ocean. Jormungandr dwelt under the sea. Whenever he tightened his coils about the world, earthquakes and tempests lashed out. In the Twilight of the Gods (*Goetterdaemmerung* or *Ragnarok*), the monster's death agonies caused a worldwide flood, part of the universal destruction that ended a former age of greatness.

Jubmel

Laplanders of the remote Arctic Circle remember a terrible god of vengeance who, like Zeus in Plato's story of Atlantis, wanted to punish all human beings for their wickedness. Their myth contains some of the most colorful descriptions of a falling comet and the awful flood that Jubmel generated:

> The lord of heaven himself descended. His terrifying anger flashed with the red, blue and green of serpents, all on fire. Everyone went into hiding, while the children wept with fear. The god spoke in his anger, "I shall gather the sea together upon itself, form it into

a towering wall of water and throw it against you wicked children of the Earth, exterminating you and all living things!" Foaming, crashing, rising to the sky rushed the wall of water over the sea, crushing everything in its path, until neither mountains nor highlands were revealed any longer by the sun, which could not shine in heaven. The groans of the dying filled the Earth, mankind's home, and dead bodies rolled about in the dark waters.

The Maya "Acropolis" at Tikal, Guatemala, where a portrayal of the Atlantis catastrophe was discovered by pioneering Mesoamericanist, Teobert Maler, in the early 20th century.

Ka'ahupahau

A Hawaiian goddess who dwells in a cave, where she guards the waters off Oahu, near the entrance to Pearl Harbor, against man-eating sharks. Ka'ahupahau was widely believed to have alerted the captain of an American destroyer, who sank a Japanese mini-submarine—a kind of 20th-century shark—endeavoring to attack the U.S. naval installation on December 7, 1941. She is described as a fair-skinned woman with long, wavy, light-colored hair, one of several mythic personalities suggesting racially alien visitors to Polynesia in the ancient past from Lemuria.

(See Lemuria)

Kaboi

A flood hero revered by the Karaya Indians, whose ancestors he led into a massive cave as a place of refuge. After the waters retreated, they followed him back into the world and were guided by the song of a bird. This bird motif recurs in several deluge traditions around the world, not only in Genesis. Kaboi is familiar throughout South America, known as *Ka-mu* to the Arawaks, *Ta-mu* to the Caribs, *Kame* to the Bakairi, and *Zume* to the Paraguayans.

Green steatite representation of a distinctly European head, recovered from the pre-Colombian ruins of Cuicuilco, outside Mexico City.

Kadaklan

Founder of Burotu, the Melanesian version of Lemuria.

(See Burotu, Lemuria)

Kahiki

The splendid, vanished island kingdom from which Lono, the white-skinned culture-bearer, arrived in ancient Hawaii. Kahiki is a Polynesian variant of the lost civilization of the Pacific better known as Mu or Lemuria.

(See Lono, Lemuria, Mu)

Kaimanawa Wall

Located immediately south of Lake Taupo, on New Zealand's North Island, the stone structure is more probably a step pyramid or terraced, ceremonial platform of the kind found throughout ancient Polynesia, although among the very largest examples. Childress, who investigated the site in 1996 when it came to the attention of the outside world, wrote (in *A Hitchhiker's Guide to Armageddon*) that:

> ...the blocks seem to be a standard one point-eight meters long by one point-five meters high. The bottom block runs straight down to one point-seven meters and beyond. The stone is local ignimbrite, a soft volcanic stone made of compressed sand and ash. The nearest outcrop of such stone is five kilometers away. The blocks run for twenty five meters in a straight line from east to west, and the wall faces due north. The wall consists of approximately ten regular blocks that are seemingly cut and fitted together without mortar (119).

For lack of any datable material, the Kaimanawa Wall's age is elusive. Century-old trees growing through the structure predate it to prehistory, but the Maori, who arrived in New Zealand 700 years ago, were not its builders, because they never erected monumental structures. It may have been raised more than 2,000 years ago by the Waitahanui, whose elders apparently preserve some knowledge of the ramparts.

The Kaimanawa Wall is almost certainly a Lemurian ruin, part of a ceremonial center created by missionaries or survivors from Mu.

(See Mu, Waitahanui)

Kalevala

"Land of Heroes," the national epic of the Finnish people, a 19th-century collection of pre-Christian ballads, lyrical songs, incantations and oral traditions.

The *Kalevala* describes an ancient cosmic disaster, in which a "fire from heaven" devastates much of the world, causing unprecedented earthquakes and unusually high tides in Finland.

Kanamwayso

In Micronesian myth, a splendid kingdom from which sorcerers very long ago sailed throughout the Pacific. The stone ruins at Nan Madol, on the island of Pohnpei, are allegedly the remnants of their work. Falling stars and earthquakes were responsible for setting Kanamwayso aflame and dropping it to the bottom of the ocean, where it is inhabited by the spirits of those who perished in the cataclysm, who still preside over the ghosts of all persons who perish at sea.

(See Mu)

Katkochila

When mortals stole the magic flute of this Wintun Indian god, he devastated the Earth with a "fire from heaven" extinguished only by a universal flood that killed off most mankind. Katkochila's South American tradition is in common with deluge stories everywhere—namely, human irreverence punished with celestial fire and earthly inundation.

Kaveripumpattinam

Described in the "Manimakalai," the Tamil epic, as a harbor city preceding the birth of civilization on Sri Lanka, Kaveripumpattinam slipped beneath the Indian Ocean, where its ghostly ruins are still alleged to lie not far from the shore at Poompuhur.

Kesara

Queen of the Fomorach and the first ruler of Ireland. She arrived with her followers from Atlantis in the late fourth millennium B.C. during a period of severe geologic upheavals that generated similar migrations to various parts of the world.

Kircher, Athanasius

German polymath of the 17th century, this Jesuit priest was a pioneering mathematician, physicist, chemist, linguist, and archaeologist; the first to study phosphorescence; inventor of, among numerous futuristic innovations, the slide projector and a prototype of the microscope. The founding father of scientific Egyptology, his was the first serious investigation of temple hieroglyphs.

Kircher was also the first scholar to seriously investigate the Atlantis legend. Initially skeptical, he cautiously began reconsidering its credibility while assembling mythic traditions of numerous cultures in various parts of the world about a great flood. "I confess for a long time I had regarded all this," he said of various European traditions of Atlantis, "as pure fables to the day when, better instructed in Oriental languages, I judged that all these legends must be, after all, only the development of a great truth."

His research led him to the immense collection of source materials at the Vatican Library, where, as Europe's foremost scholar, its formidable resources were at his disposal. It was here that he discovered a single piece of evidence which proved to him that the legend was actually fact. Among the relatively few surviving documents from Imperial Rome, Kircher found a well-preserved, treated-leather map purporting to show the configuration and location of Atlantis. The map was not Roman, but brought in the first century A.D. to Italy from Egypt, where it had been executed. It survived the demise of Classical Times, and found its way into the Vatican Library. Kircher copied it precisely, adding only a visual reference to the New World, and published it in his book, *Mundus Subterraneus: The Subterranean World*, in 1665.

His caption states it is "a map of the island of Atlantis originally made in Egypt after Plato's description," which suggests it was created sometime following the 4th century B.C., perhaps by a Greek mapmaker attached to the Ptolemies. More probably, the map's first home was the Great Library of Alexandria, where numerous books and references to Atlantis were lost, along with another million-plus volumes, when the institution was burned by religious fanatics. In relocating to Rome, the map escaped that destruction.

Similar to modern conclusions forced by current understanding of geology in the Mid-Atlantic Ridge, Kircher's map depicts Atlantis, not as a continent, but an island about the size of Spain and France combined. It shows a large, centrally located volcano, most likely meant to represent Mount Atlas, together with six major rivers, something Plato does not mention. *Kritias* describes large rivers on the island of Atlantis, but does not indicate how many. Although the map vanished after Kircher's death in 1680, it was the only known representation of Atlantis to have survived the Ancient World. Thanks to his research and book, it survives today in a close copy. Kircher was the first to publish a map of Atlantis, probably the most accurate of its kind to date.

Curiously, it is depicted upside down, contrary to maps in both his day and ours. Yet, this apparent anomaly is proof of the map's authenticity, because Egyptian mapmakers, even as late as Ptolemaic times, designed their maps with the Upper Nile Valley located in the south ("Upper" refers to its higher elevation) at the top, because the river's headwaters are located in the Sudan.

Kitchie Manitou

The Muskwari Indians of North America recounted that this widely known god destroyed the world first with heavenly fire, then a great flood. The Potawatomi version, like Plato's account, cites the immorality of the inhabitants of a great island. Kitchie Manitou had made their homeland a veritable paradise, but because men became "perverse, ungrateful and wicked," he sank it, drowning the sinners. Only one man and his wife survived by escaping "in a big canoe."

Kleito

Literally "famous," or "splendid." According to Plato, she was an early inhabitant of the Atlantic island that would eventually become Atlantis. After the death of her parents, Kleito was visited by the sea-god Poseidon. Their children—five sets of twin boys—formed the royal house that ruled Atlantis until its destruction. Her home was on a hill not far from the sea and south of a prominent mountain. It was here that Poseidon encircled her dwelling place, thereby defining it as a holy precinct, with a concentric canal. Two others were later added to form three additional land rings, from and around which the city of Atlantis grew over the centuries.

Kleito represents the pre-civilized natives of the Atlantic island, just as Poseidon less certainly may signify the arrival of an early sea-people already in possession of the civilized arts. A shrine dedicated to her was certainly the oldest structure on Atlantis, and preserved at its central, most sacred island. It might have been simply an ancestral monument or the chapel for an unknown religion, one of many cults practiced by the Atlanteans, but certainly its most venerable.

Kmukamtch

The Klamath Indians of south-central Oregon and northern California say this shining demon from the sky endeavored to destroy the Earth with a celestial flame followed by a worldwide deluge. In mythic traditions among numerous cultures, a frightening comet is often described as a bright demon or angry god. Among the California Modoc, Kmukamtch is, literally "the Ancient Old Man from Mu," the creator of mankind

(See Hathor, Mu)

Kodoyanpe

The ancestral flood hero of California's Maidu Indians and creator of the first human beings from wooden images.

Krakatoa

A 6,000-foot (above sea-level) volcano on Pulau Rakata Island in the Sunda Straits of Indonesia. At 10 a.m., on August 27, 1883, Krakatoa exploded, sending ash clouds to an altitude of 50 miles, and generating shock waves registered around the Earth several times. The detonation could be heard in Australia, 2,200 miles away. Some 5 cubic miles of rock debris were discharged, and ash fell over 300,000 square miles. The volcanic mountain collapsed into the sea, spawning tsunamis (destructive waves) as far away as Hawaii and South America, reaching heights of 125 feet, and claiming 36,000 human lives on Java and Sumatra. Krakatoa's geological history not only makes the destruction of Atlantis credible through close comparison, but demonstrates how the Earth energies common to both events were brought about.

Krantor of Soluntum

A 4th-century neo-Platonist, a contemporary and colleague of Iamblichos, who played a important part in confirming Plato's account of the sunken civilization by personally traveling to the Nile Delta, where he found the same Temple of the Goddess Neith, inscribed with identical information presented in the Dialogues.

(See Iamblichos, Plato, Solon)

Krimen

South America's Tupi-Guarani Indians tell how three brothers—Coem and Hermitten, led by Krimen—escaped the Great Flood, first by hiding in caves high up in the mountains, then by climbing trees. As in the Greek version of Atlantis, the brother motif plays a central role.

Kritias

The second of two Dialogues composed by the Greek philosopher, Plato, describing the rise and fall of Atlantis, left unfinished a few years before his death in 348 B.C. The text is formed from a conversation (more of a monologue) between his teacher and predecessor, Socrates, and Kritias, an important fifth-century B.C. statesman. He begins by saying that the events described took place more than 9,000 years before, when a far-flung war between the Atlantean Empire and "all those who lived inside the Pillars of Heracles" (the Mediterranean) climaxed with geologic violence. The island of Atlantis, according to Kritias, was greater in extent than Libya and Asia combined, but vanished into the sea through a series of earthquakes "in a day and a night." Before its destruction, it ruled over an imperial system from the "Opposite Continent" in the far west, to Italy in the central Mediterranean, including other isles in its sphere of influence and circum-Atlantic coastal territories.

The beginnings of this thalassocracy occurred in the mythic past, when the gods divided up the world between themselves. As part of his portion, Poseidon was given the Atlantean island. Its climate was fair, the soil rich, and animals—even elephants—were in abundance. There were deep forests, freshwater springs, and an impressive mountain range. The island was already inhabited, and Poseidon wed a native woman. The sea-god prepared a place for her by laying the foundations of a magnificent, unusual city. He created three artificial islands separated by concentric moats, but interconnected by bridged canals. At the center of the smallest, central island stood his wife's original dwelling place on a hill, and it was here that the Temple of Poseidon was later erected, together with the imperial palace nearby.

Poseidon sired five sets of twin sons on the native woman, and named the island after their firstborn, Atlas. These children and their descendants formed the ruling family for many generations, and built the island into a powerful state, primarily through mining. The completed city is described in some detail, with emphasis on the kingdom's political and military structures. Although their holdings kept expanding in all directions, the Atlanteans were a virtuous people ruled by a beneficent, law-conscious confederation of monarchs. In time, however, they were corrupted by their wealth and became insatiable for greater power. The Atlanteans built a mighty military machine that stormed into the Mediterranean World, conquering Libya and threatening Egypt, but were soundly defeated by Greek forces and driven back to Atlantis.

Kritias breaks off abruptly when Zeus, observing the action from Mount Olympus, convenes a meeting of the gods to determine some terrible judgement befitting the degenerate Atlanteans.

Kukulcan

The Mayas' version of the "Feathered Serpent," known throughout Middle America as the leading culture-bearer responsible for Mesoamerican civilization. According to their epic, the *Popol Vuh*, he was a tall, light-eyed, bearded, blond ("his hair was like corn silk") visitor from his homeland, a great kingdom across the Atlantic Ocean. It reports that he arrived at the shores of Yucatan on a "raft of serpents," perhaps a ship decorated with serpentine motif, or as Dr. Thor Heyerdahl suggested, a vessel whose reed hull twisted in the waves like writhing snakes.

Kukulcan was accompanied by a group of wise men who taught the natives astrology-astronomy, city-planning, agriculture, literature, government, and the arts. He put an end to human and animal sacrifice, saying that the gods accepted only flower offerings. Unfortunately, the Mayan words for "flower" and "human heart" were almost indistinguishable, and the Mayas eventually returned to human sacrifice and ritual removal of the heart. Kukulcan was much beloved and built the first cities in Yucatan. In time, however, he got into political trouble of some kind, and disgraced himself through drunkenness and sexual excesses, the common course of civilizers alone (or almost) among so-called primitive natives. He was forced to leave, much to the distress of most people. They wept to see him board his ship again, but he promised that either he himself or his descendant would come back someday. With that, he sailed, not to his homeland in the east, but into the Pacific Ocean, toward the setting sun.

Kukulcan was doubtless an important, though not the only nor necessarily the first, culture-bearer from Atlantis, probably before the final destruction of that city, because the Mayas' account makes no mention of any natural disaster. They portrayed him in temple art as a figure supporting the sky, the archetypical Atlas. In any case, Kukulcan represents the arrival of Atlantean culture-bearers in Middle America.

Lowland Yucatan pyramid dedicated to Votan, a flood hero from the Maya version of Atlantis, Valum.

Kuksu

Revered by South America's Maidu and Pomo Indians as the creator of the world, he later, in response to the wickedness of mankind, set the Earth ablaze with celestial flames, then extinguished the conflagration with an awful deluge. Such native versions, while similar to the biblical version, differ importantly with the addition of a "fire from heaven" immediately preceding but inextricably bound to the flood.

A North American tribe known by the same name told of a turquoise house on a large island, long ago, on the other side of the western horizon. Before it was gradually engulfed by the Pacific Ocean, sorcerers who lived in the house took ship for California, where their descendants still make up a shamanistic society among the Kuksu.

Kumari Kandam

In Tamil tradition, the "Land of Purity," a sophisticated kingdom of high learning, south of Cape Comorin, in the distant past. Like Mount Atlas, after which Atlantis derived its name, Kumarikoddu, the great peak of Kumari Kandam, gave its name to the "Virgin Land." During a violent geologic catastrophe, Kumarikoddu collapsed into the Indian Ocean, dragging the entire island kingdom to the bottom of he sea. Survivors migrated to the subcontinent, where they sparked civilization in the Indus Valley.

(See Mu)

Kumulípo

A Hawaiian creation chant in which the *kumu honua*, or origins of the Earth, are described in connection with a splendid island, where humans achieved early greatness, but were mostly destroyed by a terrible flood, "the overturning of the chiefs." The *Kumulipo* is a folk memory of the Pacific Ocean civilization overwhelmed by natural catastrophe, as affirmed by repeated references to Mu.

Kung-Kung

A flying dragon in the Chinese story of creation, which caused the Great Flood by toppling the pillars of heaven with his fiery head. In the traditions of other ancient peoples, most particularly the Babylonians, sky-borne dragons are metaphors for destructive comets.

(See Asteroid Theory)

Kurma

The avatar of Vishnu, in Vedic myth, as a turtle in the "second episode" of the deluge story. Following the cataclysm, Kurma dove to the bottom of the sea, where he found treasures lost during the Great Flood. He returned with them to the surface, and led the survivors to life in a new land. Remarkably, his myth is virtually identical to numerous Native American versions—Ho Chunk, Sioux, Sauk, and so on—which refer to the North American Continent as "Turtle Island" after the giant turtle that saved their ancestors from drowning in the Great Flood.

Kusanagi

A magical sword originally belonging to Sagara, a dragon- or serpent-god living in an opulent palace at the bottom of the sea. It passed for some time among various members of Japan's royal household, to whom it brought victory, but was eventually returned to its rightful owner. The Kusanagi sword appears to have been a mythic symbol for some technological heirloom from lost Lemuria. Sagara also possessed the Pearl of Flood, able to cause a terrible deluge at his command.

Kuskurza

Flood hero of the Hopi Indians in the American Southwest. He and his people fled the cataclysmic destruction of their magnificent homeland formerly located far out in the middle of the Atlantic Ocean. As the flood began to rise, Kuskurza led them westward from island to sinking island until they reached safety on the eastern shores of North America. The Hopi account of what appears to be the Atlantean catastrophe reads in part, "Down on the bottom of the seas lie all the proud virtue, and the flying patuwvotas, and the worldly treasures corrupted with evil, and those people who found no time to sing praises to the Creator from the tops of their hills."

(See Hemet Maze Stone, Vimana)

Ladon

The serpent who guards the Tree of Life in the Garden of the Hesperides, scene of a mystery cult in Atlantis known as "The Navel of the World." When Ladon entwines his length around its bough he becomes the Kundalini snake winding about the human spinal column, the symbolic force of rising consciousness and spiritual power. The Golden Apples of immortality he protects are the fruits of enlightenment. These concepts, so long associated with Eastern thought, originated in Atlantis, where even their appearance in classical Greek myth still predated Buddhism by centuries. Ladon was also the name of a Trojan warrior, another linguistic connection between the Trojans and their Atlantean ancestry.

Lak Mu-ang

A pillar venerated in its own small shrine at the spiritual center of Thailand, in the capital city of Bangkok. It is a copy of the original brought to southeast Asia by the Thens from their drowned homeland in the Pacific Ocean. They managed to carry away just one column that belonged to the most important temple in Lemuria before the entire structure was engulfed by the sea. Arriving on the shores of what much later became Thailand, the Thens set up the Lak Mu-ang at the center of their new capital, Aiyudiya. During centuries of subsequent strife, the city was sacked and its sacred souvenir lost, but memory of it persisted with the relocation of various Thai capital cities, each one erecting a simulacrum of the original pillar.

In 1782, King Rama I, who traced his royal descent from the lost motherland of Mu, erected a ceremonial column at the precise center of the city. The original La Mu-ang was so ancient, however, no efforts succeeded to preserve it against decay, and it was eventually replaced with a replica by Rama VI. Today's Bangkok Lak Mu-ang is continually decorated with gold-leaf by anyone wishing to pay homage to their country's sacred center. The shrine itself is decorated with symbols and images of the Lemurian homeland from which the column was brought so long ago, such as stylized swastikas and scenes of a tropical island suggestive of the land of Mu itself. The small shrine in which it stands is an elaborate pavilion with intricate gold-inlayed doors and is set, untypically, below ground level in a sunken court, suggesting the undersea condition of the civilization from which the pillar was taken.

The name recurs at important monumental sites in Thailand: Mu-ang Fa Daet, Ban Mu-ang Fai, Mu-ang semay, and Mu-ang Bon, where the original Lak Mu-ang may have been installed by immigrants from Mu.

(See Thens)

Lam Abubia

The "Age Before the Flood," preserved by Babylonian and Assyrian scribes from their Sumerian predecessors, it described a highly advanced land of wise men and sorcerers who ruled the world until a natural catastrophe annihilated their oceanic kingdom. Only a few survivors managed to reach Mesopotamia, where they worked with native residents to build civilization anew.

Lankhapura

In ancient Hindu tradition, the capital of a great empire believed to have been swallowed by the sea toward the end of the *Treta yuga*, 1621 or 1575 B.C. Lankhapura's demise corresponds with the cataclysmic eruption of Thera, in the Aegean, and the penultimate destruction of Atlantis.

Lapita People

An archaeological term for a sophisticated culture that flourished throughout the western Pacific for 1,000 years after 1500 B.C. The Lapita People are associated with the survivors of Mu, who dispersed after its destruction in the 16th century B.C.

Lara

Along with thousands of other refugees, he escaped the late fourth-millennium B.C. seismic upheavals of Atlantis to settle with his wife, Balma, in Ireland, where these earliest Atlantean immigrants were known as the Fomorach. Lara was the son of their leader, Fintan.

Law of One

According to Edgar Cayce, this monotheistic cult arose in Atlantis as a reaction to the Followers of Belial, who made a religion of materialism. Tenets of the Law of One included social service for the less fortunate, acts of charity, abstinence, and humility. Although more of a social service creed than a theology with any original spiritual ideas, Cayce regarded it as a forerunner of Christianity. In any case, both the Law of One and its opposite number in the Followers of Belial were symptoms of the overall decline of Atlantean civilization during its final phase, when the former quest for enlightenment degenerated into a narrow-minded religious struggle for ascendancy. The Followers of Belial finally triumphed politically, only to have the technology they idolized blow up in their faces. Both sides were intolerant of opposing views, and together they contributed, despite their intense mutual animosity, to the social chaos of Atlantis in its latter days.

(See Cayce)

le Cour, Paul

French professional Atlantologist who, in 1926, stated that Atlantis was not a "continent," but a large island not far outside the Strait of Gibraltar.

Lemmings

Every three or four years, hundreds of thousands of lemmings (*Lemmus lemmus*) head away from the Norwegian coasts, swimming far out into the Atlantic Ocean, where they thrash about in a panicky search for dry land, then drown. The small rodents do not begin to move in packs, but usually head out individually, their numbers growing into a large mass. After rejecting overpopulation versus food resources as the cause, animal behaviorists do not understand why the self-destructive migrations take place. But it is the singular manner in which the process occurs that points to something special in their migratory pattern.

Lemmings have a natural aversion to water and hesitate to enter it. When confronted by rivers or lakes, they will swim across them only if seriously threatened, and otherwise move along the shore or bank. Their mass-migrations into the ocean dramatically contradict everything known about the creatures. Natural scientists recognize that lemmings seek land crossings whenever possible, and tend to follow paths made by other animals and even humans. Their suicidal instinct may be a persistent behavioral pattern set over thousands of years ago, when some land-bridge, long since sunk, connected the Norwegian coast to a former island in the Atlantic. The other three lemming genera (Dicrostonyx, Myopus, and Synaptomys), whose habitats have no conjectured geographical relationship to such an island, do not participate in migratory mass-suicides.

Nostophilia is a term used to describe the apparent instinct in certain animals which migrate to locations often very great distances from their usual habitat. Perhaps some behavioral memory of a large, lost island that for countless generations previously sheltered and nurtured the lemmings still survives in the evolutionary memories and compelling instincts of their descendants.

Lemuel

Literally, the "king" (*el*) of Lemu(ria), the contemporary civilization of Atlantis in the Pacific. His royal identity is underscored in the Old Testament (Proverbs, viii, 31), where he is described as a monarch. The 18th-century American revolutionary, Thomas Paine, wrote in *The Age of Reason* that the verse in which he appears "stands as a preface to the Proverbs that follow, and which are not the proverbs of Solomon, but of Lemuel; and this Lemuel was not one of the kings of Israel, nor of Judah, but of some other country, and consequently a Gentile" (134). The Lemurians reputedly proselytized the tenets of their spirituality far and wide, so the biblical "proverbs" associated with King Lemuel may have been remnants of Pacific contacts in deep antiquity.

(See Lemuria)

Lemuria

An ancient civilization of the Pacific predating both the emergence and destruction of Atlantis. The name derives from a Roman festival, celebrated every May 9, 11, and 15, to appease the souls of men and women who perished when Lemuria was destroyed by a natural catastrophe. These dates probably represent the days during which the destruction took place. The Lemuria festival was believed to have been instituted by the founder of Rome, Romulus, as expiation for the murder of his twin brother, Remus. During the observance, celebrants walked barefoot, as though they had fled from a disaster, and went through their homes casting black beans behind them nine times in a ritual of rebirth; black beans were symbolic of human souls which were still earthbound (that is, ghosts), while 9 was a sacred numeral signifying birth (the nine months of pregnancy).

The ritual's objective was to honor and exorcise any unhappy spirits which may haunt a house. This part of the Roman Lemuria is identically observed by Japanese participants in the Bon Festival, or "Feast of Lanterns," when the head of the household walks barefoot through each room of his home exclaiming, "Bad spirits, out! Good spirits, in!" while casting beans behind him.

Obviously, both ancient Rome and Japan received a common tradition independently from the same source, when Mu was destroyed in a great flood. A graphic reenactment of that deluge occurred on the third day of the Roman Lemuria, when celebrants cast 30 images made of rushes into the River Tiber. What the images represented (perhaps human beings?), and why they were put together from rushes is not precisely known, but they were plainly meant to simulate loss in a torrent of water. Nor is the specific significance of 30 understood, although Koziminsky (citing Heydon's similar opinion) defines it as appropriately calamitous (49).

The name, "Lemuria," is not confined to Rome, but occurs as far away as among the Chumash Indians of southern California. They referred to San Miguel

Island, site of an un-Indian megalithic wall, as "Lemu." Laamu is in the Maldives, south of the Indian subcontinent at the equator, featuring the largest *hawitta*, or stone mound, in the islands, constructed by a foreign, red-haired, seafaring people during prehistory. Throughout Polynesia, Lemu is the god of the dead, who reigns over a city of beautiful palaces at the bottom of the sea. On the Polynesian island of Tonga, Lihamui is the name of the same month, May, just when the Roman Lemuria was celebrated.

In some of these names, "l" and "r" become interchangeable. The Roman festival may also have been called "Remuria," just as Polynesia's god of the dead was sometimes prayed to as "Remu." Lima, the Peruvian capital, was preferred by the Spanish conquerors over the native "Remu," which was probably itself a linguistic twist, like the others, on the name of a pre-Inca city, originally known as "Lemu." If so, it represents another Lemurian influence on coastal Peru. "Lemuria" is a variant of "Mu," which, according to Churchward, means "mother." "Lemuria," then, may have been an equivalent of "motherland."

(See Bon, Mu)

Le Plongeon, Augustus

French physician (1826 to 1908) who lived for many years among the Lacadone Indians, descendants of the Mayas, learning their language, customs, and oral traditions firsthand. Dr. Le Plongeon was first to excavate the pre-Columbian ruins of Yucatan, amassing important artifact collections that became valuable additions to some of the leading museums of Mexico and the United States. He was also an early pioneer in decipherment of the Mayan hieroglyphs, which his academic contemporaries found utterly inscrutable.

It was his ability to achieve at least their partial translation with the help of his Lacadone friends that sabotaged his professional standing, because Le Plongeon found references among a few of the carved steale to the sunken civilization of Mu. After its destruction, survivors arrived in Central America, he read, where they became the ancestors of the Mayas.

He believed the story was preserved in the *Tro-Cortesianus*, or *Troano Codex*, one of only three books that survived the wholesale incineration of Mayan literature by Christian zealots in the 16th century. While his literal translation was erroneous, it was at least vaguely correct, because the *Troano Codex*, while not a history of the Lemurian cataclysm, is a kind of astrological almanac describing natural catastrophes as the delineators of world epochs.

Le Plongeon's *Sacred Mysteries Among the Mayas and Quiches 11,500 Years Ago* and *Queen Moo and the Egyptian Sphinx* were important influences in the work of James Churchward, who brought the subject to a wider reading audience beginning in the early 20th century, and they remain valued, if flawed contributions to Lemurian studies.

(See Churchward)

Lesser Arrival

The Mayan epic, the *Popol Vuh* ("The Book of Counsel") records two major immigrations of white-skinned foreigners from over the Atlantic Ocean. The earlier is the Greater Arrival, and corresponds to large-scale, although not total, evacuation of Atlantis in the late 4th millennium B.C., during a period of geologic upheavals. The Lesser Arrival took place some 2,000 years later, when Atlantis was utterly destroyed and some of its survivors made their way to the shores of Yucatan. According to the *Popol Vuh*, the leading personality of the Greater Arrival was Itzamna, the founding father of Mesoamerican Civilization. Votan led the Lesser Arrival. He was described as saving sacred records written on deer hide that chronicled the early history of his people from Valum before its destruction by a natural catastrophe.

(See Greater Arrival)

Peru's Emerald Pyramid is adorned with the motif of an over-arching rainbow through which a fair-skinned foreigner arrived with the gifts of civilization, following a catastrophic deluge.

Leucaria

A Latin version of the ancestress cited in Plato's account of Atlantis, she and her husband founded the city of Rome.

(See Italus, Kritias, Leukippe)

Leukippe

"The White Mare," the first woman of Atlantis mentioned briefly by Plato in *Kritias*. A white mare motif in association with Atlantean themes appears in various parts of the world. The most prominent example appears at England's *Vale of the White Horse*, north of the Berkshire chalk downs, in Uffington. The 374-foot long hill-figure depicts a stylized horse cut into the turf. It is traditionally "scoured" by local people, as they tramp around the outline of the intaglio seven times every Whitsunday to preserve the image. Whitsunday, or "Pentecost," is a festival celebrated every seventh Sunday after Easter. It commemorates the descent of the Holy Ghost on Christ's disciples after his crucifixion, resurrection, and ascension to heaven, and marks the beginning of the Church's mission throughout the world. "Whitsunday" supposedly derives from special white gowns worn by the newly baptized. But all this may be a Christian gloss over an original significance that was deliberately syncretized by Church officials anxious to dilute and absorb "pagan" practices.

While the seven annual scourings of the White Horse parallel the seven Sundays following Easter and ending with "White Sunday," 7 was, many centuries before, regarded as the numeral of the completion of cycles by the Greek mathematician Pythagoras, and his followers, including Plato, throughout the Classical World. Moreover, the British hill-figure is deeply pre-Christian, even pre-Celtic, dating to 1200 B.C. This is also the most important time horizon in Atlantean studies, because it brackets the final destruction in 1198 B.C. Some survivors from the catastrophe may have immigrated to England, where they created the White Horse intaglio to commemorate the first lady of their lost homeland while celebrating their renewed life in Britain. These were possibly the original sentiments taken over by the analogous death and resurrection of Christ at Pentecost. Even the very term, "Whitsunday," may not have been occasioned by Christian baptismal garb, but more likely arose from the White Horse itself. Pentecost is only known in Britain as "Whitsunday" (that is, "White Sunday").

The cult of the white horse persisted throughout Celtic times, Roman occupation, and centuries after in the British worship of Epona, from which our word "pony" derives. White horse ceremonies rooted in prehistory are still performed at some seaside villages in the British Isles, and are always associated with sailing. A particularly Atlantean example is *Samhain*, (pronounced *sovan* or *sowan*), or "end of summer" celebration, a survivor from deep antiquity. In parts of Ireland's County Cork, the Samhain procession features a man wearing the facsimile of a horse's head and a white robe. In this costume he is referred to as the "White Mare," and leads his celebrants down to the seaside. There he wades out into the water, pours a sacrificial libation, then recites a prayerful request for a good fishing harvest. This ritual occurs each November 1, the anniversary of the destruction of Atlantis.

The Greeks commonly envisioned foaming waves as "whites horses," so Leukippe was appropriately named. The Earth Mother Goddess Demeter was sometimes referred to as Leukippe, the White Mare of Life. As Demeter was part of the Atlantean mystery cult, The Navel of the World, Leukippe may have been its original and central figure. In a North American plains' version of the Great Flood, ancestors of the Lakota Sioux were saved by a sea-god who rises up from the waves riding a great white horse.

Lifthraser and Lif

In Norse myth, the husband and wife who survived a world-ending flood to repopulate the world. Every Scandinavian is a descendant of Lifthraser and Lif.

Limu-kala

Hawaiian for the common seaweed (*Sargassum echinocarpum*), distinguished by its toothed leaves, used as a magical cure. A lei of limu-kala was placed around the neck of the patient, who then walked into the sea until the waves carried the garland away and, with it, all illness. It was also eaten by mourners as part of funeral rites. Limu-kala leis still adorn fishing shrines and ancient temples, or *heiau*, throughout the Hawaiian Islands. Its name and functions clearly define limu-kala's Lemurian origins.

(See Hina-lau-limu-kala, Lemuria)

Ling-lawn

The supreme sky-god worshiped by the Shans, a tribal people inhabiting northeastern Burma (Myanmar). Offended by the immorality of his human creations, Ling-lawn dispatched the gods to destroy the world. His myth relates, "They sent forth a great conflagration, scattering their fire everywhere. It swept over the Earth, and smoke ascended in clouds to heaven." With all but a few men and women still alive, his wrath was appeased, and Ling-lawn extinguished the burning world in a universal flood that killed off all living things, save a husband and wife provisioned with a bag of seeds and riding out the deluge in a boat. From these survivors, life gradually returned.

The fundamental similarities of Ling-lawn's flood story with accounts in other, distant cultures is particularly remarkable in view of the obscure Shans' remote isolation. Doubtless, their ancestors experienced the same natural catastrophe witnessed by the rest of humanity.

Llyn Syfaddon

Also remembered in some parts of Wales as *Llyn Savathan*, Llyn Syfaddon was the great kingdom of Helig Voel ap Glannog, which extended far out into the Atlantic Ocean from Priestholm, until it sank entirely beneath the sea. Another name for the drowned realm, *Llys Elisap Clynog*, seems related to Elasippos, the Atlantean king in Plato's dialogue, *Kritias*.

Llyon Llion

Remembered as the "Lake of Waves," which overflowed its banks to inundate the entire Earth. Before this former kingdom was drowned, the great shipwright Nefyed Nav Nevion completed a vessel just in time to ride out the cataclysm. He was joined in it by twin brothers, Dwyvan and Dwyvach who, landing safely on the coast of Wales, became the first Welsh kings. This myth is less the slight degeneration of an obviously earlier tradition than it is an example of the Celtic inclination toward whimsical exaggeration, making a mere lake responsible for a global flood. In all other respects, it conforms to Atlantean deluge accounts throughout the world, wherein surviving twins become the founding fathers of a new civilization.

Llys Helig

A stony patch on the floor of Conway Bay, sometimes visible from the shore during moments of water clarity, and regarded in folk tradition as the site of a kingdom formerly ruled by Helig ap Glannawg. He perished with Llys Helig when it abruptly sank to the bottom of the sea. The stones taken for the ruins of his drowned palace are part of a suggestive natural formation that recalls one of several Welsh versions of the Atlantis disaster. Others similarly describe Llyn Llynclys and Cantref-y-Gwaelod. A large, dark pool of fathomless water in the town of Radnorshire is supposed to have swallowed an ancient castle known as Lyngwyn. So many surviving mythic traditions of sunken kingdoms suggest that the Atlanteans made an enduring impact on Wales.

Llyn Savathan

Known in other parts of Wales as *Llyn Syfaddon*, it was the extensive kingdom of Helig Voel ap Glannog, whose great possessions, extending far into the sea from Priestholm, had been suddenly overwhelmed by the sea. His name is remarkable, because it contains the "og" derivative of Atlantean deluge heroes in other parts of the world. Another Welsh flood tradition, Llys Elisap Clynog, repeats the "og" theme.

(See Llyn Syfaddon, Ogma, Ogriae)

Lono

The white-skinned man-god who arrived long ago by ship in the Hawaiian Islands, bringing the first `uala, or sweet potato to the natives. His name is still invoked at every stage in its planting, tending, and harvesting. Lono instituted and presided over the makahiki celebrations, which began every late October or early November, the same period used for ceremonies commemorating the dead in various parts of the world, such as Japan's Bon, Thailand's Lak Krathong, Christian Europe's and pre-Columbian Mexico's All Souls' Day, and so on. This is the time of year associated with the final destruction of Atlantis.

Like these foreign celebrations, the dating of the makahiki, a new year's ceremony, was determined by the first appearance of the Pleiades, or "Atlantises," above the horizon at dusk, because it was at this time that Lono traditionally arrived from Kahiki, one of several names by which the sunken kingdom was known throughout the Pacific. Ironically, the famous British explorer, Captain James Cook, landed at the same anchorage, Kealkekua, in Hawaii's Kona District, where Lono first appeared. Cook was not the only white man to have followed so closely in the footsteps of a prehistoric predecessor. Both Cortez in Mexico and Pizarro in Peru were identically mistaken by the indigenous people for Quetzalcoatl, the "Feathered Serpent," and Viracocha, "Sea Foam," earlier white-skinned visitors. Clearly, these vastly separated traditions establish a form of prehistorical meeting common to them all.

Carried throughout the makahiki was a ritual image of Lono consisting of a tall upright wooden pole, at the top of which was a crosspiece from which were hung sheets of white bark cloth and lei of fern and feathers. The carved figure of a bird surmounted "Father Lono," or this *Lonomakua*. Its resemblance to the chief symbol for Mu, as described by James Churchward, is remarkable. Lono's identification with this sunken kingdom is underscored by his title, *Hu-Mu-hu-Mu-nuku-nuku-apua'a*, which indicates he could "swim" from Mu between the islands like a fish, a reference to his skill as a transoceanic mariner. His myth is the folk memory of an important culture-bearer from the lost civilization of the Pacific.

(See Bon, Hiva, Lak Krathong, Mu, Pleiades, Viracocha, Quetzalcoatl)

The Lost Garden

Published in 1930, G.C. Foster's witty spoof of all "lost continent" theories has reincarnated Atlanteans hotly debating the real or imagined existence of Lemuria, employing all the standard arguments used to either support or discredit a historical Atlantis.

Luondona-Wietrili

The original homeland of the Timor people, who universally claim descent from this sunken kingdom. According to them, the little islet of Luang is the only dry land surviving from the much larger island. Luandona-Wietrili was destroyed by natural catastrophes in the form of a monstrous sailfish for the divisiveness of its leaders.

Lycaea

A Greek ceremony conducted at Mount Lycaeus commemorating the destruction of a former human epoch by a worldwide catastrophe. Each Lycaea reenacted the story of an antediluvian monarch, Lycaon, who tried to deceive the king of the gods into committing cannibalism. Seeing through the trick, Zeus punished both Lycaon and his degenerate people with a genocidal flood.

Of the three distinct deluge myths known to the Greeks, the Lycaea seems closest to Plato's account of Atlantis, which likewise grows degenerate and is annihilated by Zeus with a watery cataclysm. The deeply pre-Platonic roots of this rendition tend to thus confirm at least the fundamental veracity of both *Timaeus* and *Kritias* and the Lycaea itself. The previous Deucalion and Ogygean floods belonged to geologic upheavals and mass migrations of Atlantis in the late fourth and third millennia B.C.

(See Deucalion, Ogriae)

Lyonesse

In British myth, the "City of Lions" was the capital of a powerful kingdom that long ago dominated the ocean. Like Plato's description of Atlantis, Lyonesse was a high-walled city built on a hill which sank beneath the sea in a single night. Only a man riding a white horse escaped to the coast at Cornwall. Two families still claim descent from this lone survivor. The Trevelyan coat-of-arms depicts a white horse emerging from the waves, just as the Vyvyan version shows a white horse saddled and ready for her master's flight. While both families may in fact be direct descendants of an Atlantean catastrophe, Lyonesse's white horse connects Leukippe, "White Mare," mentioned in Plato's account as an early inhabitant of Atlantis, with the White Horse of Uffington, a Bronze Age hill-figure found near Oxford. Tennyson believed Camelot was synonymous for "the Lost Land of Lyonesse." Indeed, the concentric configuration of Atlantis suggests the round-table of Camelot.

In another version of the Cornish story, Lyonesse's royal refugees sailed away to reestablish themselves in the Sacred Kingdom of Logres. While the medieval Saxon Chronicle impossibly dates the sinking of Lyonesse to the late 11th century A.D., its anonymous author nonetheless records that the event occurred on November 11, a period generally associated with the destruction of Atlantis. Traditionally, the vanished kingdom is supposed to have sunk between the Isles of Scilly and the Cornish mainland, about 28 miles of open sea. A dangerous reef, known as the Seven Stones, traditionally marks the exact position of the capital. These suggestive formations appear to have helped transfer the story of Atlantis, recounted by survivors in Britain, to Cornwall.

(See Leukippe)

The ruins of Lixus, coastal Morocco, associated with Atlantean king, Autochthones.

Macusis

The survivor, together with his wife, of a great flood that destroyed the world and from whom an Indian tribe in British Guiana derived its name.

Madolenih-Mw

The eastern half of Ponape, which features the island's largest state. The Micronesian location is the site of Nan Madol, an extensive megalithic ceremonial center which resembles the Indus Valley cities of Harappa and Mohenjo Daro. Madolenih-Mw suggests the name of the lost Pacific civilization that gave rise to both Nan Madol and the Indus Valley cities.

Maeldune

A legendary Irish voyager, he was actually a poetic device to epitomize pre-Celtic and early-Celtic knowledge of the sea. In one adventure, Maeldune sails to an unknown, mist-shrouded, abandoned island with tall mountains and a strange city laid out in concentric circles of alternating land and water connected by canals. Each ring of land was surrounded by walls decorated with gold, silver, and an unfamiliar precious metal —*bath*, which gleamed brighter than shiny copper or bronze.

Maeldune's nameless island is doubtless the same as Atlantis, from its mountains to the circular city plan and richly covered walls. Bath is Plato's orichalcum, the gold/copper alloy he said the Atlanteans delighted in displaying. That the island was depicted as hidden by mists and uninhabited are metaphors for its disappearance.

(See Findrine, Orichalcum)

Sacred gateway, Machu Picchu. Photograph by William Donato.

Mag Meld

An island in the Atlantic Ocean from which the Family of Partholon immigrated to pre-Celtic Ireland before the "Pleasant Plain" disappeared in a "storm."

(See Partholon)

Magog

Cited in the Old Testament (Genesis 10: 2) as the grandson of Noah, who led his family and followers in post-Deluge times. Magog is also mentioned in the New Testament (Revelation 20:8). Gog and Magog appear to have been less formal than descriptive names referring to mighty kingdoms at either ends of the world—"in the four corners of the Earth." They "went up over the breadth of the Earth" before a "fire from heaven came down out of heaven and devoured them," together with their "beloved city." The Atlantean implications of these lines seem inescapable, especially in view of the "og" appellation identified with Atlantis in Celtic traditions in Ireland, Britain, and the European Continent. Gog and Magog may be associated, respectively, with Lemuria and Atlantis.

The 17th-century Swedish savant, Olaus Rudbeck, concluded that the tribe of Magog was the biblical name for Atlantean survivors of the Second Cataclysm who arrived in Scandinavia during the mid-third millennium B.C.

(See Rudbeck)

Mahabalipuram

In ancient Indian scriptures, "City of the Great Bali" was copied after the palace of the gods, which its architect and ruler, Bali, visited. For this impropriety, Mahabalipuram was entirely swallowed by the sea in a terrible flood.

The cataclysm was commanded by Indra. Like Zeus in Plato's account of the Atlantean destruction, he was a sky-god, who convened all the other deities of heaven to call down a watery judgement on the blasphemous inhabitants. Bali was described as a "giant," just as the first ruler of Atlantis, Atlas, was a Titan.

Mahapralaya

"The Great Cataclysm," among the oldest surviving Hindustani legends, describes the rapid approach of a comet as it grows in size:

> By the power of God there issued from the essence of Brahma [the sky] a being shaped like a boar, white and exceedingly small; this being, in the space of an hour, grew to the size of an elephant of the largest size, and remained in the air. Suddenly [it] uttered a sound like the loudest thunder, and the echo reverberated and shook all the quarters of the universe. Again [it] made a loud sound and became a dreadful spectacle.
>
> Shaking the full-flowing mane which hung down his neck on both sides, and erecting the humid hairs of his body, he proudly displayed his two most exceedingly white tusks. Then, rolling about his wine-colored eyes and erecting his tail, he descended from the region of the air, and plunged head-foremost into the water. The whole body of water was convulsed by the motion, and began to rise in waves, while the guardian spirit of the sea, being terrified, began to tremble for his domains, and cry for mercy.

(See Asteroid Theory)

Maia

An Atlantis, daughter of Atlas by Pleione, called "Grandmother," because she is the oldest of the Pleiades. In Greek myth, Maia's husband, Hephaestus, crafted the golden and silver dogs in front of King Alkynous's palace at Phaeacia, in the *Odyssey*. "Alkynous" is a male derivation of another Pleiade, Alkyone, further establishing Homer's Phaeacia as Atlantis. Her son is perhaps the most Atlantean of all the gods, Hermes-Thaut, who carried the Emerald Tablets of Civilization to the Nile Valley after the Flood, which he memorialized in building the Great Pyramid. Our month of May, the birthstone of which is still the emerald, derived from Maia, whose name means "the Maker." Her feast-day, the first day of May, continues to be celebrated around the world, as the workers' international holiday.

In Hindu myth, Maia is also known as "the Maker," the personification of civilization. She was likewise worshiped by the Guanches, the ancient inhabitants of the Canary Islands, off the northwest coast of Africa. A Guanche statue of Maia was of such high caliber workmanship, the Christian Spaniards preserved it in the mistaken belief that it represented the Virgin Mary. To them, the statue was "our Lady of the Candalaria." Its original location was in a seaside cave or grotto on Tenerife, and featured an inscription at its base. Leading Latin scholars for four centuries struggled and failed to translate it, concluding that the words belonged to a wholly unknown written language. The statue portrayed a nude female, so Catholic priests draped the figure with specially sewn garments. Interpreted as a representation of the Catholic Blessed Virgin, it stood 3 1/2 feet tall and was carved in light red wood, the hair arranged in plaits of beaten gold hanging down to the shoulders.

To the female figure's right, holding a little bird of gold, was seated a small, naked boy, identified by Church officials as the Infant Jesus. He might just as well have been Herupkhart, "Horus the Child," the sun-god usually appearing as a naked youth. His Egyptian myth told how he first crossed the sky from east to west in the company of Maia, the goddess of truth and embodiment of the eternal order of the universe. The golden bird, a common solar symbol, held by the boy of the Candalaria statue was probably a falcon, the avatar of Herupkhart. In any case, the statue's close resemblance to Maia and Horus the Child rendered it more Egyptian than Christian, especially in view of the Guanches' name for the image: Maia.

In November, 1826, a monstrous tidal wave crashed over Tenerife, and swept the Lady of the Candalaria and her boy into the sea, never to be seen again. The statue may have been a local Guanche creation, or perhaps it had been preserved as a holy image from lost Atlantis. The boy accompanying her was an appropriate addition, considering the function of each one of the Pleiades as the ancestors of post-deluge founders of new kingdoms.

It is tempting to see in Maia the eponymous ancestress of the Mayas specifically and Mesoamerican civilization generally. The female progenitor of the Aztecs was Coatlicue, "Our Grandmother," the same title given to the eldest Pleiade, Maia. The Ge-speaking Indians of Brazil's northern coasts worshiped Maira, their ancestress. In the ancient past, she was said to have set fire to a beautiful city on an island far out at sea, then sank it to punish its sinful inhabitants. Interestingly, "Maira" is the European gnostic name for the Star of Isis, later used as a title for the Virgin Mary. The Greeks knew Maia similarly as "The Grandmother of Magic." In Hindu tradition, Maya is the mother of Buddha, in keeping with the role of the Atlantean Pleiades as the mothers or grandmothers of great men.

The goddess of the Canary Islands, Egypt, Greece, India, and the Americas was one and the same deity: the Atlantis, Maia. In the Atlantean Empire, Maia was the name of an allied kingdom or colony including Lowland Yucatan and Guatemala. It is here, at the Maya city of Tikal, that the Austrian archaeologist, Teobert Mahler, discovered a sculpted frieze representing the destruction of Atlantis on the front facade of the Acropolis.

(See Maler, Pleiades)

Maidu

A California Indian tribe, whose deluge story tells of Talvolte and Peheipe, the only survivors of a natural catastrophe that destroyed their earthly paradise after its inhabitants, grown corrupt, had offended heaven, the same cause presented in Plato's account of Atlantis.

Mai-Ra

Still venerated by the Ge-speaking Indians as the "Walker," or "Maker," Mai-Ra was the last and former king of the "Land Without Evil." Its inhabitants did not live up to his high standards of morality, however, so he set the island on fire, then sank it beneath the sea. Before these calamities, Mai-Ra left with a small fleet of survivors chosen for their goodness. In time, they landed on the shores of Brazil, where they interbred with native peoples to sire the present Indian race.

The story of Mai-Ra is a clear folk memory of the final destruction of Atlantis.

Makila

The ancestral hero of North America's Pomo Indians. Makila and his son, Dasan, leaders of a bird clan, arrived from "a great lodge" across the Atlantic Ocean to teach wisdom, healing, and magic. The Atlantean features of this myth are clear.

Makonaima

In Melanesian tradition, the last king of Burotu before it sank beneath the Pacific Ocean. He survived with his son, Sigu.

(See Burotu, Lemuria, Mu)

Maler, Teobert

An important Mayanist in the late 19th and early 20th centuries who discovered physical evidence for an Atlantean presence in Mesoamerica. Over the course of several decades, he accumulated a vast treasury of exceptionally skillful photographs depicting numerous, previously unrecorded Maya sites in Mexico and Guatemala. These provided a seminal stimulus to the development of Mesoamerican archaeology, and still remain a unique source of material for epigraphic, iconographic, and architectural studies prized by modern archaeologists. Maler has long been recognized as one of the two great archaeological explorers active in the Maya area at the dawn of professional studies in Middle American history, the other being Alfred Maudslay. Had it not been for them, later scholars would have been seriously handicapped by a lack of reliable data, and the development of Maya archaeology would have been delayed by decades.

Austrian-born Teobert Maler came to Mexico in 1864 as a volunteer in an Austrian military expedition supporting the imperial claims of Archduke Maximilian. Although Maximilian was toppled in 1867, Maler made Mexico his adoptive home, where he became a professional nature photographer. His subject matter eventually included the country's pre-Columbian ruins, which so fascinated him that he was eventually recognized as a self-taught but brilliant expert in local archaeology. Documenting these structures soon evolved into his life's work, and he traveled widely throughout Mexico and Central America in search of ancient sites, some of which he discovered himself.

During 1885, he settled in the quiet little Yucatan town of Ticul, and there established a photographic studio, while becoming proficient in the Mayan language. Throughout the course of his studies and explorations, he was a valued contributor to the German geographic-ethnographic magazine, *Globus*, and other scientific journals. His sets of large prints, uniformly mounted, supplemented by site plans and other information, were sought after by museums and universities in both Europe and America, including Harvard's Peabody Museum, which sponsored his survey—the first ever—of Palenque and its environs.

Although vaguely familiar with Plato's account of Atlantis, Maler, like most scholars, then and now, dismissed the lost civilization as mere fantasy. However, while photographing the so-called "acropolis" at the ninth century Maya ceremonial city of Tikal, in Guatemala, he discovered, in his words, "a water scene with a volcano spouting fire and smoke, buildings falling into the water, people drowning." It was at the start of a sculpted frieze that ran around the uppermost part of the building in an apparent visual representation of Maya history. Until Maler's photographic expedition to Tikal, the extensive ruins there were virtually unknown to the outside world. Astounded by the "water scene," he was convinced it depicted Maya origins in Atlantis, and removed the panel to the Voelkerkunde Museum, in Vienna. It was part of the institution's permanent Mesoamerican display until 1945, when it disappeared among the general looting by invading Soviet troops at the end of World War II. Fortunately, his photograph of the Atlantean panel survives at the University of Pennsylvania.

Long after his death on November 22, 1917, in the Yucatan city of Merida, Maler is still recognized by the academic community for his invaluable photographic and surveying services to Mesoamerican archaeology, although deplored for his courage in describing evidence of Atlantis among the Mayas he knew so well for most of his adult life.

Mama Nono

Before their extinction through exposure to European diseases against which they had no immunity, Caribs of the Antilles told the Spaniards that Mama Nono created the first new race of human beings. She achieved this act of regeneration by planting stones in the ground after a great flood that wiped out all life on Earth.

In Greek myth, the deluge heroes, Deucalion and Pyrrha, were counseled to repopulate mankind by throwing stones over their shoulders. As the stones fell to the ground, men and women sprang up in their place. This myth, known in its variants among widely scattered cultures around the Earth, is a shared metaphor for the repopulation of a badly wounded world by survivors of the Atlantean holocaust. In Britain, local traditions often recount that the standing stones of megalithic circles are petrified humans, such as the "Whispering Knights."

Mama Ocllo

Also called "Mama Oglo," she was the companion of Manco Capac, who survived a great flood by seeking refuge among the high Bolivian mountains, at Lake Titicaca. Children born to her in South America were the progenitors of all Andean royalty.

(See Manco Capac)

Man Mounds

Two effigy earthworks, of gigantic proportions, in Wisconsin. They represent the water spirit that led the Wolf Clan ancestors of the Winnebago, or Ho Chunk Indians, to safety in North America after the Great Flood. One of the geoglyphs still exists, although in mutilated form, on the slope of a hill in Greenfield Township, outside Baraboo. Road construction cut off his legs below the knees around the turn of the 20th century, but the figure is otherwise intact. The giant is 214 feet long and 30 feet across at his shoulders. His anthropomorphic image is oriented westward, as though striding from the east, where the Deluge was supposed to have occurred. His horned helmet identifies him as Wakt'cexi, the flood hero.

The terraglyph is no primitive mound, but beautifully proportioned and formed. Increase Lapham, a surveyor who measured the earthwork in the early 19th century, was impressed: "All the lines of this most singular effigy are curved gracefully, and much care has been bestowed upon its construction."

A companion of the Greenfield Township hill-figure, also in Sauk County, about 30 miles northwest, was drowned under several fathoms of river by a dam project in the early 20th century. Ironically, the water spirit that led the Ho Chunk ancestors from a cataclysmic flood was itself the victim of another, modern deluge.

The Atlantean identity of Wakt'cexi as materialized in his Wisconsin effigy mounds is repeated in an overseas' counterpart. The Wilmington Long Man is likewise the representation of an anthropomorphic figure—at 300 feet, the largest in Europe—cut into the chalk face of a hill in the south of England, about 40 miles from Bristol, and is dated to the last centuries of Atlantis, from 2000 to 1200 B.C. Resemblances to the Wisconsin earthwork grow closer when we learn that the British hill-figure was originally portrayed wearing a horned helmet obliterated in the early 19th century. A third man-terraglyph is located in the Atacama desert of Chile's coastal region. Known as the Cerro Unitas giant, it is the largest in the world at 393 feet in length. It, too, wears a horned headgear, but more like an elaborate rayed crown.

The Old and New World effigy mounds appear to have been created by a single people representing a common theme—namely, the migration of survivors from the Atlantis catastrophe led by men whose symbol of authority was the horned helmet. Indeed, such an interpretation is underscored by the Atlantean "Sea People" invaders of Egypt during the early 12th century, when they were depicted on the wall art of Medinet Habu, wearing horned helmets.

(See Navaho Child Initiation Ceremony, Pipestone, Ramses III)

Manco Capac

Described as a bearded, white-skinned flood hero, who arrived at Lake Titicaca, where he established a new kingdom. In time, however, the native peoples rose against him, massacring many of his followers. These events forced him to relocate the capital to Cuzco, where all subsequent Inca emperors were obliged to trace their lineal descent from Manco Capac.

(See Ayar-chaki)

Mangala

As described in Benin and Yoruba myth, he was deliberately left behind to die on a kingdom in the Atlantic Ocean when the island sank beneath the sea, but survived in a water-tight vessel built for himself and his followers. They arrived on the shores of West Africa, where an earlier flood survivor, Amma, had already installed herself as the first ruler. After her death, Mangala's claim to the throne was opposed by a twin brother. Pemba was eventually banished, however, and Mangala became West Africa's first king, from whom all subsequent dynasties trace their descent.

In many lands touched by the Atlantis phenomenon, ruling families commonly traced their lineage to escaped royalty from a cataclysmic deluge

(See Amma)

Manibozho

The Algonquians' great creation hero and survivor of the Deluge which submerged the Earth. From his place of refuge atop the tallest tree at the center of the world, the Tree of Life encountered in universal tradition, Manibozho sent forth a crow, but it returned after several days to say that the waters had not yet receded. Another failed attempt was made with an otter. Finally, a muskrat was able to report that land was beginning to emerge. Manibozho swam to the new territory, where he reestablished human society, and became the founder of the Algonquians' oldest, most venerated tribe, the Musk-Rat.

Manibozho was the Algonquian forefather from Atlantis. His Native American version of the Great Flood bears some resemblance to the Genesis account, in which Noah dispatches birds to inform him about the receding waters.

Manoa

The Portuguese royal historian, Francisco Lopez, recorded his account of an oceanic capital which once sent "visitors" to the Brazilian natives:

> Manoa is on an island in a great salt lake. Its walls and roof are made of gold and reflected in a gold-tiled lake. All the serving dishes for the palace are made of pure gold and silver, and even

the most insignificant things are made of silver and copper. In the middle of the island stands a temple dedicated to the sun. Around the building, there are statues of gold, which represent giants. There are also trees made of gold and silver on the island, and the statue of a prince covered entirely with gold dust.

Manoa's resemblance to Plato's opulent Atlantis, with its Titans and oceanic location "on an island in a great salt lake" is apparent.

Manu

India's flood hero. In the *Matsyu Purana*, his version of the deluge features a rain of burning coals. Warning Manu of the catastrophe to come, the god Vishnu, in the guise of a fish, says, "the Earth shall become like ashes, the aether too shall be scorched with heat." Oppenheimer observes that "the details suggest a grand disaster, such as may follow a meteorite strike."

(See Asteroid Theory)

Marae Renga

A homeland in the east from which the chief culture-bearer, Hotu Matua, with his family and followers, arrived at Rapa Nui, or Easter Island, to replant civilization there. Marae Renga was itself an island belonging to the larger kingdom of Hiva, before it was sunk by the earthquake-god, Uwoke, with a "crowbar."

(See Heva, Mu)

Marerewana

The Arawak Indians' foremost culture hero, who escaped the Deluge in a "great canoe" with his followers. Spanish Conquistadors in the 16th century noted occasional blondism, somewhat European facial features, and light eyes among the Arawak—physical throw-backs to their ancient Atlantean genetic heritage.

Marumda

Together with his brother, Kuksu, he virtually destroyed the world by fire and flood, according to the Pomo Indians of Central America. The savior of threatened humanity was the Earth-Mother goddess, Ragno.

Marumda combines a celestial cataclysm with the deluge common in Atlantean traditions around the world.

Masefield, John

Early 20th-century British poet laureate renowned for his innovative verse. In his 1912 "Story of a Roundhouse," he told how "the courts of old Atlantis rose."

Mataco Flood Myth

The Argentine Indians of Gran Chaco describe "a black cloud that came from the south at the time of the flood, and covered the whole sky. Lightning struck and thunder was heard. Yet the drops that fell were not like rain. They fell as fire." Here, too, a celestial event coincides with the deluge in a South American recollection of the Atlantean catastrophe.

Medinet Habu

The "Victory Temple" of XX Dynasty Pharaoh Ramses III at West Thebes, in the Upper Nile Valley, completed around 1180 B.C. It is the finest, best preserved example of large-scale sacred architecture from the late New Kingdom, and built as a monument to his important triumph over a massive series of invasions launched by the "Sea People" against the Nile Delta at the beginning of the 12th century B.C. The exterior walls of Medinet Habu are decorated with lengthy descriptions of the war and illustrated by incised representations of the combatants.

Recorded testimony of captured "Sea People" warriors leaves no doubt about their Atlantean identity. The text quotes them as saying they came from an island the Egyptians transliterated as "Netero," like Plato's Atlantis, a "sacred isle," in the Far West after it had been set ablaze by a celestial event identified with the fiery goddess Sekhmet and sank into the sea. Medinet Habu's profiles of various "Sea People" invaders are the life-like portraits of Atlanteans in the Late Bronze Age.

The grand entrance of Medinet Habu, Ramses III's monument to his victory over Atlantean invaders.

Medinet Habu as it appeared when approaching final construction, around 1180 B.C. A gigantic Ramses III, impersonating Amun-Ra, presents the captured armies of Atlantis to his fellow gods. Model, Milwaukee Public Museum, Wisconsin.

Mee-nee-ro-da-ha-sha

The Mandan Indians' annual "Settling of the Waters" ceremony commemorating the Great Flood from which a white-skinned survivor arrived in South Dakota.

(See Nowah'wus, Okipa)

Meg

"Before the second of the upheavals," this priestess, according to Edgar Cayce, "interpreted the messages that were received through the crystals and the fires that were to the eternal fires of nature" (natural energies). In Meg's time, there were "new developments in air, in water travel...there were the beginnings of the developments at that period for the escape." Although the first examples of this evacuation technology were becoming available, "when the destructions came, the entity chose rather to stay with the groups than to flee to other lands" (3004-1 F.55 5/15/43).

In ancient British myth, Meg was a giantess able to throw huge boulders over great distances. Her memory still survives in the Royal Navy, where battleship guns are referred to as Mon Megs, from Long Meg. It is not inconceivable that Cayce's Meg and the Atlantean cataclysm were transmuted over time into the British Meg, whose myth seems to describe an erupting volcano at sea.

(See Cayce, Vimana)

Megas

See Saka Duipa

Meh-Urt

Literally "The Great Flood," she was the Egyptian "Goddess of the Watery Abyss," from whose deluge all life sprang. She was usually portrayed as "the Celestial Cow" wearing a jeweled collar and a sun disk resting between her horns. At other times she appeared as a woman with the head of a cow, while carrying a lotus-flower scepter. Me-Urt represented creative destruction, which annihilated older forms to bring forth new ones, such as Nile civilization from the early Atlantean "Great Flood" in the late fourth millennium B.C.

Memnon

Described in the *Posthomerica*, by Quintus of Smyrna (circa 135 A.D.), as an Ethiopian king who, with his 10,000-man army, came to the aid of besieged Troy after the death of its foremost commander, Hector. "Ethiopia" was, in pre-classical and early classical times not associated with the East African country south of Egypt, but another name for Atlantis, according to the Roman scholar, Pliny the Elder. Memnon said of his own early childhood, "the lily-like Hesperides raised me far away by the stream of Ocean." The Hesperides were Atlantises, daughters of Atlas, who attended the sacred, golden apple tree at the center of his island kingdom. Having been "raised" by them indicates that Memnon was indeed a king, a member of the royal house of Atlantis.

At his death, he was mourned by another set of Atlantises, the Pleiades, daughters of the sea-goddess Pleione, by Atlas. His mother, Eos, or "Dawn," bore him in Atlantis, and his father, Tithonus, belonged to the royal house of Troy; hence, his defense of that doomed kingdom. His followers, the Memnonides, wore distinctive chest armor emblazoned with the image of a black crow, the animal of Kronos, a Titan synonymous for the Atlantic Ocean. Even during the Roman era, the Atlantic was known as "Chronos maris," the Sea of Kronos.

(See Atlantean War, Hesperides, Kronos, Pleiades)

Men Like Gods

A novel about Atlantis by the early 20th-century British author of the better known *War of the Worlds* and *The Time Machine*, H.G. Wells.

Gerardus Mercator

The 16th-century cartographer and inventor of the modern globe with its "Mercator lines," who compared the abundant native flood traditions he heard firsthand in Mexico with Plato's account of Atlantis to conclude that the lost civilization was fact, not fable. Like many of his contemporaries, he identified America with Atlantis itself.

Merlin

Famous as King Arthur's magician, his Atlantean, or at any rate, Celtic (even pre-Celtic), origins are widely suspected. The legendary character was probably modeled on a real-life bard who went mad after the Battle of Ardderyd, in 574 A.D., and spent the rest of his life as a hermit in the woods, known for his eccentric genius. "Merlin" was likely derived from *Mabon*, the all-powerful Lord of the Animals known on the Continent as *Cernunnos*. He is depicted on Denmark's second-century Gundestrup Cauldron as a horned stag holding a serpent in one hand and a golden torc (neck ornament) in the other. These symbols appear to signify mastery over the forces of death and regeneration: the horns and snake shed their skins to rejuvenate themselves, while the torc is associated with the eternal light of the sun.

According to Anna Franklin, in her encyclopedic work on world myth, "Some say Merlin came out of Atlantis, and that he and the other survivors became the Druid priests of ancient Britain." Indeed, he was said to have disassembled Stonehenge and rebuilt it on the Salisbury Plain. His earliest known name, Myrddin, Celtic for "from the sea," certainly suggests an Atlantean pedigree.

Merope

An Atlantis, daughter of Atlas, one of the seven Pleiades. Her name and variations of it appear in connection with Atlantis among several cultures over a long period of time. Euripides, Plato's contemporary, who was considered the most realistic of classical playwrights, wrote in "Phaeton" of an island in the Distant West called Merope, a possession of Poseidon, the sea-god creator of Atlantis. Aelian's *Varia Historia* (Book III, Chapter XVIII) quotes the fourth-century B.C. Theopompous of Chios on an island beyond the Pillars of Heracles ruled by Queen Merope, described as a daughter of Atlas. The Merops, according to Theopompous, launched an attack on Europe, first against Hyperborea (Britain).

But the war was lost, and the kingdom of Merope received a sudden increase in population immediately following the fall of Troy. Queen Merope was supposed to have been contemporary with Troy's Laomedon, King Priam's father, so she would have lived around the turn of the 14th century B.C., a time when the Atlanto-Trojan Confederation came into effect. These events are dimly shadowed in myth and the name of an historical people, the Meropids, who occupied the Atlantic shores of northern Morocco in the first century B.C. Merope was probably the name of an allied kingdom or colony of the Atlantean Empire in coastal North Africa, perhaps occupying the southern half of present-day Morocco.

Mesentiu

The "Harpooners," sometimes called "Metal Smiths" in ancient Egyptian tradition, who, along with the "Followers of Horus," escaped in the company of the gods from their oceanic homeland sinking in the Distant West. They arrived at the Nile Delta, where they created Egyptian Civilization, a fusion of native culture with Atlantean technology. The Mesentiu were a particular group of survivors from one of the Atlantean catastrophes, perhaps the late fourth-millennium event.

(See Sekhet-aaru, Semsu-Hor)

Mestor

In Plato's *Kritias*, an Atlantean monarch of which nothing is known. Only the meaning of his name, "The Counselor," suggests Mestor's kingdom may have been in Britain, where that foremost Atlantean monument, Stonehenge, gave counsel through its numerous celestial alignments. "Merlin" was perhaps a linguistic variant of "Mestor."

(See Stonehenge)

Miwoche

A "Master" with whose birth in 1917 B.C. the history of Tibet officially began. Miwoche is described in the pre-Buddhist Boen religion as directly descended from the spiritual hierarchy that dominated Mu.

Monan

Literally, "the Ancient One" of Brazil's Tupinamba Indians, who believe he long ago destroyed most of mankind with a "fire from heaven" extinguished by a worldwide flood. Chronologer, Neil Zimmerer, writes that Monan allegedly "enjoyed watching the humans suffer until the island of Atlantis sank."

(See Irin Mage)

Montezuma

Flood hero of the Piman or Papgos Indians of Arizona and Sonoroa, Mexico. He came from a "great land" over the ocean, in the east, where an awful deluge drowned most of his people. His name appears to have been passed down to two Aztec emperors. Moctezuma I was the earliest Aztec emperor, while Moctezuma II was the last such ruler, captured by the Spaniards and stoned to death by his fellow countrymen.

Mo-o

In western Micronesia, an Oleai glyph comprising a smaller circle at the center of a larger one connected at the top and bottom by two vertical lines extending from the outer rim of the inner circle to the inner rim of the larger. It appears to represent the lost civilization of Mu, an island in the middle of the ocean culturally connected to circum-Pacific territories.

Moriori

The white-skinned natives of Chatham Island, lying several hundred miles east of New Zealand. When questioned about their origins by British explorers in the late 18th century, they told how their ancestors arrived at Chatham from a great island kingdom in the west after it sank beneath the sea. The Moriori were shortly thereafter exterminated through their exposure to European diseases, against which they possessed no immunity.

(See Mu)

Moselles Shoals

Lying at the same depth, 19 feet, as the Bimini Road, and approximately 5 miles further away to the northeast, Moselles Shoals is a jumbled collection of squared, granite "columns," resembling the collapsed ruin of a temple or public edifice of some kind. This manmade appearance is enhanced by a total absence of any other stones, megalithic or otherwise, on the sea bottom. At about 30 feet across and perhaps 200 feet long, the "ruin" approximates the dimensions and configuration of an elongated building. Moselles Shoals lies in the same waters with the Bimini Road, but the structures are wholly unlike one another, although they may share a common Atlantean identity. As of this writing, Moselles Shoals has received only a fraction of the attention won by the more famous Road, but concerted investigation there could prove surprisingly rewarding for Atlantologists.

(See Bimini Road)

Mu

A Pacific civilization, also known as *Lemuria*, *Kahiki*, *Ku-Mu waiwai*, *Horai*, *Hiva*, *Haiviki*, *Pali-uli*, *Tahiti*, and *Rutas*, that flourished before Atlantis. Far less is known about Mu, but its influence from Asia through the Pacific to the western coasts of America appears to have been prodigious, particularly in religion and art. References to Mu appear among hundreds of often very diverse and otherwise unrelated societies affected by its impact, including Tibet, Easter Island, Olmec Mexico, Indonesia, Australia, Hawaii, Japan, pre-Inca Peru, and so on.

Atlantis and Mu engaged in some cultural interchange, but the peaceful Lemurians mostly regarded imperialist Atlanteans with a veiled mixture of dread and contempt. For their part, the Atlanteans looked down on the people of Mu as members of a backward but colorful and even spiritually valuable, although pre-civilized, society. There were no "cities," as such, in Mu, but ceremonial centers appeared across the land. Unlike the concentric designs favored by Atlantean architects, monumental construction in Mu was squared and linear, with less spiritual emphasis on the sky (Atlantean astrology) than on Mother Earth. Maritime skills were high, but long voyages were mostly conducted for missionary work.

Nothing in the numerous traditions related to Mu suggests a military of any kind. Its society was unquestionably theocratic, similar perhaps to Tibetan Buddhism, which is, in any case, descended from Mu, with additional alien religious and cultural influences. Also unlike Atlantis, Mu may have actually been "continental," or, at any rate, a large, mostly flat landmass approaching the size of India, located in the Philippine Sea, southwest of China.

The destruction of Mu is not as well attested as the Atlantean catastrophe, although both events seem to have been generated by a related cause—namely, a killer comet that made repeated, devastating passes near the Earth with increasingly dire consequences for humanity, from the 16th through 13th centuries B.C. A particularly heavy bombardment of meteoritic material around 1628 B.C. may have ignited volcanic and seismic forces throughout the Pacific's already unstable "Ring of Fire" to bring about the demise of Mu. In Hawaiian myth, a fair-haired people who occupied the islands before the Polynesians and built great stone structures are still remembered as "the Mu."

Mu'a

An island in western Samoa, featuring prehistoric petroglyphs, burial mounds, and ceremonial structures. Its name and ancient artifacts are associated with the lost Pacific Ocean civilization of the same name.

Mu-ah

Shoshone name, Mu-ah, "Summit of Mu," for a sacred mountain in California. Mount Mu-ah may have been chosen by Lemurian adepts for the celebration of their religion, and regarded as holy ever since by native peoples.

(See Shoshone)

Muck, Otto Heinrich

Austrian physicist (University of Innsbruck) who invented the snorkel, enabling U-boats to travel under water without surfacing to recharge their batteries, thereby escaping enemy detection in World War II. He later helped develop German rocketry on the research island of Peenemunde, in the Baltic Sea. Published at the time of his death in 1965, *The Secret of Atlantis* was internationally acclaimed for its scientific evaluation of Plato's account, helped revive popular interest in the lost civilization, and remains one of the most important books on the subject.

Mu Cord

An ancient Lemurian flying vehicle described in Tibetan traditions.

(See Lemuria, Vimana)

Mu-Da-Lu

Celebrated in Taiwanese folk tradition as the capital of a magnificent kingdom, an ancestral homeland, now at the bottom of the sea. Like Atlantis, Mu-Da-Lu was supposed to have been ringed by great walls of red stone.

Legend seemed confirmed by an underwater find made by Professor We Miin Tian, from the Department of Marine Engineering at National Sun Yat Sen University, in Kaohsiung City, Taiwan. During August, 2002, he discovered a wall standing about 4 feet high, perpendicular to the seafloor. The stone structure is approximately 30 feet long, and 60 feet beneath the surface, among the Pescadores Islands, near the Pen-hu Archipelago, between the small islands of Don-Jyu and Shi-Hyi-Yu, 40 miles west of Taiwan. Twenty years before Professor Tian's discovery, another scuba diver from Taiwan, Steven Shieh, found a pair of consistently 15-foot high stone walls underwater near Hu-ching, or "Tiger Well Island." At estimated 2,000 feet long, they run at right angles to each other, one oriented north/south; the other, east/west, terminating in a large, circular structure.

The Pescadores' sunken walls and tales of Mu-Da-Lu are cultural and archaeological evidence for Lemurian influences in Taiwan.

(See Sura and Nako)

Mu-gu

A Chumash village in southern California: "place (*gu*) near water," signifying "beach," although its actual meaning is more likely, "Place near (or toward) Mu." Variations of "Mu" are more common among the Chumash than any other Native Americans, appropriately so, since their tribe evidenced many Lemurian influences, not the least of which was facial hair among North America's otherwise beardless peoples, together with their singular skills as boatwrights and mariners.

Mu-Heku-Nuk

"Place-Where-The-Waters-Are-Never-Still," the oceanic origins of the Algonquian Indians, suggests the geologically unstable, sunken Pacific "Mother-land" of Mu.

A 17th-century statue of Mu Kung, the mythic ruler of a Pacific Ocean paradise (from which he derived his name) before the island was overwhelmed by the rising sea.

Mu Kung

In Chinese myth, god of the immortals who ruled over the East, the location of the Pacific civilization of Mu. Mu Kung was an earlier version of Hsi Wang Mu, likewise associated with immortality. He dwelt in a golden palace beside the Lake of Gems, where a blessed peach tree provided fruit from which was distilled the exilir of immortality. Several Lemurian themes are immediately apparent. Chinese explorers actually went in search of the elixir at Yonaguni, a Japanese island where a sunken citadel dated to the 11th millennium B.C. was discovered in 1985. Yonaguni is also known for *cho-me-gusa*, a plant still revered by the islanders because of its alleged life-extending properties. Moreover, the Japanese myth of "peach boy" concerns a sunken palace of gold, where he never ages.

Chronologist Neil Zimmerer writes that Mu Kung "formed a special group of eight humans, who were given fruits from the Tree of Life. They were known as the 'Immortals.'" According to Churchward, the Tree of Life, the embodiment of immortality, was Lemuria's chief emblem. As millennia began to fade clearer folk memories of Mu, the "Motherland," Hsi Wang Mu's palace was changed to Kun Lun, the western paradise.

Mu-Lat

California Chumash for "bay," implying a Lemurian influence.

Mu-luc

Literally, "Drowned Mu," meaning "flood" in the Mayan language.

Mu-Mu-Na

In Australoid myth, the flaming rainbow serpent, also known as Mu-It, that fell from heaven to cause a world flood. Mu-Mu-Na's description and name reference the cometary destruction of both antediluvian civilizations, Mu and Atlantis.

Mu Museum

In the aftermath of World War II, Reikiyo Umemto, a young monk, while engaged in deep meditation at the southeastern shores of Japan, experienced a powerful vision of the ancient land of Mu. More than some archaeological flash-back, it transcended his traditional Buddhist thinking with the sunken realm's lost mystery cult, which he refounded as the "World's Great Equality" in Hiroshima prefecture. For the next 20 years, he lived and shared its principles with a few, select followers, until some wealthy backers put themselves at his disposal. With their support, he built a 12-acre temple-museum with surrounding, landscaped grounds closely patterned after structures and designs recalled from his postwar vision. Work on the red and white complex adorned with life-size statues of elephants and lively, if esoteric murals was undertaken at a selected site in Kagoshima prefecture because of the area's strong physical resemblance to Mu and the location's particular geo-spiritual energies. Construction was completed by the mid-1960s.

A large, professionally staffed institute with modern facilities for display and laboratory research, the Mu Museum is unique in all the world for its authentic artifacts and well-made recreations associated with the lost civilization which bears its name. Although open to the general public, spiritual services at its temple are restricted to initiates. Reikiyo Umemto passed away in 2002 at 91 years of age.

Mungan Ngaua

According to chronologist, Neil Zimmerer, a Lemurian monarch who perished with his son, Tundum, in the Great Flood.

Mu-Nissing

Among Michigan's Ojibwa, an island (Mu) in a body of water (nissing).

Mu-nsungan

Known as the "Humped Island" among the Algonquian-speaking native people of Maine.

Murias

Antediluvian capital of the Tuatha de Danann, described in the *Book of Invasions*, a collection of oral histories written during the Middle Ages, as a "sea people" who arrived in ancient Ireland 1,000 years before the Celts, circa 1600 B.C. They were immigrants, survivors of a cataclysm that sank Murias beneath the sea. Some researchers conclude from this characterization, together with its name and alleged location in the far west, that Murias was an Irish version of the sunken Pacific civilization, Mu, or Lemuria.

Before the disaster, the surviving Tuatha de Danann were able to save their most valuable treasure, a mysterious object called "Un-dry," also known as the "Cauldron of Dagda," the "Good God," who led them away from the catastrophe. The same vessel is implied in the most sacred artifact from Murias, "a hollow filled with water and fading light." The renowned Atlantean scholar, Edgerton Sykes, believed Un-dry was "possibly the origin of the Grail."

The story of drowned Murias is not confined to Ireland, but known in various parts of the British Isles and the European Continent. In Wales, it is remembered as *Morvo*, and it is known as *Morois*, in French Normandy.

(See Falias, Finias, Gorias, Mu, Tir-nan-Og, Tuatha da Danann)

Mu-ri-wai-o-ata

Known throughout Polynesia as a legendary palace at the bottom of the sea, home of the divine hero, Toona, an apparent reference to the lost Pacific civilization of Mu.

Murrugan

A god whose worship was carried from Mu to India, where it still flourishes. (See Land of the Kumara)

Musaeus

Listed in Plato's *Kritias* as an Atlantean king. He appears to have been deified as Muyscas, the "Civilizer" of the Chibchas. They were a people not unlike the

Incas who occupied the high valleys surrounding Bogotá and Neiva at the time of the Spanish Conquest. Also known as the "White One," the bearded Muyscas laid down ground rules for Colombia's first civilization, then departed, leaving behind four chiefs to govern through his authority and example (Blackett, 274). The Chibchans referred to themselves, after Muyscas, as the Muisca, or "the Musical Ones." Musaeus, the fifth Atlantean king in Plato's account, means "Of the Muses," divine patrons of the arts.

Blackett wrote, "On the common interpretation of mythic traditions, these Atlantides ought to be provinces or places in South America" (215). The Atlantean kingdom of Musaeus was in Colombia, where the native culture came to reflect his name and origins in Atlantis.

Cretan Knossos shared some architectural similarities with monumental construction in Atlantis, because both evolved into contemporary Bronze Age cities.

Mu-sembeah

A mountain sacred to the Shoshone of Wyoming. Like its California counterpart, Mu-sembeah received its holy character from Lemurian missionaries.

Mu-sinia

The Ute Indians' sacred "white mountain," in Utah.

Mu-tu

Tahitian for "island," possibly derived from the sunken Pacific Ocean island of Mu. Interestingly, its reverse, *tu-mu*, is Tahitian for "tree," which may again refer to Mu. According to researcher, James Churchward, Mu was alternately known as the "Tree of Life."

Mu-tubu-udundi

A secret martial art known only to masters directly descended from the first king of Japan's Ryukyu Islands. He brought the regimen with him from his island kingdom in the east, where it was overwhelmed by the sea. Adepts avoid physical confrontation, seeking rather to exhaust their opponents through an intricate series of controlled postures and dance-like movements, striking a blow only after all other options have been exhausted. Like China's tai-chi, its Japanese precursor is also a form of mediation aimed at putting human bio-rhythms in accord with so-called "Earth energies." Its name, Mu-tubu-udundi, or "the Self-Disciplined Way of Mu," derives from the lost Pacific civilization of Mu, similarly known for the spiritual disciplines and peaceful worldview of its inhabitants.

Mu-tu-hei

In Marquesan cosmology, the worldwide void or "silence" that existed during the remote past immediately after the annihilation of a great Pacific kingdom, an apparent reference to the disappearance of Mu.

Mu-tul

A Mayan city founded by Zac-Mu-tul, whose name means, literally, "White Man of Mu." The name "Mu-tul" seems philologically related to the Polynesian "Mu-tu" (Tahiti) and "Mu-tu-hei" (Marquesas), all defining a Lemurian common denominator.

(See Mu, Mut-t, Mu-tu-hei)

Mu-yin-wa

The Hopi "maker of all life," he appears during ritual events known as Powamu, every February. A white line signifying his skin color appears down the front of his arms and legs. Mu-yin-wa's personification of the Direction Below (sunken Mu?), and the recurrence of "Mu" in his name, to say nothing of the suggestive Powamu, define him as a mythic heirloom from the lost Pacific civilization.

Mu-yu-Moqo

Site of the earliest known working of precious metal in the Andes. Located in the Andahualas Valley, archaeological excavations at Muyu-Moqo uncovered a 3,440-year-old stone bowl containing metallurgical tools and gold beaten into thin foil. The Lemurians were renowned metalsmiths, and the discovery of fine gold work at Muyu-Moqo echoes not only the site's derivation from Mu, but coincides with the probable destruction of the island civilization, around 1628 B.C.

Naacals

Literally, "Serpents" or "Serpent People," denoting wisdom, the spiritual/scientific elite or missionary "brotherhood" of Mu, who traveled to India in the west and Mexico in the east, following the destruction of their oceanic homeland.

Nacxit

The "Great Father" of Patulan-Pa-Civan, the Quiche Mayas' ancestral realm across the sunrise sea. Before some of its inhabitants left on their transoceanic voyage to Yucatan, he presented a power-crystal to their leader, **Ballam-Qitze**. This sacred stone from Patulan-Pa-Civan and the kingdom's Atlantic location are foremost identifiable details in any description of Atlantis. "Nacxit" would appear to be an authentically Atlantean name.

(See Ballam-Qitze, Crystal Skull, Patulan-Pa-Civan, U Mamae, Tuoai Stone)

Nagaitco

The ancestor of North America's Kato Indians. He was discovered floating on the waters of the Great Flood, clinging to the branches of a tree. Nagaitco was said to have arrived on the mainland from a distant island that no longer exists.

Nammu

A Sumerian birth-goddess, personification of the primeval sea from which human life emerged. Nammu is also known to Canada's Haida Indians as the whale upon whose back mankind first resided, until it sank beneath the waves under savage attacks from the sky. Many drowned, but some floated to the Pacific-coastal shores of British Columbia, where they became the Haidas' ancestors. Both versions reflect the story of Mu.

(See Mu)

Nana Buluku

Described in Yoruba and Benin folk traditions as a royal personage belonging to the "Sea Peoples" who conquered the West African kingdom of Aja around 1200 B.C. This is the same period when Egyptians on the other side of Africa were fending off invasion by warriors who Pharaoh Ramses III identically described as the *Hanebu*, or "Sea Peoples" from the sunken realm of Neteru (Atlantis). Nana Buluku similarly came from an Atlantic island overwhelmed by a natural catastrophe with her husband, Wulbari. Thanks in large measure to her reputation as a skilled physician, they were chosen as corulers to mitigate the worst effects of a famine ravaging Aja. But its severity was so widespread, Wulbari resigned under pressure, and discontented opposition, led by the "High Priest of the Sky," Aido, plotted to overthrow Nana Buluku. The conspiracy was discovered before it could succeed, however, and Aido was banished with his accomplices.

The story of serious famine associated with Nana Buluku's arrival in West Africa once again underscores its relationship with the Sea Peoples, whose appearance in the eastern Mediterranean was said to have coincided with wide-spread famine resulting from the global cataclysm that destroyed Atlantis in the Late Bronze Age.

(See Sea Peoples)

Nanabush

Flood hero of Algonquian-speaking Indians in the Central Woodlands culture area. After retrieving the corpse of his drowned brother, Nanabush led survivors of the great flood that destroyed a former world. Among the treasures he saved was the Medewiwin ceremony, which brought his dead brother back to life. Nanabush perpetuated his world's secrets in various Medewiwin societies of initiates among the Cree, Fox, Menomoni, Ojibwa, Ottawa, Potawatomi, and Sauk, who still preserve its arcane principles. He compares with the West African Nana Buluku.

(See Nana Buluku, Wallum Olum)

Nancomala

The flood hero of South America's Guayami Indians. Nancomala waded into the receding tide of the Deluge, where he found a water-maiden, Rutbe, whose children became ancestors of the Guayami. Here, as in so many similar traditions around the world, the survivor of some catastrophic inundation during the ancient past is revered as the progenitor of a whole people. In these universal folk memories culture-bearers from the destruction of Atlantis are strongly suggested.

Nata and Nena

In Mixtec myth, a husband and wife who were warned by the god Tezcatlipocha of a coming, world-destroying deluge. Like Shiva in the Hindu flood epics, he instructed them to build a large ship in which they could survive. When the natural catastrophe occurred, it eclipsed a former "Sun" (or Age), in which most of mankind was obliterated. But Nata and Nena rode out the tempest in their vessel, eventually coming to rest at what is now the east coast of Mexico. Disembarking, they promptly proceeded to repopulate the world in the normal fashion.

The resemblance of this pre-Conquest story to the Genesis flood is remarkable, even to comparisons between the Mixtec *Nata* and biblical *Noah*. Still closer to the Old Testament version was a Venezuelan flood hero of the Orinoco Indians, *Noa*.

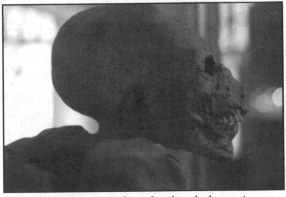

Nausicaa

An Atlantean princess, who befriended Odysseus, the shipwrecked Greek war veteran in Homer's epic. A variation of her myth has her leaving Phaeacia, the Homeric Atlantis, a few years before its destruction, to marry Telemachus, Odysseus' son.

Inca cranial remains show that head-elongation was practiced by both ancient Peruvian and Egyptial royals as a means of physically distinguishing themselves from others missing an Atlantean heritage.

Navaho Child Initiation Ceremony

It featured a masked figure wearing a red wig and horned helmet, accompanied by a woman, her face painted white. She portrayed the man's wife. Both were supposed to represent the couple which survived the Great Flood, as a reminder of the child's ancestral origins. The Atlantean and racially alien implications of the Navaho Child Initiation Ceremony are self-evident.

(See Man Mounds)

Navel of the World

The original and most important mystery religion of Atlantis, at least some of its rituals, such as initiation, were performed in selected caves representing Mother Earth's womb. The name, "Navel of the World," appears to not only refer directly to its central spiritual tenet, but was also an early title by which Atlantis itself was known; modern parallels are Chicago as "the Windy City," a characterization of its loquacious politicians; New York as "the Big Apple," representing ultimate material success; Paris as "the City of Lights," for its bright gaiety, and so forth. The leading cult-object of The Navel of the World was a large, egg-shaped stone, known to Greeks as the *Omphalos*. The Navel of the World emphasized inner illumination through spiritual experience, such as religious drama, in which actors convincingly impersonated the gods, and other theatrical devices were used to convince initiates that life was eternal, death but a momentary transition, not annihilation.

With the destruction of Atlantis, practitioners reestablished themselves at various, new centers in many other lands. Each of the different locations wherein they headquartered the cult were known as Navels of the World. These included the Aegean island of Delos, the Greek Delphi, Rome, Jerusalem, in the Azores (Homer's Ogygia, the "Navel of the Sea"), the Incas' Cuzco (Peru), Easter Island in the Eastern Pacific, and so on—wherever the Atlantean survivors resettled. Their mystery religion fundamentally influenced Hinduism, Tibetan Buddhism, even early Christian mysticism, primarily through belief in the eternity of the human soul, never in a static form, but through recurring cycles exemplified in nature's seasonal changes, a concept that resulted in the doctrine of reincarnation.

The purest survival of The Navel of the World religion was preserved in the Eleusian Mysteries.

Nawalam

A splendid island kingdom which perished in the sea during the deep past after its survivors sailed to Sri Lanka. Tamil culture traces its origins back to these immigrants, survivors from the lost Pacific civilization of Mu.

(See Mu)

Nefydd Naf Neifion

A young prince who saved his royal family from a great flood that sank their realm under the Atlantic Ocean in the distant past. He led them to Wales, where they established a new kingdom, the first in the land. Nefydd Naf Neifion is the local memory of culture-bearers from Atlantis arriving at the end of the Late Bronze Age.

Neith

Very ancient, possibly pre-dynastic Egyptian goddess, at whose Nile Delta temple in Sais the history of Atlantis was inscribed on memorial pillars. She was, in fact, worshiped as the oldest of all deities. One of her titles, *Tehenut* ("Of Libya"), according to Imel, "suggests a Western origin." Although Plato only mentions Neith in passing, the preservation of Atlantean records at her temple was appropriate in many respects.

While never entirely forgotten, her worship over the centuries had declined almost to nothing until it was spectacularly revived during the XXVI Dynasty, when Neith's city was elevated to the capital of Egypt. Pharaohs like Psamtik and Ahmose were leading a national revival after generations of neglect. To reassert their country's ancient greatness, they reopened and remodeled old temples to restore general respect and enthusiasm for Egyptian heritage. Everything important from the past was resurrected and honored. It was during this cultural house-cleaning that the Atlantis story was either installed with prominence at Egypt's most important temple, or dusted off where it had been kept for at least eight hundred years. Coincidentally, Solon, the Greek legislator on holiday along the Nile, visited the Temple of Neith. There he learned the account first-hand from Psonchis, the high priest.

Among her numerous godly duties, Neith was the divine patroness of history and prophesy, as indicated by the words inscribed on the wall of her temple: "I am all that has been, that is and that will be." In sacred art, she was symbolized by a cow in the company of 19 stars. These were the Atlantises, or daughters of Atlas: the seven he had by Pleione, the Pleiades; another seven, the Hesperides; and five by Arethusa, the Hyades. Her cow form was also known as *Meh-urt*, literally, "the Great Flood."

Nemed

Described by the Sumerian scholar Neil Zimmerer as "a grandson of Noah," leader of the eponymous Nemedians, survivors from the 17th-century B.C. cataclysm that almost destroyed Atlantis. He led his followers to Ireland, where they were opposed by the resident Fomorach, themselves descended from Atlantis. The Nemedians were defeated, but allowed to remain, so long as they paid an onerous annual tribute to their conquerors. Eventually, Nemed staged a bloody rebellion, seizing the Formorach stronghold of Tor Conaind. Losses were so heavy, however, the Nemedians lost their tribal identity and faded into the resident population.

(See Fomorach)

Ne-Mu

Demigods or giants recalled by the Kai of New Guinea, the Ne-Mu are said to have been much taller and stronger than today's men, and ruled the world before the Great Deluge. They introduced agriculture and house-building to Kai ancestors. When the Flood came, all the Ne-Mu were killed, but their bodies turned to great blocks of stone. This final feature of the myth betrays the Kai's reaction to megalithic structures found occasionally in New Guinea, often composed of prodigious stonework they identify with the pre-Flood Ne-Mu.

(See Mu)

Nemquetheba

Also Nemtherqueteba, another name of the Muysca flood hero, who arrived on the shores of Colombia following a fiery cataclysm in the Atlantic Ocean that destroyed his homeland.

(See Bochica, Zuhe)

Nephilim

Described in the Old Testament as a fallen race of giants, they ruled the world before the Great Flood, which obliterated their power. Their descendants, the Emin, "a people great, and many, and tall" (Deuteronomy 2:11), were also known as the Rephaim or Anakim, who perpetuated pre-deluge religious practices atop a sacred mountain, Seir. The Nephilim appear to have been late fourth-millennium B.C. Atlanteans.

Neptune

The Roman Poseidon. His name stems from the earlier Etruscan Nefthuns As the mythic creator of Atlantis, he symbolized either the natural forces which formed the basis of the city into alternating rings of land and water, or personified alien, pre-Atlantean culture-bearers who arrived at the island to found a hybrid civilization with the natives. In Plato's account, the sea-god mates with an indigenous woman to sire the first kings of Atlantis.

(See Poseidon)

Nereides

Daughters of Nereus and Doris, both oceanic deities. Although fleetingly mentioned by Plato, they are significant because the Nereides were poetic descriptions of dolphins ridden by very young men. The famous "Boy on a Dolphin" was the emblem of an Atlantean mystery school, which initiated male youth into personal spiritual development through intimate rapport with dolphins, what today would be understood as a kind of inter-species communication with a strong religious emphasis. Like their avatar, the dolphin, the Nereides were notable for their devoted protection of shipwrecked humans. They were also said to be oracular, a suggestion of their cultic function.

Some Nereide names are overtly Atlantean: Arethusa, after the mother of the Hyade Atlantises; Calypso, an Atlantis; Leukothe, after Leukippe, the first woman of Atlantis; Plexaura and Pasithea, after the Atlantean Hyades, Plexarus and Pasitheo, respectively; and so on. In Greek myth, the Nereides are given as 50, but in *Kritias* they number twice as many attendants of the sea-god, Poseidon, as consistent with Plato's (or possibly Solon's) error in translating numerical values from the original Egyptian account of Atlantis into Greek. As such, it represents contributing internal evidence for the overstated size and age of Atlantis in the Dialogues.

(See Plato, Solon)

Neshanu

Creator-god of the North American Pawnee Indians, he was so disgusted by man's cruelty and disrespect, he commanded a worldwide deluge to destroy all but a few individuals. These he changed into seeds. After the flood, Neshanu harvested an ear and molded it into Mother Corn. She went about the Earth, finding the hidden grains, released the survivors, then taught them the arts, ceremonies, and agriculture. Her work done, Neshanu transformed her once more into a cedar. Ever since, the tree has been venerated as a sacred, living memorial to the Great Flood and the reeducation, that is to say, cultivation of its chosen survivors, their ancestors.

The Pawnee version shares a major theme—the corruption of mankind— with Plato's Atlantis account, and explains the universal North American reverence for cedar as a holy wood. Pacific Northwest Coast tribes carve their so-called "totem poles," which sometimes symbolize the Great Flood, from cedar.

Netamaki

The Delaware Indians tell how their virtuous ancestors were subverted by Powako, a high priest, who instituted *Intake*, or self-indulgent serpent-worship. To chastise them, a terrible cataclysm drowned their luxuriant homeland. "All this happened very long ago," states the Delaware *Hymn of the Flood*, "at the first land, Netamaki, beyond the great ocean, Kitahikan (the Atlantic)." Obviously, Netamaki is a Delaware cultural inflection of Plato's Atlantis.

The New Atlantis

A 1629 utopian novel by Francis Bacon, it was the first written discussion of Atlantis since the fall of classical civilization and probably sparked Athanasius Kircher's interest in the subject, when he published his own scientific study of Atlantis in *The Subterranean World*, 36 years later. Although a work of fiction, *The New Atlantis* came about through excited discussions in contemporary scholarly circles of reports from travelers to America. They stated that the indigenous peoples had oral accounts of a land comprising numerous points in common with Plato's sunken civilization. *The New Atlantis* actually incorporates some Atlanto-American myths Bacon heard repeated in London.

(See Athanasius Kircher)

Ngaru

The leading culture hero of Mangaia Island, he was said to have defeated Miru, the Underworld god, by unleashing a flood so colossal it extinguished the fires of hell.

Nichant

The Gros-Ventre Indians remember Nichant as the god who sent a punishing "fire from heaven" to burn up sinful humanity. Those who survived were mostly killed by a global deluge he caused immediately thereafter to extinguish the conflagration, lest it incinerate the rest of the world.

Nina Stahu

In tribal myth, the name of a cavern in which the ancestors of North America's Blackfoot Indians sought refuge from the Great Flood. They later emerged reborn as a new people.

The story of Nina Stahu is the mythic background for kiva rituals, wherein participants emerge from a subterranean chamber while being doused with water, as a symbolic reenactment of ancestral survival from the Deluge.

Ninella

In Babylonian myth, the name of a mother goddess said to have been worshiped before the World Flood, in which Ninella perished.

Nirai-Kanai

A culture hero cited throughout the oral traditions of the Ryukyu Islands, south of Japan. Nirai-Kanai was said to have arrived very long ago from his enlightened kingdom, far over the sea, where it was swallowed in a tempest of fire and storm. He taught the natives how to cultivate *cho-mei-gusa*, the "plant of immortality," and built the first stone castles in the islands. Coincidentally (?), his legend is venerated at Okinawa and Yonaguni, where underwater ruins were discovered in the mid-1980s and late 90s. Nirai-Kanai is also "The Homeland Very Far Away In The Sea," regarded as a kingdom from which the forefathers of the Japanese Ama arrived after it was engulfed in the western Pacific Ocean.

(See Ama, Horai, Mu, Yonaguni)

Noah

Although he appears in Genesis, Noah is certainly not an original biblical conception. Virtually his entire story was lifted from Assyrian, Babylonian, Akkadian, Eblamite, Sumerian, and other Mesopotamian traditions which predated the bible, sometimes by thousands of years. He was cited to lend legitimacy to the pedigree of the Hebrew patriarchs, who claimed to trace their lineage from Noah.

The name is a corruption of Nu, or Nun, the Egyptian god of the primordial deep, who submerged the first "mound" on which gods and men once lived in harmony. "Noah" was taken directly from Ma-Nu, Nun's cohort and goddess of the ancient ocean, and embodiment of the Great Flood, as it was known both in the Nile Valley and the Indus Valley. The Hebrew letter, *nun*, means "fish." Even the Hebrew "ark" was originally the Sumerian *arghe*, a "moon vessel" that rode out the Deluge millennia before the Old Testament version was composed.

(See Nowah'wus)

Noatun

Literally, the "Enclosure of Ships," a variant in Germanic myth of Atlantis; palace of the Norse sea-god Njord, at the bottom of the ocean. "Noatun" is also a segment in the Nordic zodiac equivalent to Pisces, the Fish, a sign that concludes on the vernal equinox, March 21, Njord's feast day. Noatun's philological similarity to the biblical Noah suggests it is a variant on an original Atlantean name both Norse and Hebrews received independently from a common source—namely, one of the Atlantis catastrophes.

Nostradamus

Born Michel de Nostredame in Saint-Remy, France, December 14, 1503, he is history's most famous astrologer. During his mid-40s, Nostradamus began making prophecies, which he published as a book, in 1555. It is composed of rhymed quatrains, or four-lined stanzas, grouped in hundreds; each set of 100 quatrains was identified as a "century." Hence, its title, *Centuries*. Its popularity was so widespread, especially in high places, he dedicated an enlarged, second edition to the King. Having thus gained royal favor, Nostradamus was everywhere in demand. Catherine de Medici invited him to cast the horoscopes of her children, and he became the personal physician to Charles IX, who ascended the French throne in 1560.

Because of these important political contacts, Vatican hostility was postponed, but inevitable. In 1781, the Roman Catholic Church officially condemned Nostradamus, his prophecies, and any Catholics who read them, under the inquisitorial Congregation of the Index. This was a body of bishops and cardinals who busied themselves with rooting out perceived heresies. Since then, the "centuries" of Nostradamus have gained international attention for many predictions that have apparently come to pass, and especially because at least some of those which are yet unfulfilled seem strangely relevant to our time.

One of his prophecies may be an enigmatic reference to the future discovery of Atlantis. It reads:

> *Le camp Ascop de Europe partira,*
> (The Ascop company leaves Europe,)
> *S'adjoignant proche d' l'sle submergee*
> (Approaching in concert the sunken island)
> *D' Arton classe phalange pliera Nobril du Monde.*
> (with Arton's tight group of individuals united for a common purpose near the Navel of the World:)
> *plus grand voix subrogee.*
> (a greater voice will [then] be subrogated by a lesser one;
> or, a great voice will be substituted [then] for another.)

Like all his prophecies, *Century* II.22 is open to interpretation. Nonetheless, Nostradamus refers to "l'sle submergee" as "Nobril du Monde"; Atlantis, "the sunken island," was also known as the "Navel of the World." His "classe phalange" suggests highly motivated investigators working together on a common project. He implies that two different groups will cooperate: Ascop and Arton. Neither have been certainly identified with anything known before or since the 16th century. They are more like modern amalgams for industrial firms, perhaps different research companies cooperating in a common underwater investigation. "Plus grand voix subrogee" hints that the long-standing opinion, or "voice" of conventional scientists, who insist that Atlantis was strictly legendary, will be displaced by Ascop and Arton's joint discovery of archaeological evidence establishing the city's physical existence.

The two best-known prophets in history—Nostradamus and Edgar Cayce—both spoke of Atlantis.

(See Edgar Cayce, Navel of the World)

Nowah'wus

Cheyenne name for Bear Butte, a 1,200-foot high mountain standing alone in a South Dakota prairie not far from the Black Hills. Geologically, the formation is classified as a *laccolith*, an irregularly formed body of solidified magma intruded between layers of sedimentary rock, making them bulge outward, about .5 million years ago. Together with Minnesota's Pipestone, Bear Butte was and is the most sacred site dedicated to the Great Flood, and a pilgrimage center for tribes from all over North America. Bear Butte was the scene for the Mandans' *mee-nee-ro-da-ha-sha*, or "Settling of the Waters." The performance of this annual ritual was an adjunct to their Okipa commemorative ceremony intended to prevent a recurrence of the cataclysm by assuring the Great Spirit that the Mandans had kept his laws and sacrificing sharp-edged implements symbolic of the tools which made the "big canoe" in which the deluge-survivors saved themselves.

The mee-nee-ro-da-ha-sha took place when the willow leaf was in full growth at mid-spring, because it was a leaf from this plant that was brought back in the bill of a turtle dove to Nu-mohk-muck-a-na, the Mandan flood hero, as a sign that "The Settling of the Waters" had begun. He then followed the bird's flight to Bear Butte, where Nu-mahk-muck-nan instituted the commemorative mee-nee-ro-da-ha-sha ceremony. Ever since, both the dove and the willow leaf were revered as the Indians' most sacred images.

Resemblance of Nu-mohk-muck-a-na to the biblical Noah is remarkable, even to the Cheyenne name for the butte, Noawah'wus. Sioux Indians refer to the laccolith as *Mato Paha*, or "Bear Butte," supposedly because it resembles a crouching bear when seen from the northeast. Be that as it may, more cogently, the bear symbolizes regeneration after a death-like winter hibernation. It awakens with the onset of spring, when the willow leaf is in full bloom, signaling the beginning of the mee-nee-ro-da-ha-sha ceremony. So too, the Atlantean people were reborn after the death of their homeland, commemorated at Mato Paha, in the survivors who settled among the Mandan.

The site may have been originally chosen for the mee-nee-ro-da-ha-sha because of its physical resemblance to Atlantis. From the mid-spring celebration until early fall, Bear Butte stands towering among waving prairies resembling a great island in the sea.

(See Noah, Okipa)

Ntlakapamuk

A British Columbian tribe in residence at the Thompson River. Ntlakapamuk shamans speak of a time when the Earth was consumed by a fire so universal only a worldwide flood succeeded in extinguishing it.

(See Asteroid Theory)

Nuadu

He led one of several waves of refugees from the final destruction of Atlantis to Ireland, where they battled the resident Fomorach, themselves descended from earlier Atlantean settlers, led by Eochaid. In the decisive Battle of Mag Turied, Nuadu lost his left arm, so he called for a truce. During negotiations that followed, Eochaid rejected the proposed terms, so Nuadu had him assassinated before the Fomorach king could return to his people. Due to his infirmity, Nuadu abdicated thereafter.

(See Fomorach)

Numbers

In *Kritias*, Plato wrote that the numbers 5 and 6 were sacred in Atlantis, where they were encoded in architecture, art, and ceremonial life "to honor the odd and even days." The Atlanteans' choice of these numerals reflects their holistic religion, the "Navel of the World," whose adherents strove for spiritual synthesis and balance. The number 5 represents the male principle of conscious outward action, while 6 stands for female intuitive receptivity.

Numinor

Atlantis in J.R.R. Tolkien's fantasy, *Lord of the Rings*, before the kingdom vanished beneath the sea. Following the deluge, it was known as Atalante. Tolkien claimed to have been plagued since childhood by nightmares he believed were past-life memories of the Atlantean catastrophe, but they never returned to disturb his sleep after he wrote about Numinor-Atalante. His son, too, experienced similar nightmares, but they ceased, as well, with the same description. Numinor was also known as Ele'na and Westernesse.

Nu-mohk-muck-a-na

The "first" or "only man" to survive the Great Flood, impersonated by an actor in an annual religious ceremony conducted by North Dakota's Mandan Indians. He portrayed Nu-mohk-muck-a-na, his body painted overall with white clay to resemble a white man, then entered the village from the east, the direction in which their ancestors arrived from the Deluge. There he was welcomed by all the chiefs, as though for the first time. Following their official greeting, he entered a secluded medicine lodge, where he participated in secret rituals. Emerging later, the impersonated Nu-mohk-muck-a-na stopped before each family lodge, where he wailed until he was asked what ailed him. He always replied that he was sad because he was the "only man" to survive a horrible flood which destroyed the outside world. He escaped in a "big canoe" which came to rest on a mountaintop in the West.

(See Nowah'wus, Okipa Ceremony)

Nurrundere

An Australian culture hero who eventually became the supreme being. Upon attaining that august position, Nurrundere unleashed a universal deluge that drowned his own wives (an illimitable number) and their families for their wickedness.

Nyoe

The "New Land," an island that appeared from the bottom of the Atlantic Ocean several miles out from Iceland, in 1783. Nyoe was so large it featured great cliffs. Within a year of its emergence, however, it collapsed back into the sea. Atlantologists cite Nyoe to show that the former existence and final disappearance of Atlantis is within the geologic experience of the Atlantic Ocean.

Ireland's New Grange is rife with Atlantean implications.

Oak

The tree sacred to Atlas; its branches, like his arms, supported the heavens. The oak's association with Atlas implies a primeval tree cult or pillar cult, a memory of it surviving in *Kritias*, Plato's Atlantis account, when he described a ceremonial column at the very midpoint of the Temple of Poseidon, itself located at the center of Atlantis. The Atlanteans' oldest, most hallowed laws were inscribed on its exterior, and sacrificial bull's blood was shed over it by all 10 kings of Atlantis in that civilization's premiere ritual.

Oannes

Described in Babylonian myth as a bearded man dressed in a fish-like gown who brought "The Tablets of Civilization" from his kingdom in the sea to the Near East. The Maya preserved an almost identical tradition of Oa-ana, "he who has his residence in the water." Like his Mesopotamian counterpart, he was considered an early culture-bearer who sparked Mesoamerican Civilization after arriving with great wisdom from across the Atlantic Ocean. Both Oannes and Oa-ana cross-reference Atlanteans landing on both sides of the world.

Obatala

Along the Gold Coast of West Africa, fronting the Atlantic Ocean, there are several accounts of the Atlantean deluge among the Yoruba people. They tell how Olokun, the sea-god, became angry with the sins of men, and sought to cause their extinction by instigating a massive flood that would drown the whole world. Many kingdoms perished in the ocean, until a giant hero, Obatala, standing in the midst of the waters and through his *juju,* or magical powers, bound Olokun in seven chains. The seas no longer swelled over the land, and humanity was saved.

In this West African version of the flood, Obatala is the Yoruba version of the Greco-Atlantean Atlas: *Oba* denotes kingship, while *atala* means "white." Yoruba priests wear only white robes while worshipping him, and images of the god are offered only white food. Among these sacrifices are white kola and goats, recalling the Atlantean goat cults known to the ancient Canary Islanders, off the coast of northwest Africa, and the Iberian Basque. Obatala's chief title is "King of Whiteness," because he is revered as the white-skinned "Ancient Ruler" and "Father" of the Yoruba race by a native woman, Oduduwa. Like Atlas, Obatala was a giant in the middle of the sea, and the "seven chains" which signal the end of the Deluge may coincide with the seven Pleiades, associated throughout much of world myth with the Flood's conclusion. Directly across the Atlantic Ocean, in the west, the Aztec version of Atlantis—Aztlan—was referred to as the "White Island." In the opposite direction, in the east, Hindu traditions in India described ancestral origins from Attala, likewise known as the "White Island."

Olokun, the Yoruba Poseidon, is commemorated at the ceremonial center of Ife, Nigeria. Its foremost ritual feature is the *Opa Oran Yan*, a 12-foot tall stone obelisk with nails driven into its side to form a trident. The monolith also bears the Egyptian hieroglyph, *sekhet*, initial of the god Shu, the Egyptian Atlas. To the north, 2 miles away, lies the presently overgrown Ebo-Olokun, a sacred grove reminiscent of the same holy precinct described by Plato at the innermost sanctuary of Atlantis. The site was excavated in the early 20th century by the famous German archaeologist Leo Frobenius, who found a cast bronze head which "cannot said to be 'negro' in countenance, totally unlike anything Yoruban" (328). These Yoruba cultural features unmistakably point up the impact made by Atlantean culture-bearers in West Africa. Even in the remote lower Congo region, an oral tradition recalls an ancient time when "the sun met the moon and threw mud at it, which made it less bright. When this meeting happened there was a great flood."

(See Basque, Leo Frobenius, Guanche, Shu)

Oceania Deluge Tradition

Commonly related throughout the islands is the story of an octopus which had two children, Fire and Water. One day, a terrible struggle broke out between their descendants, during which the whole world was set on fire, until Water extinguished the flames with a universal flood. The myth appears to preserve the folk memory of events from 3100 through 1198 B.C., when a comet or multiple comets rained down rocky debris on the Earth. Massive, destructive waves were caused when large meteors fell into the sea.

Oduduwa II

In Yoruba folk tradition, the native queen of West Africa when her realm was invaded by Atlantean "Sea Peoples," who refrained from deposing her because she was a competent ruler.

Oera Linda Bok

Literally, "The Book of What Happened in the Old Time," a compilation of ancient Frisian oral histories transcribed for the first time in 1256 A.D., and published in Holland, in 1871. The Frisians are a Germanic people of mysterious origins. All that is known of their earliest history is that they ousted the resident Celts of what is now a northern province of the Netherlands, today's Frisia, and the Frisian Islands. They also live in Nordfriesland and Ostfriesland, in Germany. Their language is closely related to English.

The *Oera Linda Bok* tells of the ancestral origins of the Frisian people in the island kingdom of Atland. Subjected to seismic and volcanic violence, many of its residents fled to other lands. Those who arrived in Britain, according to the *Oera Linda Bok*, brought with them the *Tex*; this was the legal structure of Atland, which, in subsequent generations, came to be known as Old English common law. One of today's Frisian Islands is called Texel.

Other Atland immigrants sailed into the Mediterranean, where they reestablished their worship of Fasta, the Earth Mother, with her perpetual flame, at the Roman Temple of Vesta. Voyaging further eastward, a princess from Atland, Min-erva, founded Athens and, after her death, was worshiped in Italy, first by the Etruscans, later by the Romans, as Minerva, the goddess of technical skill and invention.

Two royal brothers of troubled Atland parted in mid-ocean. Neftunis steered along the shores of North Africa, settling at what later became Tunis in his honor. After his death, the Etruscans named their sea-god after him—Nefthuns, subsequently adopted by the Romans as Neptune. His brother, with a smaller contingent, sailed to the west, and was never heard of again. But his name, Inka, suggests he, like Neftunis, was a culture-founder who bequeathed his name to subsequent generations, this time in South America, where they became the Incas of Peru and Bolivia.

According to the *Oera Linda Bok*, the ancestors of the Frisians left Atland in 2193 B.C.. Their oceanic homeland went under the sea either at that time or sometime later; the text is not entirely clear on this matter. In any case, its late third-millennium B.C. date fits the Bronze Age context of Atlantis, and probably corresponds to the penultimate geologic upheaval and mass-evacuation described both by Edgar Cayce and Greek myth in the Ogygian Deluge, following Deucalion's Flood. Although the *Oera Linda Bok* is the only Frisian document of its kind with specific references to Atlantis (Atland), folktales of sunken islands and drowned kingdoms of old are still common throughout modern Frisia.

Oergelmir

The original name of Ymir, the Norse giant whose death caused the Great Flood. The Hrim Thursar, a race which sprang into being from the only two survivors of the catastrophe, knew him as Oergelmir, a designation in keeping with variations of "Og" recurring in the flood traditions of other cultures.

(See Hrim Thrusar, Ogma, Ogriae)

Ogma

In Celtic myth, the chief of the Tuatha da Danann, refugees from the final destruction of Atlantis, who arrived in Ireland around 1200 B.C. Ogma was known in Gaul as Ogimos and in Wales as Gwydion. He is primarily remembered for the script associated with his name, Ogham. This is a system of notches for five vowels and lines for 15 consonants. They were etched into natural stone or the walls of cut tombs to memorialize the dead and/or a visitor.

Although the earliest surviving examples of Ogham date only to the fourth century A.D., connections with runic and Etruscan alphabets imply its antiquity, whose ultimate roots as an elemental script appear to lie in the Middle-Late Bronze Age. Ogham's identity as an import is suggested by its signs for H and Z, letters which do not appear in Irish.

Ogham may be at least one of the original written languages developed and used in Atlantis, but it is more likely a later, simplified version of Atlantean script modified to accommodate Celtic speech. An Atlantean

Olmec sculpture, Villahermosa, Mexico. Mesoamerican beginnings, growth, and population surges from 3100 to 1200 B.C. parallel the rise and fall of Atlantis. Photograph by Claudette Nichols.

provenance is found not only in its use by the Tuatha da Danann. "Og," as mentioned in the following entry, is widely connected with Atlantis in Ireland (Tir-nan-Og), Homeric Greece (Ogygia), the Andean Ogllo, and the biblical Og of Noah's ark. Ogma and his people were unquestionably Atlanteans, sufficient reason to regard his script as such.

Ogriae

In a "life-reading" by American psychic Edgar Cayce, Ogriae was an Atlantean princess at a time when Atlantis was reaching the zenith of its greatness. She "kept away from those of the opposite sex, for the love was given in one of low estate and could not bring self to the conditions necessary for the consummation of the desires in each other's inner self." Doubtless, those "conditions" would have entailed Ogriae's renunciation of her high place in the royal family.

Appropriately, names comprising or deriving from "Og" are associated in Old Irish and biblical contexts with a world-class deluge, such as the former's Tir-nan-Og, a kingdom beneath the sea, and the Old Testament Og. In Genesis, he was a giant who hitched a ride on Noah's ark. According to Inca cosmology, after a terrible flood destroyed their homeland, Ogllo, together with her husband, Manco Capac, arrived in South America, on the shores of Lake Titicaca, Bolivia; there they founded Andean Civilization.

In Greek myth, Ogyges was the son of the divine creator of Atlantis, Poseidon, and the first king of Greece, who reigned during a Great Flood. Homer wrote of Ogygia (*Odyssey*, iv, v, xii), a mid-Atlantic Ocean island, where Calypso, herself an Atlantis, the daughter of Atlas, was high priestess of a magic cult that turned men into beasts, not unlike the genetically engineered "Things" Edgar Cayce said made up the unfortunate laboring classes of Atlantis. He, in fact, identified one of the three principle islands of Atlantis at the period of its final destruction as "Og."

(Cayce 2725-1 F.36 5/14/25; 364-6 2/17/32)

Okinoshima

A bay in western Japan facing the Korean Sea, where three enormous stone towers were discovered by scuba divers in 1998. Their bases stand 100 feet beneath the surface, the same depth at which a citadel-like structure was found 3 years earlier off Isseki Point, in the Ryukyu Island of Yonaguni. All of Okinoshima's cylindrical towers are 40 feet tall, but only one is entwined with a spiral staircase. This particular structure may have been long ago described in an Australian Aboriginal account, which told of the sunken "Land of Mystery." One of its features was a huge "crystal cone" with a "serpent" winding up its length from bottom to top.

(See Mu)

Okipa

The outstanding ceremony of North Dakota's Mandan Indians, whose earlier home was in the Ohio Valley. Before any significant contact with White Americans, the Mandan occasionally evidenced fairer skin, light-colored eyes, and auburn hair, with less Amerindian facial features, suggesting interracial contacts at some early period in their history. They were first brought to general attention by the American artist, George Catlin, who painted many portraits of the Mandan, and was the first white man to witness their Okipa ceremony. This was an annual event in which the whole village participated. It began with an actor covered in white clay representing a white man, a survivor of the Great Flood, approaching the village from the east, the direction in which the cataclysm was said to have occurred.

At the center of the village, occupying a circular open space 150 feet in diameter, was a barrel-like object. This was the "Okipa," about 10 feet high, made of planks and hoops. Known as a representation of "the big canoe" that rode out the Deluge, it was a kind of tabernacle containing objects sacred to folk memory of the cataclysm. These included the *Eeh-teeh-ka*—four sewn-together, turtle-shaped sacks allegedly containing the original waters of the Great Flood from the four quarters of the world, signifying the catastrophe's Earth-wide magnitude.

Families from every wigwam donated edged tools, symbols of the construction that went into the original "big canoe." They were collected in a medicine lodge for the duration of the ceremony, but on its last day were sacrificed by throwing them into the deepest place of a nearby river to at once commemorate the Deluge and spiritually prevent another from taking place. The Okipa concluded with *Bel-lohck-na-pie*, a dance of 12 men painted white, black, and yellow (representing the three major races of mankind) around the "big canoe."

(See Nu-mohk-muck-a-na)

Oklatabashih

Choctaw for "Survivor from the Great Flood," the tribe's forefather.

Olle

North America's Tuleyone Indians preserve the oral account of a time, long ago, in the days of their ancestors, when a fiery demon remembered as Sahte appeared in the sky, and incinerated most of the world. Its terrified inhabitants prayed for salvation from the gods, one of whom, Olle, came to their rescue. He was a colossal giant wearing a horned helmet. Olle saw at once that only the most radical measures could prevent Earth from being completely consumed by the conflagration, so he caused a sudden flood that submerged all land, except for the tallest mountain at the center of the world. On its summit he placed some human survivors, who later became the ancestors of a new humanity.

Among the Ho Chunk, Olle is remembered as Wakseksi. The so-called "Man Mound" near Baraboo, Wisconsin, the 90-foot-long effigy mound of a man wearing a horned helmet, represents Olle-Wakseksi. He is also portrayed in petroglyphs at Jeffers and Pipestone, both sites in southwestern Minnesota. At Jeffers, he is depicted walking away from a circle, signifying the all-encompassing flood that ravaged the world.

Omphalos

The "navel stone," shaped like an egg, at the sacred center of Delphi, the most influential oracle in the ancient world. The Omphalos was the symbolic centerpiece of the Atlanteans' "Navel of the World" reincarnation cult. With the destruction of their homeland, its principles were reinstated wherever the survivors landed. Omphalli were almost identically revered in Egypt (the *Ben-Ben*, or "Phoenix," of Heliopolis); Troy (the Palladium, of Mount Ida); Rome (the Temple of Saturn's navel-stone); Ireland (County Galway's Turoe Stone); the Canary Islands (Tenerife's *zonzonas*, or "sacred precinct" ["zone"]); North America (the Mandan Indians' *Nat-com-pa-sa-ha*, "Center of the World," at Heart River, North Dakota); and even as far away as Easter Island (known to the natives as *Te-Pito-te-Henua*, "the Navel of the World") where, in fact, an egg-shaped stone was worshiped.

(See Okipa, Navel of the World)

Ora Martima

A world history with longer, more thorough descriptions of Atlantis than Plato recorded in his account. Sections detailing the sunken capital were lost with the fall of Classical civilization, although a few references survived. *Ora Martima*'s author, the first-century B.C. encyclopedist Avienus, composed his history based on original documents salvaged from the Great Library of Carthage before its incineration during the Second Punic War.

Orichalcum

A term Plato cites in *Kritias* to describe a precious metal, second only in value to gold, manufactured in Atlantis. A strict translation of orichalcum renders something approximating "gleaming copper," or "superior copper." At the height of their cultural extravagance and material prosperity, the Atlanteans decorated whole sections of their exterior walls with broad sheets of orichalcum as flamboyant displays of wealth.

It is an important addition to Plato's account, because orichalcum links Atlantis to the Upper Great Lakes copper mines, which were operated until their abrupt shut-down around 1200 B.C., the same historical moment when the island capital was finally destroyed. Orichalcum, Plato wrote, "survives today only in name, but was then mined in quantities in a number of places throughout the island." It was an alloy invented by Atlantean metalsmiths through combining the world's richest grade of copper ore with gold.

The same precious metal was described in Old Irish accounts of Atlantis; the Celtic authors referred to it as *bath* and *findrine*. Long after Atlantis perished, orichalcum was still being manufactured by the descendants of Musaeus, an Atlantean kingdom in Colombia. There the Muysica Indians produced *tumbaga*, gold-alloy vessels outstanding for their buttery sheen of "gleaming copper."

(See Findrine, Maeldune, Musaeus)

Out of the Silent Planet

A novel about Atlantis by the early 20th-century British author, C.S. Lewis.

Outer Continent

Mentioned by Plato in his Atlantis dialogues as a large territory on the opposite side of the Atlantic Ocean, otherwise unknown to his fellow third-century B.C. Greeks, and an apparent reference to America—18 centuries before it was "discovered" by Christopher Columbus. Plato stated that its eastern shores were colonized by Atlantean imperialists.

Ova-herero

A Bantu people named after their chief culture heroes, a pair of white men who arrived in southwest Africa following a terrific deluge, from which the ancestors of the Ova-herero took refuge on mountain tops.

Cairo Museum diorama of an early dynastic pharaoh impersonating Osiris, as he blesses the soil, in preparation for planting. The Egyptians believed the principles of scientific agriculture were brought to the Nile Delta by the god of resurrection after he arrived from his sunken homeland in the Distant West.

Pacata-Mu

This huge and important pre-Inca religious center featured a complex labyrinth the size of four football fields surrounded by high walls of mud brick. The maze was apparently the scene of large-scale ritual activities, judging from the sacrificed remains of llamas and curious tiny squares of exquisitely woven cloth of no apparent utilitarian value. Such squares are still used, however, by North American aboriginals of the southwestern states to contain religious offerings of tobacco.

Pacata-Mu's name and location in northern coastal Peru, on a promontory overlooking the Pacific Ocean, underscore its Lemurian origins.

Painted Cave

A site located on the North American west coast above Los Angeles. Its interior is decorated with dozens of red, white, and black pictoglyphs and astronomical depictions created by the Chumash Indians before their extinction in the late 19th-century. Painted Cave and all such illustrated sites were revered by Chumash shamans as the spiritual centers of their ancestors, who named a number of islands and settlement after the lost Pacific civilization of Mu, such as Pismu, modern Pismo beach, at San Nicholas Island, formerly Limu.

(See Mu)

Avenue of the Sphinxes to the temple complex of Karnak, Thebes, Upper Nile. Across its pylon entrance, Pharaoh Ramses II inscribed the terms of a military alliance against an invasion of "Sea Peoples" from Atlantis.

The ruins of Medinet Habu, Ramses III's "Victory Temple" over the Atlanteans.

Khafre's Pyramid at the Giza Plateau, where refugee Atlanteans and Nile residents cooperated to create Pharaonic Civilization.

Thaut brought the Emerald Tablets of civilization from Atlantis to the Nile Delta, where he built the Great Pyramid.

Captured Atlantean marines, as portrayed on the walls of Medinet Habu.

William Donato hammering granite fragments for laboratory analysis from one of the toppled columns at Moselle Shoals, in the Bahamas.

Possible underwater ruins at Moselle Shoals, in the Bahamas.

William Donato, President of The Atlantis Organization, at Bimini, with a block from the underwater Road site.

Perhaps a pylon anciently used to tie up ships from Atlantis now encrusted with underwater coral near Long Rocks at the Bahamas' Cat Island. Photograph by William Donato.

A proper perspective of Ohio's Great Serpent Mound, the emblem of Atlantean spirituality, may only be obtained from an aerial vantage point.

Gadeiros, Defender of Atlantean Spain. Original painting by Kenneth Caroli.

Temple to Itzamna on the island of Cozumel, where he was said to have first landed in Yucatan following the watery destruction of his distant homeland.

Leukippe, First Lady of Atlantis. Original painting by Kenneth Caroli.

Sacred gateway, Machu Picchu. Photograph by William Donato.

Teotihuican's Pyramid of the Sun, where golden tablets recording the Atlantean Flood were stored.

Ireland's Turoe Stone, an Atlantean omphalos.

A symbolically decorated monolith lies before the entrance to New Grange, evidence of Atlanteans during the New Stone Age.

Stonehenge's most significant periods and physical features closely coincide with the rise and fall of Atlantis.

Guimar's step-pyramid on the Canary Island of Tenerife was made of the same black, white and red building stones Plato claimed went into raising the monumental structures of Atlantis.

The Delphic oracle, in Greece, was presided over by priests directly descended from survivors of the Atlantean Flood.

The walls of Ilios, the Trojan capital, were similar to the battlements of Atlantis.

Palatkwapi

An Atlantic island that the Patki Indians told of, on which a sorceress lived a very long time ago. Her evil powers so menaced the world, the gods drowned her by sinking Palatkwapi. The resulting tsunami destroyed almost all living things on Earth, but a few human survivors reached the eastern shores of North America to become the founders of the Patki tribe.

Pali-uli

Legendary island of plenty and joy from which the Hawaiian ancestors escaped before it was destroyed in a terrible deluge.

(See Hiva, Kahiki)

Pan

The Algonkian Atlantis. Its flood myth tells how:

> ...the Earth rocked to and fro, as a ship and sea, and the rains fell in torrents, and loud thunderings came up from beneath the floor of the world. And the vortex of the Earth closed in from the extreme, and, lo, the Earth was broken! A mighty land was cut loose from its fastenings, and the fires of the Earth came forth in flames and clouds with loud roarings. And again the vortex of the Earth is about on all sides, and the land sank down beneath the waters, to rise no more.

The Algonkian version takes a line from Plato's account: "In the same day, the gates of heaven and Earth were opened" (Churchward, 74). Pan is likewise identified with Atlantis in various *Puranas* of India. An Atlantean saga was retold in the Mexican Toltec tradition of Pantitlan.

Pandyan

Indian version of Mu.

(See Rawana, Sillapadakaram)

Partholon

In *The Book of Invasions*, a Medieval collection of Celtic and pre-Celtic oral traditions, he was the tragic leader of a lost sea people who sought refuge in Ireland. They were preceded by the Fomorach, who stubbornly opposed them. Partholon nonetheless succeeded in conquering much of the country, dividing its land into five districts, after defeating Cichol Gricenchos, the Fomorach king. Unfortunately, a plague so decimated the Family of Partholon, they were unable to defend themselves against renewed Fomorach resistance, so they evacuated Ireland and disappeared into myth.

Coming as they did some time after the Fomorach, "Partholon's people" were probably immigrants from the geologic upheavals that beset Atlantis during the late third millennium B.C. Certainly, Partholon's division of Ireland into five districts is the same kind of Atlantean geopolitics found in Plato's *Kritias*.

(See Formorach)

Patkinya-Mu

The Hopi "Dwelling-on-Water Clan" whose members anciently crossed the Great Sea from the west. The flood refugees in North America, known as the *Patki*, or "Water People," were met by Massau, a native guide, who directed them to the Southwest, where they could live in peace. All the Patki were able to save from their sunken homeland was a stone tablet broken at one corner. Massau prophesied that some day in the distant future a lost white brother, Pahana, would deliver the absent fragment, thereby signalling the beginning of a new age, when brotherhood would again prevail on Earth. Over the millennia, the stone was in the special care of the Fire Clan. When their representative gave it to a Conquistador in the 1500s, the Spaniard did not reciprocate as expected, so the Hopi continue to wait for Pahana. It is remarkably similar to *Pakeha*, a name bestowed by New Zealand natives on the first modern Europeans they met in the late 18th century. It derives from the *Pakahakeha*, the Maui version of an ancestral sea people, a white-skinned race from the sunken kingdom of Haiviki.

(See Mu)

Patulan-Pa-Civan

A Quiche Maya variant of Atlantis. The *Popol Vuh*, a Yucatan cosmology, tells how "the Old Men...came from the other part of ocean, from where the sun rises, a place called Patulan-Pa-Civan."

(See U Mamae)

Payetome

A South American version of the "Feathered Serpent" or "Sea Foam" known to various Indian tribes of coastal Brazil. Distantly removed from the high civilizations of both Mesoamerica and the Andes, their tradition of a tall, white-skinned, light-eyed, fair-haired, and fair-bearded man arriving in the ancient past is folkish evidence for a culturally formative event these less sophisticated natives shared with the materially superior Mayas and Incas. The aboriginal Brazilians remember Payetome as the leader of a "tribe" of fellow immigrants, whose kingdom across the ocean was obliterated by a world flood. He was a gentle and wise man who taught medicine, agriculture and magic.

Pelasgians, or Pelasgi

In Greek tradition, a "sea people" who entered the Peloponnesus and the islands of the Eastern Mediterranean about four thousand years ago. They were the forefathers of the Achaean or Bronze Age inhabitants of Greece, named after their leader, Pelasgus, remembered as the First Man. A third-century B.C. vase painting portrays him emerging from the jaws of a serpent, while the goddess Athena stands ready to welcome him. In Aztec sacred art, Mesoamerica's white-skinned culture-bearer, Quetzalcoatl, the "Feathered Serpent," identically appears out of a snake's mouth. In both instances, the serpent signified their hero's arrival by sea. Pelasgus was believed to have been born between the fangs of Ophion, a primeval, metaphorical snake personifying the undulating ocean. Athena's presence in the vase painting signifies the destiny of Pelasgus as the first civilizer of Greece.

Notable mariners, the Pelasgians came from the Far West, where they conquered Western and Northern Europe, just as Plato's Atlanteans were said to have done, previous to their arrival in the Eastern Mediterranean. The pre-Greek "Linear A" written language of ancient Crete and the enigmatic Phaistos Disk are attributed to the Pelasgians. The disk is a baked clay plate found at the Cretan city of Phaistos, inscribed in a spiral pattern on both sides with unknown hieroglyphs. According to the first-century B.C. Greek geographer Diodorus Siculus, writing was introduced by the Pelasgians, and the mathematical genius Pythagoras was supposed to have been directly descended from them.

Waves of immigrants from Atlantis who entered the eastern Mediterranean during the geologic upheavals of the late third millennium B.C. were referred to by the Greeks as "Pelasgians."

Pelota

A Basque ball game virtually identical to a Maya version, and cited by various Atlantologists (Muck, von Salomon, and others) to establish a cultural correspondence with Atlantis. Both Basque and Maya oral traditions are rich in references to the lost civilization.

(See Basque)

Peng Sha

In Chinese myth, a large and resplendent island kingdom in the East, far over the sea, where spiritual powers reached their fulfillment. Among the adepts were sorcerers who mastered human levitation. Peng Sha was sometimes identified with the original homeland of Kuan-Yin Mu.

(See Mu, Mu Chord)

Phaeacia

In the *Odyssey*, Calypso gives the hero sailing directions to Phaeacia. Her instructions are according to another set of Atlantises, the Pleiades, and indicate a currently blank area of the Atlantic Ocean between Madeira and the Strait of Gibraltar. Atlantologists have discovered no less than 56 details that Homer's Phaeacia shares with Plato's Atlantis, leaving little doubt that the same island is indicated by both names. ·

The king of Phaeacia was Alkynous, a male derivative of the Pleiadian Atlantis, Alkyone. His capital was Scherie, virtually a mirror-image of Atlantis, including bronze-sheeted walls, interconnecting causeways, and a centrally located Temple of Poseidon, from whom he and his royal family claimed direct descent, just as mentioned in *Kritias*. Like the Atlantean kings, he sacrificed bulls to the sea-god. The island of Phaeacia was described as remote, mountainous, agriculturally prosperous, with a year-round temperate climate and abundant natural springs of hot and cold water. Its inhabitants were rich in copper and gold, exceptional mariners, manufacturers of purple dye for royal robes, and the descendants of Titans—the same details Plato accords to the Atlanteans.

Some Phaeacian names cited by Homer, in addition to King Alkynous, are identifiably Atlantean, such as Eurymedusa (see "Gorgons") and Amphialus, Plato's Atlantean king, Ampheres. Interestingly, Homer identifies himself as the Phaeacian bard, Demodocus, "whom the Muse loved above all others, though she mingled good and evil in her gift, stealing his sight, but granting him sweetness of song." Investigators have interpreted Homer's one and only appearance in either the *Iliad* or the *Odyssey* as a self-declaration of his Atlantean descent.

His Phaeacian description of Atlantis, while so like Plato's in numerous particulars, is more detailed. Readers learn about the sumptuous palace and its surrounding garden, together with information about the Atlanteans themselves, to an extent not covered in the Dialogues. Their counterpart is the *Odyssey*, and, combined, they flesh out an in-depth portrait of Atlantis during its cultural zenith.

The uppermost chamber of Chichen Itza's Pyramid of Kukulcan is decorated with the faded images of four bearded men holding up representations of the sky, like so many Atlases.

Phaethon

In Greek myth, the Deluge survived by Deucalion and Pyrrha was supposedly triggered by Phaethon, mentioned in Plato's account of Atlantis. Phaethon was the illegitimate son of Helios, the god who drove the chariot of the sun across the heavens each day. Phaethon forced his reluctant father to hand over the reigns of this solar vehicle. Before long, however, he lost control of the powerful team of fiery horses, and they set much of the world ablaze. Hearing the commotion, Zeus hurled a thunderbolt, and Phaethon fell to Earth, his long hair in flames. The chariot crashed into the sea, causing a terrific flood that extinguished the conflagration.

As early as 1821, the German genius Wolfgang von Goethe expressed his opinion that Phaethon symbolized a natural catastrophe. Long before and since, many scholars have concluded that the myth describes a cometary collision with the Earth. In *Timaeus*, Plato quotes the Egyptian high priest, who explains that the myth was actually a metaphor for a real, natural event:

> There have been and will be many different calamities to destroy mankind, the greatest of them by fire and water, lesser ones by countless other means. There is a story which even you have pre-served, that once upon a time, Phaethon, the son of Helios, having yoked the steeds of his father's chariot, burnt up all that was upon the Earth, because he was not able to drive them in the path of his father, and was himself destroyed by a thunderbolt. Now, this has the form of a myth, but really signifies a deviation in their courses of the bodies moving around the Earth and the heavens, and a great conflagration recurring at long intervals of time.

This inclusion of the Phaethon story early in the narrative can only mean Plato intended to posit a celestial cause in his unfinished description of the Atlantis catastrophe. That Phaethon was in fact a mythic representation of an actual cosmic event appears certain. In numerous ancient accounts, comets are almost invariably referred to as "hairy," or "long-haired," recalling the tragic hero's flaming tresses, as he fell to Earth. *Phaethon* means "Shining One," or "Blazing Star," no less descriptive of an extraordinary comet. It has a similar meaning in Egyptian: *Pha-aton*, or "House of (or inheritable property belonging to) Aton," the sun-disk. This shared significance implies that both the Greeks and Egyptians, whose languages were otherwise unrelated to each other, received the name independently from an outside source—namely, Atlantean survivors who sought refuge in both lands.

Kritias ends with Zeus, master of all celestial fires, contemplating the destruction of Atlantis.

Philo Judaeus

Important first-century Alexandrine theologian, who taught that Plato based his allegorical story of Atlantis on historical reality.

Phorcys

"He Who Was Borne Away" by the Great Flood in Greek myth, son of Inachus ("Rapid Current") and Melia ("Ash"), from which was made Phorcys' ark. After the Deluge, it settled on a mountain top, and its crew, the Pelasgian "Sea People," disembarked to repopulate the world. Phorcys himself became the first king of Argos.

In his myth are the leading themes of Atlantis, including its destruction by a flood and the culture-founding destinies of its survivors.

Phoroneus

Plato mentions him at the beginning of the Atlantis account. Phoroneus was the great-grandson of Atlas by Niobe, also included in *Timaeus*. In Greek myth, she perished following the Great Flood, having been turned to stone and per-petually covered by water. Phoroneus survived the catastrophe, and fathered Pelasgus, leader of the Pelasgians, the first civilizers of Greece. His other son, Car, became the eponymous founder of another "sea people," the Carians. Their name is intimately connected with Atlantis: Caryatid, the architectural feature of a human figure supporting a lintel usually representing the sky, derives from "Caria," just as Atlas was conceived of as a man upholding the heavens. After the Great Flood, Car sailed with his followers to the shores of Asia Minor, where they established the kingdom of Caria.

Phoroneus and his sons represented a large-scale migration of Atlanteans into the eastern Mediterranean during the late third millennium B.C. geologic violence that beset the Atlantic island.

Pillars of Heracles

In Plato's Dialogues, we learn that Atlantis was located "beyond the Pillars of Heracles," known today as the Strait of Gibraltar. The "pillars" were twin columns of enormous dimensions flanking a massive cauldron of perpetual flame that not only burned in homage to the demigod Heracles, but marked the western limits of the Classical World. This monumental sacred site stood on a high cliff and could be seen for many miles out at sea by sailors aboard approaching ships, and therefore served as a kind of lighthouse beacon. Its exact location is unknown, but it must have been built in either coastal Spain, near Tarifa; or in Morocco, around Cetua or perhaps even Tangier.

Heracles' far western shrine may have survived until the collapse of the Clas-sical World, when it was finally destroyed by either earthquakes or invading Visigothic barbarians in the fifth century A.D. Who constructed it has never been clear. Because the Strait of Gibraltar was known to Phoenician sailors as the "Pillars of Melkharth," their version of the Roman Hercules, some writers believe it was set up by the Carthaginians, who were known to have venerated a pillar cult. But so did their predecessors, the Atlanteans, according to Plato. The structure may have originally been built by them, but was subsequently renamed by the Greeks and Romans after the defeat of Carthage, in 146 B.C.

Pimugnans

Original name of the southern California coast Gabrielino Indians, mixed descendants from the lost civilization of Mu.

Pipestone

A national monument located in the south west corner of Minnesota memorializing the Great Flood from which the ancestors of all Native American tribes descended. The area was carefully chosen, not only for its abundance of pipestone, but for waterfalls symbolizing the deluge and unusual rock formations resembling human heads and profiles suggesting the flood survivors.

Petroglyphs here and at nearby Jeffers confirm the version told to George Catlin, the early American artist and first white man to visit the site. It received its name after an easily quarried and malleable stone fashioned by Indian carvers into calumets, or "peace pipes," and known as catlinite, after Catlin. Shamans, tribal spiritual leaders, told him that very long ago the ancestors of humanity lived in harmony with themselves and the immortals in "a great lodge" at the center of an island far over the Sunrise Sea to the east. For many generations, human beings were virtuous. But in time, they grew corrupt, contentious, and arrogant. To punish them, the gods threw a terrible flame from heaven onto the island of offensive men and women.

Their "great lodge" was utterly consumed, but the fire spread to other parts of the world, threatening to destroy the innocent animals, as well. They prayed for salvation; the gods heard them and extinguished the conflagration by sinking the whole island beneath the sea. Only a relatively few honest persons survived. As they floated in the ocean amidst the wreckage of the "great lodge," they prayed for rescue. In answer, the gods commanded a horned giant to rise from the bottom of he sea. He scooped up as many people as he could, but there were more than anyone expected, and he could not carry them all.

The gods ordered a colossal turtle to assist him. It swam over to the giant, and the remaining survivors climbed upon its shell. The turtle swam to the west, the giant wading after. Eventually, they arrived on the shores of a new land, where the people found refuge. Ever since, in memory of their salvation, Native Americans continue to refer to North America as "Turtle Island." For the next several generations, they wandered across the unfamiliar territories, until they came to what is now the south western corner of Minnesota. They were halted by the Great Spirit, who told them that they had arrived in the most sacred place in Turtle Island. Here he had transformed the flesh of their relatives, drowned during the Great Flood, into red stone.

The survivors were to fashion it into objects commemorating that calamity. Most important of these items would be a pipe. Its bowl would represent the female principle; its stem, the male; and tobacco burned in it, the passion of creation. "Whenever you smoke the pipe," said the Great Spirit, "remember the peace that has been made between mankind and me after the Deluge. Humans once disobeyed my sacred laws, so I punished them with water. So long as you abide by my words, peace will prevail over the land. Another big trouble will come if you stray from the law. On this understanding, smoke the pipe as a reminder to live well and make peace among yourselves."

Besides peace pipes, the images most commonly rendered in catlinite are fish and turtles. The "great lodge" and its destruction by fire and flood after the degeneracy of its inhabitants closely parallel Plato's Atlantis account.

Plato

Together with Socrates and Aristotle, he was the most important philosopher in the Western World. Alexander Whitehead, a prominent 20th-century metaphysician, declared, "the safest general characterization of the European philosophical tradition is that it consists of a series of footnotes to Plato." It is impossible to imagine a more credible source for Atlantis-as-fact.

Born in Athens around 428 B.C., he inherited the story from Solon, the influential Greek legislator, who heard it narrated during a visit to the Nile Delta, early in the fifth century B.C. However, many historians believe Plato traveled to Sais himself, perhaps specifically to verify the Egyptian account. The existence of this temple record was documented by two other highly influential thinkers. The last major Greek philosopher, Proclus, wrote 800 years after Plato, but in his *Platonis theologiam* (Platonic Theology), he cited the veracity of Atlantis by pointing out that Egyptian columns inscribed with the story were visited and identically translated more than half a century after Plato's death. They were examined by yet another influential thinker, Krantor of Soluntum, described by Proclus as *amicus Plato, sed magis amicus veritas*: "Plato's friend and a powerful friend of truth." He went to Sais as part of his research for Plato's first biography, near the end of the fourth century B.C., and reported that Krantor found the Atlantis story preserved exactly as described in the Dialogues.

There may be no other account supported by men of such stellar credentials. Yet, modern skeptics, particularly archaeologists, dismiss Atlantis as entirely legendary. They fail to consider that beyond his position as the seminal philosopher of Western Civilization, Plato based his whole body of thought on ruthless pursuit of the truth. *Timaeus* and *Kritias* cannot comprise a fictional allegory for his notion of the ideal state, as some critics insist, because the Atlantis he portrays is far from his utopian conception, as developed in *The Republic*. It seems likely, however, that Plato, had he completed the Dialogue, would have used the rise and fall of Atlantis as an historical example illustrating the fatal consequences of civil degeneracy. In the *Kritias*, he did not inexplicably change from philosopher to historian, and his intended use of the lost civilization to provide factual basis for his political ideas appears probable.

Some of Plato's critics accuse him of inventing the Atlantis story out of whole cloth. Yet Greeks knew about the lost civilization before he described it. At the annual Panathenea Festival in Athens, women participants wore a *peplum*, a broad skirt embroidered with scenes depicting Athena's victory over the forces of Atlantis—not a particularly remarkable fact in itself, except that the Panathenea was celebrated 125 years before Plato was born. He was about 2 years old when "a major earthquake caused widespread destruction and tsunami inundation around the Gulf of Evvia" (Childress, 19). A nearby island partially submerged and separated from the mainland by the same geologic upheavals was renamed Atalanti, together with its equally devastated gulf, after Atlantis, whose fate it suggested.

Plato appears to have been supported in his account of Atlantis by most scholars of the ancient world, if not all, including the noted histriographer, Theopompus, and the more famous naturalist, Pliny the Elder. His Atlantis Dialogues were seconded by the renowned Greek writers Diodorus Siculus, Plutarch, and Poseidonus of Rhodes, of whom the Roman historian, Strabo, wrote, "he did well in citing the opinion of Plato that the tradition concerning the island of Atlantis was something more than fiction." Only Aristotle, Plato's adversary, was more ambiguous: "He that created Atlantis also destroyed it." Critics have interpreted this statement to mean that Plato invented the tale. But the ambiguous "he" mentioned by Aristotle might just as well have referred to Poseidon, the sea-god attributed in *Timaeus* and *Kritias* with the creation and destruction of Atlantis.

In 1956, Albert Rivand, Professor of Classical History at the Sorbonne, declared that both dialogues embodied ancient, historic traditions and contained results of the latest contemporary research carried out in Plato's day. As Ivan Lissner wrote, "That a distinguished French scholar who had spent decades studying the Platonic texts should reach this conclusion is most significant, because it invests the geographical and ontological allusions in the two books with greater weight." R. Catesby Taliaferro writes in the foreword to the authoritative Thomas Taylor translation of *Timaeus* and *Kritias*:

> It appears to me to be at least as well attested as any other narration in any ancient historian. Indeed, he (Plato) who proclaims that 'truth is the source of every good both to gods and men', and the whole of whose works consists in detecting error and exploring certainty, can never be supposed to have willfully deceived mankind by publishing an extravagant romance as matter of fact, with all the precision of historical narrative.

(See Dionysus of Miletus, Kritias, Timaeus)

Pleiades

Atlantis means "Daughter of Atlas," and the *Atlantides*, or *Pleiades*, were seven daughters fathered by him. Like the kings listed by Plato, they correspond, through their individual myths, to actual places within the Atlantean sphere of influence, and thereby help to illustrate the story of that vanished empire. The souls of the Pleiades were transformed into the constellation by which they are known because of their great services to mankind in siring the culture-bearers of post-deluge civilizations. They were known around the world for their culture-creating sons by numerous peoples who never knew of each other, but who nevertheless experienced a common impact from Atlantean survivors. Even the remote tribes of Java preserve a tradition that tells how one of the Pleiades mated with a mortal man to sire the human race.

Atlas' consort was Pleione, from the Greek word, *pleio*, "to sail," appropriately enough, because the constellation of the Pleiades is particularly visible from May to November, the sailing season. *Pleione* means "Sailing Queen"; *Pleiades*, the "Sailing Ones." By their very definitions, they exemplify the Atlanteans' outstanding cultural characteristic; namely, maritime prowess. In fact, the Pleiades appear in Odysseus' sailing instructions to Phaeacia, Homer's version of Atlantis (*Odyssey*, Book V, 307).

A common theme among the Pleiades was the extraordinary destinies of their offspring, who, like the Atlanteans themselves, were founders of new kingdoms in distant lands. Paralleling Kleito in Plato's narrative, Alkyone, the leader of the Pleiades, bore royal sons to Poseidon, the sea-god. Her sisters were no less fertile. All their sons or grandsons founded or rebuilt numerous cities and kingdoms. Maia was venerated in Rome until the last days of the Empire as the patroness of civilization itself through her son, Mercury, the god of organized society. The expanse of the Atlantean imperium was encompassed by the Pleiades and their children.

As the Greek scholar Diodorus Siculus wrote in his first-century B.C. *Geography*:

> All the rest likewise had sons who were famous in their times, some of which gave beginning to whole nations, others to some particular cities. And therefore not only some of the barbarians, but likewise some among the Greeks refer the origin of many of the ancient heroes to these daughters of Atlas. They lay with the most renowned heroes and gods, and they became the first ancestors of the larger part of humanity" (Blackett, 103).

In other words, Western Civilization was born from Atlantis. Diodorus' characterization of the Pleiades suggests they were not originally mythic figures, but real women, wives of Atlantean culture-bearers, who dwelt in kingdoms which comprised the Empire of Atlantis, and generated the royal lineages of those realms. Long after their deaths, they were regarded as divine, and commemorated as a star cluster.

The Pleiades' stellar relationship to Atlantis has been cited in Odysseus' sailing instructions to Phaecia. But their Atlantean significance predated the *Odyssey*, and spread far beyond Homer's Greece. The Sumerians associated the constellation of the Pleiades with their version of Atlas, Adad, the volcanic fire-god. The rising of the Pleiades signaled the New Year among the Mayas and Aztecs, as they did for the pre-Inca Chimu and Nazca civilizations of the Andes. Known to the Mayas as Tzab, the Aztecs sighted them along a water channel running parallel to the Sirius-Pleiades Line at Teotihuacan, the imperial capital long since covered by modern Mexico City. When the Seven Sisters ascended the middle of the sky at dawn of the winter solstice, Aztec priests assembled on the summits of the Huizachtleatl Mountains.

The Cheyenne Indians of North America believed that a mother died and took her daughters with her into the night sky to become the Pleiades. Remarkably, this is identical to the Greek version. The Lakota Sioux likewise called them "the Seven Sisters." No less remarkable was the Incas' worship of the Pleiades as the Aclla Cuna, "the Chosen Women," or "the Little Mothers." These New World interpretations of the Pleiades credibly echo Atlantean contacts with Native Americans in pre-Columbian times. Given their particular identities, the Pleiades correspond individually to the following realms within the Atlantean Empire:

> *Alkyone*: Atlantis itself, through Phaeacia's Alkyonous.
>
> *Claeno*: the Azore Islands, through her husband's reign over the "Blessed Isles."
>
> *Elektra*: Troy; her son, Dardanus, was the founder of Troy.
>
> *Merope*: North Africa, the Meropids of Morocco.
>
> *Maia*: Yucatan, the Maia Civilization:
>
> *Sterope*: Western Italy; her son founded Pisa, the Etruscan Pisae.
>
> *Taygete*: the Canary Islands, from Tegueste, a Guanche province in Tenerife.

Pohaku o Kane

The "Stone of Kane," an elongated monolith from 1 to 6 feet long, set upright to resemble a column within every Hawaiian household, where it was the center of worship by male family members only. Its location in the *hale mua*, or men's eating quarters, reaffirms its ritual association with Mu, the sunken civilization of the Pacific. Kane was a creator-destroyer god responsible for the Great Flood that overwhelmed a former kingdom of immense *kahuna*, or spiritual power, known variously as *Hiva, Haiviki, Kahiki, Pali-uli*, etc.

Each Pohaku o Kane was considered a sacred version of an original pillar from that vanished realm, as implied by its waterworn condition. Cunningham observed, "Not just any stone could be used as the *Pohaku o Kane*. Such a stone was pointed out by Kane during a dream or vision" (84). Like distant Thailand's La Mu-ang, the Stone of Kane was Hawaii's simulacrum of a column from some sacred building in lost Mu.

(See Hiva, Kahiki, Lak Mu-ang, Mu)

Poseidon

The sea-god in *Kritias* who, after the creation of the world, was given the island that would later become Atlantis. A native woman he loved provided him with five sets of male twins, progenitors of a royal line. Poseidon honored her hillside home by encircling it with a moat, thereafter creating two more sets of concentric rings of

Fifth-century B.C. *bronze of Poseidon, the sea-god of Atlantis, National Archaeology Museum, Athens.*

alternating land and water. Atlantologists endeavoring to interpret his myth have been unable to determine if Plato used Poseidon as a symbol for the natural forces which went into the configuration of the island, or as a metaphor signifying the arrival of some outside, unknown, possibly Neolithic or megalithic culture-bearers. Supporting his alien provenance, "Poseidon" is among the few identifiable examples of the long-dead Atlantean language, because the name stands out among his fellow Olympian deities as decidedly non-Indo-European. It derives from a contraction of the un-Greek *Posis Das*, "Husband of the Earth," and *Enosichthon*, or "Earthshaker," together with the very Greek *Hippios*, "He of the Horses." This synthesis implies that Poseidon did indeed come from outside Greece, where he was eventually adopted as one of the supreme divinities. With no linguistic or mythic parallels among eastern cultures, he arrived from the western direction of Atlantis, according to Herodotus: "Alone of all nations, the Libyans have had among them the name Poseidon from the first, and they have ever honored this god."

In the non-Platonic myth of Poseidon, he loses a contest with Athene for possession of Greece, which may symbolize the Atlanto-Athenian War. Underscoring this interpretation, Poseidon hurls his trident at the Athenian Acropolis, from which a flood gushes forth in a spring.

Poshaiyankaya

Leader of the ancestral Zuni into the American Southwest, following their near annihilation in the Great Flood. Some modern pottery decoration memorializing the ancient catastrophe suggest Lemurian themes, such as the hooked cross and Tree of Life.

(See The Tree of Life, The Zuni Deluge Story)

Pounamu

The "Green Stone" of New Zealand, mythically associated with the Lemurian Waitahanui. According to New Zealand archaeologist, Barry Brailsford, "It was used as ballast in the oceangoing ships, the double-hulled *waka* ships. These ships had a very large sail and went to all parts of the world." He described the Pounamu as "harder than steel," cut today only by diamond saws. "Black Elk, the great North American Indian chief, came to New Zealand to collect the ancient stones which he said his people once used" (*A Hitchhiker's Guide to Armageddon*, 121). The Green Stone's connection with New Zealand's Waitahanui and the appearance of "mu" in its name define the Pounamu as a religious relic from Lemurian times.

(See Mu, Waitahunui)

Poverty Point

The name of an archaeological find in northeastern Louisiana, the oldest city in North America, dated to circa 1500 B.C. Poverty Point was a concentric arrangement of alternating rings and canals interconnected by causeways radiating outward from a central precinct and fronted by a large earthwork built to resemble a volcano. The site is fundamentally a mirror-image of Plato's description of Atlantis, an identification reaffirmed by sudden cultural florescence at Poverty Point in 1200 B.C., just when Atlantis was finally destroyed, and some of its survivors sought refuge in what is now America.

Powako

The Delaware Indian flood hero who led their ancestors out of a natural disaster that sank "the first land, beyond the great ocean." The oldest branch of the Algonquian family, the Leni-Lenapi, displayed white racial characteristics so pronounced that some early settlers considered them members of the fabulous "Lost Tribes" of Israel. The Delaware, in fact, called themselves the *Leno-Lenape*, or the "Unmixed Men," as some distinction for their descent from white-skinned flood survivors led by Powako.

Prachetasas

"Sea-kings" whose kingdom plunged to the bottom of the ocean. Hindu myth tells of 10 Prachetasas, the same number of kings, according to Plato, who ruled the Atlantis Empire.

Pramzimas

The Lithuanian Zeus, who, fed up with the iniquities of mankind, dispatched a pair of giants, Wandu (wind) and Wejas (water) to destroy the world. Pramzimas halted the deluge just in time to save the last few people huddling together on several mountain peaks, the only dry land left on Earth. He dropped them a few cracked nut shells, which served as vessels for the survivors, who floated away under a rainbow that Pramzimas put in the sky, indicating the deluge was finished.

After the waters abated and the remaining humans scampered out of their improvised arks, he instructed them to leap "over the bones of the Earth" (stones) nine times. Having performed as they were commanded, nine additional couples appeared to sire the nine tribes of Lithuania. Elements of this deeply prehistoric myth are mirrored in the Genesis deluge (the rainbow) and Deucalion flood (repopulating the world from stones). These considerations affirm that the Pramzimas' version was likewise drawn from the same Atlantean tradition.

The Prince of Atlantis

A 1929 novel by American author Lillian Elizabeth Roy, who associated the decline of Atlantis with the lowering of both moral standards and immigration barriers.

Psonchis

Cited by the Roman historian Plutarch, in his *Lives*, Psonchis appears in Plato's account as an Egyptian high priest who narrated the story of Atlantis for his Greek guests. "Psonchis" may be the Greek rendition of a priest or servant of "Sakhmis," a name for the Egyptian goddess, Sekhmet, even though Psonchis belonged to the Temple of Neith. The two represented similar conceptions, and could have been syncretic versions of the same deity. Sekhmet, a variant of Hathor, was characterized as the celestial fire, a "shooting star," that consumed Atlantis and immediately preceded its cataclysmic inundation. If the Psonchis in *Kritias* was indeed attached to the worship of Sekhmet, Plato's version of Atlantis appears all the more credible.

Punt

A distant land of great wealth and friendly natives visited by several, large-scale mercantile expeditions from dynastic Egypt. Although conventional Egyptologists have long assumed Punt was Somalia, their supposition has been proved incorrect by both the expeditions' recorded sailing times (three years was too long a period for round-trip voyages from Egypt to East Africa) and the non-African goods imported. Moreover, Senemut, the Egyptian admiral in charge of a commercial fleet making for Punt, recorded the changing positions of the stars, as his ships rounded the Cape of Good Hope, at the bottom of Africa, on a westerly heading. After 608 B.C., Pharaoh Nekau II sponsored a circumnavigation of Africa, which similarly took three years.

"Punt" appears to have actually been a term used to define the foreign expedition itself, not any particular land visited during the course of a single, extended voyage. The "country of Punt" was actually known as "Hathor's Land," after the goddess of fiery destruction from the sky associated in the Medinet Habu wall texts with the sinking of Neteru, that is, Atlantis. Hathor, in fact, was hailed as "Lady of Punt." Although the most famous voyage to Punt was ordered by

Queen Hatshepsut in 1470 B.C., it was neither the first nor last. Her expedition was outstanding, however, because she faithfully recreated Punt architecture for her temple at Deir el-Bahri, whose un-Egyptian structures were intended to memorialize her great commercial achievement. Nothing remotely resembling this complex ever appeared in East Africa, where academic opinion erroneously locates Punt.

Many of the goods listed by Egyptian bureaucrats as Punt exports, such as amber, never came from the area of Somalia. Amber is still exported from the Atlantic islands, particularly the Canaries. Moreover, the records of Ramses II report that his largest ships, known as *menechou*, "reached the mountain of Punt." While Somalia has no mountain, Plato described the island of Atlantis as "very mountainous." The Queen of Punt, during the Hatshepsut expedition, was named Ati, a possible derivation of "Atlantis." She and her King, Parihu, were not negroid, but white-skinned, with aquiline features similar to those of the Atlantean "Sea Peoples" portrayed on the walls of Ramses III's "Victory Temple."

Ati's people, the Puntiu, "wore long beards which, when they were plaited, looked just like the beards of the Egyptian gods" (Montet, 86). Egyptian deities were associated with the rising and setting of the sun, never in the south, the direction of East Africa. The Puntiu were themselves said to have worshiped the Egyptians' supreme solar god, Ra, and built a great temple to Amun, the sky-god, none of which has ever had anything to do with Somalia. Hatshepsut's well-preserved ruins are undoubtedly the last surviving specimens of public buildings as they appeared in 15th century B.C. Atlantis, which was one of Egypt's wealthiest but farthest trading partners.

Revealingly, the last Punt expedition took place at the very beginning of Ramses III's reign, circa 1200 B.C. A short time following—two to five years, possibly even a few months—Atlantis was destroyed, and some of its survivors invaded the Nile Delta. Nekau II, mentioned previously, undertook the circumnavigation of Africa six centuries later, specifically to determine if anything was left of the Atlantean Punt, but his hired Phoenician sailors returned empty-handed. Nekau reigned at a time when his XXVI Dynasty was actively engaged in promoting a renaissance of Egyptian culture and history, when old documents describing rich expeditions to Punt were reevaluated. His capital was Sais, the same city where the story of Atlantis was preserved in the Temple of Neith. All these elements were certainly related, and strongly imply an Atlantean identity for Punt.

Pauwvota

A flying vehicle, as described in Hopi accounts of their pre-flood ancestors.

(See Vimana)

Pu Chou Shan

Literally, the "Imperfect Mountain," among the oldest recorded Chinese myths almost certainly dating from the Shang Period, circa 1200 B.C. It tells that after the primeval goddess, Nu Kua Shih, created humanity, she worked with men and women to build the first kingdom, and a golden age of greatness spread around the Earth. Many years later, one of her divine princes, out of envy, fought to overthrow her. During the heavenly struggle that ensued, his fiery head struck Pu Chou Shan. It collapsed into the sea, resulting in a global flood that obliterated civilization and most of mankind.

The story of Nu Kua Shih is a poetic recollection of the comet impact associated with the deluge of Lemuria, some 3,500 years ago.

Puna-Mu

Literally the "Stone from Mu," or "green stone," terms for jade, highly prized by New Zealand Maoris for its association with the sea that overwhelmed their ancestral homeland.

Pur-Un-Runa

The "Era of Savages" recounted in the Inca story of Manco Capac marked a time of decadence at the "Isle of the Sun." The Pur-Un-Runa immediately preceded the obliteration of this splendid island-kingdom in the middle of the Atlantic Ocean by fire and flood. Manco Capac, his wife and entourage survived by sailing to South America. His Andean version parallels exactly Plato's description of the degeneracy that befell the inhabitants of Atlantis prior to their capital's destruction.

Qamate

Supreme god of the Amoxosa Kaffir Negroes, who raise large burial mounds in his honor. These earthworks represent the mountainous island from which their ancestors arrived in Africa after he pushed it to the bottom of the sea. Since only one man and woman survived, Qamate told them to pick up stones and throw them over their shoulders. As they did so, human beings sprang from the ground wherever the stones fell. To commemorate this repopulating of the world after the flood, every passerby deposits a stone on one of the mounds. Resemblance of the Amoxosa version to the Greek deluge account is remarkable, implying a calamitous event both peoples experienced—the destruction of Atlantis.

(See Deucalion)

Q'a'mtalat

The Canadian Kwakiutl Indians' flood hero, who died in the Great Flood while successfully trying to save his children by removing them to the summit of a high mountain. They became the ancestors of a post-deluge humanity.

Here, as in other traditions among peoples more likely effected by the Lemurian disaster, the story of Q'a'mtalat describes steadily rising waters, not the more geologically violent destruction of Atlantis depicted in East coast myths.

Qoluncotun

Creator deity of the Sinkaietk, or Southern Okanagon Indians, in Washington State. Angered by the ingratitude of their ancestors, he hurled a star at the Earth, which burst into flames. Just before the entire planet was reduced to ashes, Qoluncotun extinguished the conflagration by pushing "a great land" beneath the sea, making it overflow into a world flood. From the few survivors, he refashioned mankind into various tribes.

Q'o'mogwa

"Copper-maker," leading culture hero of the Kwakiutl, native inhabitants of the Canadian Pacific coast. According to Kearsley, "His exploits are invariably associated with long sea voyages, sometimes to the Land of Ancestors, or the Upper World, beyond the West where the sun sets, or into the middle of the ocean, clearly the Pacific Ocean, where the Copper-maker was also said to exist" (50,51). Q'o'mogwa commanded a magical vessel that took him to all parts of the world, "a self-paddling copper canoe 'filled with coppers'...probably a sailing craft."

"Copper-maker" is the self-evident memory of the Lemurian captain of a sailing ship from the mid-Pacific kingdom of Mu, the Kwakiutl "Land of Ancestors," which dispatched miners to excavate North America's rich and anciently worked copper deposits. While Michigan's Upper Peninsula was dominated by Atlantean miners, Lemurian interest in metallurgy was certainly less commercial than spiritual. Adepts of the Pacific Motherland probably used copper primarily for psychic activity, due to its alleged conductivity of various energy forms, a quality still prized in many native cultures throughout the world.

Quaitleloa Festival

The Aztec legend of Tlaloc told how the god of water raised a great mountain out of the primeval sea. His Quaitleloa Festival commemorated the destruction of the world by flood: "Men had been given up to vice, on which account, it (the world) had been destroyed." Tlaloc's wife, Chalchihuitlicue, was represented as a torrent carrying away a man, woman and treasure chest, intending to portray *Otocoa*, "the loss of property." As though to emphasize the Atlantean identity of Tlaloc, the Quaitleloa Festival took place in the vicinity of Mount Tlalocan, or "Place of Tlaloc," in nothing less than a ritualized recreation of the final destruction of Atlantis.

Queevet

Worshiped by South America's Abipon Indians as the white-skinned god of the Pleiades, he long ago destroyed the world with fire and flood. The Abipon regarded Francisco Pizarro and his fellow Conquistadors as manifestations of Queevet. Their veneration did not, however, prevent the Spanish from exterminating them.

Quetzalcoatl

Toltec version of the Feathered Serpent, the white-skinned, light-eyed, blond, bearded man who arrived at Vera Cruz on his "raft of serpents" accompanied by a group of astrologers, scientists and physicians. Quetzalcoatl was the most important Mesoamerican deity, regarded as the founding-father of civilization. The kingdom from which he came across the Atlantic Ocean was called Tollan, the Toltec Atlantis, described as a powerful, island-city of great, red-stone walls, recalling Plato's portrayal of Atlantean walls constructed of red tufa.

Quetzalcoatl was commonly depicted in sacred art as an Atlas-figure: a bearded man surrounded by symbols of the sea, such as conch shells, and supporting the sky. It is not clear which of the three major migrations from Atlantis with which Quetzalcoatl was associated. In his Maya guise as Kukulcan, he was preceded in Middle America by Itzamna, and must therefore have arrived in either the late third millennium B.C. or after 1200 B.C.

Quihuitl

Literally, "the Fire from Heaven," third of the global catastrophes depicted in its own square on the Aztec Calendar Stone as a sheet of descending flame. It closed a former "Sun," or world age, from which a few survivors rebuilt society. The date 4-Quihuitl refers to the penultimate Atlantean cataclysm, in 2193 B.C.

Quikinna'qu

Revered by Native American tribal peoples like the Koryak, Kamchadal, and Chuckchee of coastal British Columbia as "the first man." He was the only survivor of an island that had been transformed into a whale by the Thunderbird. To escape attack from its talons, the whale dove to the bottom of the sea, drowning everyone on its back except Quikinna'qu, who floated on a log to what is now Vancouver Island. There he married a native girl, whose children became the tribes of the Pacific Northwest.

(See Mu)

Stone frieze from the ceremonial megalopolis at Teotihuacan, depicting the culture-bearer of Mesoamerican civilization, the Feathered Serpent.

Ragnarok

The Norse "Twilight of the Gods," the destruction of the world that has been and will be again, over and over, as part of the cyclical nature of destiny. With its vivid descriptions of fiery skies and sinking land-masses, Ragnarok undoubtedly reflects folk memories of Atlantis. It reads in part, "Already the stars were coming adrift from the sky and falling into the gaping void. They were like swallows, weary from too long a voyage, who drop and sink into the waves."

Ramses III

XX Dynasty Pharaoh who defeated the "Sea People" invasion of the Delta in 1190 B.C., and subsequently raised a great Victory Temple, Medinet Habu, to his success in the Upper Nile Valley, West Thebes. On its walls, Ramses documented his military campaigns in incised illustrations and hieroglyphs. They still exist and document a serious attempt by Atlantean forces to subdue Egypt eight years after the capital of their island empire had been obliterated by a natural catastrophe. The wall texts explain that Sekhmet, the goddess of fiery destruction, "pursued them like a shooting-star" and incinerated their homeland, which immediately thereafter "vanished beneath the waves." The Sea People's head city was referred to as *Neteru*, defining a sacred place; Plato likewise characterized Atlantis as "sacred." The Medinet Habu account is accompanied by various scenes from these events, including realistic representations of enemy warships and the Sea People themselves in various poses of defeat and captivity. They are the only portraits from life of Atlanteans soon after their capital was engulfed by the ocean.

Ramses displayed his military genius and personal courage in terrible adversity. The navy of Atlantis had brushed aside the Egyptians' defenses at the mouth of the Nile Delta, and its troops of invading marines stormed ashore. They overcame all initial resistance to capture major cities, such as Busiris. Ramses withdrew his forces and regrouped, observing how the invaders advanced concurrently with their ships, which they relied on for support. At the southernmost end of the Nile Delta, he threw virtually all of his surviving naval units against the Sea People. The much smaller Egyptian crafts were not only out-classed, but out-numbered, as well. On the verge of being overwhelmed, Pharaoh's warships suddenly turned and fled in retreat, with the whole invading fleet in hot pursuit.

Ramses had his littler vessels lure their cumbersome enemies into narrower, shallower areas of the river familiar to the Egyptian captains, but unknown to the Sea People. The Atlanteans suddenly found themselves unable to freely maneuver and began grounding on unseen shoals. The Egyptians now plied the big warships with a barrage of fire-pots, just as thousands of archers abruptly appeared along the shore to launch endless flights of arrows at the outmaneuvered invaders. Cut off from their floating supplies, the Sea People were routed back up the delta toward its Mediterranean shores, where they disembarked in their remaining ships.

But the war was far from over. The invasion had consisted of a three-pronged attack from the north against the Delta, westward across Libya, and at the Egyptian colony of Syria, in the east. Infantry held the Libyan assault at Fortress Usermare, near the Egyptian frontier, until Ramses was able to bring up his forces, enduring almost annihilating losses in the process of defense. Pharaoh never spared a moment for celebration. He moved with great speed. Before they could effect a landing, he met the Sea People on the beaches at Amor, where they suffered their final defeat. Ramses personally participated in this last battle, drawing his great bow against the invaders.

The wall texts at Medinet Habu record that the captive Sea People warriors were bound at the wrists behind their backs or over their heads, together with their allies, including Trojan War veterans from Libya, Etruria, Sicily, Sardinia, and other parts of the Mediterranean. They saw the Atlantean invasion as an opportunity for plunder, and had joined as pirates. Thousands of these unfortunate prisoners-of-war were paraded before the victorious Ramses III and his court. After interrogation by his scribes, they were castrated, then sent to work for the remainder of their lives as slave laborers at the Tura limestone pits. Thus ended the imperial ambitions of Atlantis in the eastern Mediterranean.

Ramman

A Babylonian god whose destruction of the world describes the Atlantean catastrophe. The Deluge engulfed mankind when "the whirlwind of Ramman mounted up to the heavens and light was turned into darkness." His cataclysmic function was still recognized by the Assyrian king, Hammurabi, who invoked him with the words, "May he overwhelm the land like the Flood! May he turn it into heaps and ruins! And may he blast it with a bolt of destruction!" In the Old Testament, Ramman appears as "Rimmon."

Ramu

The capital city of Lemuria, located in what later became the Hawaiian Islands, according to a past-life memory experienced by actress and author, Shirley MacLaine.

Ra-sgeti-Mu

A Maldive island at the Equator, south of the Indian subcontinent, its name contains both that of the worldwide sun-god, Ra, and Mu, the sunken Pacific civilization from which Ra-sgeti-Mu's first culture-bearers arrived in prehistory.

(See Mu, Redin)

Rawana

Described in a Tamil religious text, *Sillapadakaram*, as the lord of a resplendent "citadel," Kumari Nadu, comprising 25 palaces with 4,000 streets, "swallowed by the sea in a former age." The myth probably refers to ruins of a city discovered 120 feet under the Gulf of Cambay, 25 miles off the coast of Gujarat, India, in May, 2001, by researchers with India's National Institute of Ocean Technology. They found stone pillars, walls, pottery, jewelry, sculpture, human bones, and even inscribed evidence of a written language. The site appears to have been part of Harappa-Mohenjo Daro Civilization that flourished in the Indus Valley from around 2800 to 1500 B.C. The island on which Rawana's "citadel" was located most likely sank under the Gulf of Cambay during the Late Bronze Age with the same worldwide cataclysm that destroyed Atlantis.

Redin

Racially alien seafarers who sailed from their distant kingdom, bringing civilization to the Maldives in the Indian Ocean. Remembered as red-haired and blue-eyed, with sharply defined noses, the Redin were probably the "Rutas" described in Tibetan tradition as culture-bearers from the sunken Pacific lands of Mu. This identification is reinforced by the names of islands where the Redin erected monumental structures, including stone mounds (*hawitti*), pyramids, and baths: Ra-sgeti-Mu, Laamu, Utimu, Timu and Utimu—all variations of the lost homeland.

(See Mu)

Revolving Castle

A Celtic memory of Atlantis, in which "revolving" is a mythic elaboration of "circular," referring to the city's concentric layout. The Brythonic otherworld, Annwn, with its distinctly Atlantean features, was *Caer Sidi*, a "revolving castle" surrounded by the sea. The Old Irish Catair Cu Roi, was a "revolving fort," where the first heroes of Ulster competed for the rank of champion.

R'lyeh

In H.P. Lovecraft's 1926 short story, "The Call of Cthulhu," a huge stone city built during the deeply ancient past, but since sunk beneath the Pacific Ocean following a natural catastrophe that affected much of the world. R'lyeh was based at least in part on accounts of Mu, then being popularized by James Churchward.

The underwater Delta formation, possibly a harbor facility for Atlantean ore ships, in Wisconsin's Rock Lake is clearly visible from 3,000 feet. Photograph by Steven Dempsey.

Rock Lake

A small body of water in southern Wisconsin, located between Milwaukee and the state capitol, Madison. Rock Lake is notable for the sunken stone structures it contains—pyramidal burial mounds of men who worked the copper mines of Michigan's Upper Peninsula from 3000 B.C. to 1200 B.C. The mines were excavated and operated by engineers from Atlantis, so at least some of the underwater tombs probably contain the remains of Atlantean workers.

Rongo-mai

Still venerated in the Lake Taupo districts of New Zealand as a war-god who, in the deep past, attacked the world in the guise of a comet. After bringing great destruction upon humankind, he transformed himself into a gigantic whale which sank into the sea.

(See Asteroid Theory)

Rongo-Rongo

An indecipherable written language preserved by the natives of Easter Island, in the eastern Pacific Ocean, on wooden tablets known as *kohau*. Most of the thousands of such tablets were burned by Christian missionaries, but very few surviving specimens are virtually identical to the no less mysterious Indus Valley script from nearly 13,000 miles away, precisely half-way around the globe. In between India and Easter Island, rongo-rongo appears only in rarely isolated characters among the Gilbert and other scattered Pacific islands. Comparison between the two syllabaries is less complicated by the great distances dividing them than by their broad separation in time. The Indus Valley script was in use by the late fourth millennium B.C., dying out with the Aryan invasions of 1500 B.C., while the kohau have not been dated earlier than the fifth century A.D. These are apparently copies made of earlier "talking boards."

Variations on the name "Rongo" are associated throughout Polynesia with a fair-haired flood hero from a sunken kingdom. The culture-bearer, Hotu Matua, was said to have brought a library of 67 kohau to Rapa Nui, or Easter Island, from Marae-Renga, an island satellite of the larger kingdom, Hiva, which sank beneath the sea. His "talking boards" were alleged to have included histories, proverbs, songs, and genealogical tables. Because traditions in both India and Easter Island describe arrivals of culture-bearers from a high civilization destroyed by a natural catastrophe, the written languages unique to either location are probably legacies from the sunken land of Mu. No other conclusion better explains the close resemblance of these two written languages otherwise parted by thousands of miles and several millennia.

(See Hotu-matua, Mu, Rongo-mai)

Root race

An Anthroposophical term for an ancestral race of modern man. The Atlantean is one of several such races.

(See Steiner)

Rudbeck, Olaus

Living from 1630 to 1702 , Olaus Rudbeck was a Swedish scientific genius, Professor of Medicine (Uppsala), discoverer of the lymphatic system at just 22 years of age, inventor of the anatomical theater dome, designer of the first university gardens, initiator of Latin as the lingua franca of the scientific world community, astronomer, architect, shipyard builder, musician, historian of early Sweden, and on and on. Rudbeck's ambition to create a life-size woodcut of every plant known to botany resulted in more than 7,000 carved images. He financed and personally led the first professional expedition beyond the Arctic Circle to bring back numerous plant and animal specimens previously unknown to science. A brilliant scholar fluent in Latin, Greek, and Hebrew, Rudbeck possessed a grasp of classical literature nothing less than encyclopedic.

Combining his vast knowledge of the ancient world with personal archaeological research in his own country, he concluded during a long period of investigation (1651 to 1698), that Atlantis was fact—not fiction—and the greatest civilization in prehistory. From 1679 until shortly before his death 23 years later, he composed *Atlantica*, published in a bilingual Latin-Swedish edition. According to the four-volume work, Norse myths and some physical evidence among his country's megalithic ruins show how a relatively few Atlantean survivors may have impacted Sweden, contributing to its cultural development, and laid the foundations, particularly in ship construction, for what would much later become the "Viking Age" from the ninth to 12th centuries A.D.

Although Atlantologists have since dismissed Rudbeck's chauvinist belief that Sweden and Atlantis were synonymous, the main thesis of *Atlantica*—that Scandinavia was among the first lands occupied by Atlantean survivors—continues to persuade through the vast amount of still-valid cultural evidence he marshalled on behalf of his argument. He identified some Atlanteans with the biblical tribe of Magog, whose members migrated after the catastrophe far across the Black Sea, following Russian rivers to the Kimi districts in northern Finland, moving on to the plain around Uppsala in the middle of what would much later become Sweden. "Magog" features the "og" associated with Atlantis in several ancient Old World cultures: the Bronze Age British *Gogmagog*, the Celtic *Ogimos*, the Old Irish *Ogma* and *Tir-nan-Og*, the Greek *Ogyges*, and so on.

Rudbeck's tracing of Atlantean influences appeared to have been verified more than 250 years later, during the early 1960s, when Swedish archaeologists identified Scandinavia's earliest known Bronze Age site in digs at Uppsala. Radiocarbon testing revealed a habitation date circa 2200 B.C. The Swedish savant had stated that the Atlanteans arrived at Uppsala around 2400 B.C. This time parameter is particularly significant, because it has been identified with the second Atlantean flood, brought about by the near-miss of a debris-laden comet in 2193 B.C.

Rudbeck's Atlanto-Nordic researches were taken up by another 18th-century scholar, the French astronomer Jean Bailey, who concluded that Spitzbergen, in the Arctic Ocean, was all that remained of Atlantis. Bailey was a victim of the French Revolution.

It says something for the credibility of Atlantis that many of the most eminent thinkers in the history of Western Civilization—Solon, Plato, Strabo, Plutarch, Bacon, Kircher, Muck, Blake, Rudbeck, etc.—have been among its most prominent advocates.

Rutas

Another name for Mu or Lemuria found among a few scattered Polynesian tales, mentioned by some Brahman traditions and in Beon-Buddhist monastery records of Tibet. "Rutas" may have derived from *Rudra*, the "Cosmic Fire," or life-energy and title of Murrugan, one of Lemuria's chief deities, described in an Indian purana, the *Shrimad Bhagavatam*. Like Mu, Rutas was supposed to have been a very large island located in the eastern Pacific, where dwelt a race of spiritually advanced sun-worshippers before their land was destroyed by a terrific flood. Survivors arriving in India established what eventually became the elite Brahman caste.

(See Jacolliot, Sillapadakaram)

Ruty

An epitaph meaning a "pair of lions." They are represented in temple art facing away from each other, their tails opposed, while Shu, the Egyptian Atlas, appears in between them, thus defining Atlantis as the sacred center, the Navel of the World. "Ruty" would also appear to have a philological relationship with "Rutas," one of the names or titles of Lemuria. Such a connection would be appropriate, because the two civilizations shared some fundamental spiritual beliefs. Indeed, the Navel of the World appears at two important cult centers in the Pacific during post-Lemurian times; namely, Easter Island as Rapa-nui, and Hawaii's "Navel of Kane," the creator-god. Ruty's twin lions might have even signified the two sunken civilizations, Atlantis and Lemuria, which both shared a related spirituality.

Sacsahuaman

A skillful arrangement of several thousand colossal blocks rising in three tiers to 60 feet, located outside the city of Cuzco. Many of the finely cut, meticulously fitted stones weigh about 100 tons each. The largest single block is 9 feet thick, 10 feet wide, and 20 feet tall, with an estimated weight of nearly 200 tons.

According to conventional archaeological dogma, Sacsahuaman was raised as a fortress around 1438 A.D. by the Incas. But they only occupied the site long after it was built by an earlier people remembered as the Ayar-aucca, a race of "giants" who arrived in Peru as refugees from a cataclysmic flood. Sacsahuaman was used as a quarry by the Spanish throughout the 16th century to furnish construction material for churches and colonial palaces, so its original appearance and actual purposes were obscured. Even some mainstream archaeologists tend to believe the intentions of its creators were less military than ceremonial or spiritual.

The superb workmanship evidenced at Sacsahuaman is matched by the daunting tonnage of its blocks. Even with the aid of modern machinery, positioning them with equal precision and finesse would present severe challenges. Their cutting, moving, lifting, and fitting during pre-Columbian times seems far beyond the limited capabilities of any pre-industrial people. Modern experiments to replicate construction using the primitive tools and means supposedly available before the Europeans arrived invariably produce ludicrous results. Clearly, some unimaginable, lost technology was used by the Ancient Peruvians. Their Atlantean identity in the Ayar-aucca is underscored by Sacsahuaman's uncanny resemblance to an underwater site in the Bahamas, a suspected outpost of Atlantis.

(See Ayar-aucca, Bimini Road)

The Saga of Ninurta

A Sumerian epic describing the destruction of Atlantis: "From the mountain [Mount Atlas] there went forth the pernicious tooth [eruption] scurrying, and at his [Ninurta's] side the gods of his city cowered on the Earth."

Sagara

In Japanese myth, a dragon-god of an undersea kingdom and possessor of a magical sword and a "pearl" able to cause catastrophic floods. Sagara appears to reference the sunken civilization of Mu.

(See Kusanagi)

Saka-duipa

Cited in the Sanskrit *Suria Adanta* as pre-deluge Atlantis, home of the sun-worshiping Megas, Atlantean priests or adepts who carried the esoteric principles and "magic" of their solar cult to India and other parts of the world.

Salinen Deluge Story

According to this California tribe, humanity perished in a world flood. Only a single diving bird survived. It dove to the bottom of the ocean and fetched up a beak-full of muck from the bottom of the sea. Seeing this performance, Eagle God descended from the sky to fashion a new race from the retrieved mud.

The Salinen myth describes the rebirth of mankind after its near-extinction in the Late Bronze Age catastrophe that destroyed Atlantis.

Samatumi-whooah

The Okanagons of British Columbia taught that their ancestors came from Samatumi-whooah, literally "White Man's Island," which sank in the midst of evil wars, drowning all its inhabitants, save a man and his woman. The Maryland Indians claimed that the whites were an ancient generation who, perishing in a great deluge, were reborn and had returned to claim their former holdings in America. Both traditions are tribal memories of the Atlantean war and flood described by Plato, with the addition of survivors arriving in the New World.

Samudranarayana

A temple standing on an embankment above the Gomati River where it flows into the Indian Ocean. Although the name of the sea-god Samudra, to which Samudranarayana has been dedicated, suggests the lost Pacific Motherland of Mu, the sacred structure's circular design resembles the concentric layout of Atlantis, as described by Plato. Samudranarayana may have been a blending of both sunken civilizations.

Sa Na Duniya

An early king in Hausa oral tradition of Nigeria, head of the "Sea Peoples" who invaded around 1200 B.C., following the Great Flood which engulfed his former kingdom.

(See Sea Peoples)

Saracura

"Water Hen," a goddess who saved the ancestors of the Karaya and Ges Indians from a universal flood by leading them to the peak of a mountain at the center of the world. This deluge-myth suggests the Atlantean Navel of the World cult.

(See Navel of the World)

Schliemann, Paul

Described as either the grandson or great nephew of Heinrich Schliemann, the renowned discoverer of Troy and Mycenea. Paul Schliemann's published article, "How I Discovered Atlantis, The Source of All Civilization," appeared in a 1912 edition of the *New York American*. It claimed that Heinrich, while excavating Trojan ruins on the hill at Hissarlik, in Turkey, found a large bronze vase covered with a Phoenician inscription that read, "From King Cronos of Atlantis." Paul promised readers that a book fully explaining his discovery of Atlantis would be published shortly thereafter, but he was never heard from again.

Most skeptics and even Atlantologists believe the article was a hoax, if only because records exist of neither a grandson nor great nephew for Heinrich Schliemann named Paul. But some investigators point out that, if it were a hoax, no one appears to have benefited from it in any way. And Paul Schliemann's disappearance may have been explained by his death as a soldier in World War I, which followed publication of his story by two years. They also cite some internal evidence he provided, such as the association of Cronos, the Greek Titan synonymous for the Atlantic Ocean, with Atlantis. In any case, until written verification of Paul Schliemann's existence and fate comes to light, his *New York American* article remains a mystery.

(See Kronos)

Scomalt

The North American Okanaguas' ancestral "Medicine Woman," who ruled over "a lost island" at the time of the Deluge. In the Hopi version, she was called *Tuwa'bontumsi*.

Sea Peoples

In Egyptian, the *Meshwesh* or *Hanebu*. In 1190 B.C., they mounted a major invasion of the Nile Delta. After initial success, they were defeated and taken captive. The testimony of Sea People prisoners-of-war, recorded in the wall-texts of Pharaoh Ramses III's Victory Temple at Medinet Habu, in West Thebes, showed them to be the same aggressors described in Plato's account of Atlantis. The Greeks claimed their land was first civilized by the Pelasgians, a "sea people" from the Far West.

In North America, the Menomonie Indians of the Upper Great Lakes remember an alien race of white-skinned "Marine Men" or "Sea People," who arrived from over the Atlantic Ocean long ago to "wound Earth Mother by extracting her shining bones,"—that is, they mined copper.

(See Bronze Age, Pelasgians, Ramses III)

Sekhet-Aaru

The Egyptians' realm of the dead, but also their ancestral homeland on an island in the Distant West, from which their forefathers arrived at the Nile Delta in the *Tep Zepi*, or "First Time," at the start of dynastic civilization. On the other side of the world, the Aztecs believed their ancestors came from an island kingdom in the Distant East, called Aztlan. Both *Sekhet-Aaru* and *Aztlan* mean "Field of Reeds." To the Egyptians and the Aztecs alike, reeds, employed as writing utensils, were symbolic of literacy and wisdom, implying that Sekhet-Aaru/Aztlan was a place of extraordinary learning.

(See Aztlan, Aalu)

Sekhmet

Egyptian goddess of fiery destruction credited in the wall texts of Medinet Habu with the destruction of Neteru (Atlantis). Sekhmet was actually identified with a threatening comet, "shooting-star," or awesome celestial phenomenon of some kind.

Semu-Hor

In ancient Egyptian tradition, "The Followers of Horus," they were culture-bearers who arrived at the Nile Delta from Sekhet-aaru, "the Field of Reeds," their sunken homeland in the Distant West. The Semsu-Hor were survivors from the upheavals that beset Atlantis in the late fourth millennium B.C.

(See Menentiu, Sekhet-aaru)

Sequana

Celtic goddess of the River Seine, who reestablished her chief shrine at or near Dijon after the destruction of Atlantis, which is specifically mentioned in her French folk tradition. Alternate versions describe Sequana as a princess who sailed to the Burgundian highlands directly from the Great Flood that drowned her distant island kingdom. Its name, *Morois*, compares with *Murias*, the sunken city from which the pre-Celtic Tuatha da Danann arrived in Ireland.

Traveling up the Seine, Sequana erected a stone temple near Dijon. In it she stored a sumptuous treasure—loot from lost Atlantis—in many secret chambers. After her death, she became a jealous river-goddess. There is, in fact, a megalithic center near Dijon made up of subterranean passage ways that are still sometimes searched for ancient treasure.

Sequana was reborn in the Sequani, a Celtic people who occupied territory between the Rhein, Rhone, and Saone Rivers. The Romans referred to the area as *Maxima Sequanorum*, known earlier as *Sequana*.

(See Murias)

Seri Culture-Bearer Tradition

The "Come-From-Afar-Men" were revered by the Seri Indians of Tiburon Island as powerful but kindly sorcerers who arrived in a "long boat with a head like a snake" that ran aground and was ripped apart on a reef in the Gulf of California, "a long time ago, when God was a little boy." Tall, with red or white hair, the "Come-From-Afar-Men" taught compassion and healing. They interbred with a local people, the Mayo, who still occasionally evidence anomalous Caucasian features. Until the 1920s, the Mayo expelled tribal members who married outside the group.

The Seri tradition appears to be a revealing folk memory of Lemurian priests shipwrecked on the shores of southern California.

Shan Hai Ching

Ancient Chinese cosmological account that describes a prehistoric catastrophe that occurred when the sky tipped suddenly, causing the Earth to tilt in the opposite direction. The resulting flood sent a vast kingdom to the bottom of the ocean.

(See Mu)

Shasta

A volcanic California mountain described in several local American Indian myths as the only dry land to have survived a worldwide flood. Building a raft, Coyote-Man sailed over great expanses of water to arrive at its summit. There he ignited a signal fire that alerted other survivors, who gathered at Mount Shasta, from which they repopulated the Earth. Into modern times, mysterious lights sometimes seen on the mountaintop are associated with ceremonies of a "Lemurian brotherhood," whose initiates allegedly perform rituals from the lost civilization. These lights, like that of the Indians' flood hero, Coyote-Man, are probably electrical phenomena known to occur at the peaks of seismically active mountains bearing strong deposits of crystal. As earth tremors squeeze the mineral, it emits electrical discharges, similar to the piezeo-electrical effects of a crystal radio receiver.

The intensity of negative ions generated by this phenomenon can interface with the bio-circuitry of the human brain, inducing altered states of consciousness related to spiritual or shamanic experiences. Hence, the mystical character of Mount Shasta for Native Americans and modern visitors alike is not difficult to understand.

Shawnee Deluge Story

This American Indian tribe occupies much of southern Illinois, where massive stone walls atop precipitous bluffs form a broken chain, nearly 200 miles long, across the bottom part of the state from the Mississippi to Ohio Rivers. According to the Shawnee, these structures were built by immigrating giants who survived the Great Flood. An area of the Shawnee National Forest is still referred to as "Giant City" in memory of these ancient deluge immigrants. According to Shawnee tradition, this catastrophe killed every human being, save for a single, old woman. In despair at being alone in the world, she sadly molded clay dolls into anthropomorphic shapes to help her remember vanished mankind. Taking pity on her, the Great Spirit turned the clay figures into living men and women, and the Earth was repopulated. Hence, the Shawnee revere Old Grandmother as their ancestress.

The Shipwrecked Sailor

An Egyptian "tale" with strong Atlantean overtones, thought to date to an early dynastic epoch, but repeated and elaborated upon even in Ptolemaic times. An original papyrus of the story is in the possession of Russia's Saint Petersburg Museum, and dates to the XX Dynasty, circa 1180 B.C. Significantly, this is the same period in which Egypt defended herself against the "Sea People" invasion. The final destruction of Atlantis is believed by investigators to have occurred in 1198 B.C.

The story of the shipwrecked sailor opens with a terrible storm, far out at sea. A freighter carrying miners is lost, and only one man clinging to some wreckage is eventually washed ashore at some distant island.

"Suddenly, I heard a thunderous noise," he says. "I thought it must have been a great wave striking the beach. Trees swayed and the Earth shook." These stirrings announced the arrival of the Serpent King, a huge, bearded creature overlaid with scales of gold and lapis lazuli. He carefully picked up the hapless sailor in his great jaws and carried him to his "resting place." There he told the man about "this island in the middle of the sea, an Isle of the Blest, where nothing is lacking, and which is filled with all good things, a far country, unknown to men." After a four-month stay, the king loads his guest down with gifts. "But when you leave this place," he warns, "you will never see this island again, because it will be covered by the waves."

Interestingly, the Serpent King referred to his island kingdom as "Punt." This is the same ambiguous land generations of pharaohs visited with commercial expeditions, returning with rich trade goods, until the late 13th-century B.C. destruction of Atlantis, with which it has been identified. Moreover, the Serpent King's island is seismic ("the Earth shook"), "in the middle of the sea," and "a far country unknown to men." He calls his kingdom "the Isle of the Blest," the same epitaph used by Greek and Roman writers to characterize Atlantis. His description of this island kingdom as rich in natural abundance ("where nothing is lacking and which is filled with all good things") is reminiscent of Plato's version of Atlantis: "The island itself provided much of what was required by them for the uses of life. All these that sacred isle lying beneath the sun brought forth fair and wondrous in infinite abundance" (*Kritias*). In fact, the Serpent King himself leaves no doubt of his island's Atlantean identity: "You will never see this island again, because it will be covered by the waves."

The Serpent King's portrayal as a fabulous beast is transparently symbolic of a powerful monarch. *The Pyramid Texts* read, "Thou, Osiris, art great in thy name of the Great Green [the ocean]. Lo, thou art round as the circle that encircles the Hanebu." Howey commented, "Osiris was thus the serpent [dragon] that lying in the ocean, encircled the world"—that is, had power over it (164). The *Hanebu* were the "Sea Peoples" of Atlantis reported by the scribes of Ramses III in the wall-texts of his Victory Temple at Medinet Habu. The Serpent King's appearance points up his royal provenance. The beard was an emblem of sovereign authority. Even Queen Hatshepsut had to wear a false beard during her reign. And his "scales" of gold and lapis lazuli represented his raiment. The sailor's transportation to the Serpent King's "resting place," (the palace) in the "great jaws"—the edged weapons of his guards—is a metaphor for the power of command.

The ancient Egyptian artist commissioned to portray the war fought by his Pharaoh against invading Atlanteans conveyed something of the campaign's vast scope and carnage, as reflected in this partial tracing from Medinet Habu.

These mythic images shed light on the Feathered Serpent, the legendary founding-father of Mesoamerican Civilization from across the Sunrise Sea. The Quiche Mayas' foremost culture hero was Votan, from Valum, the Kingdom of Serpents. Both Coatlicue and Mama Ocllo, the leading ladies of Aztec and Inca legend, respectively, belonged to "the race of serpents." Amuraca, the Bochica Indians' first chief, means "Serpent King." Like the Egyptian Serpent King, Amuraca once ruled over an island in the midst of the sea.

The Serpent King tells his shipwrecked guest about "a young girl on whom the fire from heaven fell and burnt her to ashes." Why this curious aside should be included in the tale, if not as an allusion to the celestial impact responsible for the Atlantean catastrophe, is otherwise inexplicable.

(See Punt, Quetzalcoatl, Sea People)

Shen Chou

In Chinese myth, a very ancient kingdom, preceding the creation of China itself. Before Shen Chou disappeared beneath the Pacific Ocean, the goddess of mercy, Hsi Wang Mu, carried away the Tree of Immortality to her fabulous palace in the remote peaks of the K'un-lun Mountains. There she tends it for gods and only the most virtuous human beings. At a periodical banquet, the P'an-t'ao Hui, or "Feast of the Peaches," these select individuals achieve immortality by eating the blessed fruit.

Shen Cho is an apparent Chinese reference to the lost Pacific civilization, as underscored by the goddesses' name, Hsi Wang Mu, and the Tree of Life, with its sacred peaches, the same fruit mentioned in Japanese myth describing Lemuria.

(See Garden of the Hesperides, Mu, Urashima-Taro)

Shikiemona

Sky-god of Venezuela's Orinoco Indians. They believed Shikiemona unloosed "The Great Water," a worldwide flood, to drown the first humans, who transgressed his sacred laws.

Shinobazu

A large pond fringed with rushes and inhabited by varieties of water fowl, formerly an inlet of Tokyo Bay, until its creation in imitation of the Chikubujima Shrine on Lake Biwa, near Kyoto. At the center of the pond is a small island with a temple dedicated to the sea-goddess, Benten, the mythical culture-bearer who brought civilization to Japan from the sunken Motherland of Mu. Her arrival is symbolized at Shinobazu by statues of fish and emblems of a pyramid surrounded by threateningly high waves of the sea. With the political and cultural shift to Tokyo in the 17th century A.D., the new capital declared its Lemurian legacy by creating its own version of Chikubujima at Shinobazu. Its artificial island, connected by causeways to the shore, is a symbolic representation of the lost Pacific Motherland.

(See Benten, Chikubujima, Mu)

Shoshone Deluge Story

In the Great Flood that drowned the world, the ancestors of this North American tribe found refuge in an enormous cave called the Sipapu. After the Deluge abated, they emerged to regenerate mankind. Today, the Sipapu is the Shoshone "Navel of the World," a hole at the center of their sacred precinct, the kiva, and the most important feature of their religion. The Navel of the World, with its cavernous ceremonies, was the primeval mystery cult of Atlantis.

(See Navel of the World)

Shu

The Egyptian Atlas, he was portrayed in temple art as a bearded man supporting the heavens while guarding the Four Pillars of the Sky. These were comparable to the Pillars of Heracles, or the Strait of Gibraltar, which defined the Mediterranean limits of Atlantean influence, and a concept that placed Shu at the center of the world. In ancient Egypt, obelisks were known as "Pillars of Shu." As Atlas meant "the Upholder," so Shu was known as "He Who Holds Up." He shared the title, "God of the Air," with Ehecatl, his Aztec counterpart. According to the renowned Egyptologist Schwaller de Lubicz, Pharaonic prehistory was dominated by the twins, Shu and Tefnut" (211).

Sigu

The flood hero of Arawak myth, he saved all of Earth's animals from a planet-wide deluge by sealing them up in a huge cave. Sigu then climbed to the top of the tallest tree at the center of the world. After the waters abated, he descended and freed the animals. The same myth was known to the Mayas, who venerated the Ceibra above all others, because it was the sole tree to have survived the Flood at the center of the world. Repeatedly signified in both the Arawak and Maya accounts is the Atlantean Navel of the World mystery cult, with its central Tree of Life.

Interestingly, Sigu appears in the Melanasian rendition of the flood that destroyed Lemuria. It recounts that he was a prince, who, together with his father, the king, escaped the inundation of Burotu.

(See Burotu, Makonaima, Navel of the World)

Sillapadakaram

A Tamil religious text that describes Kumari Nadu, also known as the Pandyan Kingdom. Before it disappeared under the Indian Ocean during a natural catastrophe, the "Land of the Kumara" was the birthplace of Shiva-worship in pre-Hindu times. A teacher, Agastyr, escaped to establish the cult in the south of India, where he built an ashram in the Pothigai Hills, from which it spread throughout the subcontinent. "Kumara" is a title, "The Forever-Young Boy," referring to the androgynous Murrugan, another god whose spiritual principles Agastyr brought from Kumari Nadu.

Murrugan was a savior-deity some investigators (Mark Pinkham, Kersey Graves, etc.) believe was a model upon which the myth of Christ was fashioned. As a sage of Murrugan, Agastyr was referred to as "the Son of Mitra"; *mitra* means "contract" or "friendship" with God. As such, Murrugan's influence on Mithraism, phonetically and philosophically, is apparent. No less so is Murrugan's philological relationship with Mu, where his concept originated. His Kumari Nadu, or "Land of the Kumara," is an Indian version of Lemuria.

(See Rawana)

Silustani

A pre-Inca ceremonial area located not far from the shores of Bolivia's Lake Titicaca. It features a skillfully laid-out circle of standing stones unlike anything comparable in South America, but strongly reminiscent of megalithic sites common in Western Europe. More famous are the Chulpas of Silustani. These are enormous, well-made towers archaeologists believe, on paltry evidence, were used exclusively for funerary purposes. The Chulpas bear an uncanny resemblance to equally massive stone towers standing under 100 feet of water in the Sea of Korea, off Japan's western coast, approximating the island of Okinoshima. Connections between the Okinoshima structures and those on land, near water at Silustani, are suggested through the lost, intermediary civilization of Mu, although early Atlantean influences may also be present, as evidenced in the anomalous stone circle.

Sing Bonga

Sky-god of the Mundaris, a tribe from Chota Nagpur, West Bengal, in central India. He covered the Earth with streams of "fire water" to wipe out a sinful mankind. Only a brother and sister were saved when Sing Bonga put a serpent in the sky, which, puffing itself up, turned into a rainbow and shielded the children from the last drops of the deluge.

The Inca and pre-Inca peoples of South America likewise associated a rainbow "sky-serpent" with the great deluge which brought successive waves of culture-bearers from over the sea after the destruction of their island kingdom. So too, the biblical account of Noah's Flood has Yahweh put a rainbow into the sky as a sign that the deluge was ended.

Siriadic Columns

Thaut, or Thoth, set up two columns—one of brick, the other of stone—on which were inscribed a pre-deluge history. They were meant to survive both fire and flood, and erected "in the Siriadic land," a reference to Egypt, where the rising of Sirius coincided with the annual inundation of the Nile Delta. In Egyptian myth, Thaut arrived at the Delta after cataclysmic flooding destroyed a former age, the *Tep Zepi*, or "First Time." Doubtless, that ancient deluge symbolically correlated with the yearly rising of the Nile, because the results of both were abundance. With Thaut's arrival, pharaonic civilization bloomed again following an excess of nature, just as the yearly overflowing of the river brings fertile, alluvial soil.

He carried "emerald tablets" on which were engraved the documented wisdom of the First Time. The word "emerald" may not be literally understood, but intended to imply a precious stone of some kind, or, more probably, it meant that the information preserved on the stones was precious. Thaut is credited in both Egyptian and Arab myth as the builder of the Great Pyramid. The story of his Siriadic Columns was told by two leading historians of classical times: Manetho, a third-century B.C. Egyptian priest commissioned to write a chronicle of Dynastic Civilization by the Ptolemies, and Flavius Josephus, prominent Jewish scholar of the first century A.D. Josephus ascribed the twin columns to Seth, who he described, not as a god, but a "patriarch." Although worshiped from pre-dynastic and early dynastic times in Upper Egypt, Seth was thereafter demonized by the Followers of Horus, so little of his original cult may be inferred. Unique to the rest of the gods, however, he was a redhead, like many Atlanteans.

The memorial pillars may have been the same stele inscribed with the history of Atlantis that were seen by Solon and Krantor, the Greek visitors to Neith's temple at Sais in the Nile Delta, and upon which Plato's Atlantean account was based. *Kritias* describes a sacred column inscribed with ancestral laws at the center of the Temple of Poseidon in Atlantis. It seems related to Thaut's "Siriadic Columns" and those mentioned by Plato.

Slaying of the Labu

A Babylonian description of the Atlantean flood predating Plato's account by 1,000 years, it reads in part: "the mighty Irra seized away the beams [of the dams], and Ninurta coming caused the locks to burst. The Annunaki bore torches, making the land to glow with their gleaming. The noise of Adad [a volcanic mountain] came unto heaven, and a great water-spout reached to the sky. Everything light turned to darkness. For in one day, the hurricane swiftly blew like the shock of battle over the people." Ishtar wailed, "Like a brood of fish, they [the people] now fill the sea!" After six days, "the sea became calm, the cyclone died away, the Deluge ceased. I [Xiusthros] looked upon the sea, and the sound of voices had ended."

(See Xiusthros)

Sobata

Seafarers who covered great distances in small wooden vessels known in Okinawan dialect as *Sabani*, or *Sa-bune*, after which the sailors are still remembered in Japanese oral traditions. These Sabani are remarkably similar to craft used by Polynesians, and may still be seen occasionally plying the waters between the Hawaiian Islands. Sobata dwelling sites have been radio-carbon dated to the mid-fifth millennium B.C. from Hokkaido in the north to the Ryukyu Islands in the south. Their prodigious feats of navigation almost perfectly parallel the distribution of Jomon earthenware finds made along the East China Sea and the Sea of Japan, and may account for Jomon pottery shards found on the other side of the Pacific Ocean, in Ecuador.

Professor Nobuhiro Yoshida, President of The Japan Petroglyph Society, states, "If they (the Sobata) were not after all navigators from Mu itself—spreading its cultural influences to both sides of the Pacific—then they may have been the direct inheritors of a thallasocratic tradition from the Motherland after its geologic demise."

(See Ama, Mu)

Solon

One of the "Seven Wise Men of Greece," he introduced social reforms and a legal code which formed the political basis of classical civilization. Solon was also the first great poet of Athens. In the late sixth century B.C., he traveled to Sais, the Nile Delta capital of the XXVI Dynasty, where the Temple of Neith was located. Here a history of Etelenty was preserved in hieroglyphs inscribed or painted on columns, which were translated for him by the high priest, Psonchis. Returning to Greece, Solon worked all the details of the account into an epic poem, *Atlantikos*, but was distracted by political problems from completing the project before his death in 560 B.C. About 150 years later, the unfinished manuscript was given to Plato, who formed two dialogues, *Timaeus* and *Kritias*, from it. As one of the very greatest historical figures in classical Greek history, Solon's early connection with the story of Atlantis lends it formidable credibility.

(See Etelenty, Neith, Plato, Psonchis)

Sotuknang

In Hopi Indian myth, a god who long ago drowned the world, sending all human treasures to the bottom of the sea.

Spence, Lewis

Born James Lewis Thomas Chalmbers Spence, on November 25, 1874, in Forfarshire, Scotland, he was a prominent mythologist, who inherited Ignatius Donnelly's position as the world's leading Atlantologist of the early 20th century. An alumnus of Edinburgh University, Spence was made a fellow of the Royal Anthropology Institute of Great Britain and Ireland, and elected Vice President of the Scottish Anthropology and Folklore Society. Awarded a Royal Pension "for services to culture," he published more than 40 books. Many of them, such as his *Dictionary of Mythology*, are still in print and sought after for their incomparable source materials.

Spence's interpretation of the Mayas' *Popol Vuh* won international acclaim, but he is best remembered for *The Problem of Atlantis* (1924), *Atlantis in America* (1925), *The History of Atlantis* (1926), *Will Europe Follow Atlantis?* (1942), and *The Occult Sciences in Atlantis* (1943). During the early 1930s, he edited a prestigious journal, *The Atlantis Quarterly*. *The Problem of Lemuria* (1932) is still probably the best book on the subject. Lewis Spence died on March 3, 1955, and was succeeded as the leading Atlantologist by the British scholar, Edgerton Sykes.

(See Sykes)

Statius Sebosus

A Greek geographer and contemporary of Plato mentioned by the Roman scientist Pliny the Elder, for his detailed description of Atlantis. All works of Statius Sebosus were lost with the fall of classical civilization.

Steiner, Rudolf

Born in Kraljevic, Austria, on February 27, 1861, he was a scientist, artist, and editor, who founded a gnostic movement based on comprehension of the spiritual world through pure thought and the highest faculties of mental knowledge. Steiner's views on Atlantis and Lemuria are important if only because the educational Waldorf movement that he founded still operates about 100 schools attended by tens of thousands of students in Europe and the United States.

In his 1904 book, *Cosmic Memory: Prehistory of Earth and Man*, he maintained that before Atlantis gradually sank in 7227 B.C., its earliest inhabitants formed one of mankind's "root races," a people who did not require speech, but communicated telepathically in images, not words, as part of their immediate experience with God. According to Steiner, the story of Atlantis was dramatically revealed in Germanic myth, wherein fiery Muspelheim corresponded to the southern, volcanic area of the Atlantic land, while frosty Nifelheim was located in the north. Steiner wrote that the Atlanteans first developed the concept of good versus evil, and laid the groundwork for all ethical and legal systems. Their leaders were spiritual initiates able to manipulate the forces of nature through "control of the life-force" and development of "etheric technology." Seven "epochs" comprise the Post Atlantis Period, of which ours, the Euro-American Epoch, will end in 3573 A.D.

Cosmic Memory went on to describe the earlier and contemporary Pacific civilization of Lemuria, with stress on the highly evolved clairvoyant powers of its people. But Steiner defined Atlantis as the turning-point in an ongoing struggle between the human search for community and our experience of individuality. The former, with its growing emphasis on materialism, dragged down the spiritual needs of the latter, culminating eventually in the Atlantean cataclysm. In this interpretation of the past, he opposed Marxism. To him, spirit, not economics, drives history.

Steiner died on March 30, 1925, in Dornach, Switzerland, where his "school of spiritual science" had been founded 12 years earlier.

Sterope

The third Pleiade, an Atlantis ("daughter of Atlas"), she was synonymous for the Atlantean occupation of Etruria, in west-central Italy, through her son's foundation of Pisa, the Etruscan Pisae.

(See Etruscans, Pleiades)

Stonehenge

The world's most famous megalithic site, located on England's Salisbury Plain, evidences several important Atlantean features. For example, the sacred numerals, 5 and 6, incorporated in Atlantean architecture, according to Plato, recur throughout Stonehenge. The structure even resembles the concentric city-plan of Atlantis itself.

Stonehenge was first laid out by 3000 B.C., began to reach the apex of its construction 1,500 years later, and was suddenly discontinued around 1200 B.C. Its development, use, and abandonment parallel Atlantean immigration at the close of the fourth millennium B.C., the zenith of Atlantis as the foremost Bronze Age civilization, and the final destruction in 1198 B.C.

(See Mestor)

Stonehenge's most significant periods and physical features closely coincide with the rise and fall of Atlantis.

Strath-Gordon, Alexander Edmund Ronald

Internationally renowned speaker and founder of a society for the investigation of Atlantis, which both influenced and networked important, early 20th-century Atlantologists.

Dr. Strath-Gordon was born in 1873, in Aberdeen-Huntly, Scotland, and educated at Rugby school. Following graduation with highest honors from the Edinburgh University medical school, he entered the British Army which stationed him with the Cree Indians of northwest Canada. During his seven years in the

Yukon, tribal elders told him about their folk memories of a great flood that long ago engulfed a large island, their ancestral birthplace. The Cree account sparked Strath-Gordon's life-long interest in Atlantis, and, throughout the course of his world-travels, he collected similar traditions among various other peoples.

With the onset of the Boer War, he was transferred as a medical officer with the rank of major to South Africa. There, he was surprised to learn native versions of the same flood described by Canadian Indians. He concluded that these different, though similar accounts were nothing more than cultural inflections on the same Atlantean theme. A few years later, Strath-Gordon made colonel in the British Army's medical corps, in France, where he was stationed from 1914 to 1918. During lulls in the carnage, he kept his ears open for local French deluge legends, and learned of several sunken realms, such as Ys.

After the war, he headed up the British passport control service in New York, where, following his retirement, he became a U.S. citizen. By then, he possessed a worldwide collection of folk materials, and was proficient in 32 languages, including Sanskrit. Such multiple fluency served him well in penetrating the core meaning of numerous flood traditions. During the early 1920s, he met at least several times with Edgar Cayce, the famous "Sleeping Prophet." During 1928, Strath-Gordon formed the Atlantean Research Society, in Orange, New Jersey, which served as a base for his lectures across the United States and Canada. His eloquent talks acquainted audiences with a credible rendition of Atlantis. At the onset of another international conflict, he was a medical instructor at Portland, Oregon's Hill Military academy. Following World War II, he resumed his lecture tours until his death in 1952.

Although little more is known about Dr. Strath-Gordon, researchers speculate his scholarly prestige may have at least helped to form Cayce's conception of Atlantis, and even influenced James Churchward's views on its Pacific counterpart, Mu.

(See Cayce, Ys)

Sueka

Flood hero of the Native American Pima peoples, who escaped a mountainous tsunami that arose to destroy the world when a colossal "lightning bolt" struck the sea.

(See Asteroid Theory)

The Sunken World

A 1928 novel about Atlantis by Stanton A. Coblentz, who has its inhabitants surviving the ancient destruction of their homeland under a glass dome on the sea bottom.

Sura and Nakao

Flood heroes of the Ami tribe, dwellers of central Taiwan. They alone survived a world-class deluge in a wooden vessel, which landed them safely atop Mount Ragasan after the waters abated. From Sura and Nakao descended modern mankind.

The catastrophe from which they escaped was said to have begun during a full moon accompanied by the sound of loud explosions coming from the sea, suggesting volcanic and/or meteoric origins for the flood, which had been brought about by the gods to destroy human beings for their impiety. This moral imperative, together with the landing of Sura and Nakao on a mountaintop, is likewise found in the distant deluge traditions of the biblical Noah and the Greek Deucalion. The Ami myth is underscored by the discovery of underwater ruins off the western shores of Taiwan.

Surid

In Arab histories, the pre-deluge king of Egypt, who built the pyramids of Giza specifically to preserve the written knowledge of his time. This information included texts on astronomy, a history of the world, and prophecies for the future. Surid foresaw that the Earth was about to be incinerated by "a fiery planet" with resulting universal destruction by water. He appears in several Arab accounts of the Flood, in Masoudi (1000 A.D.), and the Akbar Ezjeman Collection, at Oxford. Surid may be the same as the Atlanto-Egyptian Thaut.

(See Siriadic Columns)

Susa-no-wo

Japan's god of the ocean and natural destruction. Susa-no-wo battled a gigantic sky-dragon, who had devoured seven sisters and was about to dine on an eighth, when he was slain by the hero. In so doing, the dragon's blood gushed over the Earth, but the souls of the consumed maidens were freed to rise among the heavens, where they became a constellation known in the West as the Pleiades.

Even here, on the other side of the world from Ancient Greece, the stars were regarded as sisters connected with a cosmic-induced deluge after it has done its worst. The great antiquity of such historical myth is emphasized by its appearance among the Ainu, an aboriginal people, originally Caucasoids, whose presence on the islands goes back beyond the fourth millennium B.C.

Sykes, Edgerton

Trained as an engineer, he was an invaluable foreign correspondent for the British press because of his quadrilingual fluency. During his long life in the diplomatic service and as a fellow of the Royal Geographical Society, he published an estimated three million words in numerous books and magazine articles, many of them devoted to a rational understanding of the Atlantis controversy. Sykes's erudite journals and encyclopedias of comparative myth went far to sustain and expand interest in Atlantis throughout the mid-20th century. As such, he succeeded his predecessors, Lewis Spence and Ignatius Donnelly, as one of the three greatest Atlantologist scholars of modern times. He died in 1983, just before his 90th birthday, but a legacy in the form of his large library of Atlantis-related material is preserved in its own room at Edgar Cayce's Association for Research and Enlightenment, in Virginia Beach, Virginia.

(See Donnelly, Spence)

Szeu-Kha

The Pima Indians' flood hero, he led their ancestors to North America after a flaming serpent fell from the sky with its fiery brood to burn up the original homeland of all mankind, located in the middle of the Atlantic Ocean. Fearing that the conflagration would spread throughout the Earth, Szeu-Kha pushed the burning island beneath the sea, creating a world-wide deluge. He led the early Pima away from this catastrophe before too many were drowned.

First Dynasty stone representation of Horus, the divine patron of kings, wearing the Red Crown of Lower Egypt. Atlantean culture-bearers arriving at the Nile Delta were known as "Followers of Horus."

Tahiti

A mountainous South Pacific island, the original homeland of all Polynesian peoples, which was destroyed by a world-class catastrophe of hurricane gusts and a rain of stones falling from the sky. The entire island sank beneath the sea, killing every living thing, save for a husband and wife, who piled with their animals into a boat and landed atop the highest mountain peak, O Pitohito, the only remaining dry land. Later, after the waters abated, descendants of the surviving couple named a new island after the drowned homeland, today's Tahiti.

Talli

Flood hero of North America's Lenape Indians. He and his followers survived the Deluge by riding it out in "great canoes." They landed at the Land of Snakes, where Talli led them successfully in battle.

Talvolte

In Maidu Indian myth, head of the Tortoise Clan, because he led his family to North America following the Great Flood that destroyed the rest of mankind. The tortoise is symbolic of the Deluge in many Native American traditions. The Mandan version recounts that "the world was once a great tortoise, borne on the waters and covered with earth. One day, in digging the soil, a tribe of white men who had made holes in the earth to a great depth, digging for badgers, at length perceived the shell of the tortoise. It sank, and the water covering it drowned all men with the exception of one, who saved himself in a boat." Donnelly wrote, "The holes dug to find badgers were a savage's recollection of mining operations; and when the great disaster came, and the island sunk in the sea amid volcanic convulsions, doubtless men said it was due to the deep mines, which had opened the ways to the central fires."

Among the Arapaho, Turtle Woman is a creator-goddess, who dredged up mud from the bottom of the universal deluge to remake the Earth.

(See Bronze Age)

Tamil Sangham

In oral traditions from the south of India, an exclusive academy for spiritual initiates located on a distant island of mountain ranges, beautiful rivers, lush vegetation, abundant animals and 49 provinces. Tamil Sangham was destroyed in a sudden convulsion of nature that pulled the island to the bottom of the sea. Some of its students survived, however, to pass their wisdom on to Hindu mystics.

Ta-mu

Literally "the Man from Mu," he was a deluge hero of the Carib Indians. Ta-mu was described as a fair-complected, light-haired, and light-bearded "sorcerer," who escaped a terrible catastrophe at sea. It was Ta-mu with whom the 16th century Spanish conquerors were compared by the natives.

(See Mu)

Tangis

According to the Berber scholar, Ouzzin, Tangiers was named after Tangis, a princess who founded the Moroccan city before she was lost at sea. Later, her husband was involved in the Greek war against Atlantis.

Taprobane

Known to classical Greeks and Romans, the famous geographer Strabo described it as the "beginning of another world." They believed Taprobane was located, at most, 20 days sail from the southern tip of India. A number of unspecified islands, probably the Cocos, were supposedly passed en route to the large island with its 500 towns. Taprobane may have been Australia but was certainly not Mu, as some modern investigators speculate.

Tara

A pre-Celtic archaeological site used for public ceremonies during megalithic times, located 20 miles northwest of Dublin, and the ancient political capital of Ireland. It was originally named *Tea-mhair* after Queen Tea, the wife of Eremon, the "Euaemon" listed by Plato as a king from Atlantis. Together with her sister, Tephi, Queen Tea made Tara the spiritual hub for the Atlantean Navel of the World mystery cult, and the sacred center of Ireland itself. A huge oval enclosure called the *Rath na Riogh*, the "Fortress of Kings," sits atop the "Mound of the Hostages," stressing its identity as an *omphalos*, the metaphysical cosmic egg of eternal rebirth.

Beside this passage-grave still stands the *Lia Fail*, the "Stone of Destiny," a later addition to Tara brought by the Tuatha da Danann, who arrived from the final destruction of Atlantis after 1200 B.C. Irish kings were crowned on or beside the monolith to demonstrate their Atlantean lineage, hence the name of another Tara earthwork known as *Forradh*, Gaelic for the "Seat of Kings." The Atlantean character of their inauguration was demonstrated by the five druid priests involved in selecting a royal candidate, and the bull sacrifice they performed. In Plato's description of ritual practices undertaken by kings at the Temple of Poseidon in Atlantis, a bull was sacrificed over a pillar not unlike the *Lia Fail*, and 5 was their sacred numeral.

The *Feis Teamhra* was another ceremony in which the new king was united with Ireland by symbolically marrying the goddesses of Irish sovereignty, Etain and Madb, both impersonated by a white mare. In the *Kritias*, Plato reported that the first lady of Atlantis was Leukippe, "White Mare."

Tara's "Mound of the Hostages" has been dated to circa 2100 B.C., coinciding with the second Atlantean catastrophe, in 2193 B.C., when refugees from Atlantis instituted their kingly rituals in Stone Age Ireland.

(See Eremon, Euaemon, Leukippe, Navel of the World, Tuatha da Danann)

Tavwots

The Ute Indians tell of Little Rabbit, who very long ago picked a fight with the Sun by hurling his penis at it. The great disk exploded into thousands of burning fragments which crashed to Earth, igniting a terrific conflagration. Try as he might to escape the cataclysm, Tavwots was dismembered by falling solar debris. His head went rolling around the planet, tears gushing from his swollen eyes in such great quantities of remorse that they caused a universal flood that extinguished the flaming holocaust, but almost obliterated all life in the process.

Little Rabbit's myth is the means by which a preliterate people preserve the memory of the world-wide Bronze Age catastrophe that destroyed Atlantis.

Tawantisuyu

A term by which the Incas referred to their South American empire. It derived from the collective name for their ancestors who migrated to the Andes as survivors from a Great Flood (Zorate, 9). The word may have the same Atlantean root as *Tawy*, which the ancient Egyptians used to describe Nile Civilization.

Tawiscara

North American flood hero of the Huron Indians, said to have "guided the torrents into smooth seas and lakes" following the disaster.

Tayasal

Sunken homeland of Yucatan's Itza Indians. Before its watery demise, Tayasal dominated an island in the middle of the Atlantic Ocean.

Taycanamu

The Lemurian city father of Chan Chan, a pre-Inca megalopolis on Peru's northern coast. In fact, his name appears to mean, literally, "Taycan from Mu," just as some Europeans used to be known by the places in which they were born: Francisco de Leon, Goetz von Berlichen, and so on.

(See Chimu)

Taygete

Fifth Atlantis of the Pleiades, daughters of Atlas by the goddess Pleione. Taygete was an Atlantean kingdom in the Canary Islands, where the native name for a Guanche sacred province on their largest island, Tenerife, was originally known as *Tegueste*.

(See Pleiades)

Tazlavoo

An early emperor of Atlantis, the first to possess a special crystal of alleged mystical properties, according to "ancient Asian chronicles," cited by J. Saint-Hilair, of the Roerich Museum, in New York.

(See Chintamani Stone)

Tehom

The Sumero-Babylonian term for the Great Flood.

Tenmadurai

One of several "sunken civilizations" described in Hindu scripture, the inundation of Tenmadurai signaled the end of a golden age, just as the destruction of Atlantis closed the Bronze Age.

Tephi

A name helping to establish the Atlantean identity of the Milesians who occupied pre-Celtic Ireland. *Tephi* is a derivative of *Tefnut*, the divine wife of the Egyptian Atlas, *Shu*.

Thens

In Thai folk tradition, a people who fled across the Pacific Ocean from their sinking kingdom during the ancient past. All they managed to salvage from the rising waters was a single column from their chief temple. It was set it up at the center of their new city in Southeast Asia, where the Thens blended Lemurian mysticism and technology with the native peoples.

(See Lak-Mu-ang)

Thera

The ancient Greek name of modern Santorini, a small Aegean island north of Crete, synonymous in the minds of some conventional archaeologists for Atlantis. They argue that a volcanic eruption experienced by Thera during the Middle Bronze Age was garbled in Plato's account and subsequently remembered, imperfectly, as the fate of the lost civilization. While a Minoan

The column from an unidentified structure at Ilios, the Trojan capital, represents the same Late Bronze Age style found in the clean, monumental architecture of Atlantis. Troy Museum, Cannikale, Turkey.

settlement was indeed located on Thera, it was too small to exert any significant cultural, economic, or much less, military influence. Skeptics still sometimes attempt to use Thera and Crete to explain away Atlantis, but they represent a dwindling voice shunned even by most mainstream scholars.

They Found Atlantis

A 1936 novel by Dennis Wheatley.

Third Reich

A view largely promoted by conventional scholars (Colin Renfrew, Donald Feder, et al) and authors with more interest in the occult than science, who insist that a belief in Atlantis as the lost homeland of an Aryan "super race" was aggressively championed by the leaders of Nazi Germany. This view has, in large measure, been sensationalized by television producers of several pseudo-documentaries depicting Atlantis as a fantasy with no basis in historical reality.

Hitler, Hess, Himmler, and Rosenberg are particularly singled out for their fanatic interest in "the lost continent," and the post-World War I Thule Society—a mystical club—is sometimes cited as evidence of an early connection between interest in Atlantis and the Nazis.

But the Thule Society's emphasis was far more Germanic than Atlantean. True, one of its members was Rudolf Hess, but the A-word cannot be found in any of his public speeches or private letters. *The Myth of the 20th Century*, Alfred Rosenberg's magnum opus, contains not a single reference to the sunken civilization. Throughout millions of recorded statements made by Adolf Hitler from 1919 to 1945, including his voluminous "Table Talk," the subject appears just twice, and then only in casual after-dinner remarks about the German cosmologist, Hanns Hoerbiger.

Contrary to portrayals by some television producers, Heinrich Himmler never ordered expeditions to search for surviving populations from Atlantis, nor included the study of Atlantis in the curriculum of his SS corps. No prominent Nazi leader ever described Atlantis as the homeland of the Aryan race. Still, the German Navy did name one of it surface raiders the *Atlantis*, although the name does not otherwise appear to have been used by the Kriegsmarine.

During the 1930s, both German and non-German anthropologists believed the Indo-European peoples originated in either the Steppes of Central Russia or Northern Europe, perhaps a region roughly corresponding to the Baltic States. A volume that did postulate German origins in Atlantis was *Unser Ahnen und die Atlanten , Nordliche Seeherrschaft von Skandinavien bis nach Nordafrika* (*"Our Ancestors and the Atlanteans, Nordic Seamanship from Scandinavia to North Africa,"* published by Kinkhard and Biermann, Berlin, 1934), by Albert Herrmann (1886–1945). His was principally the examination of an old Frisian manuscript describing survivors from the Atlantis catastrophe in Northern Europe, Nordic maritime technology, and a contemporary discovery in Libya at Schott-el-Djerid, where the concentric ruins of a buried archaeological site suggested Atlantean influences. Nowhere throughout its 164 pages does the author state that either the Atlanteans or the Germans were a "master race."

Four years after the publication of his popular book, Herrmann used his prestige as a professor of historical geography at Berlin University to stage a large-scale exhibit about Atlantis in the nation's capital. Although the 1938 event attracted favorable notice across the country and outside Germany, it was not sponsored by any Nazi organization. He may have contributed to the production of *Wo liegt Atlantis?* ("*Where is Atlantis?*"), a popular film examining possible Atlantean impact on Central America, released in 1933, just after the Nazis assumed power. Herrmann's illustration for *Atlantis in Unser Ahnen und die Atlanten*, banned in Germany since 1945, is still well-known and continues to be republished in several Atlantology books, almost invariably without credit.

Other well-known Third Reich Atlantologists included Ernst Moritz Arndt (*Nordische Volkskunde*, "Nordic Folk Message," 1935); Alexander Bessmertny (*Das Atlantis Raetsel*, "*The Atlantis Riddle*," Leipzig, 1932); Rudolf Brunngraber (*Der Engel in Atlantis*, "*The Angel in Atlantis*," Frankfurt, 1938); Heinrich Pudor (*Voelker aus altes Athen, Atlantis, Helgoland*, "*Peoples from old Athens, Atlantis, Helgoland*," Leipzig, 1936); Herrmann Wieland (*Atlantis, Edda und Bibel*, "*Atlantis, Edda and the Bible*," Nuremberg, 1922); and Herbert Reichstein (*Geloeste Raetsel: Geschichte von Edda, Atlantis und der Bibel*, "*Solved Riddle: The History of the Edda, Atlantis and the Bible*," Berlin, 1934). They were part of worldwide interest in Atlantis, as attested by contemporary Atlantologists in other countries, such as Britain's Lewis Spence and Colonel Braghine of the United States. Unfortunately, the works of early 20th-century German Atlantologists, regardless of their political content, were lost when they were uniformly proscribed by Allied occupation authorities after World War II.

Atlantis has always attracted especially broad interest in Germany, as Ignatius Donnelly, the American father of Atlantology, pointed out during the last decade of the 19th century, long prior to Herrmann's exhibition, and many years before Hitler wrote *Mein Kampf*. In an attempt to silence their critics, skeptics lump Atlantologists together with "Nazi mass-murderers," even though consideration of Atlantis, save on a single public occasion (Herrmann's 1938 exhibit), was never part of the Third Reich.

Thonapa

Either another name for Viracocha, the Andean flood hero, or a distinctly different, though similar, survivor associated with an earlier arrival of technologically gifted foreigners. The Incas told of four major waves of alien immigration to South America during the ancient past, all prompted by terrific natural catastrophes. Thonapa is commonly associated with the *Unu-Pachacuti*, or "World Over-Turned by Water," the third Atlantean cataclysm around 1628 B.C.

(See Ayar-aucca, Ayar-chaki, Ayar-manco-topa, Unu-Pachacuti, Viracocha)

Thoth

Also known as *Thaut* (Egyptian), *Taaut* (Phoenician), *Hermes* (Greek), and *Mercury* (Roman), he was mortal, later deified, and a prominent leader of Atlantean refugees into the Nile Valley. He is the Atlantean deity of literature, magic, and healing most associated with civilization. In Greek myth, Hermes is the grandson of

Atlas by the Atlantis, Maia. The Theban Recension of the Egyptian *Book of the Dead* quotes Thaut as having said that the Great Deluge destroyed a former world-class civilization: "I am going to blot out everything which I have made. The Earth shall enter into the waters of the abyss of Nun [the sea-god] by means of a raging flood, and will become even as it was in the primeval time."

His narration of the catastrophe is related to the *Edfu Texts*, which locate the "Homeland of the Primeval Ones" on a great island that sank with most of its inhabitants during the Tep Zepi, or "First Time." Only the gods, led by Thaut, escaped with seven favored sages, who settled at the Nile Delta, where they created Egyptian civilization from a synthesis of Atlantean and native influences. The *Edfu Texts* are, in this regard at least, in complete accord with Edgar Cayce's version of events in Egypt at the dawn of pharaonic civilization.

(See Siriadic Columns)

Thule

After Plato's story of Atlantis became generally known during the early fourth century B.C., a contemporary Greek natural scientist, Pytheas, set out on a voyage of discovery to locate remnants of the sunken civilization. His account, which still exists, tells how he sailed into the Atlantic Ocean, going north toward the Arctic Circle. Historians are uncertain whether Pytheas reached Iceland, the Shetland Islands, or visited Norway's coast above what is now Bergen. In any case, he called this land *Ultima Thule*, the "farthest land." Its native people told him they did indeed know of a great island that had collapsed under the sea many ages ago, when its survivors, their forefathers, sailed north and east to save themselves. The new land was named after their lost homeland, Thule, just as, during the 17th-century, Englishmen arriving from York on the eastern seaboard of North America named their settlement, "New York."

Tiahuanaco

An Aymara Indian rendition of the older *Typi Kala*—"Stone-in-the-Center," in the native Quechua language—suggesting the city's prominence as an omphalos. "Tiahuanaco" derives from *Wanaku*, "Powerful Spirit Place," referring to an island, now sunk beneath nearby Lake Titicaca, formerly the center of the Andean culture-founder Kon-Tiki-Viracocha and his followers. Whether this Aymara tradition refers to Atlantis or the actual stone ruins found beneath the surface of Lake Titicaca, or both, is not clear. The Spanish chronicler, Cieza de Leon, recorded a local Bolivian legend to the effect that "Tiahuanaco was built in a single night after the Flood by unknown giants."

The ruins comprise an important archaeological site, a pre-Inca ceremonial center, featuring spacious plazas, broad staircases, colossal statuary, and monumental gates.

(see Navel of the World, Viracocha)

Tiamuni

The Acomas claimed that their ancestors were white people washed ashore on the east coast of North America by the Deluge. The chief who led these hapless survivors was Tiamuni. The name compares favorably with Tiamat, the Babylonian personification of salt water (the ocean), itself derived from the older Sumerian version. Tiwat was a sun-god of the primordial flood known to the Luvians, a people kindred to the Trojans, in west-coastal Asia Minor.

Tien-Mu

In Chinese myth, a range of mountains far across the Pacific Ocean. According to Churchward, Mu was a mountainous land.

Tien Ti

China's Imperial Library featured a colossal encyclopedia alleged to contain "all knowledge" from ancient times to the 14th century, when additions were still being made. The 4,320-volume set included information about a time when Tien Ti, the Emperor of Heaven—ancient China's equivalent to Zeus—attempted to wipe out sinful mankind with a worldwide deluge: "The planets altered their courses, the Earth fell to pieces, and the waters in its bosom rushed upwards with violence and overflowed the Earth."

Another god, Yeu, taking pity on the drowning human beings, caused a giant turtle to rise up from the bottom of the ocean, then transformed the beast into new land. Remarkably, this version is identical to a creation myth repeated by virtually every tribe north of the Rio Grande River. Native American Indians almost universally refer to their continent as "Turtle Island," after a gigantic turtle raised up from the sea floor by the Great Spirit for their salvation from the Deluge.

Another Chinese text explains how "the pillars supporting the sky crumbled, and the chains from which the Earth was suspended shivered to pieces. Sun, moon, and stars poured down into the northwest, where the sky became low; rivers, seas, and oceans rushed down to the southeast, where the Earth sank. A great conflagration burst out. Flood raged."

(See Pipestone, Asteroid Theory)

Timaeus

The first of Plato's Dialogues describing Atlantis. It is presented as a colloquy between Socrates, Hermocrates, Timaeus, and Kritias (whose own Dialogue immediately followed).

In *Timaeus*, Solon visits the Temple of Neith, in Sais, at the Nile Delta. There, the high priest tells him that 9,000 before, the Athenians saved Mediterranean civilization and Egypt from the invading forces of Atlantis. Located on a large island "beyond the Pillars of Heracles," or Strait of Gibraltar, the kingdom was greater than Libya and Asia Minor combined, and exercised domination over all neighboring islands, together with the "opposite continent." The Atlantean sphere of influence stretched eastward as far as Italy and the Libyan border with Egypt. But in the midst of its war with the Greeks, the island of Atlantis sank "in a single day and night" of earthquakes and floods.

The information presented by *Timaeus* is entirely credible, with most details verified and supported by geology and the traditions of dozens of disparate cultures in the circum-Atlantic region. The only and consistent exception concerns the numerical values applied to Atlantis: they are unmanageably excessive; Atlantis was supposed to have flourished more than 11,000 years ago, its canals were said to be 100 feet deep, and so on. The difficulty is clearly one of translation. The Egyptian high priest who narrated the story spoke in terms of lunar years for the Greeks who knew only solar years. The discrepancy perpetuated itself whenever numerical values were mentioned. Given the common error in translation, the impossible date for Atlantis comes into clearer focus, placing it at the end of the Late Bronze Age, around 1200 B.C.

One of the most revealing details of *Timaeus* is its mention of the "opposite continent," an unmistakable reference to America. Its inclusion proves not only that the ancient Greeks knew what lay on the other side of the Atlantic Ocean 2,000 years before Columbus rediscovered it, but underscores the veracity of Plato's Atlantis account.

Timu

One of five islands among the Maldives at the Equator, located directly south of the Indian subcontinent, named after the lost Pacific civilization of Mu. The Maldives feature numerous stone structures, many of them similar to pyramidal examples in Yucatan, said to have been built long ago by a powerful, seafaring people.

(See Mu, Redin)

Tiri

Flood-god of Peru's Pacific coastal Yurukare Indians. They recounted that their ancestors hid in a mountain cave during two worldwide cataclysms that destroyed a former age. All other humans were killed by a fire that fell from the sky, followed by an all-consuming deluge. Tiri alone, of all the other deities, took pity on the survivors of a sinful mankind by opening the Tree of Life, from which new tribes stepped forth to repopulate the world. His myth refers to the destruction of Lemuria, where a sacred tree cult was venerated.

(See Mu, Tree of Life)

Tir-nan-Og

The Celtic "Island of Youth," a tradition adopted from pre-Celtic Irish in-habitants and associated with Atlantean invaders of Ireland, the Tuatha da Danann. Its philological correspondence to Homer's Ogygia, the biblical Og, the Greeks' Ogygian Flood, and so on, are all transparent references to Atlantis—an identification supported by Tir-nan-Og's eventual demise beneath the sea. In a Scottish version, Tir-nan-Og was sunk when a wicked servant girl, Bera, the springtime-goddess, uncapped its sacred well. The widespread association of "og" with an Atlantis-like catastrophe defines its impact on various peoples.

(See Ogma)

Tistar

In the Iranian cosmogony, the Bundahis, an angel personifying Sirius, the Dog Star, battles with the Devil for mastery of the world, shape-shifting from a man and horse to a bull. In these guises, the angelic Tistar creates a month-long deluge, from which the Evil One's offspring seek refuge in caves. Although the rising waters found them out and drowned them all, their combined venom was so great that it made the ocean salty.

Tistar's assumed forms suggest the conjunction of constellations at the time of the Great Flood, which is clearly depicted as the result of a major celestial disturbance.

(See Asteroid Theory)

Tlaloc

The Aztec rain-god, portrayed in temple art and illustrated books as a bearded man supporting the cross of the sky on his shoulders, like the bearded Atlas. According to chronologer, Neil Zimmerer, Tlaloc was originally an Atlantean monarch who improved mining conditions by providing a fresh water system for workers.

Like Atlas, the Aztec Tlaloc carries the cross of the sky on his shoulders.

Tlavatli

A popular 1920s novel about the survival of an Atlantis princess into then modern times, by the German author, Otto Schultz.

Tlazolteotl

Described in Maya myth as the Earth Mother, "the Woman who sinned before the Deluge." Tlazolteotl signified the seismic upheavals that wracked Aztlan and accompanied the Great Flood. According to the mestizo chronicler Enrique Camargo, Tlazolteotl came from "a very pleasant land, a delectable place, where are many delightful fountains, brooks and flower gardens. This land was called Tamoanchan, the Place of the Fresh, Cool Winds." It was here, at Tamoanchan, that Tlazolteotl committed some offense against the gods, who destroyed the "Place of the Fresh, Cool Winds" with a terrific flood. Sailing with a remnant of her warrior women, she eventually arrived on the shores near Veracruz.

The Aztecs also knew her as Toxi, "Our Grandmother," a reference to their sunken, ancestral homeland.

(See Tamochan)

Tobacco

A variant of the story of the Great Flood familiar to many Native American tribes tells of a long-haired god who was sleeping near a campfire, or star in the night sky. A demon crept up on him, then suddenly pushed his head into the flames. The god's hair instantly caught fire, and he dashed wildly throughout the heavens until the demon tripped him, and he fell to Earth. There he ran around the world, causing terrible conflagrations wherever he went. Finally reaching the ocean, he jumped into the water to extinguish his flaming hair. But in so doing, he caused a massive flood that killed off almost all mankind. Afterward, the survivors discovered that at each place where his burning hairs had fallen to the ground, tobacco was growing. Henceforward, they used it in sacred rituals to commemorate their escape from the deluge.

Comets are traditionally described as "hairy" or "long-haired," and its association here with the Great Flood suggests the Atlantis cataclysm.

(See Pipestone, Asteroid Theory)

Tollan

Topiltzin, the Toltec version of the "Feathered Serpent," was a prince in Tollan, the glittering capital of a magnificent empire located on an island in the middle of the Atlantic Ocean. After its destruction by a natural catastrophe, he led Toltec ancestors to the shoes of Mexico.

Toxi

The Aztec "Grandmother" synonymous with Atlantis.
(See Tlazolteotl)

Tree of Life

A mythic allusion to the human spinal column as the bearer of seven major energy centers known as *chakras*, or spiritual "wheels" in Indian kundalini yoga. The concept originated in Atlantis, with its seven Hesperides, daughters of Atlas, and the golden apples of eternal life they guarded. Its Atlantean roots are also found in the Mayas' Imix Tree, symbolic of the Great Flood from which their ancestors, Ixchel and Itzamna, came from across the Atlantic Ocean. Yucatan's Ceibra was revered for its association with the Imix. In Norse myth, the goddess, Iduna, likewise tended a tree bearing apples filled with immortality.

(See Hesperides)

Tripura

The most famous Indian epic of its kind is the *Mahabharata*. According to the *Encyclopaedia Britannica*, it was based on actual events which took place from the 15th to 11th centuries B.C., the same time parameter framing the zenith and fall of Atlantis. Beginning in the *Drona Parva* (Section XI), the destruction of Tripura is set forth. It is described as a wealthy and powerful oceanic kingdom, whose eastern shore faced the coast of Africa. The *Mahabharata* calls it "the Triple City" after its trident presented to the residents by Shiva, the island's creator, as a national emblem.

The city itself was designed by a Maya "of great intelligence," who raised two more, configuring each one on a massive, opulent scale and "shaped like a wheel [*Chakrastham*, Sanskrit for "circular"]. And they consisted of houses and mansions and lofty walls and porches. And though teeming with lordly palaces close to each other, yet the streets were wide and spacious. And they were adorned with diverse mansions and gateways. Each of these cities, again, had a separate king."

Tripura's Bronze Age time frame, location in the near Atlantic Ocean, circular design, luxury, and Poseidon-like trident could only describe Plato's Atlantis.

Tsuma

Familiar to the Cuna Indians of Venezuela as the fair-haired survivor of a great deluge that wiped out the rest of his people in the Atlantic Ocean during the deep past, Tsuma belonged to the "Feathered Serpent" accounts known all along the eastern coast of the Americas—a clear reference to culture-bearers from Atlantis.

Tsunokiri

A ceremony conducted from mid-October to early November at the Kasuga Taisha in Nara, Japan. Sacred bucks are lassoed by priests, who carefully saw off the antlers of the animals corralled at the shrine. As Churchward observed, deer were the holy symbols of mankind's emergence from Mu, the Pacific Ocean civilization destroyed probably between the 18th and 16th century B.C. Deer symbolism likewise plays a central role in Tibetan Boen-Buddhism, with its roots deep in traditions of Mu. In the Japanese practice, trimming of the antlers, which gradually grow back, commemorates the death of Mu but also its partial resurgence in prehistoric Japan.

That the annual Tsunokiri should take place in Nara is particularly significant, because the city is generally believed to be the oldest one in the country. Moreover, the Tsunokiri service between mid-October to early November coincides with the final destruction of Atlantis, suggesting the Lemurian and Atlantean cataclysms were combined or somewhat confused in Japanese tradition.

(See Mu)

Tuaoi Stone

The "Fire Stone" allegedly represented the epitome of Atlantean crystal technology, because it was able to harness and direct the natural energies of the physical universe for material and spiritual purposes. "It was in the form of a six-sided figure," according to Edgar Cayce:

> ...in which the light appeared as the means of communication between infinity and finite; or the means whereby there were the communications with those forces from the outside [outer space?]. Later, this came to mean that from which the energies radiated, as of the center from which there were the radial activities guiding the various forms of transition or travel through those periods of activity of the Atlanteans.

A special structure housed the Tuaoi:

> The building above the stone was oval, or a dome, wherein there could be or was the rolling back, so that the activity of the stone was received from the sun's rays or from the stars; the concentrating of the energies that emanate from bodies that are on fire themselves—with the elements that are found in the earth's atmosphere. The concentration through the prisms or glass, as would be called in the present, was in such a manner that it acted upon the instruments that were connected with various modes of travel, through induction methods—that made much the character of control through radio vibrations or directions would be in the present day; through the manner of the force that was impelled from the stone acted upon the motivating forces in the crafts themselves.
>
> There was the preparation so that when the dome was rolled back there might be little or no hindrance in the application directly to the various crafts that were to be impelled through space, whether in the radius of the visioning of the one eye, as it might be called, or whether directed underwater or under other elements or through other elements. The preparation of this stone was in the hands only of the initiates at the time.

Cayce spoke of "a crystal room" in Atlantis, where "the tenets and the truths or the lessons that were proclaimed by those that had descended to give the messages as from on High" were received by the initiates of a mystery cult. They "interpreted the messages that were received through the crystals." Atlantean adepts achieved levels of proficiency in all the transformational arts and mastery of psychic powers through their understanding and use of crystals, a lost science of the paranormal only just beginning to be reclaimed in our times, almost instinctually, it would seem, through growing popular interest in the spiritual qualities of quartz crystal. (Cayce: 2072-10 F.32 7/22/42; 440-5 M.23 12/20/33; 3004-1 F.55 5/15/43; 440-5 M.23 12/20/33)

Possible confirmation of his statements describing the "Fire Stone," the name Cayce gave to the Tuaoi, occurs in the languages of several peoples directly influenced by Atlantis. For example, the Mayan word *tuuk* means "fiery." Cayce said "the records [describing the Tuaoi] were carried to what is now Yucatan, in America, where these stones are now."

On the other side of the world, the Sumerian counterpart to the Mayas' seafaring culture-bearer, Kukulcan, the "Feathered Serpent," was Utnapishtim, another deluge hero who rode out the watery destruction of a former age in an ark. He belongs to the oldest Mesopotamian mythic traditions, which also include a mysterious, sacred object called "the Stone that Burns," "the Fire Stone," precisely the same term used by Cayce. Remarkably, its original Sumerian word is *Napa-Tu*, from which the English word *naphtha* derives through Persian.

Roughly midway between the Mayas of America and the Sumerians of Mesopotamia lie the Canary Islands off the coast of North Africa. Until their extermination by the Spaniards, beginning in the 15th century, indigenous inhabitants who called themselves the Guanches likewise told of a catastrophic flood; well they might, situated as they were in the immediate vicinity of lost Atlantis. The Guanche word for "fire" was *tava*; through phonetic evolution, a standard linguistic process, "tava" may be traced back to the sound-value from which it originally sprang: *tua* or *tuoh*.

According to James Churchward, the leading symbol of Mu—the Pacific counterpart and contemporary civilization of Atlantis—was a T-sign, pronounced *Ta-oo*, signifying the emergence of the island from the sea. Several Polynesian folk traditions speak of the wide use of crystals for high spiritual purposes on a Lemurian kind of lost kingdom. Australian aboriginals still refer to its sunken towers of crystal. In central Ireland, a white crystalline granite omphalos sculpted with patterns suggesting energy forms is known as "the Turoe Stone." Although conventional scholars speculate about its Celtic identity, the Turoe Stone suggests an earlier Bronze Age provenance.

These widely disparate peoples, separated by vast distances and many centuries, never knew each other. Yet, they shared common accounts of a world-class flood associated with a "fire stone" described, despite the otherwise complete dissimilarity of their languages, by the same word-value: *Tuuk, Napa-Tu, Tava (Tua, Tuoh), Turoe, Ta-oo*—cultural-linguistic variants of Edgar Cayce's Tuaoi.

(See Cayce, Crystal Skull)

Tuatha da Danann

Variously translated as "Followers of the Goddess Danu," the Celtic divine patroness of water, or the "Magicians of the Almoners" (those who dispense sacred wisdom), the Tuatha da Danann are described in medieval Irish chronicles, such as the *Annals of Clonmacnoise*, as a "sea people." Encyclopedist Anna Franklin states that Danu was an Indo-European water-god, appropriate for an Atlantean sea people. According to O'Brien, they arrived on the south coast of Ireland in 1202 B.C., closely coinciding with the final destruction of Atlantis; its late Bronze Age date was not known in O'Brien's time (1834).

The Tuatha da Danann's Atlantean identity is further emphasized by a philological resemblance of their name to the Tuaoi, the sacred stone of Atlantis. They may have represented the class of initiates responsible for its care or operation, as implied by O'Brien's interpretation of their name as "almoners." He points out that the Tuatha da Danann practiced the same religion as the Fomorach, an earlier Atlantean people who settled in Ireland at the end of the 4th millennium B.C. He competently argues that the strange, obelisk-like towers still found in Ireland were erected by the Tuatha da Danann, citing the 10th-century *Book of Leccan*, which tells of "the Tuathan tower." Ruins of several such towers are found, appropriately enough, in County Roscommon, at Moy-tura, where the Tuatha da Danann decisively defeated their immediate predecessors, the Fir-Bolg. Known more correctly as Moye-tureadh, the battle-area is translated as "the Field of Towers." Edgar Cayce mentioned that the Tuaoi stone was set up in a special tower. Perhaps those erected in Ireland by the Tuatha da Danann ("Keepers of the Tuaoi Stone"?) were raised after their prototype in Atlantis. Ireland's Turoe Stone, a granite omphalos, may signify a correlation between Cayce's Tuaoi and the Tuatha da Danann.

Interestingly, the three major cataclysms of Atlantis with their attendant migrations in the late fourth and third millennia B.C. and Late Bronze Age are respectively paralleled in Old Irish tradition of the Fomorach, Fir-Bolg, and Tuatha da Danann.

(See Fomorach, Fir-Bolg, Tuoai Stone)

Tulum

The Mayas' only walled ceremonial center is a Late Classic site overlooking the Yucatan coast. Its walls feature sculpted images of the Diving God, representing survivors jumping into the water to escape the destruction of Valum. This was the unseen Atlantic kingdom from which Votan—one of the Mayas' overseas culture heroes—arrived on the coast of Yucatan. Tulum was raised to commemorate his arrival, which signaled a new dawn for Mesoamerican civilization. There is, moreover, a philological resonance between "Tulum" and "Valum." Both appear to be native versions, like the Toltecs' "Tollan," of the Greek "Atlantis." Votan, the Atlantean culture-bearer, is perhaps symbolized by the Diving God himself.

(See Wotan)

The Maya ceremonial city of Tulum, on the Yucatan shore.

Tundum

According to chronologer Neil Zimmerer, Tundum was a Lemurian prince who perished along with his father in the Great Flood.

(See Lemuria, Mungan Ngaua)

Tutulxiu

The Mayas' "Land of Abundance," or "the Bountiful," original oceanic homeland of their white-skinned ancestors, who arrived en masse in a fleet of ships "carving twelve paths through the sea," according to their cosmological book, the *Popol Vuh*.

Tutulxiu is an obvious recollection of Atlantis and the appearance its culture-bearers on the shores of Yucatan.

(See Ah-Auab, Halach-Unicob)

Tyche

An Atlantis, a Hyade, daughter of Atlas by Arethusa.

Ualuvu levu

In Pacific island myth, a cataclysmic flood that occurred after the beginning of time, engulfing some territories, while sparing the mountain peaks of others. The deluge was said to have carried an ancestral people from their homeland at Nakauvadra throughout all parts of Fiji. Interestingly, Degei, an angry spirit that caused the Ualuvu levu, took the form of a serpent in the sky, an allusion to a destructive comet found in many other cultures around the world.

Uassu

Deluge hero of several Amazon tribes—the Abederys, Katauhys, and Parrarys—in eastern Brazil. Tradition states, "Once on a time, folk heard a great rumbling above and below ground [exploding meteors and earthquakes]. The sun and moon turned red [ash fall]. Our forefathers heard a roar and saw darkness ascending from the Earth to the sky [volcanism], accompanied by thunder and heavy rains which blotted out the Earth and made day into night. The waters rose very high, until the Earth was sunk beneath them." Uassu and his wife alone survived when they climbed to the top of a tall tree.

(See Asteroid Theory)

U Mamae

The Quiche Mayas' *Chilam Balam* reports that "the wise men, the Nahuales, the chiefs and leaders, called *U Mamae* ["the Old Men"], extending their sight over the four parts of the world and over all that is beneath the sky, and, finding no obstacle, came from the other part of the ocean, from where the sun rises, a place called Patulan. Together these tribes came from the other part of the sea, from the east, from Patulan." The civilizing mission of these U Mamae and their arrival over the Atlantic Ocean leave little doubt that they came from the same island capital described by Plato, a conclusion broadly underscored by the obvious philological resemblance between the Quiche "Patulan" and the Greek "Atlantis."

U-Mu

Literally "He of Mu," Tahitian for "high priest," an apparent linguistic heirloom from the sunken Pacific Ocean kingdom of Mu.

(See Mu)

Unnefer

"He Who Is Continually Happy," an epitaph for the Egyptian Osiris in his role as the god of resurrection, a concept originating in Atlantis. The final scene of *The Book of Gates*, an illustrated scared text inscribed on the alabaster sarcophagus of Pharaoh Sety I, at Abydos, depicts the distended body of Osiris encircling Sekhet-aaru, the Egyptian "Atlantis."

According to Tibetan records examined by James Churchward around the turn of the 20th century, Unnefer, having been educated in the Navel of the World mysteries, undertook a worldwide mission to spread his own interpretation of the cult. Churchward concluded that the Osirian concept of survival after death was misunderstood and degraded by the Egyptians into the lucrative business of mummification. Unnefer is described in Egyptian myth as "a world traveler."

Unu-Pachacuti

Literally, "The World Overturned by Water," the Inca version of the Great Flood, associated with the penultimate Atlantean destruction in the early 17th century B.C. and the coming of a prominent culture-bearer, Thonapa.

(See Thonapa, Viracocha)

Unuycit

Mayan for the Great Flood that destroyed a former "world" from which the founding-fathers of Mesoamerican Civilization sailed to Yucatan.

Ushnu

The central plaza, today's Plaza de Armas, of Cuzco, Peru, the Incas' capital and "Navel of the World," where ceremonies were held to commemorate the Great Flood. A variety of offerings—water, milk, fermented cactus juice, beer, etc.—was poured into the Ushnu at the center of a ceremonial area known as the *Haucaypata*. Ushnu was a poetic metaphor signifying the ability to consume prodigious amounts of liquid, and referred to someone drinking copious amounts of alcohol without getting drunk. It was into this ritual hole in the ground that the waters of the Deluge were said to have drained after the arrival of the Ayar-aucca, who brought civilization to the Andes in the ancient past. The Ushnu was believed to be the entrance to the sacred underworld.

Precisely the same significance was attached by the Etruscans to holes dug into ground at the precise midpoints of their cities, such as Tarquinia or Populonia. Each hole was referred to as a *mundus*, a feature for the ritual deposit of holy water commemorating the Deluge. Identical offerings to a shared purpose were made at the Greek Hydrophoria and by the Phoenicians at Hierapolis, in Syria. Among the Anasasi, Hopi, and other native peoples of the American Southwest, ritual players in an ancestral ceremony were doused with water, as they tried to climb up out of an underground chamber known as a *kiva*. They symbolized the "emergence" of survivors from the Great Flood.

The vast cultural and geographical differences separating the Inca, North American Indian, Etruscan, Greek, and Phoenician participants in these sacred dramas contrasts with their close similarity, which may only be explained in terms of an actual experience shared independently, but in common by them all.

There may be more than a phonetic relationship between the Inca *Ushnu* and the uniquely oval Maya pyramid *Uxmal* (pronounced *ush-mal*), even though these languages have nothing else in common. Perhaps both shared an Atlantean word describing the Deluge that destroyed Atlantis.

(See Ayar-aucca, Etruscans, Hydrophoria, Navel of the World, Uxmal)

Urashima-Taro

According to Japanese folklore, a boy whose compassion for an afflicted turtle saved its life. In gratitude, the creature took him to the bottom of the sea, where he was the guest of friendly spirits in a magnificent palace, the center of a once-powerful kingdom, before its tragic demise beneath the waves. As a parting gift, he is given the Peach of Immortality.

Plants or fruits (particularly peaches) are common elements in Asian, as well as Western myths about sunken, antediluvian civilizations. The very old legend of Urashima-Taro is today widely regarded as a reference to the lost kingdom of Lemuria.

(See Mu)

Uti-Mu

Site of an early landing by racially alien culture-bearers among the Maldive Islands, in the Indian Ocean, at the equator. The name derives from their sunken homeland, the lost Pacific civilization of Mu.

(See Mu, Redin)

Utnapishtim

Flood hero of the Babylonian Deluge. Warned in advance of the coming disaster by Anki, the god of wisdom, Utnapishtim built a ship for his family and livestock. When the flood came, they rode out the raging seas until their vessel finally came to rest on Mount Nizir, in Mesopotamia.

The Babylonians traced their direct descent from Utnapishim. He is associated with the Late fourth-millennium B.C. geologic upheavals which prompted mass migrations of Atlanteans from their oceanic homeland throughout the world.

Uxmal

"Thrice-built" is the designation of a ceremonial center raised by the Mayas in Yucatan. Local legends recount that its oval pyramid was constructed by a dwarf sorcerer after a great flood; hence, its name, "Pyramid of the Magician." The elliptical design was intended to simulate the cosmic egg, repeated in a frieze on its flanks, where it is shown regurgitated from the mouth of a serpent. The same image appears some 1,500 airline-miles away, atop a high ridge in the Ohio Valley, at the Great Serpent Mound.

A proper perspective of Ohio's Great Serpent Mound, the emblem of Atlantean spirituality, may only be obtained from an aerial vantage point.

An identical motif was emblematic of the Pelasgians, a "sea people" from Atlantis, who brought civilization to the Eastern Mediterranean. Even earlier, the egg-serpent symbol originated with the Atlantean Navel of the World mystery cult. Its practitioners regarded the snake as a metaphor for the immortality of the human soul, based on the serpent's ability to slough off its old skin for a new one. The egg was the omphalos, the "Navel Stone," signifying life perpetually reborn from the self-renewing demiurge implicit in the snake.

The recurrence of this imagery throughout Atlantis' former sphere of influence (the Atlantean kingdom of Azaes dominated Yucatan) implies that the tenets of its chief mystery cult survived and flourished among the Mayas, whose Uxmal pyramid embodies its esoteric symbols. The monument's legendary dwarf is perhaps reflected in the Old World Cabiri. According to the Carthaginian writer Sanchoniathon, these were gods descended from the Rephaim, or Titans, "that is, Atlas and his kin," and worshiped in sacred mysteries at Samothrace, Thebes, Macedonia, Lemnos, Phrygia, together with parts of the Peloponnesus (Spence, 174). The Cabiri themselves were envisioned as dwarves, great builders, and metallurgists armed with hammer tools, through which they were connected to Hephaestus, the divine artificer.

A pre-deluge antiquity associated with the Cabiri and the similarity of their cult to the Osirian mysteries underscores an Atlantean provenance. These are the same esoteric principles sculpted in serpentine symbolism on the flanks of

The massive stairway fronting Uxmal's Pyramid of the Magician.

Uxmal's foremost structure. Yucatan's "Pyramid of the Magician," so unique among all the other sacred architecture of Maya Civilization, appears to have been built by descendants of cult-bearing immigrants from Atlantis—descendants who preserved and monumentalized the Cabiri tenets of spiritual regeneration for many centuries after the Atlantis catastrophe.

The entire ceremonial complex is oriented to various risings and settings of Venus, the "star" associated with Kukulcan, the fair-haired "Feathered Serpent," who brought civilization to Yucatan from across the Atlantic Ocean. This symbolic celestial alignment accents the post-deluge, Atlantean character of Uxmal's founders and users.

(See Kukulcan, Navel of the World, Venus)

Vediouis

According to the Sumerian scholar Neil Zimmerer, Vediouis was a prince, who overthrew his aged father to become an early king of Atlantis, then suffering from an acute labor shortage. Vediouis attempted to solve the national dilemma by large-scale slave raids into Europe and Africa. These criminal acts were opposed by an Indo-Aryan leader of the Aegean World, Poseidon, much later deified as the Greek sea-god. He led a successful invasion of Atlantis, killing Vediouis in combat.

Venus

It was the personal symbol of the most important Atlantean culture-bearers and a telling link between the Old and New Worlds through the story of Atlantis. The Evening Star belonged to Osiris, "the Westerner" from Aalu, who was on a civilizing mission throughout the world. Inanna, the Babylonian "Ishtar," was a Sumerian goddess who carried the Tablets of Destiny from Atu to Mesopotamia. She was represented by a twilight Venus in the center of a six-rayed circle, recalling the Atlantean sacred numeral of female energy and the divisional zones of Atlantis itself.

Quetzalcoatl, the "Feathered Serpent" founding-father of Mesoamerican Civilization, was symbolized by Venus. In his guise as Ehecatl, he was represented in Aztec art as a man emerging from a tsunami at Panco, the Vera Cruz port where he was said to have landed from his home kingdom across the Atlantic Ocean. As *Ce Acatl*, his Atlantean identity becomes clearer still. Plato described in *Kritias* how the kings of Atlantis performed bloody sacrifices over a sacred column located at the center of their most holy precinct in the Temple of Poseidon. This column, inscribed with the ancestral laws of the land, embodied the cultic concept of Atlas, who supported the sky on his shoulders. Quetzalcoatl was likewise often represented holding up the heavens. But as Ce Acatl, the planet Venus, a pillar cult was dedicated to him at the Aztec capital of Tenochtitlan. At the very center of the city was erected a free-standing column over which bloody sacrifices were conducted. This column had the highly Atlantean name of "In the Midst of the Heavens."

The association of Venus with some primordial culture spread to the North American Plains Indians. The Iowas' story of the Deluge begins, "At first, all men lived on an island where the day-star is born."

The Greek Hesperus, from whom evening vespers derives, was synonymous for Venus as it appears shortly after sunset; in other words, the Far West. According to Hesiod, the fifth-century B.C. Greek mythologist, he was the brother of Atlas and founder of Italy, known originally as *Hesperia* (Virgil, *The Aeneid*). His myth conforms with Plato's Atlantis account, wherein Italy was specifically mentioned as the Etruscan extent of Atlantean power in Europe. The non-Platonic myth of Hesperus accentuates his Atlantean identity. It described his sudden disappearance in a "great tempest" (a volcanic eruption), while standing at the summit of Mount Atlas, as he observed the motions of the stars. The Atlantean connection is again stressed by his daughter, Hesperis, also associated with the Evening Star: She bore a trio of daughters to Atlas, the Hesperides, three additional Atlantises.

Classical European tradition associated the coming of civilization with Venus in the West (Osiris, Inanna, Ishtar, Hesperus), where it was seen as the Evening Star. Pre-Columbian myth connected the arrival of civilization with Venus in the East (Ce Acatl), where it appears as the Morning Star. The source of those widely geographically separate but fundamentally similar arrivals lay on a lost island in the mid-Atlantic, the Hesperides of Atlantis, between the Old and New Worlds.

Vimana

A flying machine capable of carrying human beings plus cargo. Examples were allegedly common at some early period in Atlantis, where they were invented. Evidence for Vimanas is found in abundance throughout Hindu literature. Its name, "That Which Measures," may define the Vimana's function as a device "measuring" territory over which it flies.

As David Hatcher Childress explains in his own research of the subject:

> Ancient Indian texts on Vimanas are so numerous it would take several books to relate what they have to say. The *Vaimanika Sasta*

[sometimes spelled *Vimanika Shastra* or *Vymaanika-Shaastra*], perhaps the most important ancient text on Vimanas, was first reported to have been found in 1918 in the Baroda Royal Sanskrit Library. Swami Dayananda Saraswati in his comprehensive treatise on the Rig veda, dated 1875, references the *Vaimanaik Sastra* in his commentary, as well as other manuscripts on Vimanas. The *Vaimanaik Sastra* refers to about ninety seven past works and authorities, of which twenty works deal with the mechanism of aerial flying machines.

None of these sources claim Indian origins for the Vimana, but assign its creation to a remote period of earlier civilization before the Great Flood. From descriptions such as these, Childress and other researchers conclude the device was invented in Atlantis.

Hopi accounts of the flood hero, Kuskurza, tell how a pre-deluge, Atlantean-like people "made a *Pauwvota*, and in their creative power made it fly through the air. On this many of the people flew to a big city, attacked it, and returned so fast no one knew where they came from. Soon the people of many cities and countries were making Patuwvotas and flying in them to attack one another."

In the Boen religion of pre-Buddhist Tibet, monarchs during ancient times were said to have had a power that enabled them to fly through the sky from one kingdom to the next. They called it the *dmu dag*, *rmu tha*g, or "The Cord of Mu." Remarkably, here is preserved not only the memory of prehistoric aviation, but an Atlantean contemporary, the lost Pacific civilization of Mu.

Edgar Cayce, who was presumably unfamiliar with Tibetan traditions, Hopi myth, or Hindu literature describing Vimanas, often spoke of aircraft in Atlantis. He said the Atlanteans possessed "things of transportation, the aeroplane, as called today, but then as ships of the air, for they sailed not only in the air but in other elements also" (Cayce 2437-1 1/23/41).

Many Atlantologists regard Indian and Hopi stories of Vimanas as early science fiction. To them, Cayce's statements about airships in Atlantis were influenced by contemporary fantasy writers. Others point out his more convincing description of Atlantis in so many additional details, arguing that he may have been accurate here, too. And they find it difficult to dismiss the surprisingly large number of admittedly authentic ancient Indian texts which mostly depict Vimanas in unadorned, straightforward language.

There were certainly no aircraft in the Late Bronze Age, when Atlantis reached the zenith of its material greatness. During their life-and-death struggle in the eastern Mediterranean, the Atlanteans could have certainly used a squadron of Vimanas to stave off defeat. If such machines ever existed during ancient times (which is unlikely in the extreme), they were utterly forgotten by subsequent ages, except in Indian literature and Hopi and Tibetan myth. The earliest suggested period for Atlantis, and out of which it appears to have evolved, was the Neolithic. It is difficult to imagine any relationship between megalithic and aeronautical technologies.

(See Cayce, Mu)

Viracocha

The Incas' leading culture hero, believed to have escaped a world-class deluge that obliterated everyone else in his kingdom. He hid in the Cave of Refuge, emerging to found Andean Civilization. In a later variant of his myth, Viracocha rose from the depths of Lake Titicaca and recreated humans by breathing life into great stones lying about, a process that resulted in the pre-Inca city of Tiahuanaco. His action is similar to the transformation of stones into a post-deluge population achieved by the Greek deluge hero, Deucalion, suggesting a shared flood tradition. Viracocha's name, "Sea Foam," implies the bow wave of an arriving ship. He was described as fair-skinned, red-haired, and robed in a long garment decorated with a red flower motif. Viracocha taught the natives everything they needed to build the first Andean civilization, then sailed away from Peruvian shores into the west and was never seen again. It would appear that a culture-bearer associated with the Atlantis catastrophe around 2100 B.C. may have moved on to Lemuria after making his mark in Bolivia and Peru.

The mere appearance of Francisco Pizarro and his Conquistadors in South America during 1531 caused widespread confusion among the Incas. Emperor Atahualpa and his people were unsure if these bearded white men in the possession of magical technology were descendants of the beneficent Viracocha. The Spanish soon enlightened them on that account by kidnapping and executing Atahualpa, looting the Inca temples of their gold, demonizing their religion, and dismantling their empire. The paralysis that had gripped the Incas at the sight of Pizarro was identical to the Aztecs' disabling uncertainty when confronted by Hernan Cortez, who they imagined might be their own white-skinned culture hero, Quetzalcoatl, the "Feathered Serpent."

(See Quetzalcoatl)

The Voguls

A Finno-Urgic-speaking people residing on either side of Russia's Ural Mountains, whose tradition of the Great Deluge tells how the world was engulfed in waves of boiling hot water, suggesting a volcanic cataclysm.

von Humbolt, Alexander

Famous in the early 19th century as an explorer, the author of a 30-volume encyclopedia of the natural sciences, and organizer of the first international scientific conference, von Humbolt is remembered today as the founder of ecology and the modern earth sciences. Across the more than 6,000 miles that von Humbolt traveled through Central and South America, numerous flood traditions he learned first-hand from native speakers made him a firm believer in the historical reality of Plato's Atlantis, which he identified with America itself. Von Humbolt is but one of the important scientific personalities who lend Atlantology significant credibility through their sympathetic understanding of the investigation.

Vue

An extinct race of fair-haired foreigners who passed thorough Melanesia in the wake of a cataclysmic flood. Described in folk tradition as the possessors of powerful *mana*, or magic energy, the Vue are believed to have built the megalithic structures scattered throughout the Pacific islands.

Machu Picchu from the Inca gate.

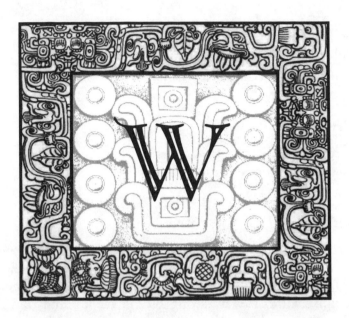

Wai-ta-hanui

New Zealand's oldest known tribe, said to have arrived more than 2,000 years ago. Of the original 200 tribes that dominated the islands, only 140 mixed descendants were still alive in 1988. The Waitahanui were supposed to have been prodigious mariners who navigated the world in oceangoing sailing ships, and raised colossal stone structures, of which the Kaimanawa Wall is the last surviving example. Also known as the *Waitaha*, or *Urukehu*, the "People of the West" were fair-skinned, hazel-eyed redheads, who came from a splendid kingdom overwhelmed by the sea.

(See Mu, The Kaimanawa Wall)

Wai-Tepu

The Brazilian Indians' forefather, who arrived long ago after his island home in the Atlantic Ocean caught fire. As he and his family sailed away to South America, their burning homeland collapsed under the sea. His name, "Mountain of the Sun," implies volcanic Mount Atlas. Wai-Tepu's story suggests the final destruction of Atlantis.

Wakt'cexi

In Native American oral traditions of the Upper Midwest, a horned giant who gathered up survivors of the Great Flood and carried them to safety on the eastern shores of Turtle Island (North America).

(See Man Mounds, Wilmington Long Man, Wolf Clan)

Wallanganda

A monarch who built the first cities in the Lemurian kingdom of Baralku, according to chronologer Neil Zimmerer.

Wallum Ollum

The "Red Record" is a preserved oral tradition of the Lenni Lenape, or Delaware Indians. It tells of the Talega—"strangers" or "foreigners"—who arrived on New England shores after a deluge overwhelmed their homeland across the Atlantic Ocean: "All of this was long ago, in the land beyond the great flood (book 1). Flooding and flooding, filling and filling, smashing and smashing, drowning and drowning" (book 2, line 7).

Led by Nanabush to the North American coast, the survivors formed a new state with their "Great Sun" as monarch. He ruled over "lesser suns," nobles, "honored men," and the vast majority of native peasants and laborers contemptuously known as "stinkers." The Talega eventually intermarried with these "stinkers," and their "sun kingdom" dissolved into chaos, leaving behind impressive earthworks in abandoned ceremonial centers. Thus, the so-called "mound builders" are depicted as Atlanteans (the Talega) by the Delaware Indians.

The same story is related by a Shawnee dance ceremoniously performed in Oklahoma forest groves. The Mayas' flood hero, as described in the cosmological epic, the *Popol Vuh*, arrived in Yucatan following a deluge that overwhelmed his island kingdom across the Atlantic Ocean. It was called *Valum*, which appears to be a Mayan contraction of *Wallum Ollum*—doubtless one and the same location.

(See Nanabush, Wotan)

Washo Deluge Story

The Washo are a native California people who recounted an early golden period of their ancestors. For many generations, they lived in happiness on a far away island, at the center of which was a tall, stone temple containing a representation of the sea-god. His likeness was so huge, its head touched the top of "the dome." This part of the Washo account is found, perhaps surprisingly, in the *Encyclopaedia Judaica*, and virtually reproduces Plato's description in *Kritias* of the Temple of Poseidon at the center of Atlantis, where a colossus of the sea-god was "so tall his head touched the roof." It seems no less remarkable that the Washo, whose material culture never exceeded the construction of a tepee, would have even known about an architectural feature as sophisticated as a dome.

Their deluge story tells that violent earthquakes caused the mountains of their ancestral island to catch fire. The flames rose so high they melted the stars, which fell to Earth, spreading the conflagration around the world. Some fell into the sea, and caused a universal flood that extinguished the flames, but threatened humanity with extinction. The Washo ancestors tried to escape the rising tide by climbing to the top of the sea-god's temple, but were changed into stones. This transformation is reminiscent of the Greek Deluge, in which Deucalion and his wife, Pyrrha, threw stones over their shoulders; as the stones struck the ground, they turned into men and women—an inverse of the Washo version.

Wegener, Alfred L.

Austrian founder of the continental drift hypothesis, which transformed established notions of geology more than any other theory in modern times. While Wegener was advocating his ideas in the early 20th century, he was no less ridiculed by his scientific contemporaries for insisting that Plato's Atlantis was a victim of the same violent earth changes associated with plate tectonics.

Wekwek

In the North American Tuleyone Indian deluge account, Wekwek, in the guise of a falcon, was sent by a sorcerer to steal fire from heaven. But the gods pursued Wekwek, who, in his fright, dropped a burning star to Earth, where it sparked a worldwide conflagration. The Coyote-god, Olle, extinguished the flames with a universal flood.

The celestial catastrophe associated with the destruction of Atlantis appears in this Tuleyone account.

Westernesse

One of three versions of J.R.R. Tolkien's Atlantis.
(See Numinor)

Wesucechak

Alaska's Cree Indians of the Subarctic Circle preserve traditions about a catastrophic flood that destroyed most of the world long ago. Wesucechak was a shape-shifting shaman who escaped the flood he caused when he got into a fight with the water-monsters who murdered his brother, Misapos.

Widapokwi

The Yavapai Indians of the American Southwest preserve a folk memory of Lemurian origins in their most important mythic figure, the Creatrix, or "Female

Maker." Long ago, all humanity dwelt in an underworld, from which the colossal Tree of Life grew to pierce the sky. But when the time came for men and women to emerge into the outer world, they neglected to close the hole through which they passed after them. The ocean gushed out, flooding the whole world to drown most of mankind. Widapokwi survived by riding out the cataclysm in a "hollow log," in which she had provisioned herself with a great number of animals. After the waters subsided, she used these creatures to repopulate the Earth.

Mu was synonymous for the Tree of Life.

(See Tree of Life)

Wigan

As told by the Ifugao, a Philippine people residing high in the cordillera of Luzon, Wigan and his sister, Bugan, were lone survivors of the Great Flood. The Ifugao version is similar to Babylonian and other accounts which describe an unusual period of extreme drought immediately prior to the deluge, accompanied by a sudden darkness, the result of volcanic eruptions and/or meteorite collisions.

Wilmington's Long Man, in the south of England, has Atlantean counterparts in North and South America.

Wigan and Bugan, as in accounts of flood heroes everywhere, floated safely to the top of the world's tallest mountain. But here its name suggests the destruction of Mu: *Amuyao*.

Wilmington Long Man

The colossal, chalk outline of a man apparently pushing his way through a portal in the green side of a hill outside Bristol, in the south of England. He has been tentatively dated by archaeologists to the Iron Age, although evidence of nearby flint manufacturing from the late fourth millennium B.C. suggests a Neolithic provenance. Like Britain's other hill-figures—the Cerne-Abbas Giant and Uffington Horse—the Long Man's Atlantean identity is implied by the horned helmet with which he was originally adorned before it was obliterated on orders of churchmen convinced it made him seem demonic.

A comparable figure is found on the other side of the world, in southern Wisconsin. On a hill in Greenfield Township, outside Baraboo, the Man Mound is still revered by Ho Chunk and other tribal peoples as Wakt'cexi, a horn-headed giant who saved their ancestors from the Great Flood. Resemblance between these two effigies is unique, in the world, and demands comparison. Under the Atlantic Ocean that separates them lies their common source: the sunken civilization of Atlantis, from which survivors spread in both directions, leaving the same image in England and America, where folk memory still tells of survivors from a catastrophic deluge.

(See Cerne-Abbas Giant, Man Mounds, Uffington Horse, Wolf Clan)

Wintun Deluge Story

This native California tribe told how a shaman stole the magic flute of Katkochila, the sky-god. With this instrument, he could make his people the most powerful in the whole world. Katkochila, in a rage, showered the Earth with fire from heaven, but doused the conflagration before humanity was utterly exterminated.

(See Asteroid Theory)

Wisaka

The first ancestor of the Sac and Fox Indians, who so offended a pair of powerful Manitous, or great spirits, they set the whole world on fire. But Wisaka escaped by finding refuge atop a mountain. Still intent on destroying him, the Manitous drowned the Earth in a universal flood. Once again, Wisaka survived, this time in "a big canoe."

(See Asteroid Theory)

Whishaw, Ellen

U.S.-born director of Spain's prestigious Anglo-Spanish-American School of Archaeology during the post-World War I era. Whishaw was widely respected by her peers as one of the outstanding archaeologists of her time until she went public with the results of her findings after extensive excavation of a pre-classical site near the Andalusian town of Niebla. She declared that the evidence clearly defined an important cultural impact made there by civilizers from Atlantis, who established a rich colony in southern Spain.

(See Gadeiros)

Witana

A Lemurian monarch who developed mining and the damming of rivers, according to chronologist Neil Zimmerer.

Wiyot Deluge Story

A California tribal account of the creator, Gudatri-Gakwitl ("Above-Old-Man"), who sent a worldwide flood to extinguish mankind and most animals.

Condor survived to find only his sister, some birds, and a single raccoon were left alive. A new humanity was born from the incestuous relationship of Condor and his sister. Wiyot tradition mandated that a chief take his sister as bride, a custom reminiscent of the Egyptian pharaohs, if only ritually, to commemorate his people's descent from the ancestral pair that escaped the flood.

Wolf Clan

The Worak, a tribal history of Wisconsin's Ho Chunk or Winnebago Indians, tells of their ancestral Wolf Clan, whose leader dwelt in "a great lodge" on an island in the ocean where the sun rises. This progenitor had 10 sons, one of whom came to Turtle Island (North America) with his fellow clansmen and women. In time, they intermarried with the natives and established four clans: the White Wolf, Green Hair, Gray Wolf, and Black Wolf. The quartet was so named in association with the four cardinal directions which streamed outward from their old oceanic homeland at the center of the world. Their first child born in the new land was called "Wave," after the bow-wave of the vessel that brought them from the great lodge. Likewise, Plato told how the sea-god, Poseidon, sired 10 sons to become the kings of Atlantis.

In an alternate version of the Winnebago myth, "the original Wolf brothers appeared from the bottom of the ocean," where their ancestral island had been swallowed up in a terrible deluge. As the disturbed seas began to calm down, the *Wakt'cexi*, a water-spirit, arose from the waves, wearing a horned helmet, and led the survivors across the ocean on improvised rafts to the new land. Thereafter, all the Wolf clans were known as "water clans." Anthropologist Paul Radin writes, "There may be some significance in the origin legends of some of the clans which claim that they came from over the sea, but it is utterly impossible to determine whether we are here dealing with a myth pure and simple, or with a vague memory of some historical happening."

But as though to confirm the Ho Chunk story of the horned *Wakt'cexi*, two effigy mounds of gigantic proportions were found in Wisconsin. They represent the water-spirit that led the Wolf Clan ancestors of the Winnebago from the Great Flood. One of the geoglyphs still exists, although in mutilated form, on the slope of a hill in Greenfield Township, outside Baraboo. Road construction cut off the legs below his knees around 1901, but the hill-figure is otherwise intact. He is 214 feet long, 30 feet across at the shoulders, and oriented westward, as though walking from the east and the flood that drowned "the great lodge." His horned helmet identifies him as the *Wakt'cexi* deluge hero. The companion figure, also in Sauk County, about 30 miles northwest, was drowned under several fathoms of river by a dam project in the 1930s. In any case, these two horned geoglyphs clearly memorialize the Atlantean beginnings clearly defined by the Worak tradition of Wolf Clan origins.

(See Man Mounds, Wilmington Long Man)

Wotan

His name derived from the German *wut,* "to rage," which defined his identification with the dynamic forces of creation and destruction over which he had almost complete control. Also known as *Odin, Wodan, Vodan,* and *Votan* to the Germanic peoples of Northern Europe since deeply prehistoric times, he was chief deity of *Asgaard,* the abode of the gods in the Norse pantheon. He was also the great culture-creator and culture-bearer, who invented the civilizing gifts of poetry, literacy, wisdom, the arts, law, and medicine and brought them to mankind. Sometimes he appeared among mortals dressed in the great cloak and broad-brimmed hat of a traveler, his spear made to resemble a walking stick. At such times, he was the Wanderer, who roamed the world. He was known as the most potent sorcerer. Secret magic enabled his godhood and brought supernatural power to anyone with whom he shared some of his runic mysteries. In the cyclical myth of *Ragnarok,* the "Breaking of the Gods," Wotan perishes or disappears in a worldwide conflagration extinguished by a universal flood. Eventually, the cycle begins all over again.

The West Africans of Dahomey still worship Vodun, a powerful sorcerer who brought their ancestors great wealth and wisdom from over the waves, but soon after returned to his palace at the bottom of the sea. Before he departed, he confided his wisdom to a secret spiritual society of select initiates. In his honor, they named the cult *vodu,* which signifies various deities called upon in their ecstatic rituals. The Gold Coast was the main source for black slavery, so when the enslaved cultists arrived in the New World, their vodu beliefs went with them, and thrive today in the "voodoo" magic of the Caribbean.

Directly across the Atlantic from West Africa, the Quiche Mayas of Mexico's Lowland Yucatan region venerated the memory of Votan, a tall, bearded, fair-skinned, light-haired man-god. He landed at Laguna de Terminos with his family and followers from the East in a great ship, then built the first stone cities in Yucatan, taught written language to the Mayas' ancestors, and instituted the sciences of astronomy, medicine, and government.

Nunez de la Vega, the Bishop of colonial Yucatan in 1691, made a deep study of the Quiche Mayas' religion, all the better to convert them to Christianity. He learned more about the mythic Votan than any Spaniard before or since, and was so impressed with the legend's historical credibility, he concluded the ancient culture-bearer had been a son of Noah! When his native informants recounted that Votan knew of "a great wall that reached to the sky," de la Vega assumed it must have been the Tower of Babel. But he realized that a biblical interpretation of the foreign hero did not entirely mesh with the Indians' story.

Among Votan's titles was, according to the Bishop, "El Corazon de los Pueblos," meaning "the Heart of the Cities." After the Deluge and his subsequent arrival on the shores of Yucatan, he was said to have recorded details of the catastrophe, his survival, and prophesies for the Fifth Age following the Flood on a deer hide hidden in a sacred cave. Later, he went to the city of Palenque, where he transcribed this information onto golden sheets, which were dispatched to the great capital at Teotihuacan. There, they were preserved at the Temple of the Jaguar. Thanks to de la Vega, the Mayas' Votan is adequately described as an alien civilizer.

Votan was known to another Yucatan tribe, the Chiapenese, who claimed they were the first human beings in Middle America. To them, he was the grandson of a man who built a great "raft" to save his family from the Deluge that ravaged the world. "He came from the east," they said, then went on to found a great city known as Chan. On Peru's north Pacific coast lie the ruins of Chan-Chan, a pre-Inca megalopolis. In fact, wall friezes at its Palace of the Governor display a pyramidal city sunken beneath the sea. The Chiapenese recounted that seven families arrived with Votan from over the "Ocean of the Sunrise."

The occurrence of this figure on three continents forms a curious triangle. His name appearing at such widely separated locations is remarkable enough. But that three peoples as culturally different from one another as the Norse, Dahomey, and Mayas should share complimentary aspects of his myth exceeds mere coincidence, indicating an experience common to them all. Wotan/Vodun/Votan is not found outside the areas mentioned, so he was not part of some extra-historical phenomenon common to humanity in general. On the contrary, his appearance is very specific, as is his myth, among just those peoples dwelling close to the ocean who were obviously visited by the same "Wanderer," a culture-bearer from some central point and from which he impacted the three continents separately. Today, that central point is only open sea, where several thousand years ago there flourished a maritime Asgaard.

These intercultural connections through Wotan are reenforced by his early characterization in Norse myth as god of the winds. So too, the Egyptian equivalent of Atlas was Shu, likewise portrayed as controller of the winds supporting the heavens. The Aztec Ehecatl—containing the indicative "atl" of Atlas—who was said to have arrived on the shores of Mexico near Vera Cruz, was the wind-god depicted in sacred art holding up the sky. Additionally, Wotan wore an azure cloak and was venerated as the patron of sailors. In Plato's *Kritias*, the maritime kings of Atlantis wore sacred blue robes. The palatial estate of Wotan in Asgaard was, of course, the famous Valhalla, originally, *Valhal*. Remarkably, both the Quiche Maya and Chiapenese Indian versions of their Votan portray him arriving from his Atlantic home, known as *Valum*. Reason rebels at the dismissal of comparisons between the Norse Wotan-Valhal and the Central American Votan-Valum as "purely coincidental."

In what may be correlating evidence, Rene Guenon, one of the greatest mythologists of the 20th century, reported that Hindu priests preserve traditions of Atlantis. In a description of the Atlantean written language, astrological glyphs stood for specific characters. They referred to this kind of "astral-alphabet" as *Watan* or *Vatan*. Was that alphabet named after a culture-bearer from Atlantis? Since the Atlanteans were supposed to have been the inventors of astronomy-astrology and continued to excel foremostly in that science, their use of astrological symbols for letter values is credible.

Wotan, Vodun, Votan, Watan, Vatan, Valhal, Valum—their interrelating themes seem to describe the same Atlantean figure.

Xelhua

The flood hero of the Aztecs' creation legend, in which he sought refuge from the Deluge by climbing to the top of Tlaloc's mountain. Tlaloc, together with Quetzalcoatl, was a version of Atlas, depicted in temple art as a bearded man supporting the four quarters of the sky as a cross on his shoulders. He was identified with a mountain, like Atlas, one of the Titans. Xelhua was also a giant who, just before the Great Flood, went with his followers to central Mexico, where they built the most massive structure in Mesoamerica.

Today, the Cholula pyramid is mostly overgrown and surmounted by a Catholic church which substituted an Aztec temple. It used to enshrine a meteorite fragment, a relic of the Deluge "which had fallen from heaven wrapped in a ball of flame." Before the pyramid was completed, "fire fell upon it, causing the death of its builders and the abandonment of the work." The original caption in Nahuatl, the Aztec language, to a native illustration of the Cholula temple read, "Nobles and lords, here you have your documents, the mirror of your past, the history of your ancestors, who, out of fear for a deluge, constructed this place of refuge or asylum for the possibility of the recurrence of such a calamity" (Nuttall, 269).

Cholula's enshrined meteorite and related deluge tradition represent compelling evidence for an Atlantean catastrophe brought about by a celestial event.

The oldest date for the pyramid goes back to late pre-Classic times, no earlier than 400 B.C.; it was probably completed in its ultimate form around 200 A.D. These construction periods are many centuries after the 12th-century B.C. destruction of Atlantis, which the Cholula pyramid was intended to memorialize, thereby demonstrating how seminal the cataclysm continued to be regarded by subsequent generations of Mesoamericans.

(See Asteroid Theory)

Xi Wang Mu

The Chinese goddess of compassion, also known as *Kuan Yin*, whose name and function as protectress of the Tree of Life from a sunken kingdom suggest Lemurian origins. She mythically represents an actual event—namely, the transference of Lemurian spirituality to China after the inundation of the Pacific realm.

(See Mu, Tree of Life))

Xicalancans

Described in the Cakchiquel Manuscript, a collection of ancient Mexican traditions collected for Spanish conquerors by Aztec chroniclers in the mid-16th century. The Xicalancans were said to be Mexico's first civilized people, "forerunners of the races that followed; they came from the East in ships or barks" after the Third Sun. This was one of four epochs in Earth's history defined by universal catastrophes. The Third Sun ended with the near-destruction of the world by "the fire from heaven." Such an event places the arrival of the Xicalancans at sometime in the late third millennium B.C., when Atlanteans were fleeing the second series of their island's major geological upheavals.

The Xicalancans were doubtless the same people archaeologists refer to as the "Olmecs," who experienced a sudden increase in population about 1200 B.C., when Atlantis was finally destroyed. The progenitors of Mesoamerican civilization, the Olmec were believed to have developed their first ceremonial centers at La Venta, circa 1500 B.C., but further research by writer Zecharia Sitchin and others implies a more probable date around 3000 B.C.

Xmucane and Xpiyaoc

Cited in the Mayas' great cosmological book, the *Popol Vuh*, as the god and goddess who made the first animals and human beings. The beasts, however, grew into ferocious monsters, while men degenerated into mean, selfish perversions. Regretting their own creations, Xmucane annihilated the whole lot in a universal flood. In Plato's account, the Atlanteans' decadence similarly prompted their punishment.

Xochiquetzal

The Aztec mother of mankind after the Fourth Sun, or Age, when a former humanity was exterminated by the Great Flood. She was said to have been its only survivor, together with a mortal man, Coxcoxtic, with whom they repopulated the world. Their offspring were born without any capacity for speech, however, so Xochiquetzal called down the birds of the sky to lend their voices to her mute children. Her sons and daughters eventually grew up to wander all over the world, a myth that was used to explain the different languages of mankind.

Her sacred flower, the marigold, was a souvenir of the solar worship that mankind observed before the Deluge. In this, she suggests the antediluvian Golden Age mentioned by the Greek mythologist Hesiod. The Atlantean deification of the sun that Hesiod describes is the same veneration found in the Aztec myth of Xochiquetzal. Her name means "Feather Flower," and she was believed to have preserved some pre-Flood dances, music, and crafts, so that they might be restored in Mesoamerican culture. If so, then some Aztec performing arts may have been handed down directly from their Atlantean forebears.

(See Coxcoxtic)

At the southern tip of Isla Mujeres, off the coast of Yucatan, stands a shrine to Ixchel, the Mayas' flood heroine.

Yamquisapa

A fabulously rich and powerful island kingdom in the Atlantic Ocean sunk to the bottom of the sea after having been set on fire with "Thonapa's celestial flame" for the idolatry of its sinful inhabitants. The resemblance of this Inca account to Plato's story of Atlantis could not be more clear.

(See Thonapa)

Yima

In the Zoroastrian religion, the man who was told of a coming world-flood by the god of light. Thus "enlightened" with Ahura Mazda's instructions, Yima went up into the mountains of Persia, where he sought refuge at the Var. Into this huge "enclosure" he sheltered his family and "all classes of living things." As the Earth and most of humanity were inundated, the cave protected Yima and his charges.

The eminent Atlantologist Edgerton Sykes observed, "The disaster legend is of interest, as it shows that the cave motif is not confined to the Americas alone." Indeed, some Guanche versions of the Great Flood have the native Canary Islanders seeking refuge in large caves.

After the deluge, Yima released the *Karshipta*, a bird which no longer exists, with instructions to bring news of his whereabouts to others who happened to survive. Ahura Mazda reappeared and asked him to become a religious reformer. Yima refused, but promised to pass down the story of the Great Flood to "the right man." That happened to be Zarathustra, the founder of Zoroastrianism.

The Genesis account of the Flood was obviously indebted to the Persian story of Yima.

(See Zend-Avesta)

Ymir

In Norse myth, a cosmic colossus whose violent death at the hands of Odin, the Sky-Father, unleashed a universal deluge, in which perished a race of giants, save Bergelmir and his wife, who escaped in a ship. A variant of the story describes other giants sailing safely away in the *Naglfar*, an enormous vessel captained by Hrim.

Ymir is possibly related to the Sanskrit *Yama*, an Indian god of the Underworld and creator of all things. In any case, Ymir's sudden death and subsequent flood caused by violence descending from the sky refers to the celestial origins of the Atlantean catastrophe, as similarly described in numerous folk traditions around the world.

(See Asteroid Theory)

Ynys Avallach

"Land of the Apples of Eternal Life"—Atlantis in Welsh folk tradition.
(See Avalon, Ynys Vitrius, Ys)

Ynys-vitrius

"Land of Glass or Crystal"—the British version of Atlantis.
(See Avalon, Tuoai Stone, Ynys Avallach, Ys)

Yokut Creation Myth

The southern California Yokut tribe recounts that mankind was born on an island in the middle of a primeval sea. Here, Eagle and Coyote fashioned the first men and women. The Yokut myth is one of many in the circum-Pacific region suggesting human origins in Lemuria.

Yonaguni

A small island among the Ryukyus, the southernmost territories of Japan. In 1985, off Isseki Point, or "Monument Point," scuba divers discovered an apparently man-made stone structure not unlike the ruins of prehistoric citadels found on Okinawa. The ruin, with a base 100 feet beneath the surface, may have been built during an early phase of Japan's Jomon culture, circa 10,000 B.C., when the site was last above the surface of the ocean. Because evidence of seismic activity in the area is insufficient, sea-level rise occasioned by the close of the last Ice Age appears to be the only credible geologic mechanism for its inundation.

Yonaguni's terraced feature, approximately 750 feet long and 75 feet high, appears to have been terra-formed from the native rock into a ceremonial center, judging from somewhat similar but much smaller Jomon building style elements on the Japanese mainland, most notably at Masada-no Iwafune, Cape Ashizuri, and Mount Nabeyama in Gifu Prefecture. The Yonaguni structure is not alone, but part of a chain of known underwater ruins stretching for hundreds of miles on the seafloor in an arc from off nearby Taiwan to Okinawa. Doubtless, more are yet to be found. Some investigators conclude this collection of sunken monuments is nothing less than the lost kingdom of Mu.

(See Horaizan, Nirai-Kanai, Mu)

Part of the underwater monument near Yonaguni.

Ys

Also known as *Ker-is*, the story of Ys is a pre-Celtic myth with a Christian gloss through which Celtic details appear, famous throughout Brittany, and even the subject of an evocative tone-poem for piano, *Le Cathedrale Egoulte* ("The Engulfed Cathedral"), by Claude Debussy, which was later scored for full orchestra by Leopold Stokowski. Eduard Lalo actually turned the legend into a grand opera, *La Roi d'Ys*—"The King of Ys."

Ys was an island kingdom in the North Atlantic ruled by Gradlon Meur; *Meur* is Celtic for "great." His capital was an ingenious arrangement of interconnected canals constructed around an immense "basin." In other words, similar if not identical to the alternating rings of concentric land and water Plato described as the city-plan of Atlantis. A central palace was resplendent with marble floors, cedar roofs, and gold-sheeted walls, again recalling Plato's opulent sunken city. Suspended by a chain around Gradlon Meur's neck was a silver key the monarch alone possessed to open and close the great basin's sluice gates, thereby accommodating the rhythm of the tides.

One night, however, his sinful daughter, Dahut, stole the key from her father while he slept, and tried to open the sea-doors for one of her numerous lovers. The legend describes her as having "made a crown of her vices and taken for her pages the seven deadly sins." Unskilled in their operation, Dahut inadvertently sprang open the city's whole canal system, thereby unleashing a huge inundation. Awakened by an admonishing vision of Saint Gwennole, King Gradlon swung on his horse, and galloped down one of the interconnecting causeways, the swiftly rising torrent close behind. He alone escaped, for Ys with all its inhabitants, including Dahut, disappeared beneath the ocean.

His horse swam to coastal France, where Gradlon Meur finally arrived at Quimper. A very old statue of him once stood there, between two towers belonging to the cathedral. But in 1793, the monument's head was violently removed as part of the anti-aristocracy hysteria then sweeping France. A new head was affixed 66 years later, or the original restored. Like the Greek flood hero Deucalion, Gradlon introduced wine to Europe. During the Middle Ages, the story of Gradlon was reenacted every Saint Cecilia's Day, when a chorus sang of lost Ys. While engaged in their musical narrative, an actor would climb up on his statue to offer the ante-diluvian king a golden cup of wine. This done, he wiped the statue's mustache with a napkin, drank the wine himself, then tossed the empty cup into the crowd. Whoever caught it before it could strike the ground and returned it to the acting company received a prize of 200 Crowns.

Dahut still does mischief, but as a mermaid who tempts unwary fishermen, dragging them into the waters covering the city she also drowned. The Ys myth describes her as "the white daughter of the sea," recalling the first lady of Atlantis in Plato's account, Leukippe—the "White Mare," for foaming waves. The Breton legend's pre-Christian origins appear in a Welch version of Ys, whose king was remembered as Gwyddno.

As the renowned mythologist Lewis Spence concluded, "If the legend of Ys is not a variant of that of Atlantis, I am greatly mistaken" (226).

Yurlunggur

Remembered by the Australian Aborigines as a colossal serpent in the sky. It deluged the whole Earth with a flood that drowned large tracks of land. Afterward, Yurlunggur signaled an end to the catastrophe by twisting himself into a rainbow—the same imagery found in the Hebrew Genesis and among the South American Incas.

(See Asteroid Theory)

Zac-Mu-until

Literally a "White Man" who founded the Maya city of Mu-tul. Both his name and the city's, as well as foreign racial characterization, bespeak fundamental influences brought to bear in Middle America by culture-bearers from the sunken civilization of Mu.

(See Mu, Mu-tul)

Zalmat-quqadi

A people, also known in Babylonian myth as the *Ad-mi*, or *Ad-ami*, "who had fallen" because of their sinfulness prior to a terrible flood, and from whom the biblical "Adam" was taken. As the founder of modern Atlantology Ignatius Donnelly observed, "The name Adam is used in these legends, but as the name of a race, not a man." The Zalmat-quqadi are equivalent to Atlanteans endeavoring to evacuate the geologic violence afflicting their island in the mid- to late fourth millennium B.C.

Zend-Avesta

The "Interpretation of the Avesta," sacred books of the Persian religion, compiled by the prophet Zarathustra, or *Zoroaster*. Its Vendidad section narrates the story of a worldwide deluge. The *Zend-Avesta* is recognized as the repository of traditions going back many centuries earlier than the lifetime of its writer in the sixth century B.C. Zoroastrianism may be the only surviving religion, at least in part, from Atlantis, specifically, the Law of One described by Edgar Cayce. Both have important features in common, including a monotheism fire-worship.

Zer-panitu

"Lady of the Abyss," in Babylonian myth, Zer-panitu is the divine personification of the sea, "creatrix of the seed of mankind." Zer-panitu signifies the Atlantean origins of civilized humanity.

Zeu-kha

Deluge hero of the Patagonian Indians, philologically similar to the Sumerian flood hero *Ziusudra* and not unlike the Greek *Zeus*. Perhaps these and other mythic figures around the world derived from a single Atlantean progenitor.

(See Ziusudra, Zuhe, Zume)

Ziusudra

The Sumerian flood hero, the 10th pre-diluvial king. The particulars of his myth, composed at least 2,000 years earlier than the Old Testament, closely parallel Noah's version in Genesis. Ziusudra's deluge is associated with the first mass migrations from Atlantis, which took place around 3100 B.C. Some investigators have endeavored to see in his name the evolution of the Greek King of the Gods, Zeus. As Walker writes, Ziusudra carried the seeds of new life "between destruction of one world and the birth of the next" (1101). He is the Babylonian "Utnapishtim."

Zschaetzsch, Karl Georg

Born in 1870, he was a prominent German Atlantologist during the interwar period. His 1922 book, *Atlantis, Urheimat der Arier* (*"Atlantis, Primeval Homeland of the Aryans"*) was a national best-seller. Zschaetzsch and his generation were a link between previous German Atlantologists, such as turn-of-the-20th-century anthropologist Leo Frobenius; the early photographer of Maya ruins in Yucatan, Teobert Mahler; and popular postwar investigators Jurgen Spanuth and Otto Muck.

(See Maler, The Third Reich)

Zu

A Sumerian sky-god who brought the Tablets of Destiny from Lemuria.
(See Har-Sag-Mu)

Zuhe

Flood hero of the Muysca and Chibcha Indians. "Bearded, he was unlike a man of any race known to them," according to Wilkins. "He carried a golden scepter." Zuhe arrived on the shores of Colombia as the only survivor of a cataclysm that destroyed his kingdom in the Atlantic Ocean. The sky had fallen down on his homeland in a deluge of fire that was extinguished only when the island sank beneath the waves. He established the first guidelines for agriculture, law, and religion. The Chibcha greeted each Spanish visitor in the early 16th century as "Zuhe." Like Kukulcan, Quetzalcoatl, Votan, Itzamna, and all the other progenitors of pre-Columbian civilization, Zuhe was one people's mythic response to culture-bearers from Atlantis.

(See Bochica)

Zume

The Paraguayan Indian version of the "Feathered Serpent"—the fair-haired, bearded leader of fellow survivors from the "Place of the Sunris," a lost island kingdom in the Atlantic Ocean. His obvious philological and narrative resemblance to the Muyscan *Zuhe* of Colombia demonstrates the scope of the impact made on pre-Columbian South America by what must have surely been waves of immigration from Atlantis.

(See Quetzalcoatl)

Zuni Deluge Story

This Pueblo Indian people preserve the tribal memory of a pair of rocks known as "Father and Mother." They were a boy and girl turned to stone after having been sacrificed during the Great Flood, which their transformation subsequently memorialized. People turned into stone and vise versa is a motif found in many other flood myths around the world. In the Greek version, the deluge heroes, Deucalion and Pyrrha, tossed stones over their shoulders; as they hit the ground, the rocks became men and women. The children comprised an offering and appeal to the gods for rescue from the Flood. Meanwhile, the Zuni's ancestors sought refuge in caves. They were afterwards led forth by the founder of their tribe, Poshaiyankaya. Like most deluge stories in general, the Zuni trace their lineage from a culture-creator who survived the cataclysm.

Another version of the flood story is particularly Atlantean. It depicts the Zuni ancestors as given over to sexual excesses condemned by the virtuous son of a priest, who warns them that their incestuous behavior will prompt the gods to bring destruction. Divine penance comes in the form of fire and flood. The people climb to the mountain tops for refuge, but the whole land is engulfed by the Deluge, in which they mostly perish.

AFTERWORD
BY PROFESSOR NOBUHIRO YOSHIDA
PRESIDENT, THE JAPAN
PETROGRAPH SOCIETY, KITA-KYUSHU

The very word, "Atlantis" conjures powerful images, albeit usually indistinct, of the deep past. So does another haunting name, "Lemuria." Both seem to linger in our genetic memory, what Carl Jung called the "collective unconscious." The Okinawa version of a sunken kingdom known as Nirai-Kanai has the same effect in Japan. These and hundreds of other evocative names are brought back to life by Frank Joseph in this comprehensive book.

Since 1996, he has been my guest on half-a-dozen visits to Japan, where I accompanied him on investigative expeditions to some of the most remote areas of my country seldom visited by Japanese, let alone Westerners. He shared his research into our Atlantean and Lemurian folk traditions as a featured guest speaker at several conferences of The Japan Petrograph Society in Tokyo, Kagoshima, Kyushu, Fukuoaka, and Ena. He is well known in Japan for his lectures and the Japanese language publication of his books, beginning with *The Destruction of Atlantis*, in 1997. His sincere and consistently logical approach to this controversial topic has lent it a new level of credibility and attraction, the same qualities apparent in *The Atlantis Encyclopedia*.

But skeptics dismiss the lost civilization as a fantasy, even though it was described some 24 centuries ago by the most influential mind of the Classical World. These same doubters claim Plato simply invented the story of Atlantis as an allegory for his notion of the ideal state. However, a familiar image associated with the drowned empire, from which the city derived its name, belongs to Atlas. He was portrayed in Greek myth as a bearded Titan bearing the sphere of the heavens on his shoulders. Few skeptics realize that this same representation was already known to the ancient Chinese. A rare, 2-foot high statuette from the Arisugawa Collection in Kyoto depicts a man supporting a vase signifying the sky, while he rides on the back of a sea-serpent. The bronze figure dates to Late Shang Dynasty times, before 1000 B.C. This means that knowledge of Atlas was current in China some six centuries before Plato was born.

The sunken realm portrayed in his Dialogues and symbolized by the Shang Dynasty statuette still lies under the sea somewhere beyond the Pillars of Heracles, as he and his time characterized the Strait of Gibraltar. Until its actual discovery, this important Encyclopedia is our guide to understanding the story of this lost civilization, its Pacific Ocean counterpart, and the lingering impact made on our world by the two empires before a similar fate overwhelmed them both.

BIBLIOGRAPHY

Aelianus, Claudius. *His Various Histories*. London: Dring, 1665.

Ammianus, Marcellinus. *Roman History*. London: Bohn, 1862.

Anderson, Johannes C. *Myths and Legends of the Polynesians*. New York: Farrar and Rhinehart, 1928.

Andrews, Shirley: *Atlantis: Insights from a Lost Civilization*. St. Paul, Minn.: Llewellyn Publications, 1998.

Bailey, Jim. *The God-Kings and the Titans*. London: Hider & Stoughton, 1973.

——. *Sailing to Paradise*. New York: Simon & Schuster, 1994.

Baran, Michael. *Atlantis Reconsidered*. New York: Exposition Press, 1981.

Bellamy, H.S. *The Atlantis Myth*. London: Faber & Faber, 1948.

Berlitz, Charles. *Atlantis: The Eighth Continent*. New York: Faucett Books, 1984.

Blackctt, W.S. *A Lost History of America*. London: Treubner & Co., 1883.

Boylan, Patrick. *Thoth, the Hermes of Egypt*. Chicago: Ares, 1979.

Braghine, Alexander P. *The Shadow of Atlantis*. 1940. Reprint, Kempton, Ill.: Adventures Unlimited Press, 1997.

Brinton, Daniel G. *The Books of Chilan Balam*. Philadelphia, Pa.: Stern, 1882.

Brooks, John. *The South American Handbook*. Bath: Trade & Travel Publications, 1975.

Budge, E.A. Wallis. *The Book of the Dead: The Papyrus of Ani*. 1895. Reprinted, New York: Dover, 1967.

Cayce, Edgar. *Atlantis*. Vol. 22 of *The Edgar Cayce Readings*. Virginia Beach, Va.: Association for Research and Enlightenment, Inc., 1987.

Cayce, Edgar Evans. *Edgar Cayce on Atlantis*. New York: Warner Paperback Library, 1968.

Chatwin, C.P. "The Lost Atlantis." *The South-Eastern Naturalist & Antiquary* XLIV, (March 1940): 469–88.

Childress, David Hatcher. "Has Plato's Atlantis Been Found?" *World Explorer* 1, no. 8 (1996): 19.

———. *A Hitchhiker's Guide to Armageddon*. Kempton, Ill.: Adventures Unlimited Press, 2001.

———. *Lost Cities of Atlantis, Ancient Europe and the Mediterranean*. Kempton, Ill.: Adventures Unlimited Press, 1996.

———. *Vimana Aircraft of Ancient India & Atlantis*. Kempton, Ill.: Adventures Unlimited Press, 1991.

Christie, Anthony. *Chinese Mythology*. New York: Barnes & Noble, 1996.

Churchward, James. *Books of the Golden Age*. Albuquerque, N.M.: BE Books, 1927.

———. *The Children of Mu*. Albuquerque, N.M.: BE Books, 1988.

———. *The Lost Continent of Mu*. Albuquerque, N.M.: BE Books, 1988.

———. *The Sacred Symbols of Mu*. Albuquerque, N.M.: BE Books, 1988.

Clark, R.T. Rundle. *Myth and Symbol in Ancient Egypt*. London: Thames and Hudson, 1959.

Cunningham, Scott. *Hawaiian Religion and Magic*. St. Paul, Minn.: Llewellyn Publications, 1994.

Daniel, Glyn, ed. *The Illustrated Encyclopedia of Archaeology*. New York: Thomas Y. Crowell Co., 1977.

De Camp, L. Sprague. *Lost Continents: The Atlantis Theme in History, Science, and Literature*. Hicksville, N.Y.: The Gnome Press, 1954.

Derlech, Walter, trans. *Homer's Iliad and Odyssey*. London: Houghton House, Ltd., 1933.

de Zorate, Augustin. *The Discovery and Conquest of Peru*. Lima Treasury Publishers, 1968.

Donato, William. "Bimini and the Atlantis controversy: What the Evidence Says," *Ancient American* 1, no. 3 (November–December 1993): 4–13.

———. *A Re-Examination of the Atlantis Theory*. Buena Park, Calif.: The Atlantis Organization, 1979.

Donnelly, Ignatius. *Atlantis: The Antediluvian World*. New York: Harpers, 1882.

———. *Ragnarok: Age of Fire and Gravel*. New York: Whittim, 1883.

Drews, Robert. *The End of the Bronze Age*. Princeton, N.J.: Princeton University Press, 1993.

Ebon, Martin. *Atlantis: The New Evidence*. New York: New American Library, 1977.

Emery, W.B. *Archaic Egypt*. London: Penguin Books, 1971.

Firman, George. *Atlantis: A Definitive Study*. New York: Hallmark, 1985.

Fix, William R. *Pyramid Odyssey*. New York: Mayflower Books, 1978.

Folliot, Katherine A. *Atlantis Revisited*. London: Information Printing, 1984.

Fornander, Abraham. *An Account of the Polynesian Race*. Rutland, Vt.: Charles E. Tuttle Company, 1885.

Franklin, Anna. *The Illustrated Encyclopaedia of Fairies*. London: Vega, 2002.

Gill, Sam D. and Irene F. Sullivan. *Dictionary of Native American Mythology*. Santa Barbara, Calif.: ABC-CLIO, Inc., 1992.

Glavin, Terry. *A Death Feast in Dimlahamid*. Vancouver, British Columbia: New Star Books, 1990.

Graves, Robert. *The Greek Myths*. 2 vols. Harmondsworth, Middlesex: Penguin Books, 1984.

Guenon, Rene. *Fundamental Symbols: The Universal Language of Sacred Science*. Cambridge, England: Quinta Essentia, 1995.

Hansen, L. Taylor. *The Ancient Atlantic*. Amherst, Wis.: Amherst Press, 1969.

Hope, Murry. *Atlantis, Myth or Reality?* New York: Arkana, 1991.

Howey, M.O. *The Encircled Serpent in Myth and Magic*. London: Ashington Press, 1968.

Imel, Martha Ann and Dorothy Myers. *Goddesses in World Mythology, A Biographical Dictionary*. New York: Oxford University Press, 1993.

Jacolliot, Louis. *Historie des Vierges*. Paris: Lacroix, 1879.

Jimenez, Randall C. and Richard B. Graeber. *The Aztec Calendar Handbook*. Saratoga, Calif.: Historical Science Publishing, 2001.

Jobes, Gertrude and James Jobes. *Outer Space: Myths, Name Meanings Calendars*. London: Scarecrow Press, 1964.

Joseph, Frank. *Atlantis in Wisconsin*. Lakeville, Minn.: Galde Press, Inc., 1995.

———. *Destruction of Atlantis*. Rochester, Vt.: Inner Traditions Press, 2002.

———. *Edgar Cayce's Atlantis & Lemuria*. Virginia Beach, Va.: ARE Press, Inc., 2001.

———. *Sacred Sites of the West*. Blaine, Wash.: Hancock House Publishers, Ltd., 1997.

———. *The Survivors of Atlantis*. Rochester, Vt.: Inner Traditions Press, 2004.

Judd, J.W. "The Eruption of Krakatoa and Subsequent Phenomena." Pt. 1. *Report of the Krakatoa Committee of the Royal Society*, ed. G.J. Symons. London: Treubner, 1888.

Kearsley, Graeme R. *Mayan Genesis, South Asian Myths, Migrations and Iconography in Mesoamerica*. London: Yelsraek Publishing, 2001.

Kennedy, Gordon. *Nordic Antiquities in the Tropical Atlantic*. Ojai, Calif.: Nivaria Press, 1998.

Knappert, Jan. *Pacific Mythology*. London: Diamond Books, 1992.

Kozminsky, Isidore. *Numbers Their Meaning and Magic*. New York: Samuel Weiser, 1977.

Kramer, Noah. *The Sumerians*. Chicago, Ill.: University of Chicago Press, 1969.

Las Casas, Enrique. *Guatemala Excavations*. Translated by Hubert Willis. Boston: Collegiate Publishers, 1960.

Leach, Maria, ed. *Funk & Wagnalls' Standard Dictionary of Folklore, Mythology and Legend*. New York: Harper & Row, 1972.

Lee, Desmond, trans. *The Timaeus and the Kritias*. London: Penguin Books, 1977.

Leonard, Cedric. *The Quest of Atlantis*. New York: Manor Books, 1979.

Le Plongeon, Augustus. *Queen Moo and the Egyptian Sphinx*. London: Kegan, Paul, Trench, Truebner, 1896.

————. *Sacred Mysteries Among the Mays and Quiches 11,500 Years Ago*. New York: Macoy, 1886.

Little, Gregory L. *Search for Atlantis*. Memphis, Tenn.: Eagle Wing Books, 2003.

Lucas, J. Olumide. *Religion of the Yorubas*. Lagos, Nigeria: C.M.S. Bookshop, 1948.

Mackenzie, Donald A. *Mythology of the Babylonian People*. London: Bracken Books, 1915.

MacCullow, Canon John. *Myths of All Races*. Vol. 2. London: Marshall Jones Co., 1930.

Matthew, William Diller. "Plato's Atlantis in Paleogeography." *Procedures of the National Academy of Sciences* 6 (1920): 17f.

Mercatante, Anthony S. *Who's Who in Egyptian Mythology*. New York: Clarkson N. Potter, Inc., 1978.

Mertz, Henriette. *Atlantis, Dwelling Place of the Gods*. Chicago: Mertz, 1976.

Miller, Max and Juan Rivera. *Myths and Legends of Pre-Spanish Mexico*. Chicago: Paul Revere Press, 1956.

Motet, Pierre. *Lives of the Pharaohs*. New York: World Publishing Company, 1968.

Muck, Otto. *The Secret of Atlantis*. New York: Times Books, 1978.

Murphy, Westbrook, trans. *The Complete Hesiod*. New York: Macmillan, 1958.

North, F.J. *Sunken Cities*. Cardiff, Wales: University of Wales Press, 1957.

Nuttall, Zelia. *The Fundamental Principles of Old and New World Civilizations*. Vol. 2. Cambridge, Mass.: Peabody Museum, Harvard University, 1900.

O'Brien, Henry. *The Round Towers of Atlantis*. Kempton, Ill.: Adventures Unlimited Press, 2002.

Ogilvie-Herald, Chris. "Native Folk Memories Recall Ancient Cataclysms." *Quest for Knowledge* 1, no. 2 (May 1997).

Oppenheimer, Stephen. *Eden in the East: The Drowned Continent of Southeast Asia*. London: Weidenfeld & Nicolson, 1999.

Paine, Thomas. *The Age of Reason*. New York: Herald Publishers, Inc., 1924.

Petrie, W.M. Flinders. *A History of Egypt*. 3 vols. New York: Charles Scribner's Sons, 1905.

Pinkham, Mark A. *The Truth Behind the Christ Myth*. Kempton, Ill.: Adventures Unlimited Press, 2002.

Pukui, Mary Kwena. *New Pocket Hawaiian Dictionary*. Honolulu: University of Hawaii Press, 1992.

Radin, Paul. "The Winnebago Tribe." *37th Annual Report of the Bureau of American Ethnology*. Washington, D.C.: Smithsonian Institution, 1923. Reprint, Lincoln, Nebr.: University of Nebraska Press, 1970.

Roberts, Anthony. *Atlantean Traditions in Ancient Britain*. London: Rider & Co., 1975.

Seleem, Ramses, trans. *The Illustrated Egyptian Book of the Dead*. With comments by Ramses Seleem. New York: Sterling Publishing Co., 2001.

Shinn, Eugene A. "A Geologist's Adventures with Bimini Beachrock and Atlantis True Believers." *Skeptical Inquirer* 28, no. 1 (January–February 2004).

Spanuth, Juergen. *Atlantis of the North*. London: Rheinhold, 1979.

Spence, Lewis. *The History of Atlantis*. New Hyde Park, N.Y.: University Books, Inc. 1968.

———. *The Occult Sciences in Atlantis*. London: Rider & Co., 1945.

———. *The Problem of Atlantis*. London: Rider & Sons, 1924.

———. *The Problem of Lemuria*. London: Rider & Co., 1930.

Steiger, Brad. *Atlantis Rising*. Garden City, N.Y.: Doubleday & Co., Inc., 1971.

Stuart, Preston. *Animal Behaviorism*. New York: Harper & Row, 1977.

Sykes, Edgerton. *Atlantis*. Brighton, England: Markham House Press, 1974.

———. *Who's Who in Non-Classical Mythology*. New York: Oxford University Press, 1993.

Thompson, Gunnar. *American Discovery: The Real Story*. Seattle, Wash.: Misty Isles Press, 1992.

Tompkins, Peter. *Secrets of the Great Pyramid*. New York: Harper & Row, 1971.

Walker, Barbara G. *The Woman's Encyclopedia of Myths and Secrets*. San Francisco: Harper San Francisco, 1983.

Waters, Frank. *Book of the Hopi*. New York: Penguin Books, 1963.

Wegener, Alfred Lothar. *The Origins of Continents and Oceans*. New York: Dutton, 1924.

Whishaw, Ellen. *Atlantis in Spain*. Kempton, Ill.: Adventures Unlimited Press, 1996.

Whitmore, Frank C., Jr. et al. "Elephant Teeth from the Atlantic Continental Shelf," *Science* 156: 1477.

Williams, Mark R. *In Search of Lemuria: The Pacific Continent in Legend, Myth and Imagination*. San Mateo, Calif.: Golden Era Books, 2001.

Williams, Michael. "The New Atlantis." *Fate* 52, no. 5 (May 1999): 34.

Williams, Richard. *Mysteries of the Ancients*. Pleasantville, N.Y.: The Readers's Digest Association, 1993.

Yoshida, Nobuhiro. "Stone Tablets of Mu, 'The Motherland of Mankind.'" *Ancient American* 3, no. 21 (November–December 1997).

Zimmerer, Neil. *The Chronology of Genesis*. Kempton, Ill.: Adventures Unlimited Press, 2003.

Zimmerman, J.E. *Dictionary of Classical Mythology*. New York: Bantam Books, 1971.

Zink, David D. *The Stones of Atlantis*. Englewood Cliffs, N.J.: Prentice Hall, Inc., 1978.

Zorate, Salazar. *The Empire of the Sun*. Translated by Ernst Hiemer. London: Piccadilly Press, 1954.

ABOUT THE AUTHOR

Frank Joseph is the editor-in-chief of *Ancient American*, a popular science magazine describing overseas visitors to our continent centuries before Columbus. He is the author of 14 published history and metaphysics books released in a dozen foreign language editions. His numerous articles and reviews appear in *Fate*, *Atlantis Rising*, *Asian Pages*, *Piloting Careers*, *Aviation Heritage*, and others, as well as various foreign periodicals, including *Hera* (Italy), *Air Classics* (Britain), and more. Nominated a "Professor of World Archaeology" by the Savant Institute of Japan, Joseph is a member of California's Atlantis Organization.

He lives with his wife, Laura, and cat, Sally, in Wisconsin.